RITA nominated and *New York Tim*
author of the Killer Instincts novels, E
grew up in the suburbs of Toronto, Onta
holds a BA in English from York University.
an early age, she knew she wanted to be a wri
and actively began pursuing that dream when she was a teenager. She loves strong heroines, alpha heroes, and just enough heat and danger to keep things interesting!

Visit Elle Kennedy online:

www.ellekennedy.com
www.facebook.com/AuthorElleKennedy
www.twitter.com/ElleKennedy

PRAISE FOR ELLE KENNEDY

'Takes readers on a terrific emotional roller-coaster ride full of relentless action, heated sexual tension, and nailbiting plot twists . . . Breathless passion will leave the reader begging for more.'
Publishers Weekly

'Each book has been suspenseful, heartbreaking, and full of sexy times.'
Fiction Vixen

'As sexy as it is exciting. Elle Kennedy hits all the right notes in . . . her outstanding Killer Instincts series . . . spellbinding romantic suspense.'
Joyfully Reviewed

'[Kennedy] shows a real flair for penning thrillers that are passionate, gritty, and extremely suspenseful.'
RT Book Reviews (top pick)

'Seduction, sex, and suspense—Elle Kennedy is a master at blending all three. . . . [The] Killer Instincts series is dark, sensual, and extremely compelling.'
Romance Junkies

'Fans will be eager to see what Ms. Kennedy has in store for her mercenaries.'
Shannon K. Butcher

'The entire series is a recommended read for those who enjoy romantic suspense with a dark, dangerous edge.'
Fresh Fiction

'This book embodied raw sexual chemistry and then look it up a few notches. Be careful when handling it, because you might get scorched!'
Under the Covers

'An exciting, fast-paced read.'
Book Binge

'Flat-out spectacular . . . a series filled with strong heroes and heroines, sinfully hot love scenes, and adrenaline-filled action.'
Wit and Sin

'Elle Kennedy, please write faster!'
The Book Pushers

CLAIMED

AN OUTLAWS NOVEL

Elle Kennedy

piatkus

PIATKUS

First published in the US in 2015 by Signet Eclipse, an imprint of New American Library, a division of Penguin Group (USA) LLC.
First published in Great Britain in 2015 by Piatkus

1 3 5 7 9 10 8 6 4 2

A CIP catalogue record for this book is available from the British Library.

ISBN 978-0-349-41192-7

Printed and bound in Great Britain by
Clays Ltd, St Ives plc

Papers used by Piatkus are from well-managed forests and other responsible sources.

FSC
www.fsc.org
MIX
Paper from responsible sources
FSC® C104740

Piatkus
An imprint of
Little, Brown Book Group
Carmelite House
50 Victoria Embankment
London EC4Y 0DZ

An Hachette UK Company
www.hachette.co.uk

www.piatkus.co.uk

CLAIMED

1

"I need to get drunk and laid—not necessarily in that order," Rylan announced as the group crossed the threshold into the bar.

Connor had to duck his head to clear the top of the doorway. So did the others. All five of them stood well over six feet tall, making an imposing sight as they entered the candlelit room. Every head turned their way, but fear dissolved into mild apprehension and disinterest once the patrons discerned that the men didn't have Enforcer logos on their clothing. Most turned away, refocusing their attention on their companions or the alcohol in front of them.

"And look at that," Rylan said in delight. "The bartender's cute. Must be new, 'cause I'd definitely remember those tits."

Connor followed his friend's gaze to the long metal counter tended by a thin blonde with serious cleavage. Yeah, Ry would remember screwing her. Skinny and big-busted was his flavor of choice. Blondie glanced up and winked at the men, her pouty red lips lifting in a sensual come-hither-and-fuck-me smile.

A sense of desperation hung in the air and mingled with the cloud of tobacco smoke hanging over the room like a canopy. Sex, booze, and cigarettes—rare luxuries these days, unless you knew where to find 'em. And hell, you didn't even have to pay to fuck anymore. Currency meant shit outside the city, and besides, most women were as eager to get screwed as the men who wanted to screw them. But Connor wasn't here for sex. He was looking forward to a nice date with Jack Daniel's. It'd been way too long since he'd felt the burn of alcohol coursing through his veins.

The bar used to be a morgue, and the compartments where stiffs had once been stored now contained bottles of alcohol and supplies that the owners of the establishment had amassed over the years. They'd brought in mismatched furniture, tables and old couches, splintered wooden chairs. No power in the joint, so they'd lit dozens of candles, which danced on the cinder-block walls and shrouded most faces in shadow. The small hospital on the floors above them lay deserted, because hospitals were a thing of the past. You got sick or injured, you died. *Population control,* the fuckers in the "government" called it.

Connor chose a seat that allowed him to monitor both the door and the smoky main room, while Rylan, Pike, and Xander scrambled for the rest. Kade got stuck facing away from the door, which meant he'd be the first one to get a bullet to the back of his head if trouble arose.

The tabletop was scratched and stained with shit Connor didn't even want to know about. Without any discussion, Rylan went up to the counter to order their drinks. That meant he'd be the one paying the tab, but he didn't seem to mind in the slightest. Blondie over there was right up his alley. In a barter-and-trade era, you sometimes paid a high price for whatever you were trying to acquire, but this was win-win for Rylan—he'd get the booze *and* the pussy. Which made him a damn lucky bastard, because the last time they'd come here, the bartender had been male and Connor had been forced to trade a rifle for a bottle of Jack.

Fate smiled on the attractive and horny, he supposed.

"So . . . do we move?" A trademark scowl twisted Pike's face as he voiced the question they'd all been thinking.

Connor rubbed the stubble coating his jaw. He wished like hell he had a razor, but the one back at camp had rusted to shit, and their next raid wasn't scheduled until tomorrow. "Don't know. I think we should wait it out. The rumors might be bullshit."

"Word is Dominik is heading south," Pike reminded him. "He did a sweep last week, cleared out an entire camp only a few hundred miles from here."

Bastard sure had, and damned if that didn't make Connor uneasy. Of all the Enforcers in the Colonies, Dominik and his band of bloodthirsty psychos were the worst. They were vicious, determined, and damn good at their job. Dominik answered only to West Colony's Enforcer commander, who in turn answered to the council members above him. The group's orders were simple: round up every last outlaw in the colony, force them to rejoin society, or kill them if they refused.

If Dominik really was closing in on them, the smart move would be to get the fuck out. Head for South Colony, or try to find a ship heading east, but traveling was a bitch these days. More checkpoints, more Enforcers, more bandits.

Kade spoke up. "I say we stick it out. We've got a good thing going here."

Connor couldn't disagree as he thought about the abandoned wilderness resort they'd been living in for the past year. Tucked in the foothills of the Rockies, the camp consisted of two dozen cabins and a main lodge nestled in the trees. After scouting the area for weeks, the men had claimed the old place and promptly turned it into a fortress. The resort was more secure than a military facility, just the way Connor liked it.

Rylan returned to the table with a full bottle of whiskey and five shot glasses, which clinked together in his hand. Unscrewing the bottle, he poured a stream of alcohol over the glasses, the excess liquid joining the other stains on the rotting wood.

"Hey, don't waste it," Xander grumbled. "Who knows when we'll have another chance to get shit-faced?"

Rylan flopped down in his chair, slugged back a shot, then poured himself another. "So what's the final consensus?"

Xander rubbed the thick beard covering his jaw. "Pike thinks we should go. Kade wants to stay. Con is undecided."

Rylan was quick to throw in his two cents. "I vote for staying. I like it here. And by the way, brother, what's with the beard? You know it's like a gazillion degrees out, right?"

"If your pretty-boy face were capable of growing a beard, you'd look like me too right now." Xander sighed. "Shit. I hope we find some razors on the raid tomorrow. Maybe even an electric one."

"And candy," Kade added, brightening at the thought. "Some real sweet shit. It's been ages since we came across any chocolate."

"And some really filthy porn," Rylan added with a grin.

Connor didn't join in, mostly because he was scared he'd snap and piss everyone off. But seriously, chocolate and porn? A war had ravaged the entire globe, for fuck's sake. Bombs had fallen on cities like raindrops and eliminated entire populations, and those who survived were now prisoners—sorry, *citizens*—of the Colonies.

And Kade's biggest problem was that he couldn't satisfy his sweet tooth?

They're making the best of this shit.

Yeah, maybe. Maybe Connor was a negative motherfucker for dwelling on the chaos and destruction, but what was he supposed to do—act like everything was fine and dandy? Pretend that his life was filled with rainbows and lollipops?

Fuck that.

He raised his glass to his lips and gulped the alcohol. It burned his throat on the way down, heating his stomach in a familiar, welcoming way. Screw candy and porn—the only thing he wanted from the raid tomorrow was a crate of booze. Even cheap wine would do. Anything to numb the angry, powerless feelings swirling in his gut.

"You know what? Who needs porn when you can settle for the real thing?" Rylan scraped back his chair. "'Scuse me, boys."

Rylan headed to the counter, where he leaned forward and murmured something that made the bartender giggle. A few seconds later, the blonde eagerly followed him toward a corridor in the back, but not before tossing a not-so-discreet look at Connor and the other men.

"Think she'd be down for some company?" Kade wondered aloud.

Xander grinned. "One hundred percent yes. Did you see the way she looked back just now? That hot little number is dying to be tag-teamed."

"Can you assholes forget about your goddamn cocks for one goddamn minute?" Pike snapped. "We've gotta make a decision. If Dominik's on his way here, I say we go."

"Since when are you scared of a fight?" Xander taunted.

Pike scowled at him. "Some battles aren't worth fighting. Let Dominik do his thing, as long as he leaves us alone."

And right there was the problem—Connor didn't *want* Dominik to leave him alone.

He was itching for a face-to-face with that bastard, and if he didn't have the other guys to think about, he would've taken off and fed his hunger for vengeance ages ago. But his men looked to him for guidance. Somehow, despite his many protests, he'd become their leader. They did what he said, even Pike, who didn't like to take orders from anybody. Connor didn't want any of them getting killed just so he could satisfy the bloodlust that had been poisoning his body for years.

Getting to Dominik was virtually impossible. Not only was he constantly surrounded by his legion of soldiers, but nobody knew where the West Colony Enforcers were headquartered. It wasn't in the city, where those who survived the war had been shipped off to after the Global Council took control. Rumor had it the Enforcers moved around constantly, never making themselves targets. This was the first time Connor had an inkling of where Dominik was going to be. It was an opportunity he refused to let pass, but . . . did the men who trusted him deserve to die during his own quest for revenge?

Uncertainties rolled through his head like tumbleweed, then faded as the creak of the door grabbed hold of his senses. His head jerked up, hand instinctively reaching beneath his jacket to hover over the butt of his pistol.

Even after he decided the threat level was low, he still couldn't look away.

The woman who appeared in the doorway held his gaze captive. Tall, slim, with wary gray eyes and long hair the color of warm honey. She wore tight black pants that showcased a spectacular pair of legs and a white tank top that revealed plenty of mouthwatering cleavage. A leather jacket and knee-high boots completed the bad-girl ensemble.

Connor's mouth went dry.

Christ, he wanted her naked.

It'd been a long time since he'd experienced such a sudden, visceral attraction to a woman. His cock strained against his zipper, but another look in the woman's direction and he knew the eager bulge in his pants wouldn't be getting the attention it demanded.

She might be dressed like a bad girl, but she sure as shit wasn't one. The fearful desperation clouding her eyes revealed her for what she was—a lost little lamb who'd wandered into a den of wolves. And yet . . . there was also determination flickering in her gaze. A sense of to-hell-with-you bravado that gave her a purposeful stride as she stepped into the room.

"Dibs," came Xander's low voice.

"Don't even think about it," Connor muttered.

He registered the surprised faces around the table

realizing what his command had sounded like. Possessive. Like he was staking a claim. But that hadn't been his intention. His body might be throbbing like crazy at the moment, but he had no desire to claim the woman. Every instinct he possessed told him to stay away from her. To keep his guys away too.

He watched as she approached the counter and spoke to the young man who'd taken over for the girl who probably had Rylan's cock in her mouth at the moment.

The conversation was hushed, the blonde's shoulders going rigid as the bartender said something she clearly didn't like.

A flash of movement caught his eye. She'd slid something toward the kid, but Connor couldn't make it out. A moment later, the bartender tucked the item in his pocket and slid a beer bottle across the counter. The blonde took it and went over to a table in the corner of the room.

Connor tore his eyes off her. He was still semihard and not at all happy about it. He shouldn't be thinking about fucking, not when Dominik was finally within his grasp.

He could get off any damn time he wanted, but revenge? That was something he could carry with him for the rest of his life.

Hudson couldn't believe she'd been forced to trade a Swiss Army knife for a measly bottle of beer. It wasn't her last weapon, or one she was especially fond of, but handing it over to the bartender still grated. She hadn't realized the wad of cash in her pocket was useless beyond the city walls, and that was just another disheartening item to add to the growing list of things she didn't understand about this world.

She found an empty table and sat down, twisting off the beer cap and swallowing the lukewarm alcohol. She didn't like the taste of beer much, but she wasn't in the mood for anything stronger. She had to stay alert. And she definitely needed to find a place to sleep tonight.

Panic bubbled in her throat as she imagined spending the night outdoors again. She kept expecting bandits to pop out of the shadows, which made it impossible to fall asleep. She'd been in outlaw territory for nearly a week now, and she wasn't even close to adapting to her rough, dangerous surroundings. She'd thought her training would help her survive out here.

She hadn't expected to be this damn afraid all the damn time.

Taking a breath, she glanced around the room. Despite the low chatter and occasional chuckles, nobody looked relaxed. Shoulders were stiff and gazes were guarded. She was beginning to suspect this kind of behavior wasn't uncommon. Since she'd left the compound, she'd realized that nobody was immune to the Global Council's control. Even those who considered themselves free—the outlaws—continued to look over their shoulders.

When the GC had taken over four decades ago, they'd decided the only way to avoid another war was to rule with an iron fist. The council members insisted that the devastation of the world would not have happened if a strong global regime had been in place, so they'd eliminated conflict-causing factors like class, religion, free will. The new system worked, to some extent. Hudson couldn't deny she'd been happy in the city, at least before Dominik had turned her into a prisoner in her own life.

She supposed she was an outlaw now too. A target like the rest of them. It was a culture shock to be thrust into this new world, surrounded by people who were determined to cling to whatever freedom they could.

Her gaze drifted to a table near the door, where four men spoke in hushed tones. They made a formidable sight. Gorgeous, masculine, oozing deadly intensity.

One in particular captured her attention. Late twenties, early thirties maybe, with cropped brown hair, cold hazel eyes and muscles galore. He wore a fitted olive green jacket that most likely hid a slew of weapons beneath it, and everything about him screamed *warrior*. The broad set of his shoulders, the way his hawklike gaze swept over the room even as he carried on a conversation with his companions.

Her breath hitched when the object of her perusal turned his head and looked at her.

Heat.

Holy crap. Nothing cold in his gaze anymore, just bold, undisguised fire.

He wanted her.

Ignoring the sudden pounding of her heart, Hudson wrenched her eyes away and gulped down some more beer. She felt flushed, her hair like a heavy curtain smothering her shoulders and back, but she didn't dare pin it up. Even though the tattoo at the base of her neck was buried under layers of makeup, she still wasn't taking any chances. If anyone so much as suspected who she was, she'd be killed in a heartbeat.

A high-pitched giggle sounded from the other end of the room, and Hudson turned to see a woman with blond hair and double D's emerge from a dark corridor, flanked by a tall man with piercing blue eyes and a killer grin. He had the arrogant swagger of a guy who'd just gotten laid, and his companion's bee-stung lips and tousled hair confirmed it. The man gave the woman's ass a playful spank, then sauntered over to the table Hudson had been observing.

Surprise, surprise. Sexy blond guy was with the sexy foursome.

As he sat, his gaze collided with hers, and a faint smile lifted the corner of his mouth. It faded when the dark-haired outlaw she'd been trying not to ogle muttered something that silenced the group.

Hudson sighed. Now definitely wasn't the time to get all hot for a sinfully sexy stranger. She had more pressing matters to deal with, so many of them her head was starting to spin.

Find a place where she could lie low for a while. Scavenge some supplies. Figure out how to get the hell out of West Colony. Evade Dominik, who'd no doubt sent an army after her.

Maybe the folks who ran this place would help her find a safe haven—

"Down on the floor, assholes!"

She'd been so lost in thought she hadn't sensed the danger until it was too late. She didn't have time to unsheathe the knife on her hip, because cold fingers grabbed her arm and yanked her to the dirty cement floor.

"Stay down, bitch!"

There was a blur of movement, loud expletives, and angry shouts as a dozen men stormed the bar and advanced on its patrons.

Bandits.

Shit.

The man who'd thrown her down had neglected to search her for weapons, so she still had possession of her knife, along with the rest of the sharp steel blades strapped to her body. She gripped the bone handle and slowly slid the hunting knife down to her side, lifting her head to assess the situation. She'd heard of bandits, but this was her first encounter with them.

They looked a lot like the homeless people she'd seen in her father's photographs of prewar Los Angeles. Threadbare clothing, dirty, reeking of booze. The Enforcers didn't differentiate between bandits and outlaws, but Hudson needed only two seconds to recognize the difference. Outlaws fought for freedom, and sure, they raided GC supply compounds when it was needed, but they were fighting against a government they opposed, not with one another.

These men were scavengers. Broken, desperate vultures that didn't belong, not in GC society and not among the rebels. She'd heard that bandits had no consciences, no remorse about robbing and killing and raping anything in their paths.

Her heartbeat accelerated as she stayed flat on the floor while the bandits manhandled the patrons in the smoky room, kicking anyone who so much as yelped. The leader of the band, a man with dark hair and a bushy overgrown beard, hopped the counter, assault rifle in hand.

"We want all the booze," he snapped at the bartender.

Hudson slithered under the table. From the corner of her eye, she noticed that the five outlaws had remained seated and were watching events unfold with bored expressions on their respective handsome faces.

"Get down on the ground!" shouted one of the bandits. He was a short, skinny man with a shaved head, his unimposing physique made deadly only by the gun he waved at the group.

"No, thanks," the outlaw with black hair and an even blacker scowl replied.

"You wanna die? Is that it?" The bandit cocked his pistol. "Because I'm perfectly happy to—"

The five men sprang into action. One second the table was upright; the next it was whipped on its side with two of them diving behind it for cover. Hudson saw a blur of arms and legs, flashes of steel and silver.

An outraged moan cut the air as the skinny bandit suddenly found a knife lodged in his upper arm. He staggered forward while his fellow robbers launched themselves at the men, their quest for alcohol forgotten.

It was a bloodbath. A gunshot boomed, sending one of the bandits crashing to the floor two feet from her head. More shots echoed in the room, making her ears ring.

She watched the scene unfold in morbid fascination. The outlaws didn't even break a sweat, and they were completely unfazed by the fact that they were outnumbered. Fists connected with jaws. Grunts heated the air. Another explosion of gunfire took chunks out of the cement wall.

A furious male curse made her wince, and she twisted her head in time to see the blond outlaw stumble backward. He lifted a hand to his neck in amazement, and even from across the room she saw his hand come back stained with blood. He'd been hit. And yet he didn't even miss a beat as he raised his gun and fired twice, eliciting a shriek of agony from the long-haired bandit who'd been attempting to finish him off.

A thud. Two. The bandits were dropping like flies.

Silence finally descended over the room, broken only by the groans of those lucky enough to be alive.

"Well, that was fun," the man with the black eyes remarked. He sounded thoroughly bored.

A scuffed boot crossed her line of vision. She shifted in time to see the thick sole stomp on the chest of the bandit leader, the one with the beard. When she raised her gaze, she discovered that the boot belonged to the man with the smoldering hazel eyes.

"I suggest you round up your buddies—the ones who are still breathing—and get the hell out of here," he said coolly.

"Fuck you," was the strangled reply.

With a heavy breath, the man hauled the bandit to his feet. "Fine, we'll do it the hard way."

He grabbed the guy's arm and broke it with a sickening *crack*.

Hudson flinched at the bandit's shriek of pain, watching in amazement as the outlaw manhandled the injured man to the door. He stopped, glanced over his shoulder in an unspoken command, and his men wasted no time hauling the remaining intruders out of the bar.

Patrons slowly got to their feet. Dazed. The bartender rushed toward the blond man, but he brushed off her arm and continued toward the door, an unconscious man hanging over his broad shoulder.

Hudson stood up on shaky legs and stared at the bodies littering the floor. Eight in total. A bloody massacre. She wasn't surprised when a few customers made a beeline for the dead, frantically rummaging through pockets and looting the lifeless men.

She was sheathing her knife when the outlaws returned. The blond had his palm clamped over his neck, and she could see blood oozing between his fingers.

"Everybody all right?" their leader asked gruffly.

The bartender hurried over. "Thank you," she blurted out.

He ignored the declaration of gratitude. "Two of my guys will stay here tonight in case those assholes decide to push their luck and come back. But I suggest you close up shop. Location's been compromised, which means you're bound to encounter more of this shit."

She nodded rapidly. "We will. We'll close up tomorrow."

"Good."

He glanced around the room, his hazel eyes resting on Hudson. Warmth instantly flooded her belly, traveling through her body until every inch of her felt hot and achy.

After a long moment, he broke the eye contact. "Let's move out," he barked at his friends. "Xander, you and Pike take care of the bodies and make sure these folks stay safe."

"No problem. Oh, and, Connor," the other man added dryly, "get Ry cleaned up. He's bleeding like a stuck pig."

Connor. The name suited him.

Hudson couldn't take her eyes off him as he turned and marched to the door, providing her with a nice view of his taut backside. It wasn't until he disappeared through the doorway that she snapped out of her trance.

Ignoring the startled looks from the other people in the bar, she raced out the door, blinking to adjust to the darkness. The lights that had once illuminated the parking lot of the hospital had been knocked out, and parts of the pavement were black and cracking, most likely from the fires or explosives that had been set off by the looters all those years ago.

Everything beyond the walls of West City looked this way—dead trees and blackened earth, crumbling buildings and overgrown neighborhoods, and the coastal cities that hadn't ended up underwater were still flooded to shit.

Hudson stopped only to grab the duffel bag she'd stashed in the bushes, then raced across the parking lot. She caught up with Connor just as he reached the beat-up Jeep parked in the lot.

"Wait!"

He froze. Turned his head slightly, greeting her with suspicion.

She stumbled toward the vehicle, aware of how foolish she was being. How reckless.

But she knew without a shred of doubt that the answer to all her problems was standing right there in front of her. This man, with his warrior body and cold eyes and military precision—*he* was the solution.

"Yeah?" he muttered.

"You . . . What you guys did back there . . . I just wanted to . . ."

A soft chuckle sounded from behind her. She spun around as the blond guy with the bloody neck—Ry?—approached the Jeep, tailed by another dark-haired outlaw.

"See, I told you chicks got off on violence," Ry told his friend. He fixed his blue eyes on her. "But listen, gorgeous, don't bother with Connor. He's too bossy in bed. Me, on the other hand . . . I'll let you do *whatever* you want to me."

She couldn't help but smile. "Thanks, but that's not what I want from him."

"Your loss," he said lightly before hopping into the backseat.

"What the fuck *do* you want?" Connor demanded.

Their gazes locked, and a rush of awareness sailed through her again.

"Say whatever you want to say so we can get the hell outta here." Irritation crept into his deep, raspy voice.

"I . . ." She swallowed. "I—"

"Spit it out, sweetheart."

She opened her mouth, and four desperation-laced words flew out of it. "Take me with you."

2

Take me with you.

Definitely not the words Connor had expected to hear. They were strangers to her, and in this day and age you didn't cozy up to strangers. You stayed the fuck away from them.

"Did you hear me?" She rested her hands on her slender hips. "I want to go with you."

"Didn't anyone ever tell you that you can't always get what you want? I think someone even wrote a song about it once."

"I don't care. I still want to come with you."

"Sorry, sweetheart, but this is a boys-only club."

Her agitated expression gave way to indignation. "Wow. So you're rude *and* sexist."

From the backseat of the Jeep, Rylan snorted. It wasn't every day someone stood up to Connor; no doubt his friends were totally digging this.

He didn't enjoy it one bit, though. He hated being out in the open like this. Yeah, he and the boys had scouted the area dozens of times, but the Enforcers were unpredictable. They lived in the shadows and ambushed you when you least expected it.

Connor just wanted to get back to base, where he

could finally let himself breathe. And he had no intention of taking this woman with him.

"Please," she implored when he didn't respond. "I don't have anywhere to go."

"Not my problem." He headed for the driver's door.

She trailed after him like an annoying puppy. "I saw the way you handled those bandits. Effortlessly. You guys know what you're doing. You've had training."

"What's it to you?"

"I'm all alone." Her voice wobbled. "The people I was with were killed. I need . . . protection."

He noted that her expression remained shuttered and emotionless when she mentioned that her group was dead. Not necessarily a sign of dishonesty, but the story didn't sit right with him.

"Just take me with you. I promise I won't be a nuisance."

"You already are."

She ignored the accusation. "Look, I can help your friend. I'm good at treating battle wounds—"

"So are we, sweetheart. Trust me, he'll be fine."

"Then I can cook for you guys, or . . . I don't know . . . clean, be a lookout . . ." She trailed off.

He almost laughed. Right, because they were in the market for a fucking maid.

"Tempting offer," he said, "but I'll pass."

"We don't have anything for you to cook, anyway," Kade piped up, irritating the hell out of Connor. "At least not until the next raid. So your offer for home cooking ain't needed at the moment. Appreciated, though."

Her expression brightened. "Raid? I can come along on a raid. I've had training too and—"

Connor snorted.

Those gray eyes flashed. "I have."

"Says the woman who hid under a table when the bandits showed up."

He was goading her, but he couldn't stop himself. Something about her rubbed him the wrong way. The conflicting air of vulnerability and danger. The beautiful face and out-of-this-world body. He didn't trust her.

"I could have defended myself. They just caught me off guard," she muttered.

"I'm sure you think—"

She moved so fast, he didn't even have time to blink. Next thing he knew her knee was jammed between his thighs, and she had one hand on the nape of his neck while the other held a knife to his throat.

Connor stiffened, resisted the urge to curse. Man, she was fast. And lethal, judging by the skillful way she pressed the blade to his skin. He knew he'd get nicked—or worse—if he tried to wrench away. The feel of her firm thigh between his legs got him hard, instantly, and his cock grew harder still when he peered down and glimpsed the deadly glint in her big gray eyes.

"What now?" he couldn't help but taunt. "You're gonna slit my throat to prove your point?"

Her throat bobbed as she swallowed. Didn't take a genius to figure out she felt the hard ridge digging into her thigh.

"That's right, babe. I'm hard as a rock," he murmured. Then, with a smirk, he eased closer so his erection rubbed against her pelvis.

When she made a soft noise, he chuckled. "Ah, you like it, don't ya?"

She didn't answer. The warmth of her body seared his, making his cock jerk. His gaze moved to her mouth, watched her tongue dart out to moisten her bottom lip. He could kiss her right now. Fuck her too, he realized, as she moved her groin ever so slightly over his denim-clad leg.

"Why don't you undo my pants?" He tipped his head suggestively. "You could blow me right here, right now. Hell, you could blow Ry and Kade too. I'm sure they'd enjoy it."

Heat flickered in her eyes, and he saw her pulse hammering in the hollow of her throat.

Rotating his hips, he ground harder against her. "Maybe we'll bring Pike out. He likes to watch, and I'm sure you'll give us a damn good show—won't you, sweetheart?"

The blade dug deeper into his flesh. "You know, you're kind of an asshole."

"And you're completely out of your element." His voice lowered to a menacing pitch. "So let's stop playing games, huh? Either slit my throat or suck my dick, because we don't have all night."

Damned if his dick didn't jump at the prospect of getting some attention. Fuck. His body was primed and raring to go.

"Um, Con? I'm kinda bleeding here."

Sucking in a breath, he snapped out of his lust-filled stupor. Rylan's voice was the reminder he needed, the kick in the ass to regain control of the situation.

In a lightning-fast motion, he curled his fingers around her forearm and yanked hard enough to make her cry out. He twisted her wrist, and the knife clattered to the pavement, its silver blade gleaming in the moonlight.

"What's your name?" he said roughly.

She blinked a couple of times, as if shocked that he'd managed to disarm her. "Hudson."

"Hudson. Well, it's been fun, but like I said before, we don't pick up strays." He bent down to collect her knife, then held it toward her, handle side out. "My advice? Find someone else to protect you."

Her lower lip trembled.

Shit. Was she going to cry?

To his relief, she tightened her lips and grabbed the knife instead, reaching underneath the back of her jacket to tuck it away.

"Fine," she muttered. "I guess I was wrong. Chivalry *is* dead. Have a good life, boys."

A sigh lodged in his throat as Hudson marched off in the direction of the deserted road. Refusing to be affected by the waves of disappointment she was radiating, he hopped into the driver's seat and glanced back at Rylan. "How's the neck?"

"Hurting. Just a graze, though."

"Good." Connor started the engine, but he didn't put the gear in drive. His gaze flitted over to where Hudson was walking, head held high, the strap of her duffel hanging off her shoulder. The balmy night breeze tickled her long hair, making it ripple down her back in golden waves. To his dismay, both Kade and Rylan were also looking in her direction, their expressions somber.

"I like her," Rylan remarked.

Kade voiced his agreement. "Me too. But maybe it was the home-cooking line she gave us. I can't remember the last time I actually had a good meal. Xan's bean soup makes me want to kill myself."

"Forget the cooking," Rylan grumbled. "Thanks to Con, now I can't stop thinking about that luscious mouth wrapped around my dick." Connor felt the other man's mocking eyes on him. "She got you hard, huh?"

He gritted his teeth, finally yanking on the gearshift. "Doesn't matter. We're still not taking her back with us."

Rylan sighed. "You're no fun at all, Con."

"And you're a fool if you think that woman isn't trouble. She's running from something."

"Who isn't?" Kade said with a laugh.

"I like trouble," Rylan added. He opened his palm to show them the blood dripping from it. "Trouble's fun."

Connor rolled his eyes. "Your kind of trouble gets you an infection and robs us of our last stash of antibiotics."

Without turning on the headlights—one of them had burned out a while ago, anyway—he pulled out of the lot. The Jeep bounced as it hit several potholes, hinting at the bumpy ride they'd endure on the way back to camp. It had been decades since any kind of road maintenance had been performed on areas outside the city walls, and that was the way the Global Council liked it. If they didn't rebuild, people wouldn't have anywhere to settle down and breed, and the last thing the GC wanted was for the world to get overpopulated again—resources were too scarce these days.

Since they had a good forty minutes of driving ahead of them, Connor forced himself to concentrate on the road, though it was difficult to ignore the leather-clad blonde marching along the shoulder.

"I think she gave you the finger." Rylan chortled, twisting around in the backseat to look at the woman they'd left behind.

Connor's hands tightened over the steering wheel. He didn't glance in the rearview mirror until he'd put several miles between them and Hudson. But the memory of those defiant eyes refused to leave him.

Take me with you. She'd sounded so desperate. What was she running from?

Was he a total dick for shooting her down?

"We could've let her stay for a couple nights." The frown marring Kade's face confirmed that he thought *yes*, Connor *was* a major dick. "You know how tough it is to travel alone. Especially for a woman. And she said everyone in her group had been killed."

"Keep your bleeding heart in check," Connor grumbled. "We can't take in every person who gives us a sob story. We can't afford to take anyone in, period."

"You took me in," Kade countered.

Yeah, and Connor was beginning to regret it, what with Kade's disapproving stare pinning him down. Having people who depended on him had robbed him of his independence. He'd been perfectly content roaming the colony in search of Dominik, and then he'd met Rylan and Pike, who'd become his shadows despite his numerous objections. Next came Xander, whom they'd encountered on a raid. And finally Kade, who'd escaped from the city and never looked back.

Four tagalongs were enough for Connor. Bringing a new player into the mix would only spell disaster.

So why was he easing up on the accelerator?

Rylan chuckled. "Aw, is someone's conscience making an appearance?"

"Fuck off," Connor said through clenched teeth.

He jerked the steering wheel in a U-turn, tires raising a cloud of dust. Fucking Kade and his fucking guilt trip.

"One night," he snapped. "Two, max. And then we're sending her on her merry fucking way."

Neither man said a word, but Connor saw their lips twitching. Fighting back laughter. Assholes.

Up ahead, a flash of yellow caught his eye. Sure enough, Hudson was still ambling along, her black bag swinging back and forth with each step she took. Her body immediately stiffened in a defensive posture when she heard the hum of the engine.

Connor stopped on the other side of the road. "Get in," he called, his voice carrying in the night air.

She hesitated for a moment, then dashed over without a word. She tossed the bag inside and hopped in next to Rylan, so fast that Connor had zero chance of changing his mind.

Twisting around, he scowled at her and repeated what he'd told the guys. "You can crash with us for a night or two. No longer."

She nodded. "Fair enough."

Fair? Uh-uh. There was nothing fair about this. Just seeing her again made his body tighten with arousal.

Their gazes connected, and along with gratitude and slight amusement he saw something else flickering in her eyes.

Anticipation.

Christ.

He pulled another U-turn and sped off, trying to ignore the introductions going on behind him. When Hudson leaned forward to shake hands with Kade, her arm brushed Connor's shoulder and he nearly jumped out of his seat.

He kept his eyes on the road, cursing himself for the stupid decision he'd just made. Inviting a total stranger back to their camp. What the hell was he thinking?

"Let me see."

Hudson's soft demand had him glancing at the rearview mirror. His jaw tensed when he saw her reach for Rylan, whose face was looking dangerously pale. Well, no kidding. His neck had been grazed by a bullet. Said a lot about Ry that he was only now starting to show signs of it.

"Gorgeous, I've had a lot worse than this," he told her, his Southern accent flaring as he got his flirt on. Rylan's ancestors had once lived in Texas, and although the state was now underwater, some remnants of the South still existed, at least in the form of Rylan's easy drawl.

"Well, good for you. But humor me. You look like you're about to pass out any second."

With a sigh, Rylan capitulated.

Using the mirror, Connor watched Hudson examine his friend's wound. She leaned in so close that her hair fell over his chest and her breasts pressed up against his arm, and from the way Rylan's eyes twinkled, Connor could tell the bastard was enjoying every second of it.

"It's still bleeding," she chided. "You're not putting enough pressure on it. And I think you'll need some stitches."

Connor had just refocused his attention on the road, but his gaze darted back to the mirror when he heard a rustling noise. His throat turned to dust. Hudson was wiggling out of her jacket. She dropped it on the seat, then reached for the hem of her tank top.

He was so busy watching her strip he failed to notice the pothole, a deep depression that made the vehicle bounce like a rubber ball. The Jeep wasn't the only thing bouncing, either. Nope, Hudson's mouthwatering tits bounced too, emphasizing the cleavage spilling out of her black bra.

Rylan's gaze met his in the mirror. "Eyes on the road," his friend said in a singsong voice.

Connor's fingers clenched around the wheel.

"There," Hudson said, pleased. She'd balled up her shirt and was holding it tightly to Rylan's neck. "I can take a better look when we get to your camp. You have supplies, right?"

As Kade turned to tell their guest about what she could find at their camp, Connor blocked out their voices. This whole night had been nothing but a major headache, starting with the bandits who'd decided to cause trouble in the only bar in the area and ending with the mysterious woman in his backseat.

Too many questions ran through his head. Who was she? What was she running from?

And more important, how the hell was he going to get rid of her?

One look at the men's camp and Hudson knew she'd made the right decision by imposing her presence on them.

Their place was as secure as the Enforcers' compound, with trip wires and motion sensors set up around the perimeter and C-4 strung through every inch of the place. She didn't bother asking where they'd gotten the equipment. She was simply glad they had it.

Still holding her shirt to Rylan's neck, she studied their surroundings as they drove through the camp. She spotted a dozen small A-frame cabins on the left and several more of them deeper in the forest, their wooden roofs peeking out from the trees. The buildings were old and shabby, boasting paint-chipped doors, broken porches, and boarded-up windows. The men hadn't tried to pretty the place up, but at least they'd secured the hell out of it.

"How long have you lived here?" she asked curiously.

"About a year," Rylan answered. "We stumbled on it after a group of Enforcers ambushed us on the Utah coast."

If Hudson's father were alive, he would have shaken his head at those words—the Utah coast. He was one of the rare people who'd been around when America had been divided into states, when the word *coast* referred to places like California and Oregon and somewhere else she was forgetting. But those areas were gone now—underwater, thanks to the earthquakes that had ravaged the country after the bombs were dropped.

Utah, she mused. Five hundred miles west of where they were. Dominik had visited that area a few months ago, and the Enforcers didn't sweep a region again until they'd worked their way through the entire colony first. If she went west, chances were she'd be able to evade Dominik for a while. Maybe forever.

The thought of living her life without Dominik in it brought a rush of sorrow to her chest, a knot of emotion wrapped in anger and accusation directed at her brother.

Damn it, what happened to you, Dom?

The Enforcers used to be honorable. They'd protected the citizens and given the outlaws a chance to reintegrate into society. Dominik had been a good leader. A good *man*.

So what the hell had changed? When had the Enforcers decided they *liked* killing? And raping? Ambushing camps and weeding out the sick?

When had her brother turned into a monster?

And why the hell hadn't she seen it?

Hudson choked back the pain and bitterness clawing up her throat. She had to stop thinking about Dom. When she'd orchestrated her escape, she'd known it meant that she'd never see her brother again, and dwelling on the past wasn't going to help her adjust to her future. Her fucking uncertain future.

"We keep most of the supplies in the main lodge," Kade told her as the vehicle stopped in front of the main building.

"Get Ry inside," Connor barked. "I'll stash the Jeep and check the perimeter."

Hudson's heart did a little flip at the sound of his raspy voice. The man might be a total asshole, but she was finding it impossible to rein in her body's response to him. He was so masculine, rippling with quiet power. And when she'd felt his erection pulsing against her leg earlier . . .

The second they'd come into contact, pure liquid heat had rushed to her pussy. She'd never felt anything like it.

She wanted to feel it *again*.

A door creaked open, and she realized Kade and Rylan were waiting for her.

Swallowing, she hopped out and followed them up the rickety steps to the double doors of the large log building. When she noticed Rylan swaying on his feet, she wrapped her arm around his massive shoulders, summoning a protest from his lips.

"I'm fine. Really."

She rolled her eyes. "Sure you are, big boy."

Kade flicked a light switch, and a warm yellow glow illuminated the room, revealing a wood-paneled lobby in disarray. Dust motes danced in the air, flying apart as Kade stalked forward and gestured for her to follow. They climbed a small set of stairs and walked into a large dining room littered with dusty round tables and wicker chairs. Kade kept walking all the way to the back of the room, where Hudson found three tattered couches and an enormous metal cabinet filled with supplies.

She left Rylan on one of the sofas and examined the contents of the cabinet. Dozens of pill bottles, everything from painkillers to sedatives. Another cubby held bandages and gauze and a third contained surgical tools. There were syringes and sutures and transfusion equipment, even a defibrillator.

And the possession of any one of those items was an offense punishable by death.

"Where did you get all of this?" she breathed.

Rylan chuckled from the couch. "Raids. We can open a clinic, huh?"

"And face a firing squad if the Enforcers found out about this stuff." Medicine was strictly forbidden in the Colonies—the GC held the firm belief that Mother Nature should be the only deciding factor in life and death. The sick and injured were *meant* to die, and withholding medical treatment was not only necessary to control a population that had once totaled seven billion, but it also served as motivation for citizens to be more careful.

Avoid injury, avoid disease, stay alive. The motto had been branded into Hudson's head from the day she was born.

She pulled a few items off the shelves and went back to Rylan. His blue eyes dipped to her chest, a reminder that she was wearing nothing but a skimpy bra.

She turned to Kade. "You think you can find a shirt for me to wear?"

"No problem."

Rylan laughed as his friend dashed off. "Well, nobody said he was smart."

Hudson poured iodine on a gauze square. "What do you mean?"

"Just if it were me, I wouldn't be hurrying to find you a shirt." His gaze smoldered, still fixed on her cleavage. "I'm gonna come out and say it, Blondie. Your tits are amaz— Shit! That fucking stings! Warn a guy next time."

She batted her eyelashes. "Don't be a crybaby. It's not attractive."

"Neither is what you're doing to my neck."

He continued to grumble and complain as she cleaned him up, but quieted down when she told him to shut up so she could assess the wound. She might not be schooled in the outlaw way of bartering and trading, or making camp, or dealing with bandits, but this was where she excelled. Treating battle wounds, making snap decisions and barking out orders. Although she'd been trained to fight, she'd chosen to work in the city's medical sector instead of joining the military, and a sense of relief washed over her as she realized she *could* be useful out here in this unfamiliar land. She *could* be an asset, if these men only gave her a chance.

Rylan's neck had stopped bleeding, but the bullet had taken off a nice chunk of skin. More of a burn than a cut, and it would definitely leave a scar.

"I don't think stitches are necessary. All we can do is bandage it up," she concluded, reaching for more gauze and a roll of medical tape.

Kade returned, followed by Connor, who still wore a scowl on his handsome face. Hudson gathered up her bloody shirt and iodine-stained gauze. "What should I do with these?"

"I'll take care of it. Here, this is for you." Kade took her items and handed her a flannel shirt.

She accepted it gratefully, quickly slipping it over

her shoulders and doing up the buttons. The worn fabric hung down to her knees, but it was better than nothing.

"How you doing?" Connor asked Rylan.

The other man grinned. "All better. Hudson fixed me up and kissed all my boo-boos."

Connor just frowned.

She cast him an apprehensive look. "Why aren't there more people here? You've got so much space, and the place seems secure. People could have a nice little community here."

His features sharpened. "We don't take people in."

"Why not?"

"Because we don't." His voice brooked no argument, and she decided not to keep pushing.

"Where do you get your electricity?" She awkwardly gestured to the glowing light fixtures on the ceiling.

"Generator," he said curtly. "There's a well on the property, and the plumbing works, but we try not to use hot water unless we absolutely have to, because heating the water tank drains the genny. There're a few outhouses too, and every cabin has a shower and a bathtub."

Her breath caught. A bathtub. Holy hell. The thought of sliding into a tubful of water, even *cold* water, made her shiver with pleasure. She'd been traveling for seven days, so eager to put distance between herself and Dominik that she'd barely had time to sleep, let alone bathe. She'd passed streams and lakes along the way, indulged in quick dips, but she still felt dirty and unkempt.

She sensed Connor's eyes on her. They were more green than hazel, she realized. The color of the dark leaves on the trees outside.

"You want to take a bath," he said with a sigh.

"More than anything else in the world."

She thought she saw the corners of his mouth twitch. "Fine. I'll take you to one of the cabins."

Happiness danced through her. "Really?"

"I just said it, didn't I?"

"Thank you—"

But he was already stalking off, forcing her to hurry after him.

They'd reached the door of the lodge when he spoke again. "One night," he said brusquely, his big hand landing on her arm. He squeezed her wrist as he stared at her. "One night, and then you're gone."

She nodded weakly. The response seemed to satisfy him because he released her arm and walked out the door.

Hudson trailed after him, glad that he was in front of her so he couldn't see the determined set of her shoulders. Her show of agreement hadn't meant shit, because she had no intention of staying for one measly night.

She needed to find a way to convince Connor to let her stay.

3

"Bath's ready." Connor stepped out of the bathroom and found Hudson on the edge of the double bed, bending over to unzip her leather boots. She kicked one off, then the other, while he stood there trying not to check out her endless legs.

He was getting tired of the lust surging through his veins. He'd been sporting a hard-on since the moment he'd met her, but he was determined to ignore his dick and start using his head.

He'd given her the cabin closest to the lodge, the one right next to his, mainly because he wanted to keep an eye on her, but also because the cabins in the forest were in shambles. He'd asked Kade to bring some clean sheets, fluffy pillows, and a thick duvet, and he'd even set the water temperature in the bath to lukewarm instead of frigid. Not out of the goodness of his heart, though. Oh no, he wanted her to lower her guard, to trust him, and once he lulled her into a false state of security, he would go in for the kill and get the answers he needed.

Hudson stood up. "Thanks again."

"You'll find soap and shampoo in the cabinet under the sink," he said graciously.

She disappeared into the bathroom and closed the door behind her, but Connor made no move to leave. He stood outside the door instead, waiting, listening. He heard rustling, fabric sliding over skin and softly hitting the tiled floor.

His mouth grew dry as he envisioned her naked body, imagined kicking open that door and yanking her into his arms, feeling her tits crushed against his chest, her hot pussy clamped around his cock.

The carnal image did nothing to put out the fire building in his groin. Didn't help that he couldn't remember the last time he'd fucked a woman. Months, maybe. Yeah, at least four months. He'd gotten wasted and allowed Rylan to drag him to the whorehouse in the mountains. It was no wonder his body was so out of control. Put a beautiful woman in front of it and he was bound to get worked up.

He wandered over to where Hudson had left her jacket. Curious, he picked it up and investigated the inner pockets. His eyebrows rose when he found the arsenal hidden in the various sheaths sewn into the material. He counted six sharp-as-fuck knives before dropping the jacket and unzipping the duffel bag she'd been carrying.

He rummaged through the bag, pushing aside random items of clothing, a pair of sneakers, until his hand connected with a 9 mm.

The final tally ended up being five guns and eight knives, not including the ones in her jacket. The woman was armed to the teeth. He wasn't sure if he was impressed or suspicious. Probably both.

A splashing noise caught his attention. Hudson was getting in the tub. Good.

He squared his shoulders and made his move, striding into the bathroom just as her breasts slid beneath the water.

"What are you doing?" she squeaked. She'd been tying her hair in a knot atop her head, but she let the golden mass drop the moment he walked in.

He couldn't help it—he took a good long look at her full, perky breasts with their rosy pink nipples, then the mouthwatering paradise between her legs. Her pussy was completely bare, and his cock was totally enjoying the view.

"Taking advantage of the situation." He smirked. "I want answers, sweetheart, and you're gonna give them to me."

Dismay flashed in her eyes as she attempted to shield her nudity from him. One hand splayed over her mound, while the other folded over her breasts, and the self-conscious actions triggered another jolt of suspicion. Outlaw women didn't hide their bodies—they were used to living in camps where privacy didn't exist. Where *modesty* didn't exist.

"Can you please go?" Her voice was tight with contempt.

"No." He propped his shoulder against the doorframe and fixed a hard stare in her direction. "Who are you? Where did you come from?"

She met his gaze head-on, and though her cheeks were flushed with visible embarrassment, she didn't look afraid of him. "I was living in the East with a group of people."

"Who were all killed." He recited her story back at her. "Tell me, how exactly did that happen?"

"It was during a sweep. The Enforcers ambushed us at night and dragged everyone out of their tents. I was walking in the woods when it happened. I heard the screams and gunshots and knew something terrible was going down. So I hid." She paused. "Can I have some privacy now?"

"No." He cocked his head. "Might as well soap yourself up, baby, before the water gets cold."

Hesitation creased her face. Then, letting out a resigned breath, she dropped her hand from her breasts and reached for the bar of soap on the edge of the tub.

Connor was momentarily distracted by her tits, but he forced himself to concentrate on what mattered. "What happened after that?"

She worked the soap into a lather without looking at him. Her skin was flushed, her hands ungainly as she moved the slippery bar over her body. Clearly she wasn't used to being on display, but he didn't give a shit if he was making her uncomfortable.

"Eventually the screaming stopped and the Enforcers left," she said flatly. "I went back to camp and everyone was dead."

She told the story in a faraway voice, as if the tragedy had happened to someone else. And all the while, she continued to soap up her body. "I left the camp early the next morning—"

"Yet somehow you managed to hold on to your duffel bag full of weapons," he said dryly.

"I had it with me in the woods." She scowled at him. "I never leave it behind."

"Uh-huh. Okay. Then what happened?"

"I knew I had to get as far away from the area as possible, so I ran."

One slender arm reached for the shampoo bottle on the edge of the tub. She unscrewed the top and dumped a generous amount into her palm, then dunked her head under the water. When she reemerged, she worked the shampoo into her wet hair, fingers gently moving over her scalp.

Christ, she was one spectacular-looking woman. There wasn't an ounce of fat on her long, lithe body, and yet she wasn't lacking in curves. His gaze lingered on her breasts again, saliva flooding his mouth as he imagined those firm tits filling his hands, hard little nipples straining against his palms.

She submerged herself to rinse off the shampoo, then popped up again. "I traveled at night and slept during the day, usually in the woods. I was planning on heading to the West Coast. Then I ran into a guy who told me about the bar. I went there, met you guys, and *the end*."

He didn't believe her.

Her story sounded like all the ones he'd heard hundreds of times before. Friends and families killed during sweeps, finding yourself alone in a world that wasn't safe anymore. It had happened to him, to his friends, to strangers he'd met, and there was no reason why it couldn't have happened to Hudson.

But he still didn't believe her.

"And this training you claim to have?" he prompted. "The medical knowledge? How'd that happen, sweetheart?"

"Can you stop calling me sweetheart?"

Her annoyed reply caught him off guard. Or maybe he was shaken because she was getting out of the tub, making it impossible not to notice, well, everything. Droplets pooled on her smooth pale skin, glistening on her tits and sliding down those incredible legs. He wanted to reach out and touch her. Lick those drops off her.

"You say it like an insult," she went on, "not a term

of endearment. So unless you want me to start calling you something equally insulting, like *babycakes* or some shit, call me by my name."

He fought a grin.

"Now, pass me a towel. I'm getting cold." The pink splotches on her cheeks betrayed her blasé tone.

She wasn't used to being naked in front of a man—Connor instantly sensed that. Which made him wonder . . . Shit, was she a *virgin*?

His cock twitched at the thought of being the first to slide into her tight, hot body. Jesus. He *really* needed to get laid. Soon. Before he did something seriously stupid.

He grabbed a thin towel from the rack behind the door and handed it over without a word. She wrapped the towel around her body, tucked it over her breasts to keep it closed, then marched right past him and left the bathroom.

Connor's jaw hardened. "The training," he repeated, his voice harsh.

"Some of the people I was with fought in the People's Army before it was disbanded."

Keeping her back turned to him, she pulled a few items of clothing out of her bag. Then her shoulders tensed, as if she were debating what to do next.

What she did next was let the towel drop to the floor, providing him with a torturous view of the sweetest ass he'd ever seen.

His dick pulsed with need.

Grow the fuck up, he told his attention whore of a cock.

"They taught me how to fight," she added over her shoulder. "And one of them was a medic, so he made sure I knew the basics."

She wiggled into a pair of red panties, yanked black

leggings up to her hips, and slipped into a loose T-shirt. "When the Enforcers found us, fighting back didn't get us anywhere. They have better weapons, better vehicles, better everything. My group didn't stand a chance."

It wasn't the first time Connor had heard those words. Hell, he'd uttered them himself, knew firsthand what those bastards were capable of. Dominik and his men showed no mercy.

But goddamn it, he didn't believe her.

"You're lying to me." His tone was hard, his expression even more so.

She took a step toward him, bringing with her the scent of soap and coconut shampoo. Connor held his breath, refusing to let the alluring fragrance cloud his judgment. Everything about her got to him. The way she walked, her determination, that odd paradox of fearless vulnerability.

He wanted to sink his cock inside her and fuck her blind.

"Connor—" she started.

"You're lying. I don't know why and I'm not sure I care. But you're lying."

No mistaking the flicker of panic in her eyes. "Damn it, what more do you want to hear?"

"The truth, for one."

Her shoulders slumped in defeat. "Can't you just be satisfied with the story I told you?"

He chuckled despite himself. The way she phrased it—*the story I told you*—was all but an admission of guilt.

"Sorry, sweetheart, but the truth is the only thing that'll satisfy me."

"What if the truth is too awful?" Her voice rang with uneasiness. "What if it's unforgivable?"

He shrugged. "We've all done awful, unforgivable

things. Myself included. Hell, talk to Kade about what he did in the city before he escaped. Only difference is, *we* own up to it. We don't lie to each other."

She hesitated, lips parting as if she wanted to say more. Change her tune.

But she didn't.

"I'll contribute while I'm here," she whispered. "I can help you on that raid. Cook, clean, whatever you want."

"Whatever I want?" He didn't bother disguising the seductive note in his voice, but at the same time, he wondered why the hell he was toying with her.

"Is that it?" she challenged. "You want me to screw you in exchange for a roof over my head?"

He gave another shrug. "I don't barter for sex. If I want to get laid, there are countless women who'd be happy to help me out—and they won't ask for a damn thing in return."

The relief on her face was hard to miss. But the disappointment . . . well, that was hard to see, unless you were looking for it. Which he was. He searched those silvery eyes, chuckling when he glimpsed the telltale gleam.

"You wanted me to say yes." His head slanted thoughtfully. "You wanted to have the decision taken out of your hands, didn't you?"

Her mouth tightened. "I don't know what you're talking about."

Connor took a predatory step forward. "You're aching for it."

She edged backward, until her hip bumped the corner of the table next to the bed.

He moved closer, stopping when they were less than a foot apart. "I wouldn't get a single protest from you, would I? If I bent you over this table and fucked you hard?" A dark laugh slipped out when he saw her shiver. "Oh yeah, you'd love every second of it."

Her gaze found his again. "You'd make sure I did. You strike me as a man who knows how to make a woman feel good."

Connor raised a brow in surprise. He hadn't expected an answer from her, let alone one so brazen. "I could make you feel a lot of things, Hudson. Pleasure is one. Pain is another. If you bring trouble to my door, I won't hesitate to throw you out on your ass. Or worse."

She straightened her back. "There won't be any trouble. Especially if this place is as secure as I think it is."

"Good." With a nod, he stalked to the door.

"Connor."

He stopped. Waited.

"Yes."

Frowning, he shifted around so he could see her eyes. "Yes, what?"

Her head jerked to the table beside her. "If you . . . did what you just described . . . then, yes, I'd love every second of it."

The soft, heat-laced words nearly blew the tip of his cock off.

Without a word, he stalked out of the cabin. The rock between his legs made it difficult to walk properly—and confirmed what he'd already suspected.

This woman was very, very dangerous.

"I don't like this," Pike announced the next morning. He shoved aside the cup of coffee Connor had dropped in front of him, but they both knew he wasn't referring to the coffee.

"Me neither." Xander sounded equally annoyed. "Why the hell would you bring a stranger back to camp?"

Connor frowned as he sank into the chair across from Pike's. He'd sent Kade to grab their boys from the bar, and the man had apparently used the return trip to tell Pike and Xander all about their new guest, because it was the first thing Pike had brought up when he'd entered the lodge.

"Hey, don't look at me," Connor muttered. "These two assholes guilt-tripped me into it."

"It wasn't a guilt trip. It was the truth," Kade said, his normally laid-back demeanor replaced by barely contained anger. "It's dangerous for her to be alone. It's dangerous for anyone to be alone. Dominik and his men are out of control."

Connor couldn't disagree. They'd been hearing too many nasty stories lately. More rapes, more violence, and a lot less peacekeeping. The Enforcers didn't seem interested in talking anymore, or giving outlaws the choice to rejoin society. These days they just put a bullet in your head and called it a day.

Kade went on. "Look, she's smart, and she's obviously got skills. She might be an asset."

"You forgot *hot as fuck*," Rylan said wryly.

Pike scowled. "Is that it? You brought her here to screw her? Because you can find pussy anywhere, for chrissake. You know, the kind you don't have to invite to *live with us*."

"She's not staying," Connor said firmly.

"Good. We need her gone before the run tonight," Xander answered. "It'll be risky enough without throwing an unknown variable into the mix."

"Did you speak to the people at the bar?" Connor asked.

The other man nodded. "They didn't have anything good to say about that storage facility. Apparently it's more heavily guarded than the other ones we've hit. Motion sensors, cameras, at least six Enforcers on site."

"Actually, it's only two," a female voice hedged.

The men turned as Hudson entered the lounge, and damned if Connor's dick didn't harden at the sight of her. Black leather pants were glued to her endless legs, and the fabric of her gray T-shirt—the same silvery shade as her eyes—was so worn and thin it might as well have been a second layer of skin. She wasn't wearing a bra either, and Connor knew he wasn't the only one who could see the perfectly outlined nipples straining against her shirt.

Rylan's visible approval made him stifle a sigh. Hell, even Xan's eyes had flared with heat.

Shit. He couldn't have his men getting hot for the woman. It was a distraction they couldn't afford right now.

Hudson glanced at the two newcomers. "Hi. I'm Hudson," she said shyly, then gestured to the coffee urn. "Can I have some of that?"

Xander, who had just vocally objected to her presence, was the one who hopped up to pour her a cup. Sexed-up moron even pulled out a chair for her. Fucking wonderful. Two seconds in Hudson's presence and Xan was already singing a different tune.

"Thanks." She took a sip of coffee, then continued in a tentative tone. "Anyway, like I was saying, you only need to worry about two guards."

"Yeah? And how do you know that?" Connor challenged.

She shrugged. "I ran into an Enforcer deserter a few days ago when I was making my way here. He gave me some valuable intel."

Pike's dark eyes shone with the distrust that everyone else was feeling. "That so? Because we sure as shit haven't come across any deserters around these parts."

"They don't like to advertise it, but trust me, they exist."

An edge hardened Connor's tone. "Met a lot of them, have you?"

"Just two." Another shrug. "One was a member of my group before they were killed."

"Funny, you didn't mention that last night."

"I didn't think it was important."

She took a dainty sip, but the feminine innocence of her body language was deceptive. Yeah, she'd blushed like crazy when he'd seen her naked last night, but sexual inexperience didn't mean weakness. Because the woman was tough as nails—Connor could see it just by looking at her. Even as she sipped her coffee like she had no care in the world, she was meticulously aware of her surroundings. The positions of the men, the weapons on the table, the various exits in the room, every last fucking detail. Her gaze was as sharp as his, and a crazy thought suddenly occurred to him.

Was she an Enforcer? One of the deserters she'd hinted at?

But no, that was impossible. All the Enforcers in the Colonies were marked with a compass rose. The men had it tattooed on the back of their neck. The rare women who joined the military unit were inked on their wrists.

Before Hudson could react, Connor leaned across the table and snatched both her hands. Her breath caught, and the tin cup she was holding shook wildly, dark liquid spilling over the rim and splashing the tabletop. He wrenched the cup from her hand and set it down, then twisted both her wrists so he could see the insides of them.

They were bare.

When he lifted his head, Hudson was watching him warily.

"Are you done?" she muttered.

He released her without a word. Couldn't have done it soon enough, either, because the second their flesh had made contact, a zing of heat had traveled from his fingertips straight to his balls. Hell. Maybe he ought to fuck her already. Get it out of his system so he could concentrate on what mattered—getting rid of her.

Their gazes locked, and he glimpsed a flicker of fascination in her eyes, as if she was intrigued by whatever she was seeing on his face.

"Anyway." Rylan cleared his throat. He glanced from Connor to their unwanted visitor, humor in his eyes. "So your source says security at the storage facility has been downgraded?"

Hudson shifted her gaze to Rylan. "He's certain of it. I guess the Enforcers were worried they were wasting too many resources on the storage stations and not enough on city patrols and colony sweeps. So they reduced the amount of guards." She paused. "They installed land mines to compensate for the loss of manpower."

"Shit," Rylan murmured.

"Land mines," Connor echoed. He couldn't keep the sarcasm from his voice. "Any chance your *source* knows what kind of explosives we're dealing with?"

"Sorry. That's all he told me. But I assume he meant the ones that go *boom*." Her sarcasm rivaled his.

Pike joined in with a surly scowl. "You don't have anything else we can use? Locations? Trigger mechanisms? Blast radius?"

"Sorry," she said again.

Connor bit back a curse and thought it over. He supposed they could always reschedule the raid, at least until they conducted some more recon. They'd accounted for six Enforcers, which was usually the deal. Definitely hadn't accounted for land mines, though.

But they were in desperate need of supplies. They were out of antibiotics because Rylan was an impulsive motherfucker who couldn't stop from getting hurt every time he stepped out the door. They needed more ammo too, and battery packs if they could find them. They were doing all right in the food department, but stocking up for winter would be nice. Assuming they'd be here in the winter. At the moment, their camp was secure, but that could change in a heartbeat.

"Are we holding off?" Rylan asked, reading his mind.

After a beat, Connor shook his head. "No. But we'll have to leave now."

The others looked startled. They didn't travel in the daylight if they could help it.

"Are you crazy?" Xander demanded.

"We need to be ready to move at night. That means extra recon during the day. We'll watch the rotation of the guards, however many there are—" He speared Hudson with a curt look. "And we'll assess this potential land mine situation before we even think about moving in."

The men's reluctance faded as they each nodded at his orders. The way they trusted him implicitly made him ill at ease. Technically, Rylan and Pike had more military experience. Although the People's Army had "officially" disbanded two decades ago, there were outlaw groups that continued to train and fight for the cause, waiting for their chance to wrestle the power from the GC's hands. Rylan and Pike had once trained recruits for the cause.

Connor's training had ended the second his father had taken a bullet to the head when Connor was ten years old. After that, he'd been forced to teach himself everything else he needed to know. He'd had his mother to protect, not to mention the rest of their group, which had consisted mostly of women and children because the other men had suffered the same fate as Connor's father.

He'd never wanted to be a leader. Fuck, he didn't want it *now*. He couldn't stomach the thought of having any more deaths on his conscience.

"What about her?" Pike jerked a thumb at Hudson.

"I'm right here, you know," she said irritably. "You don't need to talk about me in the third person."

"How about you shut your smart mouth, little girl?" Pike snapped. "The only reason you're even here is because my boys think with their dicks and not their brains."

Anger radiated from her body, but she wisely stayed quiet.

"He has a point," Rylan said tentatively. "We can't leave Hudson alone at camp when we go." He shot her a rueful look. "No offense."

"I get it. We're strangers." She glanced around the table. "But I meant everything I said last night. I've had training, and some knowledge of how the Enforcers operate. I can be an asset if you give me a chance."

Every pair of eyes flicked back to Connor.

Hudson smirked at him. "Wow. Look at the blind obedience you invoke in them. I'm impressed."

He ignored the barb, still thinking about what to do.

He was never *not* thinking, and fuck, it was exhausting sometimes. He hadn't asked to be in charge, and he resented his men for placing this much faith in him.

He studied Hudson's earnest face, her golden hair and flawless features. Her looks were a goddamn distraction, but despite what Pike believed, Connor didn't think with his dick. Maybe he'd fuck this woman, maybe he wouldn't. Right now he was concerned only about what she could do for him outside the bedroom. He recognized the strength in her. She'd held a knife to his throat last night. Gotten close enough to do it, which didn't happen often.

"She comes with us," he said briskly.

Gratitude and pleasure brightened Hudson's expression. "Thank you. You won't regret it."

Connor shifted his gaze in dismissal and scraped back his chair. "We leave in an hour."

4

These men could never know the truth about her.

She'd almost confessed everything to Connor last night, when he'd held her captive with his hypnotizing eyes and taunted her about bending her over the table, but common sense had prevailed at the last second. She heard the contemptuous tone they used when they spoke about the Enforcers. If they knew who she was, they'd kill her on the spot.

Or . . . send her back to the city.

No. She couldn't go back there. She might not be safe among the outlaws, but she wasn't safe with Dom anymore, either. Her brother had turned into a stranger, and the only life she'd ever known had become more dangerous than anything she might encounter in outlaw territory.

And even if Dominik wasn't looking for her, there was no doubt in her mind that *Knox* was.

A chill raced up Hudson's spine as she pictured Knox's face. Handsome and cruel. Savage dark eyes and a mouth that was always curled in a sneer. It frightened her to think what he'd do if he found her. If her own brother had refused to protect her from that monster, then nobody else in the city would.

Which meant she had to protect herself. She had to stay silent and prove to Connor and his men that she could be trusted.

Easier said than done. The fact that he'd examined her wrists this morning told her that Connor was more suspicious of her than she'd thought. In that moment Hudson had never felt more grateful to her father for marking her neck instead of her wrists. He'd wanted her to feel equal to Dominik, had thought it would please her to be treated as if she were one of the boys. But her title of "Enforcer" had always been an honorary one.

Because she *wasn't* an Enforcer. She was a nurse, and she *helped* people. She was a good person, damn it.

But even though she was currently plastered to Connor's body like glue, she could still feel deep waves of mistrust rolling off his powerful body. He'd refused to let her out of his sight, insisting that she ride with him today, and for the past two hours she'd clung to his muscular chest as the motorcycle sped down the dirt back roads they were taking to the storage facility.

The hard muscles beneath Hudson's palms were wreaking havoc on her senses. Connor's body was remarkable. Every sleek, defined muscle strained against her fingertips, and despite the wind that was battering her face and whipping her hair around, she could smell his woodsy, masculine scent, breathing it in whenever she shifted her head.

He slowed down as they rode along an overgrown stretch of road with grass and shrubs slicing up through the cracked pavement. They hadn't passed a single town or city on the way, but now they were approaching an area that showed signs of former civilization. Run-down houses and abandoned storefronts came into view, but Connor revved the engine and quickly veered onto another back road.

It was another hour before they finally reached their destination—a wooded area behind a fenced-in warehouse that looked shiny and new compared to the other structures they'd seen. The chain-link fence was tipped by barbed wire and stood twelve feet high; at the top of every fence post was an ominous black camera sweeping the perimeter.

It always startled her to see technology in use outside the walls of West City, but she knew the Global Council made sure to keep certain communication towers and satellites in operation to aid the Enforcers who worked beyond the city borders.

Her boots connected with the ground, and she flinched when Pike stalked up to her and Connor. She wasn't going to lie—Pike scared the shit out of her. Of all the men, he was the most difficult to read, and yet it was easy to figure out he didn't like her. Or trust her. Or want her around. If it were up to him, she probably would have been banished on sight.

So . . . if she wanted to stay with these men, she needed to win over Pike.

Or maybe just Connor, because Pike seemed to follow his lead even when he clearly disagreed with some of Connor's decisions. Winning them both over, however, would definitely guarantee a stress-free existence.

Except . . . who was she kidding? There was no such thing as a stress-free life, not in this unfamiliar world she'd found herself in. Not when she wanted Connor more than she wanted her next breath.

"Split up," he barked at his men. "Get in position. Cover all four quadrants, same as usual. Hudson and I will take up position here."

She marveled at how fast the others snapped to action. She'd never met a man who commanded swift obedience the way Connor did. Even her brother, who'd been leading the Enforcers for years, didn't inspire that same level of loyalty from his people.

Hudson wondered if Connor had ever heard the word *no*. If he'd ever clapped his hands the way he had now and gotten refusal instead of submission.

She honestly didn't think so.

"Tell me what you see," Connor ordered after the men had dispersed. He dropped a pair of binoculars in her hand and gestured to the warehouse two hundred yards away.

Was this a test? Taking a breath, she raised the glasses and took a good long look. The oxygen lodged in her throat when she glimpsed an Enforcer uniform: black tactical gear, with the red compass rose stitched on the right breast pocket.

She'd known that coming along for the raid was a risk because she might spot someone she knew working at the storage station, but she'd been confident Connor wouldn't let her step foot inside, not when the facility was chock-full of dangerous goodies she could use against them. She was relieved that she didn't have to worry about the perimeter guard recognizing her—the young man guarding the facility was a complete stranger.

She watched in silence for the next two minutes before handing the binoculars back to Connor. "One exterior guard patrolling the outskirts of the warehouse. Radio clipped to his belt, so he's in contact with someone, most likely the second guard posted inside."

Connor nodded and took over surveillance, the solid weight of his arm brushing her shoulder as he peered into the glasses.

Had she passed the test? She truly had no clue.

She studied his chiseled profile, swallowing the desire that fluttered up her throat. He was so incredibly sexy. Imposing as hell. Oozing power. He made her body come alive, made it ache in a way it never had before.

Sex was a common affair in the Enforcer compound. The men fucked as hard as they fought. But Hudson hadn't been granted the same privileges. Her brother's constant presence had ensured that no man would dare touch her. Only two had been brave enough to take her to bed.

Both had suffered brutal beatings at Dom's hands once he'd found out.

Connor turned his head, fixing his hooded hazel eyes on her. "You want it bad—don't you, sweetheart?"

She gulped. "I don't know what you're talking about."

A low chuckle slid in her direction. "When was the last time you got laid?"

Hudson hoped he couldn't see the flush rising in her cheeks. "None of your business," she said primly. "When was the last time *you* got laid?"

"Too long," he rasped. "Which is why you need to stop looking at me like that. Otherwise I'll do something I might regret."

A thrill shot through her, turning into a flurry of shivers when his arm shifted again and his elbow grazed the side of her breast. Her nipple instantly puckered, and she instinctively angled her body, craving the friction caused by his biceps rubbing against that tight bud.

Oh boy. She wanted this man so badly, she could scarcely breathe.

"Don't fucking tease me," he growled.

She shocked herself by whispering, "Why not?"

"Trust me, you don't want to open that door."

But she did. She really, really did.

She'd never met anyone like him. Primal and virile and sex personified. His hard edges excited her, because she knew he wouldn't be tender with her if they slept together. He wouldn't treat her like fine china the way her previous lovers had. They'd been so afraid to leave marks, so afraid that Dominik would find out what they were doing. And they were right to be afraid.

Connor didn't strike her as the kind of man who feared *anything*.

He must have glimpsed her disappointment because he chuckled again. In the blink of an eye, he reached out and cupped the breast she'd been wantonly rubbing against him.

Hudson gasped when he squeezed it. Harder than anyone else ever had, herself included. The callused pad of his thumb pressed down on her nipple, drawing a tortured moan from her lips.

"Do you want me to fuck you?"

Her breath snagged. She hadn't realized that arousal could actually *hurt*. It paralyzed her throat and throbbed between her legs, sending pinpricks of excitement racing along her flesh.

"Do you?" he prompted.

After a long, heart-pounding beat, she shocked herself again by nodding.

His eyes burned as his thumb toyed with her nipple. He stroked lazy little circles around the rigid bud, and Hudson was frozen in place, held captive by his heated gaze and the almost-painful pulsing of her clit.

"Yeah? You think you can handle me, Hudson? You

think you can handle it when I spread your legs and fuck you with my tongue? When I ride you so hard you can't walk for days afterward?"

Holy. *Shit*.

Pressure gathered in her core, a tight, hot knot that had her squeezing her legs together. She was pretty sure she'd stopped breathing a while ago. Her lungs burned. Her throat was clamped shut.

"Answer me," he muttered. "Do you think you can handle it?"

She managed another nod, then fought a dizzying rush of pleasure as he pinched her nipple.

When he abruptly released her breast, she nearly wept from the loss of his hand.

What was *happening* to her? Two days ago her sole concern had been getting as far away from West Colony as fast as possible. Now the only thing she wanted was to spread her legs and let Connor fuck her until she couldn't remember her name.

"Do you want my cock, Hudson?" His voice was low and seductive.

She nodded again, mesmerized by the naked lust in his eyes.

He licked his lips. "Where?"

"W-what?"

"Where do you want me to put it?"

She bit back a moan. "Inside me."

"You'll have to be more specific, baby."

He was taunting her now. With his eyes, and his words, and the lazy swipe of his hand over his stubble-covered jaw. She got the feeling this was another test, but damn it, she didn't know what he wanted from her. He *knew* she wanted him. He fucking knew it, so why did she have to say it?

Hudson opened her mouth, only to get cut off by static from Connor's radio.

Just like that, the heat in his gaze was extinguished like fire in the rain. "Yeah?" he barked into the radio, all business now.

Rylan's voice rippled out. "I'm thinking our girl's right about the guard situation. I'm only seeing one out here."

Relief swept through her as Rylan confirmed the information she'd given them. Good. She was another step closer to earning their trust.

"Xan's working on disabling the cameras, but he left one of his wireless gizmo gadgets in the Jeep. He needs to leave his post."

"Tell him to come back here," Connor answered. "I'll cover his post. He can stay with Hudson."

Disappointment tickled her stomach at the thought of Connor leaving her, but Hudson forced herself not to show it. Besides, it was better that he hadn't ordered her to accompany him. She had no idea who might be working inside that storage station. If it was someone who could recognize her . . .

No. She was better off staying hidden.

Even after darkness fell, Connor continued to bide his time. He'd been on enough runs to learn that patience was key. It was the difference between getting a bullet to the head and walking out with your ass intact, and Connor was pretty fucking fond of his ass.

The Enforcer patrolling the perimeter wouldn't be nearing the gate for another five minutes. They had to time it right if they wanted to hold on to the element of surprise.

Rylan stood next to Connor, a semiautomatic in his

hand and a black wool hat covering his bright blond hair. "I'm surprised you left her with Xan."

There was no need to ask who Rylan was referring to. "Why?" he asked with a frown.

"Because it's not your style. When you're hot for a woman, you don't usually hand her over to another man."

Connor shrugged.

"Not denying the *hot for her* part, huh?"

"What's the sense in denying it? We both want her naked."

"Hell yeah, we do. She's sexy."

Which was one of the few requirements Rylan had for his women. Sexy. Willing and eager. And if she liked a little rough play, all the better. Connor knew his friend well and had a lot of experience with what got Rylan off. But he knew himself, too, and he sure as shit wasn't letting a pretty face play him for a fool.

"She's lying to us." He paused. "She's from the city."

Rylan stiffened. "You sure about that?"

"Not yet, but I will be."

That earned him a low chuckle. "What do you have in mind?"

"I don't know yet. Maybe a visit to Lennox's. Maybe something else." His jaw hardened. "We're not bringing her back to camp until I know more." And he knew he wouldn't get the truth out of her by simply asking. She wouldn't tell him a damn thing. Which meant he needed to make her *show* him.

Damn this woman. He couldn't get a grasp on her, and that pissed him off. She wasn't an outlaw—that was a given. She wasn't an Enforcer; otherwise she would've been marked. That left one option.

She was a citizen.

But that didn't feel right, either. It was easy to spot West City residents—all you had to do was look for sheep. Weak, mindless people living in a bubble of false security and blissful oblivion. Sure, there were a few who recognized that their existence was nothing more than a prettily wrapped prison, but they stayed inside it because they preferred the GC to the ravaged world beyond the city walls.

And then there were the ones who'd had enough. The ones like Kade, who couldn't stomach another day behind those walls and orchestrated their own escape.

Citizens had one thing in common, though—they couldn't fight for shit. Couldn't defend themselves, couldn't protect others. It had taken Connor months to whip Kade into shape.

Hudson knew how to take care of herself like an outlaw, yet she was sheltered like a citizen. She couldn't even say the word *pussy*, for fuck's sake. She'd *blushed* when he'd taunted her about sex. Outlaw women didn't blush. If they wanted to get fucked, they said so. In explicit detail.

So who the hell was she?

Connor checked his watch, pushing all thoughts of Hudson aside. He clicked his radio and addressed Xander. "Kill the cameras. Now."

Five seconds ticked by before Xander responded. "Done."

"Go time," Connor murmured.

Rylan cocked his weapon and grinned. "Let's do this shit. My man Xan needs a new razor."

Like clockwork, the perimeter guard came ambling around the corner. A second later, Connor and Rylan burst out of the shadows.

Fear widened the young Enforcer's eyes when he spotted them. His rifle snapped up, but not fast enough—Rylan was already knocking it out of his hand. The kid's arm shot up as he tried switching his earpiece on, but he froze when Connor's knife angled over his throat.

"Nice and easy," Connor rasped in his ear. "We're not going to hurt you."

"Screw you," the kid sputtered.

Connor dug the blade deeper, but not deep enough to draw blood. They needed the guy alive. If the warehouse really was protected by mines, then this kid was the only one who knew the right path to the door.

"No need to be an asshole," Rylan drawled. "We're all buds here."

"Yup, we're about to be the best of friends," Connor agreed.

Keeping the knife in place, he yanked the guard toward the electronic panel by the gate door. He used his free hand to lift the key card from the Enforcer's front pocket, then swiped it to open the gate. A light blinked from red to green, and then the lock released with a *click*.

Rather than walk through the gate, Connor lightly dragged the blade over his captive's throat. "Here's what's going to happen. You're going to lead us inside, because a friend doesn't let another friend get ripped apart by land mines—right, buddy? And then, when we get to the door, you're going to call out to your partner and assure him that everything is all right." Connor paused. "And look, yeah, we're buds and all, but you should know—one wrong move and I'll slice your throat. And then my friend blows your head off, just for fun."

"It's overkill, I know," Rylan quipped. "But one can never be too careful these days."

Connor could feel the Enforcer trembling. Good. Fear made men a lot more amenable than anger did.

Chuckling, he nudged the guard toward the gate. "After you."

Hudson held her breath as she peered into the binoculars. The men had walked through the gate with the young Enforcer in the lead. She hoped the guard didn't do anything stupid, like blow himself up just to take out a couple of outlaws who wanted his supplies.

At the uneasy thought, she had to remind herself that the Enforcers were selfish bastards, each and every one of them. They might have sworn to sacrifice themselves for the colony if needed, but Hudson had seen more than a few of them leave men behind to save their own hides.

Xander looked over, catching the concern on her face. "Don't worry about Con and Ry, doll."

She turned toward him, a tad flustered by his handsome good looks. He was tall and muscular, with a full beard and brown eyes that twinkled playfully at her. She had no clue why these men were so happy-go-lucky all the time. They seemed completely unfazed by the dangers around them.

"They're walking into an Enforcer station—how can I *not* worry?" she retorted.

He shrugged. "They can handle themselves."

Maybe, but she didn't release her breath until she saw the three men reach the door of the warehouse in one piece. Connor kept his knife to the guard's throat, murmuring something in his ear that Hudson knew was a threat, because the Enforcer's shoulders set in a rigid line. A moment later he swiped a key card in the panel next to the door, and the men disappeared inside.

"Pike, what's doing on your end?" Xander barked into the radio.

Pike was quick to respond. "Absolutely nothing. No Enforcers in sight."

"Good." Xander clicked the radio again. "Kade?"

"All clear," came Kade's voice.

Several minutes passed before there was any more activity. Relief flooded Hudson's belly when the metal door swung open and Connor's broad frame filled the doorway. He gave a nod in the direction of the clearing, and this time it was his voice crackling over the radio.

"Move in. Follow the path Rylan laid out. Xan, bring the Jeep right up to the gate. We've got a shit ton of supplies to haul."

Xander was already heading to the vehicle. "Come on," he tossed over his shoulder.

Panic ignited inside her. "You want me to go with you?"

"Of course. It's time for you to pull your weight, doll." He gave her biceps a teasing pinch as she came up beside him. "I hope you can handle some heavy lifting."

Crap. She wasn't worried about the land mines since Rylan had apparently marked a path to the door, but what if there were more Enforcers inside the warehouse? What if one of them recognized her?

"I can wait in the car," she offered feebly.

Xander slid into the driver's seat and started the engine. "Nah. We're gonna need all the hands we can get. Con will give us twenty minutes—thirty, tops—to clean out the place."

Hudson's breathing grew shallow as she got into the passenger side. The entire drive down to the warehouse, she prayed that she didn't know anyone inside the place. That the guards Connor might have captured were blindfolded. That Xander would change his mind and decide she should wait outside.

But he didn't. He parked the Jeep and signaled for her to follow him.

Hudson drew a breath and paused at the edge of the gate, staring at the scuffed white trail zigzagging toward the entrance: chalk, crushed between Rylan's fingers and smeared onto the pavement with his boots, indicating the safe route inside.

Her heart thudded as she and Xander stepped into the fluorescent-lit entryway of the warehouse, which looked like all the other storage facilities she'd visited in the past. Usually with Dominik, or sometimes their father, when he'd felt like leaving his office to make the rounds through the colony.

Aisles and aisles of metal racks took up the cavernous space, shelves neatly stocked with an array of supplies. Several corridors branched off from the main room. Doors labeled HAZARDOUS MATERIALS and MEDICAL spanned the halls, and Xander briskly ushered her toward the latter, thrusting two duffel bags into her hands.

"Grab as much as you can," he ordered. "Antibiotics and painkillers are the priority, but take it all if there's time."

She was left in a twelve-by-twelve-foot room full of metal cabinets and freestanding refrigerators containing so many vials and pill bottles that she knew the allotted twenty minutes of scavenging would barely make a dent in the inventory. She hurriedly got to work filling the canvas bags, all the while praying she'd be able to stay out of sight during the raid.

When she'd stowed as many supplies in the bags as she was able to carry, she reluctantly left the room and made her way back to the entrance, where Xander was manning the door.

"Take those out to Kade," he told her. "He's loading the Jeep."

Hudson eagerly hurried outside, hoping that her part in all this might be over, but when she reached the Jeep, Kade simply handed her two more empty duffels, grinned, and sent her back inside.

This time she tackled the facility's pantry, pulling canned food and boxes of freeze-dried packets off the shelves and shoving them into the duffels. From the corner of her eye she saw Rylan march by with a drum of oil in his hands, which she realized was probably a critical acquisition for the men.

There weren't many operational refineries left on the globe; the few that existed were in East Colony, but West Colony did have its own pipeline, along with a solitary oil rig up north, in an area her father had told her was once called Alberta. Petroleum products were hard to come by outside the city, so she understood the relief on Rylan's face as he trudged past her.

She dropped off her second load of supplies with Kade, then made a third trek inside. She was halfway to the pantry when a sharp voice called out to her.

"Hudson."

Gulping, she turned to find Connor in the corridor.

"Come here a minute." Without awaiting a response, he stalked toward the double doors at the end of the hall. They were marked COMMAND ROOM.

Crap.

Her knees wobbled as she followed him. She was terrified that she was about to come face-to-face with the second Enforcer, that he might be someone she knew from the compound, someone who would take one look at her and—

Two dead bodies were sprawled on the cement floor when she entered the room.

The relief was instantaneous, trailed rapidly by a jolt of guilt for being relieved that the men were dead. She didn't recognize either one of them, but the neat bullet holes in the center of their foreheads made her heart ache.

She turned to Connor. "Why did you kill them?" She couldn't control the note of wary accusation in her tone.

On the other side of the room, Pike raised his head from the papers he'd been shuffling through. "Because we're not stupid," he answered for Connor. "We don't leave loose ends, especially the kind that pose a threat to us."

"You could've tied them up, or knocked them out, or . . ." She drifted off unhappily. "They didn't have to be a threat."

"Everyone is a threat," Pike corrected, then dismissed her with a hard look and continued to rummage through the desk.

Connor didn't contradict his friend's statement. Nor did he seem at all concerned about the two dead Enforcers at his feet. He pointed to a large cabinet against one of the cinder-block walls and asked, "Do you know how to use any of this shit? Xan's our tech junkie and he already took what he needed, but if there's anything you might want, grab it now."

She wandered over to the cabinet, but almost everything inside it was way too advanced for her. Technology continued to thrive in West City, evolving faster than even she could keep up with. She rifled through the shelves and was surprised when she came across a stack of computing tablets that she *did* have experience with.

"Do you guys have a way to get online?" she asked over her shoulder.

Connor nodded.

She held up one of the tablets. "Then I might be able to use these."

"Take 'em all, then."

She tucked the devices into the duffel, then left the command room. A little too eagerly, probably, but she didn't care. She wanted to get out of this facility as quickly as possible.

Rylan came up beside her as she loaded the duffel into the back of the Jeep. "So. Your intel paid off," he remarked, sounding grudgingly impressed. Then he grinned. "You're more than just a pretty face, aren't you, gorgeous?"

"Damn straight." A little burst of joy went off inside her. She'd proved herself useful to them. Now she just had to keep doing that, and maybe they'd actually let her stay.

The more time she spent outside the city, the more she realized that she couldn't survive alone. She'd thought her self-defense skills and medical knowledge would be enough for her to make a life for herself out here, but she'd been wrong. Survival hinged on finding supplies, on finding a camp, on finding other people to watch your back.

She clung to the reminder as they left the storage station less than an hour after raiding it. She *had* to prove to Connor that she could be a good addition to his group, but that conversation would have to wait until later. It was impossible to talk when they were speeding through the dark landscape on Connor's motorcycle.

She settled in for the long ride back to camp only to blink in surprise when Connor pulled off the main road less than thirty minutes later.

Her heart lodged in her throat as the road became bumpier, more and more overgrown. Eventually a faint light became visible through the dense trees, and the road smoothed out, gravel crunching beneath their tires as they followed a winding driveway deeper into the trees.

A few minutes later Connor slowed the motorcycle, and Hudson caught sight of a split-level house in the distance. All the windows were curtained, but light and shadow moved behind the thick drapes.

"What is this place?" she demanded.

Connor killed the engine and dropped the kickstand. "A house."

"Yeah, I got that," Hudson snapped. "Where are we?"

Panic flooded her belly when he didn't answer. Was he planning to leave her here?

He chuckled at her expression. "There's nothing to be scared of, sweetheart."

She swallowed. "No?"

"No." He smiled, his straight white teeth gleaming in the darkness. "This is what we always do after a run. We unwind."

"Unwind?" Her throat went impossibly dry.

"You're an outlaw, right? You know the kind of things we do to relax." His voice lowered. It was husky, raw. "The world is so fucking bleak. So much pain everywhere you look. That's why we take pleasure anywhere we can get it. It's our way . . . Isn't it, Hudson?"

Our way.

Shit. He was testing her again. He still didn't believe her story, and now he was going to . . . to what?

What on earth was she going to find inside that house?

5

Candles illuminated the front hallway. The pale yellow glow cast shadows on the dark paneled walls and danced over the hardwood floor beneath Hudson's feet. The scent of wax and incense wafted all around her. And the sounds . . .

Sex.

The house pulsed with sex.

Husky noises and soft moans echoed from the back rooms, from the corridor to Hudson's left, from the arched doorway off the entrance. It was everywhere, thickening the air and heating her skin, prompting her to look at Connor in suspicion.

Rylan and the others trudged ahead of her, ducking through the heavy oak doors that led to a room Hudson wasn't sure she wanted to enter. She grabbed ahold of Connor's sleeve before he could follow them.

"You brought me to a whorehouse?" she hissed.

He furrowed his brow. "There are whorehouses like this all over the free land. You can't tell me this is your first time visiting one."

"My group never got around to it," she answered in a tight voice.

She didn't like that he hadn't corrected her about

the purpose of the house. If anything, his cavalier tone triggered a spurt of resentment. She didn't want to be here. It reminded her too much of the Enforcer compound, where the men passed women around like pieces of gum. It didn't matter that the women had volunteered to be there. They were still treated like sex slaves and viewed as whores, and it nauseated Hudson to think that the task of pleasuring the Enforcers was deemed an *honor*.

Everyone was considered equal in the city. People got paid the same amount for hauling garbage as they did for working in the technology sector. They lived in allocated accommodations, all identical in size. They ate at assigned meal halls and were served food that met their nutritional requirements. Hudson's father had explained that the practice had once been referred to as *communism*, the idea of common ownership and the absence of social classes.

But every system had a loophole, and the Enforcers had no problem taking advantage of it. The city's women earned monetary bonuses for offering their bodies to the men. Some were even given annual vacations to South Colony. Keep the Enforcers happy, and you were excused from the job rotation to lie on a beach for a week. High-class prostitution at its best.

Hudson frowned at Connor. "You talk about the free land, but you still call this place a whorehouse. Is that how you view women? As whores?"

A slow grin lifted his mouth, as if he were genuinely amused by her accusation. "We're all whores here, sweetheart. Every single one of us."

He uncurled her fingers from his arm but didn't let go of her. Instead, he kept a tight grip on her hand and led her deeper into the house. They passed several closed doors, and Hudson's pulse sped up, because it was painfully obvious what was going on behind those doors. Groans of pleasure. The rhythmic smacking of a headboard hitting the wall. A cry of ecstasy as a woman climaxed.

Hudson drew a breath as they neared the set of doors that Rylan and the others had disappeared through. She tried to steel herself, but nothing prepared her for what she found when they entered the room.

The surprisingly large space offered an array of couches and armchairs, and there was a long bar counter spanning one wall. About two dozen people lingered in the room. Men and women, some fully clothed, some naked. Low voices engaged in conversation mingled with the throaty sounds of sex. In a shadowy corner of the room, a brunette was bent over, facing the wall, as a bare-assed man thrust into her from behind, his hands gripping her waist, his lips pressed against her shoulder.

Hudson wrenched her gaze away from the lewd display, but it just landed on another one—a tangle of naked limbs on a plush couch, a woman's fingernails scraping down the back of the man on top of her.

Did these people have no shame?

Her cheeks were on fire as she sought out a safe place for her eyes. Connor. Connor was safe. Connor wasn't naked.

And maybe she was as shameful as everyone else here, because the fact that he was still dressed brought genuine disappointment to her belly.

A dark-haired man sauntered up to them. Tall and handsome, with magnetic gray eyes that lingered on Hudson before shifting to Connor. "Well, if it isn't Connor MacKenzie. Long time, man."

"Lennox." Connor slapped the man on the shoulder. "How's it going?"

"All right." The man shrugged. "We've been hearing about a lot of the Enforcer stations being repurposed. Some are closing down altogether."

"Security is changing too," Connor admitted. "We just hit a storage facility that was outfitted with land mines."

Lennox frowned. "Well, that's no good."

"Make sure you let your people know. They'll need to change their tactics before they go on any more runs."

"Will do. Thanks for the heads-up." The man's gaze traveled back to Hudson, a smirk playing on his lips. "I see you brought some party favors tonight, Con."

Hudson's shoulders tensed. Was that it? Had Connor brought her here to . . . to be a *party favor* for his outlaw friends?

But he quickly squashed that thought by muttering, "She's not here for that."

"Pity." Lennox smiled at Hudson, and she found herself relaxing at the seductive curve of his lips. "Come find me if you change your mind, love."

As he wandered off, Hudson glanced at Connor apprehensively. "Does he own this place?"

Connor nodded. "Come on. I need a drink," he said, rounding the bar.

Apparently this was a serve-yourself kind of establishment.

She worked up the courage to take another look around and noticed that Rylan had already made himself comfortable. He was sprawled on one of the couches with a tumbler in his hand and a beautiful woman in his lap. Skintight denim encased the woman's legs, and her blond hair fell like a curtain over one shoulder, stopping right below her breasts. Her very bare breasts.

Rylan caught Hudson's eye and winked. Then his hand moved in a slow caress down the blonde's arm before curling to cup one firm breast.

Heat tingled in Hudson's nipples, almost as if Rylan had touched *her*. She squeezed her thighs together and pulled her gaze away.

"What's your poison?" Connor asked gruffly.

She stared at the top-notch alcohol lining the bar top, wondering what kind of payment Lennox demanded from his patrons for drinking his booze. Her heartbeat accelerated as a panicky notion came to mind. No. Nobody was going to lay a hand on her, damn it.

Her gaze landed on Connor's strong hands as he rifled through bottles, and her breasts tingled harder, making her amend that last thought. Nobody was laying a hand on her unless she *wanted* them to.

She unwittingly glanced in Rylan's direction again, her breath hitching when she saw his tongue dart out to taste his companion's nipple.

"Tequila," she choked out, her throat drier than dust.

"Look at those wide eyes," Connor mocked. "Makes me think you've never seen people fucking before."

"No, I . . ." She swallowed. "I have. I saw lots of things at . . . the camp."

He poured two tumblers and walked back to her, leading her to a vinyl stool. "Relax, sweetheart." He forced her to sit, then planted the glass in her hand, the mocking note never leaving his voice. "We're here to have a good time."

Was this his idea of a good time? Watching random

people have sex? She was too afraid to ask, so she lowered her eyes and clutched her drink with such force she was surprised the glass didn't shatter.

"Uh-uh, that won't do."

She flinched when his forceful grip captured her chin, yanking her head up.

"Watch," he ordered.

Her heart raced faster. She was out of her element here. She didn't want to watch. She didn't want—oh fuck, but she *did* want to. Or at least her body wanted it. Her skin felt tight and achy, her nipples harder than the icicles that formed on the compound roof every winter. And that deep pulsing in her core. It was getting worse, spiking her body temperature, making her thighs tremble. She was painfully aware of the wetness between her legs, and a shiver flew up her spine as she focused on Rylan.

His face was buried between the blonde's breasts, hands stroking up and down her bare back, hips rocking slightly as he rubbed his lips over one puckered nipple.

"Tell me what you see." Connor's rough demand was an echo of the one he'd voiced at the storage station, except it was different this time. He wasn't asking her to assess security protocols. He was asking her to describe *debauchery*.

Hudson's voice wobbled. "I see sex."

Connor laughed. "No, not even close. Not yet anyway."

He brought the tumbler to his lips, and Hudson was fascinated by the way his strong, corded throat strained as he drank.

"Don't look at me," he said sharply. "Look at Rylan. Look at *her*. And tell me what you see."

She gulped her tequila. "He's turning her on."

No, he was driving her *wild*. Rylan's cheeks hollowed slightly as he sucked the woman's nipple deep in his mouth, triggering a throaty moan from her lips. Hudson couldn't see the blonde's face, but judging by the way she arched her spine and desperately pushed her breast into Rylan's face, she was clearly enjoying herself.

"Oh, he's turning her on, all right," Connor agreed. "What about you, baby? Is he turning *you* on?"

Hudson shifted to find him watching her intently. "W-what?"

"Do you like seeing him suck on those gorgeous tits?"

The tension in her body intensified, tightening her muscles and making her heart beat erratically. "No," she lied.

Something indecipherable flicked through his eyes. Damn it. She felt like she'd failed another test. That she'd been failing from the second they'd stepped foot in this house. But she didn't know what he expected from her. What he wanted her to say, what he was hoping she'd do. Did he want her to join the party? Saunter over there and push her breasts into Rylan's face too?

A hot shiver ran through her. She could do it. The way everyone in this room was carrying on, no one would care if she joined in. They'd probably be all too happy to initiate her into this world of unadulterated sin.

Except there was one problem. The only man she wanted to be sinful with was sitting right beside her.

"Keep watching."

Hudson hadn't realized she'd turned away until a tug on her hair brought her gaze back to the couch, where the woman was unzipping Rylan's pants.

"I think you're going to like this." Connor's tone

grew downright seductive. "I've never met a woman who doesn't moan at the sight of Ry's cock."

The blonde sank to her knees in front of Rylan, dragging the denim off his muscular legs in one fluid motion. His thick erection sprang up, and a wink of silver caught the light—the barbell running horizontally through the crown of his cock.

Hudson moaned.

Loudly.

Connor grinned. "Yeah, that's about right."

Holy shit. How was any of this happening?

Connor's dark laughter heated her skin as he leaned in closer. "You like the piercing, huh? Most chicks seem to agree with you. One told me it hits a sweet spot deep in her pussy when he's fucking her."

Hudson's breathing went shallow. She squirmed on the stool, impossibly turned on. Wetter than she'd ever been in her life.

"Maybe I'll let you fuck him so you can feel it," Connor offered.

"*Let* me? You have no say in who I screw."

"Yes, I do." He took another sip of tequila. "My men follow my lead. They won't touch you unless I consent to it."

"It must be nice to have minions."

His teeth bared in a harsh smile. "I didn't ask for their loyalty, but I have it. And I'm a ruthless bastard, sweetheart. Someone gives me unconditional loyalty? Damn straight I'll use it to my advantage."

"Yeah? Well, you don't have *my* loyalty." She tilted her head in challenge. "What if I want to go over there?" She turned back in time to see the blonde swallow half of Rylan's cock in one deep gulp, and nearly fell off the stool.

"By all means, go ahead." Connor waved toward the couch. "Just don't expect him to fuck you. Jamie might, though." A contemplative note entered his voice. "You know what? That sounds beautiful, seeing her lips all over you."

Hudson's breath caught.

His warm breath fanned over her ear. "I want to hear the noises you make when her tongue touches your clit." Then he straightened up. "Yeah, let's find out. Why don't you walk your sexy ass over there and put on a show for me?"

Hudson stayed put.

"Or not," he said with a chuckle.

Damn him. He was purposely toying with her and she didn't know why. And she was trapped. Helpless. Every time she moved her head she was greeted by an even dirtier sight. On the other side of the room, Xander was enjoying himself as much as Rylan, his naked body falling back on soft cushions as a raven-haired girl with a full-sleeve tattoo climbed on top of him.

Kade was sprawled on the other end of the couch, fisting his own cock. His expression glittered recklessly, a stark change from what she normally saw on his face. She'd thought he was the sweet one, but there was nothing sweet about him right now. He was as sinful as the rest of them.

"Why did you bring me here?" she whispered.

Connor moved closer again, sending a shiver through her body. His presence was terrifying. Thrilling. She wanted to kiss him. So badly she could practically taste him on her lips.

"You know exactly why I brought you here."

Arousal tightened her throat. "To . . . have sex with me?"

He smiled, and she knew in that moment she was wrong. He hadn't brought her here for sex. He'd wanted her to watch. To *witness*. So she could . . . could what? What was his endgame? What the hell did he want from her?

"Look at Rylan's face," he coaxed. "See the way his brow tightens when she sucks him deep? He looks like he's in pain, but he's not, is he, Hudson?"

"No," she mumbled. "He loves it."

"Oh yeah, he does. He'll start fucking her mouth soon. Fast and hard, until she's choking on his dick. Rylan likes it rough."

His silky voice slid into her ear, and she was suddenly reminded of the stories her father used to tell her about God and the devil. Worshipping a higher power was banned in the Colonies, but Hudson's father had thought it was important to educate her about the religions of the past. They'd all sounded frightening to her, though. Judgmental and shameful, rooted in pain and penance.

But right now, with Connor whispering filth in her ear, it was easy to believe in the existence of the devil. A seductive creature that lured you into the flames of sin, drew you closer and closer until he burned you alive.

"*Watch*," he repeated, low and commanding. His hand curled around her neck to direct her gaze where he wanted it to go.

Hudson bit her lip to stifle a moan as she watched the blonde—Jamie—work Rylan's hard shaft. Connor was right. Rylan's features were stretched tight as if in agony, but the naked pleasure glittering in his eyes belied the pained expression. His lips parted slightly as Jamie swallowed him up again, so deep her nose bumped his tight abs, and then he threw his head back and released a husky growl that Hudson could hear even from where she sat.

"He's not coming." Connor's remark broke through her spellbound haze.

"How do you know?" she found herself asking.

"Because I know what he looks like when he does."

Oh *hell*. Why did he have to plant that image in her head? How many times had these men fucked together? Or *one another*? A hot streak of lust roared through her blood, burning hotter when Connor's fingers lightly threaded through her hair.

"I also know that if he has the choice, he'd choose to come inside a tight pussy over a wet mouth any day." Those long fingers fisted her hair, giving a playful tug. "And look at that—I guess she agrees with him."

Hudson held her breath as Jamie rose to her feet and wiggled out of her jeans. Rylan wasted no time yanking her back into his lap, his large hands splaying on her waist as she lowered herself onto his dick. Twin groans rumbled in Hudson's direction, making her thighs tremble.

It was too much. Too . . . intimate. She wrestled her gaze away, only to gasp when it landed on Kade's hand gripping the base of Xander's shaft, holding it steady as the dark-haired girl's head bobbed over Xander's erection, her hand absently stroking his thigh as she pleasured him.

Breathing hard, Hudson abruptly shifted her gaze. This time it landed on Pike, who stood in the doorway holding a bottle of amber liquid, taking in the same salacious scene she'd just stumbled upon.

"Why doesn't Pike join them?"

Connor propped his elbows on the bar counter and leaned back. "It's not his kink."

"What's his kink, then?"

"He likes to watch." Connor shrugged. "Some people get off on being watched. Others get off on watching. Some get off on both."

Her thighs clenched. "Which one are you?"

He didn't answer.

Frustration jammed in her chest. "Fine, don't tell me." She paused. "You're not going to ask what *my* kink is?"

He offered an infuriating smirk. "No need. I already know the answer."

He did? Because she'd sure as hell like to know. She'd never thought about any of this stuff before. What got her off, what got other people off. Nobody talked about sex in the city; it was done behind closed doors. And even at the compound, where it was out in the open, it wasn't something she'd witnessed often. Dominik had made sure to keep her far away from the raunchy activities his men were involved in.

"Why don't they care that everyone is watching?" she asked in dismay.

Connor's jaw hardened.

Damn it. She'd said the wrong thing again.

"Why should they? Do you want them to feel embarrassed? To worry about what people might think tomorrow?" His expression was impossible to read. "There is no tomorrow, Hudson. Right now is all that matters."

"Live in the moment," she murmured.

"That's what we do, sweetheart. You take pleasure where you can get it, because who knows when you'll get another chance? So, yes, we live in the moment." Then he chuckled, nodding at the far couch. "And what a fucking moment."

Hudson choked back a groan. The raven-haired girl was riding Xander, and Kade was . . . Oh fuck . . . Kade was kneeling behind her, his fingers wrapped around his cock as he guided it to her . . . her . . .

Hudson's pussy contracted so hard, she had to grip the side of the stool to stop from falling over.

Connor noted her reaction with a crude smile. "You like that, huh? Have you ever had a man's cock in your ass, Hudson? And another one in your pussy at the same time?"

She was on fire. She was seriously going to self-combust. The arousal constricting her core was unbearable. Excruciating. If she'd been alone, she would have slipped her hand inside her pants and eased the dull ache, made herself come until she'd screamed herself hoarse.

Connor must have read her mind, because he barked out a laugh. "What are you waiting for? Get yourself off." His eyebrows lifted in a taunt. "I know you want to."

Her heartbeat exploded, a ragged breath squeezing out of her throat. "Do it for me," she blurted out.

6

Connor had never seen a woman more ready to be fucked. Hudson's pupils were dilated, her cheeks flushed, throat straining as if she couldn't draw enough oxygen into her lungs. He could *feel* her arousal. It incinerated the air, tickling his skin and heating his balls. The tight nipples poking through the front of her shirt begged for his tongue, made his fingers itch to rip that shirt off her and feast on her tits.

He wouldn't even have to ask permission. He knew she'd let him put his tongue all over her if he wanted to. She'd spread her legs and offer herself up to him like a goddamn sacrifice.

But that wasn't why he'd brought her here. Sex could wait. Answers couldn't.

"Please." One word, rippling with desperation. Then she uttered it again, this time in the form of a whimper. "*Please.*"

He smiled. "You want me to make you come?"

"Y-yes. Please, Connor."

He dragged one finger along her bare arm. Christ, her skin was hot to the touch. "How? With my tongue? My cock?"

"Both," she choked out.

His fingers skimmed up to her shoulder, scraping the side of her neck before gripping her chin. Gray eyes, smoky with excitement, peered up at him.

"Ask me if I want to fuck you," he commanded.

Her mouth trembled. "Do you . . . want to fuck me?"

"Yes." He swiped his thumb over her bottom lip in a teasing caress. "Ask me if I'm going to fuck you."

Her voice was scarcely above a whisper. "Are you going to fuck me?"

"No." He pinched her lip before clasping both hands in his lap. "If you want to come, you can take care of it yourself."

The frustrated noise that ripped out of her throat had him fighting laughter. "Why are you teasing me?"

"You think this is teasing?" The laugh broke free. "Oh, baby, you have no idea."

Still chuckling, he grabbed her hand and placed it directly on his crotch. Her squeak of protest died as her palm met his hard-on, and when she moaned, the throaty sound vibrated in his aching dick and his body gave an involuntary upward thrust.

"Do you want this?" he muttered, rubbing that hard bulge against Hudson's palm.

She nodded wordlessly. Eyes wide as saucers.

Damn, those big eyes were hot. Sweet innocence didn't usually turn him on, but he liked it on her, liked knowing that a strong, spirited woman like Hudson could come undone just from the feel of his dick pulsing in her hand.

Locking his gaze with hers, he squeezed her hand over his erection. "If you want my cock, you'll have to give me a lot more than wide eyes and shaky little moans."

She visibly swallowed. "What do you want from me?"

"The truth."

He tucked her hand back in her own lap and turned to face the room. Rylan's woman was riding him like a champ, but Connor expected nothing less from Jamie, who ran the place with Lennox. Her tits bounced in Rylan's face as she ground her pussy all over him, and Connor's cock twitched with envy, because it knew it wasn't getting relief anytime soon.

Realizing that Hudson hadn't responded, he gave her a sidelong glance and elaborated. "I want to know what you're hiding, and I'm not giving you a damn thing until I find out what it is."

Anger flashed across her face. Anger, and a helluva lot of lust.

"I will get the truth from you," he said softly. "You know I will. But until then . . . watching you get yourself off is a start."

Her expression filled with alarm. "A start to what?"

"To finding out who you are." Connor shrugged. "You learn a lot about someone when they're panting in orgasm."

Her brows knitted. "How does that teach you anything?"

"If you don't know the answer to that, then you're lying about more than I thought."

Hudson fell silent, shifting her attention to the slick bodies writhing all around them. He heard her labored breathing. Saw her squirming on the stool from the corner of his eye. Then there was a flash of movement, and he hissed in approval when he realized where her hand had gone.

"There you go, baby." He murmured his encouragement as she undid her pants. "Make yourself feel good."

She let out a breath, her fingers trembling as she

slowly pulled her zipper down. When she delicately slipped her hand inside her pants, Connor nearly ordered her to take them off altogether. Her panties too. He wanted her to spread her legs so he could see her. So everyone could see her.

But there was something to be said for the unseen too. The erotic motion of her hand beneath her waistband. The way it curved over her mound, the way her hips bumped up to meet it.

He felt more than one person staring at them, turning to find Rylan's blue-eyed gaze fixated on Hudson's hand. Even as he met the wild thrusts of the woman impaled on his cock, Rylan looked at Connor and lifted a brow in blatant invitation. An offer for Connor to join them, to bring Hudson along for the ride.

Connor gave a slight shake of his head before focusing on Hudson. "Look at Rylan, baby. Look at how much he's enjoying what you're doing to yourself."

"I'd rather look at you," she said in a hoarse voice.

Their gazes held, and he nearly gave in and launched himself at her. He loved seeing a woman veering toward the brink of orgasm. The unbridled pleasure in her eyes, the noises she made. But something about *this* woman got him hotter than usual. His cock was an iron spike in his pants. He ached to take it out and stroke it, but he knew Hudson would like it too much, and he had no intention of giving her anything until he got what *he* wanted.

He dragged his tongue over his bottom lip. "I bet you're wishing that I were the one touching you right now. You're wishing my fingers were rubbing that hot little clit, aren't you?"

Her breathing quickened.

"Are you wet? Would my cock be soaked right now if I put it inside you?"

Her eyes went out of focus as she moaned in abandon. Her hand moved faster, but he knew she wasn't fingering herself. She couldn't, not when her pants were still on.

Christ, he wanted her naked. He wanted to shove his fingers inside her and fuck her with them while she stroked herself. But he kept his hands to himself, curled them into fists and pressed them on either side of the stool to avoid temptation.

Rylan was still watching Hudson. So were several other men, including Lennox, who met Connor's eyes with a grin of approval.

Lennox's door was always open to Connor and the others, and he asked for nothing in return except for backup when it was needed. That was how it worked in the free land. Barter and trade worked fine for material things; the rest of the time outlaws dealt in favors. Lennox didn't call in his favors often, though. Or at least not often enough to justify how much time Connor and his boys spent at this joint. So even though he hadn't brought Hudson here for Lennox, he was glad the man was enjoying the show.

Hudson made a helpless sound that went straight to Connor's cock. Shit, sometimes he wished he *did* think with his dick. At least then he could be inside her right now, fucking them both blind.

When she curled her fingers over the edge of her stool, he *tsk*ed in disapproval and grabbed her hand. Hudson jerked as if he'd shot her, her expression a haze of passion.

"So many sexy things you can be holding on to, and

you choose the chair?" He *tsk*ed again, then moved her hand to her breast and covered her knuckles with his palm, forcing her to squeeze the perky mound.

A breathy cry left her lips, and then her hand moved beneath his, rubbing her nipple in slow, light strokes.

"That's it. Get yourself nice and hot." He drew his hand back and breathed through his nose, trying to quell the arousal running rampant through his body. He absently ran his palm over his crotch, hoping the tiny bit of friction would help ease the ache, but the fleeting stroke only made his dick throb harder.

He picked up his glass instead and downed the rest of his tequila, hoping the burn of the alcohol would distract him from the burn down below. But then Hudson moaned, and he almost shot his load right then. She was almost there. He could see it in the tension of her body, hear it in her soft gasps, feel it in the trembling of her thigh against his chair.

Screw it. One taste. He just needed a taste.

Before he could stop himself, he leaned in and pressed his mouth to hers, swallowing her gasp of delight with his kiss. Except it couldn't even be considered that. It was a hard slapping of mouths and a fast thrust of tongue, no tenderness or finesse, nothing but raw desperation.

Hudson came the moment their lips touched.

Connor wrenched his mouth away in time to see ecstasy darken her eyes and redden her cheeks as she rocked into her own hand and shuddered in orgasm.

It was fucking beautiful.

He couldn't resist stealing another kiss, this time on the side of her throat. Her flesh was hot beneath his lips, quivering as he dragged his tongue over it.

When she finally grew still, her gaze came up to

meet his, and there it was—those wide eyes again. Then she looked around, blushing harder when she realized she had an audience. Rylan was watching her from the couch, his companion gone and his cock in his hand.

"I . . . can't believe I just did that."

She sounded confused and dismayed, and the reaction was enough to confirm everything Connor had already suspected.

Without a word, he dropped his empty glass on the bar top and stood up.

"Where are you going?" Her gaze rested on the very obvious bulge in his pants.

Ignoring her, he sought out Pike and nodded at the other man, issuing an unspoken command for him to keep an eye on Hudson. As Pike made his way over, Connor took a step forward and surveyed the room until he found what he was looking for.

"If you need anything, ask Pike or Ry," he muttered to Hudson.

Then he walked away.

Hudson battled a jolt of shock as Connor turned his back on her and strode across the room like he owned it. Every female head swung in his direction, but he ignored them all, moving with purpose toward a willowy redhead in a skintight black dress.

He didn't look back in Hudson's direction. Not even once.

The afterglow from the mind-shattering orgasm she'd given herself dispersed like a cloud of dust. She watched in disbelief as Connor murmured something in the redhead's ear. The woman said something in return, eliciting a deep chuckle from Connor.

Hearing him laugh with another woman hurt.

Seeing him leave the room with another woman pissed her off.

But really, what did she have to be angry about? They weren't together. They barely even knew each other. Which meant that Connor could have sex with whomever the hell he wanted and Hudson had no right to be mad.

Except . . . she *wasn't* mad, she realized.

She was jealous.

She'd just experienced the most intense orgasm of her life in a roomful of people, and she wasn't even close to being satisfied. She wanted more. She wanted to experience that heady rush again, only this time with Connor as the one bringing her to that edge.

"So who the hell are you?"

Hudson's head jerked up, and she found herself looking at one of the most beautiful women she'd ever seen. "What?" she stammered.

"Just wondering who you are," the brunette drawled. "I've never seen Con show up here with a woman before."

Hudson shot a quick glance at Pike, who stood at the end of the bar watching her like a hawk. But he didn't seem concerned to see her chatting with the curvy brunette.

The woman studied Hudson with mesmerizing brown-black eyes that tilted upward slightly enough to give her an exotic look. Long chestnut-colored hair cascaded over one shoulder and hung over the black corset she wore.

"Are you with him?" the woman asked curiously.

Hudson gritted her teeth. "He left with someone else. Does it *look* like I'm with him?"

That got her a delighted laugh. "Oh, look at that. Kitty cat still has her claws." A seductive hand caressed Hudson's bare shoulder, making her flinch. "I'm Tamara."

"Hudson," she answered reluctantly.

Tamara leaned against the bar. "How do you know Con and the boys?"

"How do *you* know them?"

"I asked you first, kitty cat."

She had to smile. "I ran into them a couple days ago," she admitted.

Tamara's gaze sharpened. "Are you staying with them?"

She knew better than to confide in a stranger, especially about the whereabouts of the men's camp, so she shrugged and said, "Nah. They've been on the move since I met them. If they have a home base, I don't know about it."

The other woman relaxed. "Yeah," she said ruefully. "I've been trying to pry the location outta them for more than a year, but the boys are very hush-hush about where they make camp."

Hudson nodded and sipped her drink. As silence fell between them, her mind wandered back to Connor and the redhead. And the wicked things Connor was probably *doing* to the redhead.

On second thought, maybe she *was* pissed off. Because . . . well, the *nerve* of that bastard. How could he sit there and watch her tremble in orgasm and then abandon her so he could get off with some other woman?

As if reading her mind, Tamara laughed softly. "Ah, don't let it get to you, honey. Connor is a hard man to land." She lit a cigarette and blew a cloud of smoke past Hudson's face, then held out the cigarette pack in offering.

Hudson wasn't much of a smoker, but at the moment she was so on edge, she welcomed the nicotine buzz. She brought the cigarette to her lips and leaned in so Tamara could light it for her.

"Honestly, you'd be amazed at the sheer volume of women that throw themselves at him," Tamara said as she pocketed the silver lighter. "I ran into him at a bar out east once, and the second his fine ass walked into the room, every girl in the place was begging to ride on his dick. But he's very selective. Oh, and he never fucks the same woman twice, so don't worry, hon. That cute little redhead will be nothing but a distant memory in a matter of hours."

Hudson took a drag and eyed Tamara pensively. "Have you ever . . . you know . . . ?"

"With Connor? Nah. He's smarter than that." She grinned. "Connor knows I'd eat him alive. But *him*—" She tipped her chin at Rylan, who was tangled up with Jamie again. "He lets me do whatever I want to him. Doesn't care how many bite marks I leave."

This time, Hudson's cheeks didn't burst into flames when she turned to watch Rylan in action. His powerful buttocks flexed as he pounded into Jamie from behind, and yet Hudson didn't even bat an eye. It was crazy how fast she'd grown desensitized to the lusty activities happening around her. The sex had become background noise.

Tamara followed Hudson's gaze. "Trust me, the man knows how to use that cock of his. And that piercing? Fan-fucking-tastic." She exhaled another puff of smoke, then gave a discreet nod toward Pike. "Now, if you're looking for someone a little more intense, you can go with Pike. Or at least, you can *try* to. He's even more elusive than Con. He's also a mean bastard sometimes, but he's your best bet if you're in the mood for a rough ride." Tamara's eyes gleamed mischievously. "Every girl needs to be manhandled once in a while."

"What about them?" Hudson gestured to the Kade-and-Xander sandwich across the room. "What do they have to offer?"

"To me? Nothing. I fuck men, not boys."

Tamara grinned again, and Hudson couldn't help but grin back. Tamara's boldness was kind of entertaining. Come to think of it, every other woman in the room was throwing off the same confident vibe. It was like they all recognized their own power. They weren't servicing the men like the women who came to the Enforcer compound. They weren't just giving pleasure—they were *taking* it. And damn if that wasn't an exhilarating notion.

She was starting to understand this world now. The idea of living in the moment and taking what you wanted. Her whole life she'd done what her father had expected of her. She'd followed his rules. Dominik's rules. The GC's rules.

But there were no rules here, and she needed to remember that. She needed to forget about the world she'd lived in before and start living in the world she was in now.

She needed to start *taking*.

Hudson wasn't surprised when Connor ordered her to ride in the Jeep with Rylan instead of taking her on the bike, and a part of her was grateful not to be plastered to his body right now. It was hard to think when Connor was around. Hard to block out her attraction to him and just *breathe*.

Luckily, Rylan didn't push her to make conversation, at least not right away. They'd been driving for more than an hour before he finally glanced over with a teasing smile.

"What's the matter, gorgeous? Someone who came as hard as you did tonight shouldn't look so troubled."

She blushed, but her embarrassment was overshadowed by the urgency she was still feeling, that overpowering need to *take*. Or rather, to learn *how* to take.

"C'mon. Tell me what's wrong," he urged.

She let out a sigh. "I'm not sure I know how to live in the moment," she confessed.

The response seemed to intrigue him. "Why do you say that?"

Hudson paused, carefully considering how much information to reveal. "I like the people I've met since I left my other group. I like *you*." She shifted awkwardly. "But I don't fully grasp the whole live-in-the-moment mentality. I . . ."

Before she could second-guess herself, she slid closer and touched the hand he was resting on the gearshift. She dragged her palm over his knuckles, and she knew from the way his breath hitched that her touch had affected him.

Hudson drew a deep breath, ignoring the nervous sensation in her stomach. "I want you to teach me."

Rylan's voice thickened. "Teach you what?"

"How to let go. How to stop fighting and start *feeling*. How to take pleasure."

Emboldened by her own words, she leaned in and pressed her lips to his neck. When he groaned softly, she took it as a promising sign and became even bolder, sliding her hand to his crotch and cupping him over his jeans.

"Teach me," she whispered.

With a sigh, Rylan covered her hand with his, stilling her movements. "If that's what you really want, I'd be happy to help you." He gently removed her hand. "But I'm not the person you need to ask."

She stiffened. "What the hell does that mean?"

"It means it's Connor's say, not mine."

Disbelief dripped from her tone. "Are you telling me he controls your cock? That you can't sleep with a woman unless he gives you permission?"

"Sometimes. It all depends on whether or not he's staked a claim."

Oh, for *fuck's* sake. She couldn't believe the sheer audacity of that statement.

She blew out an aggravated breath. "I am not a piece of land that he can *claim*."

"No, but like it or not, you belong to him. He made the decision to take you in, and now he gets to decide what to do with you. Or who can touch you."

"Bullshit." She angrily raked her fingers through her hair. "I don't belong to him."

"We all belong to him," Rylan said simply. Then he turned his gaze back to the road. "The sooner you accept that, the better off you'll be."

7

Connor never went to bed when there was still work to be done. Didn't matter that it was two in the morning when they got back to base—the supplies from the raid couldn't stay in the Jeep all night, which meant that someone needed to unload them.

But just because he happened to be an anal bastard didn't mean he expected the same from his men.

"Get out of here," he barked when he saw their weary faces. "I've got this."

Xander, Kade, and Pike nodded in relief and strode off toward their respective cabins or, in Pike's case, the run-down stables he'd claimed as his living quarters. Hudson and Rylan lingered, the former standing near the Jeep with a frown, the latter already reaching in the back to grab a crate of canned goods.

"Go to sleep, Hudson," Connor muttered. "It's late."

"Are you sure you don't need any help?"

"We're good."

Her tone sharpened. "Of course. Because you don't need anything from me, right? You've got other people at your disposal to take care of your *needs*."

She marched off before he could answer, summoning a chuckle from Rylan.

"She's pissed at you."

Connor shrugged. "She can be as pissed as she wants. Doesn't bother me."

Rylan set the crate on the steps of the lodge before heading back to the Jeep for another one. "Did you have to go off with Nell?" he asked cautiously. "You know Blondie would have done anything you wanted. Christ, did you see her face tonight? She wants it bad, brother."

Connor didn't answer. He knew damn well that Hudson would have willingly spread her legs for him tonight. He also knew that if he'd given in, it wouldn't have been about sex for her. Hudson had wanted an initiation, an introduction to the kind of kinky pleasure that was readily available in the free land.

Well, for Connor, sex was sex and nothing more. Fortunately, Nell was in total agreement about that, which was why he'd taken her to that private room tonight and drilled her so hard he'd seen stars. Asshole that he was, he'd imagined he was screwing Hudson instead, but he knew Nell wouldn't care if she found out who he'd been fantasizing about. As long as she had an orgasm, the woman was happy as a clam.

Hudson wanted more than an orgasm. She wanted an *experience*.

And he wasn't ready to give that to her.

"She asked me to teach her."

Connor's hands froze on the barrel of kerosene he was about to lift. He drew his brows together and glanced over at Rylan. "Teach her what?"

"How to let go. How to take pleasure and not stress about the consequences."

Yeah, he'd known that would happen. The outlaw lifestyle could be addictive. Sure, it was dangerous at times, definitely a hassle when you had to pick up and move at the drop of a hat, but the joys of the life were like a drug, hooking you in, tempting you to explore the dark urges that every human possessed even though they tried to pretend otherwise. Connor had given in to those urges two years ago, because after Maggie's death there'd been no reason to keep fighting them. No reason to keep trying to be the kind of man she needed him to be.

His chest clenched at the memory. Maggie might have been born in the free land, but she'd never belonged there. She'd been too damn gentle to survive the outlaw life.

Hudson wasn't gentle, and she sure as hell hadn't shied away from his harsh words or crude suggestions.

"What did you tell her?"

Rylan grinned. "What do you think I told her? That as much as I'd love to make every dirty fantasy she has come true, it's not my place."

He nodded. Rylan was a smart man, smart enough to know exactly what it meant when Connor had brought Hudson to Lennox's playroom.

Hell, that's why he'd ordered Rylan to drive Hudson back. Connor had laid the groundwork at the whorehouse with his harsh, no-nonsense approach, but Rylan had a softer touch, a seductive way of coaxing the truth from someone instead of beating it out of them.

Connor had been hoping his friend would get some answers from Hudson during the drive, but Rylan's next question squashed that hope.

"So, is she from the city?"

"Absolutely," Connor answered.

They fell into step with each other, hauling the fuel

around the side of the lodge in the direction of the large wooden shed where they stored hazardous supplies.

"What are we going to do with her, then?"

"I haven't decided yet."

"Is she a threat?"

"Yet to be seen." He set the kerosene on the dirt and reached for the key ring clipped to his belt. Then he unlocked the shed door and propped it open. "I'll talk to her in the morning. Depending on what she tells me, I'll give her the same choice I offered everyone else."

Rylan blinked. "Shit. You're going to let her stay?"

God help him, but he was leaning toward that option. Hudson's knowledge of the Enforcers' operation gave him an advantage he wasn't sure he could ignore.

"I might," he said absently. "What do you think?"

"I think she's smart. Well trained. Has medical knowledge. Any one of those skills would make her a good addition to our merry little gang." Rylan shrugged. "But only if we eliminate her as a threat."

"Don't worry. I'll figure it out before I reach any decisions."

They quit talking and started working, storing supplies in the shed before carting food and ammo into the lodge. By the time Connor trudged back to his cabin, it was three in the morning and he was dead-ass tired.

He sensed the intruder the moment he opened the door.

His hand snapped to the gun tucked in his waistband, then relaxed when he found Hudson cross-legged on his bed. She'd changed into an oversize T-shirt that left her knees bare, and her golden hair fell over one shoulder. She always wore it down. Which annoyed him, because it made his fingers itch to stroke those long, silky strands.

"Can we talk?" she asked softly.

"Do I have a choice? You already broke into my cabin."

"I didn't break in. The door was unlocked."

"But you weren't invited, now, were you?" With a mocking smile, he dropped his gun on the table by the door.

Many of the cabins that made up the resort were equipped with living rooms and kitchens, but Connor had chosen one with the simplest layout. Bed, table, armchair, and bathroom. He didn't need much more than that, but right now he regretted his choice, because the cabin felt too damn small. Three steps and he'd be on that bed with Hudson. Three steps and he could be buried inside her.

Shit. Clearly his time with Nell tonight had done nothing to erase his attraction to this woman.

Irritated by his own lust, he settled in the chair and folded his arms. "Talk."

"I've been doing some thinking and . . ."

Connor waited.

"I want . . ." She trailed off again, digging her teeth into her bottom lip.

His annoyance grew. "You want what?"

"As long as I'm here, I want everything. I want to be free." She stumbled over her next words. "I want *you*."

It was precisely what he'd expected to hear. Freedom was a drug, one that grabbed hold of you the second it entered your bloodstream. It made you giddy and reckless if you didn't know how to channel it. The hungry glint in Hudson's eyes revealed the addiction had already taken root inside her, and it wasn't all that long ago that Connor had seen the same expression on Kade's face.

"You know the deal," he said with a shrug. "You want everything? Then you've gotta give me something in return. Starting with the truth."

Hudson drew a breath, preparing herself for what she was about to do. The truth? No, Connor could never have that. Not all of it, anyway. But she could offer him parts of it, just enough to make him believe she didn't pose a threat to him. Just enough to convince him to let her stay.

Permanently.

"You're right. I'm not an outlaw." Then she shook her head to correct herself. "I mean, I haven't been one for long."

"You're from the city." It wasn't a question.

She nodded.

Sharp hazel eyes probed her face. "How did you get out? How did you get past the main checkpoint?"

"I had certain . . . privileges," she admitted. "My father was an important man before he died. He had ties to West Colony's council members. I guess you could call him an adviser."

The real story played in her head as she spoke, as she carefully edited out the details she knew would spur Connor to reach for his gun and blow her head off.

My father wasn't an adviser to the council—he was Arthur Lane, one of the founding members of the GC. He was alive for the war. He was the one who implemented the new system.

He was your enemy.

"I didn't have a city job," she went on. "I worked in the council sector."

"Doing what?" he demanded.

"Mostly nursing. You know about the clinic, right?"

Connor's lips curled. "You mean the only medical facility in the city? The one that exclusively treats Enforcers and council members while letting everyone else rot from injury and disease? Yeah, I know all about it, sweetheart."

His bitterness polluted the air, and Hudson didn't bother defending the accusations. Medical treatment wasn't available to the masses, if you could call the meager human population a "mass." The people in charge, however, reaped the rewards of the advanced medical technology in the council sector. Council members were given all the treatments or medications they needed. So did their offspring, the ones being groomed for council seats when the older generation passed on. And, of course, the Enforcers earned the privilege because of their upstanding work protecting the Colonies.

Everyone else was shit out of luck.

"I worked in the clinic, patching up Enforcers."

Connor's frown told her he didn't like that one bit, but he didn't comment on it. "Did you ever visit their compound?"

She shook her head.

I didn't have to visit it. I lived there. I am your enemy.

But no, damn it, she *wasn't* his enemy. She was never going back to that compound, to the city, to the brother who'd betrayed her. She could be Connor's ally, if only he let her.

"Sometimes the medical staff are given a pass out of the city, usually when an Enforcer gets hurt and can't be transported to the clinic. They get us out there on a chopper, or by truck if it's nearby, and we treat the injured Enforcer on site." She took a breath. "That's what happened the day I escaped. The doctor and I were called out to treat someone, and we drove out of the city in one of the response trucks."

"How'd you get away from the group?"

"When we got there, there was only one Enforcer injured, but two other men were with him, and one of them was apparently his close buddy. After we patched him up, I told the buddy that he should ride with his friend and I'd come back with the remaining soldier. So they drove back to the city with the doctor, and I was left with the other Enforcer."

"Did you kill him?" Connor asked gruffly.

"No. I knocked him unconscious when he turned his back." She swallowed the lump in her throat, but it wasn't one of regret. It was one of lingering relief. "I stole the truck and got the hell out of there. Dumped the vehicle about five hours later and traveled on foot after that."

Connor fell silent for several seconds. Then he said, "Why?"

She frowned. "Why what?"

"Why did you escape?"

"Because I had no choice."

"That's not a good enough answer." He leaned back in his chair, but the casual pose did nothing to hide the waves of distrust rolling off him. "What made you run?"

"Dominik," she whispered.

Connor's entire body tensed, the way she noticed it always did when Dominik's name came up. His hatred for Dom seemed to run deeper than the typical outlaw attitude toward the Enforcers. There was something unsettlingly personal about his hostility.

"You know him?" Connor said sharply.

I know him better than I know myself. He is part of me.

He's my twin brother.

She choked down the confession. "He came to see me at the clinic." *He came to my bedroom.* "He brought a marriage contract with him." *He brought me a death sentence.*

Connor hissed out a breath. "You were supposed to marry him?"

She blanched at the thought. "No. It wasn't his name on the contract. It was Knox's." She felt even sicker now. "Knox is Dominik's lieutenant."

"I know who he is."

"Then you know he's a monster," she said angrily. "He's a rapist and a killer and the most sadistic bastard I've ever known. I'm not scared of a lot of people, but Knox . . ." Even saying his name sent a cold shiver up her spine. "He terrifies me."

"Dominik ordered you to marry him?" Suspicion darkened Connor's eyes. "How old are you?"

She understood why he'd immediately gone there. Before the age of thirty-five, citizens were free to date and court to their heart's content, to seek out a partner they wanted to make a life with. It didn't even matter if they chose someone of the same sex, since procreation was strictly monitored, anyway.

But if a citizen remained single by the time they turned thirty-five, the council stepped in and arranged a marriage for them. Whether they wanted it or not.

"I'm twenty-four. And before you ask, no, it's *not* normal to have a marriage arranged for you when you're twenty-four. And it wasn't Dominik's decision." She swallowed the taste of betrayal in her mouth. "My father arranged it before he died. I guess he didn't think it was important to tell me."

Her insides twisted into knots, anger and hatred tangled with sorrow and guilt. She didn't want to hate her father. She'd loved him. But she'd also trusted him, and discovering what he'd been planning behind her back had stripped away a lot of that love and left resentment in its place.

"Dominik told me that the GC is forming a new colony," she started.

Connor's gaze flew to hers. "Where?"

"On the southwest coast. They're calling it the Coast Colony. West City is beginning to get overcrowded, so the council members decided it's time to branch out. Once that happens, they'll need an Enforcer to lead the new colony. Knox is being groomed for the job." Bile coated her throat. "I wasn't about to link my fate to that twisted bastard and get shipped off to a whole other colony. I'd rather die than marry him. I figured it was better to try my luck out here in outlaw land than tie myself to someone like Knox."

"Did Knox know about the marriage contract?"

She nodded weakly.

"So he probably wasn't happy when he found out you escaped."

An ironic laugh slipped out. "No *probably* about it. He's not the kind of man to let something like this go. In his eyes, I'm his possession. It doesn't matter that the marriage wasn't finalized. He'll never stop looking for me." A sense of urgency overtook her. "That's why I need to stay hidden. This place is safe, Connor. Knox won't find me here."

"There was never an outlaw group, was there? That story you fed me about everyone getting killed?"

She met his cloudy gaze head-on. "I lied."

"What about your arsenal of weapons? Where did that come from?"

"Stolen from the Enforcer truck I rode out in."

"And your training?"

"My father made sure I knew how to defend myself." A part of her wondered if he'd done that deliberately, trained her along with the boys because he'd always planned on sending her to the coast one day.

How could he have made that decision without telling her, damn it?

Yet as quickly as the question entered her brain, the answer came just as fast. Her father had always put the Colonies ahead of his family. Hudson had learned that depressing truth at a young age, when her father stood idly by and allowed her mother to die from pneumonia. Only the children of council members could eventually join the council. Wives couldn't. And Hudson's father had refused to compromise the council's ideals by providing illegal medical treatment to his wife.

Not even to save her life.

Connor was quiet again, his gaze hard and unyielding. The longer his silence dragged on, the more anxious Hudson became.

"Say something," she pleaded.

He stood up, marching over to the table against the wall. He swiped the lone bottle of whiskey on the tabletop, unscrewed the cap, and took a deep swig. Then he turned to face her, his expression thoughtful.

"Just so we're clear—you're asking for my protection?"

"I'm asking for everything," she repeated. "Your protection, your silence, your . . . body . . ." Her voice tripped over the last word.

"You're a greedy little thing, aren't you?"

"If you think that's greedy, then fine, I guess I am. But I'm not going back to the city. I want to stay here in the free land." She sighed. "I'm not stupid, okay? I've seen how dangerous it is out here, and I know I can't survive alone." She hopped off the bed and advanced on him. "But I've seen the freedom too. That house you took me to tonight . . . I liked being there. I liked what I saw."

He cocked his head. "And what did you see?"

"No shame, no fear, just people letting go of their inhibitions and giving in to . . . *everything*."

He chuckled. "So that's the word of the night, huh? *Everything*." He lifted the bottle and took another swig. "Suppose I let you stay. How do you envision your life here?"

She thought it over for a moment. "I see myself staying out of everyone's way. I see myself contributing, doing whatever you ask of me." Her gaze roamed his hard body. "I see myself in your bed."

For the first time since she'd met him, genuine laughter rumbled out of his throat. It wasn't mocking, wasn't wrapped around a taunt. It was deep and husky and made her heart skip a beat.

Until he answered, and she realized she was indeed being mocked.

"I'm not going to fall in love with you, if that's also part of your little utopian vision."

Hudson shrugged. "It's not your heart I'm interested in."

She bridged the short distance between them, feeling bolder than she'd ever felt as she placed her hand directly over his groin. The bulge of his arousal strained against her palm. Thick and male and tempting. She wanted to feel him inside her. In her mouth, in her sex, *everywhere*.

Connor's hips rocked slightly before he drew back, once again depriving her of what she so desperately craved. "There'll be ground rules if you stay."

She'd expected that. "Like what?"

"I call the shots." He smirked at her. "And that rule extends to the bedroom. I decide how fast we go, what we do, where we do it, who joins us." A wicked gleam sparked in his eyes. "I get total control."

Whoa, this man was intense.

She wasn't sure why that surprised her, though.

She also wasn't sure if she could hand over control to a complete stranger. She hadn't been raised to follow orders—she'd been raised to call the shots. The people in her family were born leaders.

She was about to answer, when her mind registered what else he'd said. "*Who joins us?* Do you mean . . . Rylan?" The prospect triggered an unexplainable burst of heat.

"You like that idea, huh?" Connor said with a knowing laugh.

It was hard to breathe again.

"I knew you would. And, yes, if you want him, you'll get him. I'll give you whatever you need, Hudson. I'll do whatever it takes to get you off." His eyes became heavy-lidded. "I'm very good at knowing what people need to get off."

She remained apprehensive. "What about the others? Xander and Kade, and . . . Pike." She swallowed. "I'm not comfortable around Pike."

"For chrissake, you're not obligated to screw someone you're not attracted to. I know it looked like a free-for-all at Lennox's, but believe me, it wasn't. People fuck only who they want to fuck, in private, in public, whatever turns them on. We don't force ourselves on anyone." His mouth tightened. "That's the way the bandits operate, not us, okay?"

The words brought a rush of relief. "Okay."

"You don't have to worry about Pike. He won't touch

you unless you want him to. And Xan and Kade? Wouldn't touch you even if you did want them. They don't share with other men."

"But . . ." She wrinkled her forehead, remembering the woman who'd been writhing between them earlier.

"With *other men*," Connor emphasized when he caught her confused expression. "They only share with each other."

It was so hard to make sense of that. To make sense of *anything* she'd seen tonight. She'd never heard anyone talk so openly about sex, at least not in West City. Sure, everyone there engaged in it, but it was done and discussed behind closed doors. At the Enforcer compound it was out in the open, but there'd been something filthy and violent about the way the Enforcers treated their women.

Hudson had been caught in the middle of both worlds. Too knowledgeable for the city, but too sheltered for the compound.

Except now there was a third world available to her. The outlaw world, where people had sex because they liked it and advertised their "kinks" without giving a damn what other people thought about them.

"There's one last rule," Connor said. "When one or both of us is no longer interested in the sex, then we call it. No arguments, no tears. We shake hands and life goes on."

She studied him. "Do you lay down these ground rules for everyone you sleep with?"

"No."

"Why me?"

"Because this isn't a whorehouse. I won't be able to sleep with you and then walk away. You'll be living in this camp, sharing meals with me, working beside me. I won't let sex complicate my life here."

"How long can I stay?" She couldn't contain the happy quaver in her voice.

"As long as you're useful."

"As long as I please you sexually, you mean?"

He gave a harsh laugh. "I told you, sex has nothing to do with camp. It's your other skills I'm concerned about. If you don't pull your own weight, you're gone. If I decide you're more of a threat than an asset, you're gone. If Knox comes pounding on my door, you're gone. Are we in agreement?"

Since it was the best offer she was going to get from this man, she nodded in response.

"Good. Now go back to your cabin. It's late."

Surprise rippled through her. He wanted her to go? *Now?* After they'd just struck a bargain that gave her permission to put her hands all over him?

She took a step closer. "Or . . . you could kiss me."

He touched her chin, his thumb drawing a teasing line up her jaw, leaving shivers in its wake. "Yeah? Is that what you think I should do?"

His mouth lowered, and warm lips brushed her cheek before retreating.

A frustrated noise slipped out. "That's not what I meant and you know it."

Something sinful passed through his eyes as he brought his lips to her ear. She gasped when his tongue darted out to circle her earlobe. "You already came once tonight, greedy girl." He drew back slightly, his breath a warm tease on her skin. "I'm sure that'll tide you over until I'm ready for you."

8

The sound of male voices and low chuckles outside her cabin woke Hudson up the next morning, a stark contrast from the foghorn that always blasted through the Enforcer compound at the crack of dawn. She definitely preferred waking up to Connor's husky laughter.

She didn't linger in her cabin long—she was too curious to see how the men passed their time when they weren't robbing supply compounds. Hudson took a quick shower, her teeth chattering under the icy-cold spray, but she was in too good of a mood to care that her lips were turning blue. Besides, the cabin didn't have air-conditioning, so she had a feeling she'd be welcoming the cold showers once the summer kicked into full gear.

Either way, she didn't care. Because Connor was letting her *stay*.

Not even last night's mocking parting words could dim the joy and relief swirling inside her. For the first time since she'd left the Enforcer compound, she felt . . . safe. Grounded. Her life had been spinning out of control before she'd escaped, moving in a direction she'd never expected, never *wanted*.

Even the guilt of abandoning her brother was beginning to wear off, because the twin she'd idolized growing up didn't exist anymore. He'd turned into a violent, reckless man. A man who'd been willing to hand his own sister over to a monster.

She swallowed a lump of resentment and focused on getting dressed. She threw on cutoff denim shorts, a tank top, and the sneakers that had been stashed in her bag.

Another wave of laughter rolled past her window, and her body heated in response. She'd noticed that Connor didn't laugh much, but he seemed to do it a lot when he was around Rylan.

She thought about what Rylan had told her, how they all belonged to Connor, but she was still struggling to make sense of that. What was it about Connor that made his men so willing to "belong" to him? It had to be all that power he exuded, she decided. The way he could make you feel protected with one look, one raspy word. He was controlled. Confident. Strong in an intense yet understated way that she couldn't help but be drawn to.

When she stepped outside, she encountered a sight that brought a smile to her lips. Connor and Rylan were bare-chested, with shovels in hand, standing on a large stretch of dirt next to a vegetable garden she hadn't noticed before. They'd been away from camp all day and night yesterday, so she hadn't had much time to explore, but she was hoping to change that, starting today.

"'Morning, Blondie," Rylan called out. "Coffee's in the lodge if you want."

Connor's gaze met hers. Something hot and sinful passed through his stare as he swept it up and down her body.

"Thanks." She headed into the lodge, where Kade greeted her with a smile and handed her a cup of coffee. Xander was across the room, his dark head bent over a computing tablet that he'd broken apart, and he was using tweezers to poke at the inner workings of the electronic device.

Coffee in hand, she drifted back outside and approached the edge of the garden. "What are you guys doing?"

"Expanding the garden," Rylan explained. "We want to plant some summer crops."

She looked around, noticing that aside from the neat, fenced-off vegetable garden, the rest of the clearing was overgrown.

"Why don't you plant any flowers?"

Rylan rolled his eyes. "Because you can't eat flowers."

"You can eat some of them," she countered, but she supposed he had a point. Sustenance was important. Aesthetics were not.

She thought about the potted plants in her bedroom at the compound, the colorful flowers she'd planted in the courtyard. Dominik had teased her about her dedication to that garden. Said it wasn't befitting of a warrior.

Damn it. She really needed to stop thinking about Dom, but it was so hard to do when every memory she had was intricately tangled with her brother.

She drained her coffee and set the cup on the fence post. "What can I do to help?"

"Just stand there and look pretty," Rylan said solemnly.

Hudson made a face. "I'm serious. Give me something to do."

Connor spoke up. "Start tilling that section over there."

She dutifully accepted the pitchfork he handed her and walked over to the patch of dirt he'd pointed to. There was something incredibly satisfying about working outdoors, doing something that mattered, without looking over her shoulder because she knew Dominik or Knox was watching. She'd never felt more at peace as she worked the fork into the soil, over and over again, getting the earth ready for the crops it would grow.

They worked for an hour before taking a break. Hudson picked a tomato right off the vine and took a bite, sighing ruefully as a shot of juice spurted between her breasts. When she noticed Rylan grinning at her, she raised an eyebrow and very deliberately used her index finger to mop up the moisture.

His blue irises darkened.

With a suggestive grin, she brought her finger to her mouth and licked it clean.

"Hey, Con?" Rylan drawled.

"Yeah?"

"She's eye-fucking me."

Connor looked over at her. "Stop distracting him, sweetheart."

Ha. *She* was the distraction? More like the other way around. How on earth was she supposed to concentrate when Connor was taunting her with his bare chest? It gleamed in the sunshine, drops of perspiration pooling between his pecs and clinging to every hard ridge of his torso. Rylan was equally sweaty and equally appetizing.

They both had tattoos. She wondered how they'd managed to get them, because as far as she knew, tattoo parlors existed only in the city. The ink on Connor's tanned flesh was mostly curved black lines and intricate flames spanning one muscular arm and half his back. Rylan had lines of text on various areas of his chest, but she was too busy ogling his roped muscles to try to read the words.

Connor stuck his shovel in the dirt. "Let's take a break. It's fucking hot out today."

The two men headed to the water cistern near the porch. Hudson watched, mesmerized, as they scrubbed their hands and splashed water on their faces. Droplets slid down their chests, and she had to fight the urge to march over and lick their glistening male flesh.

Her gaze locked with Connor's, and she knew he could see the hunger on her face. She didn't try to hide it. Didn't *want* to hide it. She wasn't in the city anymore, and it was liberating to know that she didn't have to suppress her lust. That she could admire these men and imagine all the dirty things she wanted to do to them without having to worry about anyone judging or reprimanding her.

She held Connor's gaze, waiting for him to say something. To *do* something. But he just smirked and gave a slight shake of the head, as if to say *Not now*.

Rylan came up beside her, and her gaze tracked the beads of water dripping down his chest. He didn't have an ounce of fat anywhere on him. Just tantalizing stretches of sleek, taut muscle that her fingers ached to touch.

Damn Connor and his I-call-the-shots decree. Why did *he* get to decide who she could touch and when she could do it?

Well, screw that. She was an outlaw now. She could do whatever the hell she wanted, right?

Turning her back to Connor, she met Rylan's eyes, then leaned in and licked a drop of water right off his chest.

He hissed out a breath, peering past her shoulders. She knew that Connor was behind her, but she didn't care. She'd told him last night what she wanted, and he'd promised to give it to her.

Now she was calling his bluff.

Her lips moved from Rylan's chest to his shoulder, and she had to lean up on her tiptoes to drag her tongue over his warm flesh. She nipped at his shoulder, then grumbled in annoyance when he gently pushed her head away.

"Nice try, gorgeous. But you know the deal."

She cast him an innocent look. "I must have forgotten—what's the deal again?"

"*I'm* the deal," a male voice growled, and then Connor's chest pressed up against her back. "My camp, my rules."

Hudson twisted her head to frown at him. "Yeah? Because it seems like the only rule you have is being a prude."

That got her a delighted laugh from Rylan. "Oh, man, I think that's the first time anyone's ever accused Con of that."

Her gaze stayed on Connor. "Am I wrong?"

"Damn right you are."

She shivered when a strong hand splayed across her lower back, callused fingers rubbing the strip of bare flesh where her shirt met her shorts. Another hand came around and slid upward, hovering below her breasts.

"Did you enjoy putting your tongue on him?" he asked in a low voice.

She assumed it was a rhetorical question and didn't answer, because he damn well knew she'd enjoyed it.

"You broke the rules." His lips tickled her ear. "I'll let it slide this time because I know how hungry you are for it. But it wasn't fair to tease him, sweetheart. I think you need to be punished for that."

Connor lightly stroked the undersides of her breasts, sending another shiver racing through her. "Here's how I see it. You put your tongue on him . . . so it's only fair that he gets to put his tongue on you." His palm glided over the curve of her ass. "Don't you think?"

All the oxygen got trapped in her lungs when she saw the impish gleam in Rylan's eyes. Then he peered past her again, as if waiting for permission.

Keeping her flush against his bare chest, Connor moved his hand to the button at her waistband and deftly popped it open.

She wanted to turn around and see his face, but she was far too fascinated by Rylan's expression as he watched Connor tug the shorts down her trembling legs. Blue eyes flared with heat as her skimpy black panties were exposed, but he still didn't make a move.

Connor's talented hands continued to wreak havoc on her body as he undressed her. He tugged her tank top up to her collarbone and her arms involuntarily rose to allow him to pull the shirt off.

She was in her underwear now, standing ten feet from the lodge in the middle of the day, as brilliant sunshine warmed her skin and blinded her eyes. The other men could stumble upon them at any second, but she didn't give a damn. She was too focused on the possessive glide of Connor's hands on her stomach, on the way Rylan was eating her up with his sultry gaze.

She gasped when Connor thrust his jeans-clad groin against her ass and rotated his hips.

"See what you do to me? You get me so fucking

hard." He made a strangled sound as he ground his erection against her, and when he barked out an order, it wasn't directed at her. "I want your mouth on her."

"About damn time," Rylan choked out.

He dropped to his knees so fast Hudson didn't even have time to blink. Her pulse sped up as he teasingly drew her panties down her legs and exposed her to his hungry gaze.

"Oh Jesus, Con," he mumbled. "She's got the prettiest pussy."

Connor's groan heated the back of her neck. "Taste it."

His husky command was dark and obscene and so thrilling, her thighs quivered in anticipation.

On the ground, Rylan licked his lips. Then, sporting the filthiest smile she'd ever seen on a man, he leaned forward and swiped his tongue over her folds.

Hudson nearly jumped out of her own skin. Every nerve ending in her body crackled to life as Rylan's lips traveled lower and the tip of his tongue lapped at the moisture gathered at her opening.

He groaned in approval. "So fucking sweet."

Connor growled. He grabbed Hudson's hand and shoved it between her thighs, hissing out another command. "Put your finger inside. Nice and deep."

It was hard to follow orders when her whole body was pulsing, hot and electric. Laughing, Rylan took her hand and coaxed her finger inside her pussy.

"Let me taste." Connor yanked her hand back up and brought her glistening finger to his mouth.

Hudson moaned when his lips closed around her finger. He sucked it clean, rumbling deep in his throat before releasing her.

Rylan planted both hands on her thighs. "Wider, baby. I want to see every inch of you."

Her legs parted of their own volition. She wasn't sure how she even managed to stay on her feet. Waves of sensation coursed through her, spiraling downward and centering between her legs. Her clit throbbed, tight and painful. She'd never been more turned on in her life.

Connor's strong chest provided support, the only thing keeping her from keeling over. When he cupped her breasts, she trembled hard enough to shake them both, but that was nothing compared to the way she shuddered when Rylan's tongue found her again.

"You like having his face buried in your pussy?" Connor asked, lightly pinching her nipples in time to Rylan's quick, teasing licks.

She moaned in response. Her brain was too foggy to think, her throat too tight to answer.

Rylan's tongue circled her clit and a jolt of pleasure shot through her. Connor's thumbs rubbed her nipples, slow and skillful, stroking and pinching until they were two tight points that ached every time she drew a breath. She couldn't believe how close she was. Ripples of impending orgasm pulsed inside her, seconds away from spilling to the surface.

It was too much. The hot mouth between her legs. The rough fingers on her breasts. Her blood roared in her ears, her inner muscles squeezing tight as the ache deepened, as her hips rocked into Rylan's face in search of relief.

He closed his mouth around her clit and groaned, and she felt the husky sound *everywhere*. Between her legs, vibrating up her spine, shivering through her breasts.

"He's loving every second of it." Connor's raspy voice tickled her neck, and she whimpered when his teeth nipped at the sensitive spot right below her ear.

"Hell yeah, I am." Rylan lifted his head with a grin.

The sight of his glossy lips almost did her in, but she breathed deep and fought the orgasm threatening to crash over her. She wasn't ready to come yet. She wanted to soak up the agonizing, achy, *incredible* sensations surging through her.

"You're close," Connor murmured. "I can feel every muscle in your body straining, fighting it." He chuckled. "You don't have to try to prolong the pleasure, baby. If you come too fast, I'll just ask him to make you come again."

Rylan slid one long finger inside her, then cursed loudly. "Oh Jesus. She's so tight, Con. Gonna squeeze the hell out of your cock when you're fucking her."

The crude words had her squirming against his finger, clenching even tighter around it. Connor's breathing grew heavier, heated the side of her neck as his palms squeezed her breasts. She wished she could see his face, but she knew from the thick erection pressing into her ass that he was turned on. That he liked what his friend was doing to her.

He rocked his hips, the denim of his jeans scraping her bare ass. She wanted him naked, damn it. Naked and inside her, taking her from behind while Rylan's wicked tongue did wicked things to her clit.

But he didn't give her what she wanted. He toyed with her breasts as Rylan slipped another finger inside her. Those long fingers moved, slow at first, then faster, deeper, curling suddenly to hit a spot that made her gasp. Rylan's muffled chuckle shot up her spine like an electric current.

"Are you gonna be a good girl and come for us?" Connor whispered.

"Yes," she wheezed.

"Tell Ry what it'll take to get you there. Tell him what you need."

Her head was spinning, the aching demands of her body too intense to vocalize.

Connor gave a sharp tug on her hair. "Tell him."

"My clit," she whimpered. "Suck on my clit."

Rylan proved he was equally good at following directions, because his mouth found her core again, his lips wrapping around the swollen bud, which demanded attention. He gave a hard suck, and Hudson went off like a grenade. The orgasm slammed into her, making her cry out and fall back against Connor's chest.

"That's it, baby. There you go. Ride it out." His fingers flicked her nipples as Rylan's mouth stayed latched to her clit, milking the pleasure from her body until she was weak-kneed and dazed.

Hudson blinked rapidly. For a moment she forgot where she was. She registered the sunlight beating down on her, the scent of warm earth and summer grass. Soft kisses on the insides of her thighs. A teasing lick to her clit that made her wriggle. Then Rylan rose to his feet and kissed her hard enough to make her gasp. She tasted herself on his tongue, and it was so insanely erotic that she grabbed onto his bare chest to hold herself steady.

But she didn't have to worry. Connor was still there, the solid wall of his body plastered to her spine, the anchor keeping her grounded. He rubbed his erection against her buttocks, and then he was gone, triggering a rush of disappointment that faded fast, because he simply shifted positions so he was next to Rylan, facing her.

Then he took her hand and moved it to Rylan's zipper. "Undo his pants."

Her fingers trembled, but somehow she managed to clasp the little tab and slowly pull it down. The metal teeth released inch by inch, and then Rylan's jeans popped open. When his cock sprang up, she experienced a clench of panic. If she had sex . . . with either of them . . . without protection . . .

Her anxiety eased when Connor spoke again. "Let's see how good you are at returning the favor. Give him your mouth."

Rylan's piercing glittered in the sunlight. She wondered what it would feel like against her tongue. She wondered if Connor was pierced too. At this rate, she'd never get to find out, because his jeans stayed zipped despite the very noticeable erection straining inside them.

He caught her gaze and smirked. "You're just dying for my cock, aren't you? Shame on you, sweetheart. You're gonna give Ry a complex."

"No, I'm going to give him a blow job."

Both men chuckled, but neither looked surprise by the bold response.

It surprised *her*, though. She wasn't usually so brazen, but she couldn't help herself. Not when she wanted them both so badly.

Meeting Rylan's eyes, she wrapped her fingers around his shaft and gave it a tentative pump.

His chest rose as he inhaled. "Ah. That's nice."

Connor's mocking gaze found hers. "You'll have to do better than that. When you put your hands on a man's cock, you don't want to hear him say it's *nice*."

Her nostrils flared, a spark of indignation prompting her to tighten her grip.

"Fuck," Rylan ground out.

"There you go," Connor said in approval. His hand

brushed her cheek in a tender caress before curling around her neck. "On your knees, Hudson. I want to see those sexy lips wrapped around his dick."

Her bare knees collided with the dirt as Connor guided her down with a commanding hand. Her heartbeat galloped, rattling her rib cage, pounding in her ears. She'd done this only a couple times before, with men who'd been terrified that Dom might walk in and find her mouth on their dicks. Her sexual encounters had always taken place in the dark, in secrecy. Awkward, hurried joinings with lovers who'd wanted to come as fast as they could so they wouldn't get caught.

Rylan's erection was . . . daunting. The thickness of it, the piercing, the drop of moisture pearled on the blunt tip.

"Don't be shy," Connor chided.

Hudson took a breath. Then she leaned in and licked the crown of Rylan's cock.

She was rewarded by a strangled curse and a shudder, a response that gave her the confidence to continue. She lapped up the moisture at his tip, the salty flavor combining with the metallic taste of his piercing as it bumped her tongue. She toyed with the smooth barbell, teasing it with her tongue and summoning a groan from his lips.

"Get him nice and wet," Connor said. "It'll make it easier to take him deep."

Rylan groaned again. "Not sure I'll even make it to that point, brother. I'm too worked up from feeling her ride my face."

She eagerly followed Connor's instructions, licking Rylan until his shaft glistened. She was dying to explore, to find out what made a man moan and curse and pant with pleasure, but Rylan hadn't been kidding about how close to the edge he was, and Connor was quick to bark out another order.

"He's close, baby. Suck harder. Work that cock until you get him there."

She couldn't draw Rylan in as deep as she wanted, so she curled her fingers around his base to take what her mouth couldn't. His piercing tickled the roof of her mouth as she sucked him, swirling her tongue around his head with each upstroke.

Rylan's breathing quickened, one hand tangling in her hair. She couldn't get enough of the husky sounds he was making, the hard length of him thrusting inside her mouth as he flexed his hips to meet her strokes. It was exciting and dirty, even more so because Connor was there, watching her with heavy-lidded eyes.

"Coming," Rylan mumbled, and then he let out another groan and his release filled her mouth.

She hummed around him, sucking harder as hot lust jolted through her. Lust, and a strange sense of power, because she'd made him lose control even when she was the one on her knees.

"Yeah," he ground out. "Oh yeah, that's good."

Rylan's soft grip on her head was replaced by a rough one—Connor, shoving his fingers through her hair to still her movements as his friend recovered from the orgasm.

"C'mere," Connor muttered.

Her knees wobbled as he yanked her to her feet, and she was surprised when his mouth suddenly crashed down on hers in a blistering kiss. She knew he could taste Rylan's salty flavor on her tongue, but he didn't seem to care. With a growl, he drove his tongue deep, kissing her with an urgency that sucked the oxygen from her lungs.

When he finally broke them apart, she whimpered

in disappointment. Waited for him to reach for her again, to undo his pants, to do *something*.

What he did was take a step back. "Let's grab some lunch before we get back to work," he said with a shrug.

Hudson gaped at him. "But . . ."

"But what?"

His knowing smile grated. "You're not . . ." She shook her head in dismay. "We're not . . . ?"

"No."

She stared at him for a moment. Then she glowered. "Why the hell not?"

"You started all this by licking Ry, remember? Next time, if you want me inside you, I suggest you lick *me*." He didn't sound angry, but amused, and the bastard actually had the nerve to chuckle as he stalked off.

Wide-eyed, Hudson watched him disappear into the lodge.

What. The. Hell.

Rylan's soft laughter penetrated the fog of confusion, and she turned to see him tucking his semihard cock into his pants. He zipped up and flashed her a grin. "He likes you."

"Really?" she grumbled. "Because this is the second time he's walked away from me."

"That doesn't mean anything."

Rylan picked up her discarded clothing, drawing her attention to the fact that she was still naked. Connor's rejection had made it difficult to focus on anything other than the extreme annoyance coursing through her blood.

She gritted her teeth. "It means he's an asshole who likes to leave me hurting."

"Trust me, gorgeous. Connor has a reason for everything he does. He's a calculated bastard, but he's not cruel."

"Sure as hell feels like it."

"Nah, he just has a knack for knowing what people need. And that's what he did now. He gave both of us what we needed."

She battled her confusion. "How?"

"Well, I like games." Rylan's dimples appeared as he smiled again. "Like the one we played now. He knows I need that, so he gave it to me."

"And what do I need?" She bit her lip. "What did he give me?"

That got her a chuckle. "You know exactly what he gave you."

No, she *didn't*. She had no idea what the rules were in this damn land. She had no idea why anyone acted the way they did. Connor, especially.

Rylan bent over and brushed his lips over hers. "You've got a lot to learn." He gave her another light, soothing kiss. "But Connor is an easy man to figure out, gorgeous. All you have to do is look hard enough."

9

Connor had known she'd track him down eventually. Not that he was trying to hide from her. He was in the barn because that's where he went most nights, mostly to stare at the piles of junk littering the room and wonder how to make best use of the space.

Hudson looked apprehensive as she wandered inside. "Hey," she said.

He nodded in greeting before turning to examine a weathered oak cabinet that was taller than he was. Shit, clearing the place out would be a hassle. Especially when he wasn't sure it was even worth it. A year in one camp was an eternity in the free land—most folks were lucky to get a month before they had to move on. Usually bandits drove them out, other times it was Enforcers, but either way, packing up and leaving was a fact of life.

"What are you planning on doing with all this space?" Her curious gaze rose to the hayloft above their heads.

"Not sure," he admitted. "Storage maybe. I keep coming out here to figure it out, but the thought of getting rid of all this garbage is fucking daunting."

She ran a hand over the side of the antique cabinet,

her fingers leaving tracks in the layer of dust on the wood. "You could do what your friend Lennox did," she suggested. "Turn it into a . . . playroom. Or whatever you want to call it."

He chuckled. "There aren't enough people in this camp to make it worthwhile."

"Why is that again?" She tipped her head. "I still don't see why you can't open your doors to other outlaws."

"I'm a heartless bastard, I guess."

"No. You're not." She paused. "That's why I don't understand it. I don't understand *you*."

"Do yourself a favor and stop trying to understand me." He turned away. "I'm a fucking puzzle you're never going to solve."

She laughed softly. "Rylan said you're easy to figure out if I just try hard enough."

"Yeah? Well, Rylan talks out of his ass half the time."

"I think he's more perceptive than you give him credit for." She shrugged. "And I think he's right—I'll figure you out once I put the effort into it."

"I think you should focus your efforts elsewhere." He crossed the cluttered room, settling onto an old torn-up sofa and reaching for the bottle he'd left on the table next to it. They'd scored an entire case of cheap whiskey during the raid, enough to keep him happy for a while. And he was feeling pretty damn happy at the moment, enjoying the hot buzz of alcohol traveling in his blood.

"So, anyway." Hudson stood in front of him, her body language conveying some serious unease. "I came out here to ask you something."

"All right. So ask."

Her cheeks turned pink. "Um . . . do you have condoms?"

His hand froze before the bottle reached his lips. "Why would you ask that?"

She hesitated, then spoke in a resigned voice. "Because we'll need them if we have sex." A pause. "I'm not sterilized."

Connor's breath flew out in a hiss. "What?"

"I can bear children," she said awkwardly.

"I fucking know what 'not sterilized' means, Hudson."

He was just shocked to hear it. Ninety percent of West City's women were sterilized the moment they reached childbearing age. It was another way the GC controlled the population. But the other ten percent . . .

"You're a breeder?" he demanded.

She nodded, visibly embarrassed. "I should have told you yesterday when we talked about my life in the city, but I didn't think about it. Not until today, when I realized that if we had sex, then . . ." She sighed. "I'm sorry. I honestly wasn't trying to keep it from you."

He believed her. And as the shock wore off, he realized it made sense that she'd been chosen to breed. Only men and women with desirable genes were allowed to procreate in the city, and with her role as both a fighter and a nurse, Hudson possessed a rare combination of strength and compassion that could definitely be considered desirable.

"Um . . . so yeah. If we're going to have sex, we need protection."

Damn right they did. He *always* used protection—the thought of bringing a child into this screwed-up world made him sick to his stomach. There weren't many children running around in outlaw territory. They existed, of course, but their parents tended to keep them well hidden, because if the Enforcers discovered a child outside the city walls, they carted it back to West City and killed its parents for breaking the population laws.

"Don't worry. I've got it covered," he muttered.

"Oh. Okay. Thanks." Hudson turned to leave. "Anyway, that's all I wanted to say."

"Where do you have to run off to, sweetheart? Come here."

She moved closer, pausing when she was two feet away from him. He didn't miss the flicker of excitement in her eyes.

He patted his lap. "No. *Here*."

Her eyes narrowed. "You're drunk."

"Maybe a little." Drunk enough to not care about anything but his cock's demands. Drunk enough to not give a shit about the consequences. "But that doesn't mean I don't know what I want."

She hesitated. Then, without a word, she slowly lowered herself onto him, positioning her thighs on either side of his. The heat of her core seared right through his cargo pants. He'd driven himself crazy today keeping her at a distance, but he'd wanted to teach her a lesson. To show her what happened when she ignored his rules. The downside to that was having to walk around with a hard-on all fucking day.

"Yeah?" Her voice was throaty. "And what do you want?"

He answered by yanking her head down and molding their mouths together, eliciting a squeak of surprise from her. The sound transformed into a soft sigh as his lips brushed hers in a lazy kiss. She wasted no time driving the kiss deeper by parting his lips with her tongue, and her passion caught him by surprise.

When she sucked on his tongue, his balls drew up so tight, they damn near disappeared.

Connor broke them apart with a groan. "Jesus, baby. Watching you suck Rylan today got me so hot. I haven't stopped thinking about your tongue."

He dove in for another kiss, slicking his tongue over hers in a slow, possessive glide. Then he bit it, and her whole body jerked.

"It didn't make you jealous?" she said breathlessly.

"No," he mumbled. "Just made me horny." He nipped at her neck, then kissed his way to her collarbone. When his tongue skimmed down the valley of her breasts, she shuddered in his lap.

"I don't understand this," she whispered.

He lifted his head. "This, as in what we're doing now? Or what happened earlier?"

"Earlier." Her face grew flushed again. "The men I've been with haven't liked to share."

"I don't blame them for wanting you all to themselves." He slipped his fingers under her tank top, stroking her flat belly.

"You let Rylan touch me." It wasn't an accusation. She sounded genuinely perplexed. "Why?"

"Because it turned you on." Conner drew the material up but didn't bare her breasts.

"Did it turn *you* on?"

"Yes." He rubbed his thumbs under the swell of her breasts, and her breath hitched.

"You like being in control," she mused. "You liked ordering us around."

"Mmm-hmmm." He brought his lips to her shoulder and licked it. "You liked it too."

"Yeah . . ."

She sounded confused again, and he looked up to see her teeth worrying her bottom lip.

"There's no shame in wanting to give up control for

a little while." His hands slid under her shirt to cup her breasts. They were full and soft, spilling into his palms. Christ, she felt so good. "You don't have to be afraid, Hudson."

"Really? Because you're pretty scary sometimes."

He laughed. "I'm a bastard. I'm ruthless and demanding and I wouldn't hesitate to slit someone's throat if they posed a threat to me." He pressed his lips to the center of her throat. "Yours included."

She shivered.

"But sex . . . it's a whole different game, baby. You have to trust that whatever I do, it's with the sole purpose of making you feel good."

"Trust? That's a big word to throw around, considering we barely know each other."

He flexed his hips, and his erection bumped her core. "You want me inside you, don't you? That means you already trust me, to some extent." He squeezed her breasts, his thumbs venturing close to her nipples before veering away, bringing an anguished cry to her lips.

"Please. Take me," she begged.

Connor latched his mouth on her neck in an open-mouthed kiss. Her skin was on fire, burning his lips, fogging his mind more than any amount of whiskey ever could. "I'm not taking anything from you," he corrected. "You're giving it to me." He dragged his tongue along the delicate tendon in her throat. "And I'm giving you something in return."

He peeled off her shirt and captured one nipple in his mouth, sucking hard enough to make her cry out.

"I'm giving you pleasure," he whispered against the rigid bud. "I'm going to make you come so hard, you won't remember your name."

Her moan vibrated in his lips and shot right down to his cock. As whiskey and arousal burned in his blood, he feasted on her breasts, alternating between them to lick and kiss and explore. His tongue circled one distended nipple, flicked against it before he lightly sank his teeth in, making her jerk in his arms.

"*Oh*. Do that again."

Chuckling, he gently bit her other nipple, and was rewarded by another throaty cry and another shudder of pleasure.

His erection throbbed impatiently, causing him to tighten his grip on her hips and nudge her to her feet. Her bare breasts made his mouth water. They were splotched pink from his stubble chafing against them, her nipples glistening from his tongue.

"Take those shorts off. Panties too."

She stripped so fast, he choked out a laugh, and a moment later Hudson stood naked in front of him. He admired her smooth, pale skin. The sexy indentation of her hips and the way they rounded into her gorgeous ass.

His gaze dropped to the juncture of her thighs. Her pussy was completely bare, and when she parted her legs slightly, he growled at the sight of the moisture clinging to those delicate pink lips.

"Sit on my face, baby. Rylan's not allowed to be the only one who gets to feel you come on his tongue."

She made a desperate sound and staggered forward, and he caught her hips, yanking her toward him. He positioned her knees on his shoulders, then clutched her ass and brought her pussy to his face. Hudson braced her hands on the wall behind them, moaning when his tongue slicked over her clit.

Jesus. Now he knew why Rylan was groaning like

crazy when he had his mouth on her. She tasted so sweet, and her body was so responsive. She was already wet for him. Every lazy brush of his tongue had her bucking harder against his mouth.

Connor lost himself in her. He closed his eyes and wrapped his lips around her clit, suckling the swollen bud as he clasped her firm buttocks to hold her in place. She shamelessly ground against him as he drank her up, as he worked her with his tongue until her spine arched and her body convulsed.

He'd made plenty of women come, but there was nothing hotter than the sounds Hudson was making right now. Helpless cries and breathy moans and whimpered pleas as she told him not to stop, begged him to take her higher. She hadn't responded like this to Rylan, and that brought a strange rush of dizzying satisfaction. He wasn't sure if it was *him*, or if Hudson was simply shedding another layer of inhibition, but either way he liked it. No, he loved it. He was harder than he'd ever been, every muscle in his body straining as Hudson slid down into his lap, boneless and sated as she dropped her head in the crook of his neck.

"Welcome back," he murmured.

Her eyelids fluttered open. "Holy shit. That was . . . So. Fucking. Good." Her hands started clawing at his shirt. "Why are you still wearing clothes?"

Her urgency made him laugh again. Look at that—two laughs in less than ten minutes. Maybe he was drunker than he'd thought.

He took pity on her and helped her out by removing his shirt, and then her hands were all over his chest. Stroking, petting, scraping his nipples with her fingernails. Jesus. She was like a woman possessed, impatient to touch every inch of him.

"Can I suck you?"

The pleading note in her voice made him want to snicker in disbelief. Right. Like she needed to ask—he was *aching* for her mouth. No, he was aching for a lot more than her mouth, but her condom request had thrown him for a loop. He didn't have protection on him, and no way was he taking any chances.

He'd just have to settle for the next best thing.

Connor reached for his belt, slipping the leather free of the buckle. "You want my cock? It's all yours, baby."

She unzipped his jeans, her breath hitching when his erection rose to meet her waiting hand. Her touch was almost reverent as her fingers danced along his shaft in a teasing caress that made him groan.

"Don't tease me," he rasped. "I need it too badly tonight."

She posed a wickedly sexy sight as she slid to her knees in front of him—golden hair streaming down her back, breasts flushed pink, nipples puckered tight. It'd been a long time since he'd felt such a visceral attraction to a woman, and it was more than a sexual one. More than the instinctual need to find release in her body. He wanted to claim her. Mark her any damn way he could.

The overpowering urge unsettled him, but not enough to stop him from lifting his hips in search of her mouth.

Hudson's lips closed around his cock.

Sweet Jesus.

An electric shock zipped down his spine and seized his balls. So criminally good. And so goddamn sexy, seeing her mouth gobble him up one inch at a time. She stopped just short of taking him all the way, her lips trembling. He waited, his ass cheeks clenching to stifle the urge to thrust deep.

She curled her fingers around his base, giving it a slow pump as she hummed around the tip of his cock and sucked hard enough to make him groan.

Almost instantly, she went still again, peering up at him as if to gauge his expression, as if to ask for permission.

Connor tangled his fingers in her hair and nodded in encouragement, and the hot suction on his dick returned, the grip of her hand becoming tighter. Every lick was exploratory, every soft moan tinged with desire and wonder. Her tongue traveled along his shaft as if she were mapping his cock and figuring out what got him off, and the thorough attention threatened his control.

He leaned his head back on the couch cushion and closed his eyes, the long swipes of her tongue and quick pumps of her hand deepening the ache in his balls. Normally he could hold out for a while, but not tonight. Tonight he just wanted an outlet for the tension and lust he'd been plagued with since Hudson had walked into his life. He just wanted to come, damn it.

"I'm close," he warned. "Where do you want it?"

She released him with a *pop*, looking confused by the question.

"Your mouth?" he prompted. "Those sexy tits? Where do you want me to come, baby?"

A tiny whimper escaped her swollen, wet lips. "Wherever you want." Then she lowered her head and sucked him deep, and he almost gave in and spilled into her hot, eager mouth.

But that infuriating need to mark her refused to go away. With a growl, he wrenched out of her mouth, fisting his cock as he leaned forward. One stroke was all it took before release slammed into him. His breath grew shallow, his vision blurring as pleasure spiraled through his body. He spurted on her breasts, his entire world narrowing to the sight of her wide gray eyes, hazy with desire and riveted to his face as if she loved watching him get off.

He sucked in oxygen, trying to regulate his breathing, his erratic heartbeat, then tugged her into his lap and covered her mouth with his. Hudson laughed even as she kissed him back, her breasts sticky against his chest.

"Is sex always this messy?" she asked breathlessly.

"Yup." He chuckled. "That's what makes it so great."

She pressed her lips to his in an eager kiss, her arms looping around his neck as she rocked against his lower body. His cock was already hardening again. Son of a bitch. How did this woman have the power to do this to him? To get him worked up again seconds after sucking him dry?

Their mouths broke apart when a loud pounding sounded on the door. Hudson's head shot toward the other end of the barn, but she relaxed when they heard Xander's muffled voice.

"Con, I don't mean to interrupt."

"Then get lost," he growled.

There was a bark of laughter. "I'd love to, but I kinda need you to talk some sense into Rylan."

He smothered a groan. "What the hell did he do now?"

"The she-devil came a-visiting again. She trashed his cabin and now he's pissed."

Connor blinked. Then snorted. "For fuck's sake. You've gotta be kidding me." He climbed to his feet, pulling Hudson up with him. "Where is he now?" he called at the door.

"He grabbed a rifle and tore into the woods."

Goddamn it.

"I'll be right there," he rumbled, before turning to Hudson. "I have to go."

She raised one eyebrow. "The she-devil?"

He couldn't help but snicker. There weren't too many things to laugh about in this screwed-up world, but Rylan's rivalry with the lone wolf that roamed the mountainside was undeniably hilarious.

"It's a wolf," he explained. "She shows up every few weeks scavenging for food, ever since Rylan made the mistake of throwing her some scraps one night. When she realized she wasn't getting any more freebies, she started terrorizing him."

Hudson's lips twitched. "You're kidding, right?"

"Nope. The damn beast has a vendetta. Shit gets stolen or chewed up? It's always Rylan's." He snorted again, muttering to himself as he zipped up his pants and looked for his shirt. "Trashed his cabin . . . Jesus . . ."

"You're going after him?"

He yanked the T-shirt on. "Of course. I can't have him traipsing around in the dark, shooting off rounds. It might attract unwanted attention."

She frowned. "He wouldn't randomly shoot off his gun, would he?"

"When it comes to this wolf, Ry loses his fucking head." Connor headed for the door, then halted as he realized that when a woman just gave you a blow job, it was probably rude to run off without saying . . . something. But what came out of his mouth was, "I'll see you in the morning."

"Or . . ." She bit her lip. "I can wait here until you get back."

It was a tempting offer, but he knew better than to go too far, too fast. Hudson hadn't even been out of the city a month. She needed time to adjust, to ease into the outlaw way of life without losing herself in the addictive taste of freedom.

"I think you've had enough excitement for one day," he said gruffly.

A little grin played on her mouth. "I'm greedy, remember? I don't know the meaning of *enough*."

No, she didn't. She wanted more, each and every time. She tested his control, distracted him with her pussy and her eagerness, until he dropped his guard without even realizing it.

"And I call the shots, remember?" With a smirk, he strode to the door, pausing only to repeat his earlier words. "I'll see you in the morning."

10

"Jesus fucking Christ!"

Hudson turned in amusement as Xander's expletive floated toward her. The two of them were on opposite ends of the lodge, fiddling with their respective electronics. Obviously Xander wasn't having any more luck than she was.

"Everything okay?" she called out.

"No," he grumbled. "Goddamn satellites are ruining my life."

Intrigued, she wandered over to Xander. His gaze was focused on a laptop screen, but Hudson couldn't figure out what she was seeing. Lines and lines of code, a nonsensical jumble of letters and numbers that made her eyes cross. She assumed it had something to do with the two mobile phones next to the computer, which were a lot bulkier than the razor-thin cell phones people used in the city. She couldn't fathom what use they'd have in the free land. It wasn't like cell towers were readily available to the outlaw population.

"What are you doing?" she asked curiously.

"Nothing much." He sounded distracted. "Just trying to hack into the city's defense system and peek at their satellites."

"Uh-huh, *nothing much*. So those are satellite phones?"

He nodded. "Could be useful on runs, or if we ever need to separate. Our radios don't have too far of a range." He typed something on the keyboard. A green error box popped up immediately, causing him to slam his hand on the desk. "Jesus *Christ*!"

She wrinkled her forehead. "Why do you say that?"

"Say what?" He frowned. "You mean, Jesus Christ?"

"That's the name of that god, right? The one people used to worship?"

"Not exactly. He's actually—" Xander stopped, a wry smile crossing his lips. "Nope, no point in getting into a theological discussion with a citizen."

She froze for a second, until she realized that of course Connor had told his men where she'd come from. She didn't imagine there were many secrets among the men, which only deepened the guilt already gnawing at her gut. They were providing her with shelter, food, protection, and she was lying to them. It didn't feel right. But she'd given Connor all she could. If she wanted to survive, the rest needed to stay hidden.

Still, the back of her neck tingled as she thought about the half-truths she'd told him. Her tattoo was concealed under layers of makeup, the waterproof kind that ensured the summer heat didn't smear it. As insurance, she always made sure to wear her hair down or in a braid, but she was still terrified Connor would discover the proof of her deceit.

But the thought of Knox tracking her down and forcing her into marriage terrified her more.

Swallowing, she forced her panicky brain to focus on Xander. "I don't get why you use a god's name as a curse."

"Because that's pretty much what it's become. It's a phrase now, more than anything. A way to voice frustration, or anger"—his dark eyes twinkled—"or something to say when you're coming. Trust me, you'll hear it a lot during sex."

A blush rose in her cheeks. Rylan had said it, in some form or another, when his cock had been in her mouth. So had Connor, when he'd come all over her breasts and then kissed her as if he were a starving man and she was his only source of sustenance.

After what she'd done with them—*to* them—she was surprised she could still look either of them in the eye without keeling over from mortification. She should feel sinful.

But she didn't.

If anything, she wanted to do it *again*.

She'd lain awake in her cabin last night hoping Connor would knock on her door after he tracked down Rylan, but she'd learned this morning that the two of them had spent half the night combing the woods for the wolf. To no avail, apparently, because Rylan had been spitting mad over breakfast, vowing to cut the wolf's head off and wear it like a hat.

"My dad told me that taking the Lord's name in vain used to be considered blasphemy." Xander interrupted her thoughts, shrugging at his own remark. "But it doesn't matter anymore. There aren't many folks practicing religion out here. Most people gave up on God and Jesus once the bombs started falling."

"The ones who survived the war didn't pass it on to their children?"

"Some did."

"Did your parents?"

"Not really. I mean, I know the stories, but my parents didn't take any of it seriously." He shifted around in his chair. "Talk to Kade when you get a chance."

Her brow furrowed. "About what?"

"The city. He's gonna have some questions for you."

Discomfort roiled in the pit of her stomach. "What kind of questions?"

Xander's tone went gruff. "He still has some family there. I think he wants to know if they're okay."

"Oh." She swallowed. "I don't think I'll be much help with that. I didn't have contact with a lot of people. I worked in a sector that most citizens don't have clearance for."

"Medical. Yeah, Con told us." His lips tightened. "So it's true, then?"

"What's true?"

"The council really does decide who lives and dies."

Although the accusation wasn't directed at *her*, Hudson couldn't stop another rush of guilt. Her father had founded the Colonies, after all. *He'd* made the decision to withhold medicine from society. Warranted or not, she felt like that made her responsible too.

"It's not decided on a case-by-case basis," she said clumsily. "Only the Enforcers get the treatments. And the children of council members. And, well, the council members, of course."

What was the matter with her? The people in West City accepted the practice because . . . well, because they'd never known anything else. But Hudson had witnessed the injustice firsthand, watched her father receive house calls from doctors while denying his own wife the same privilege. It was so much easier to grasp the unfairness of it when you saw both sides of the screwed-up system. So why was she *defending* it?

"The fact that you listed three different groups who are *deserving* of lifesaving treatments confirms what I already knew," Xander muttered. "The GC are sadistic motherfuckers."

"I'm sorry. I'm not sure why I got defensive. Believe me when I say that I absolutely agree with you. It *isn't* fair."

"Life seldom is."

She couldn't argue with that, so she pointed at the laptop instead. "If you manage to hack into this system, will you be able to get the phones to work?"

"That's the plan."

"I'll let you get back to it, then."

Nodding, Xander shifted his attention back to the computer, his fingers flying over the keyboard as he attempted to . . . do whatever the hell he was trying to do. Hudson was proficient with technology, but not to the extent of hacking into global satellites.

She watched him work for a moment, smiling at his intense concentration. Then her face heated, because she realized the last time she'd seen that crease in his brow was when a woman's mouth had engulfed his dick.

The clench between her legs sent her stumbling back to her stack of tablets, but the idea of going through them again suddenly sounded tedious. She'd much rather ogle Connor as he worked in the garden.

Since she couldn't go out there empty-handed or he'd know her true intentions, she popped into the cellar first to fill up a few bottles from the cistern that stored cold water.

The men were bare-chested and hard at work when she stepped outside, but they all glanced up at her approach.

She held up the bottles. "I thought you guys could use a water break."

Rylan and Kade set down their tools and wandered over gratefully, Rylan winking at her as he took the bottle. Connor stayed put, and when his gaze met hers, it was obvious he'd seen right through her. Heat unfurled in his eyes and rippled in her direction, going straight to her core.

She stared at his chest, remembering the way she'd touched it last night, how his muscles had tightened beneath her fingers. She was nowhere near close to having her fill of him, and she didn't understand it. Why wasn't it like that with Rylan too? She found Rylan attractive and liked being with him, but she didn't crave him the way she craved Connor.

Connor was . . . *addictive*. She wanted to lick every inch of his body, to find out what it would take to summon that deep rumble from the back of his throat again. He'd made that sexy sound when her mouth was on his cock, but what if she licked his nipple? His earlobe? Bit his neck?

She was dying to find out.

Connor made his way toward her and took the bottle from her suddenly shaky fingers. "Thanks."

"You're welcome."

He offered a knowing look. "Anything else you want to give me?"

Hudson gulped. "Nope. Just . . . the water. I'll be inside if you need me."

His soft chuckle followed her back into the lodge, where she resumed the annoying task of exploring the contents of the tablets. She was trying to access the communication system that the Enforcers used, but although the icon for it was right there on every screen, she couldn't find the link that would normally take her to the password page, and she was too afraid to ask Xander for help because she didn't want to explain *how* she knew about the program.

She spent the rest of the day alternating between working on the tablets and popping outside with any excuse to see Connor. By the time late afternoon rolled around, she gave up on the tech and busied herself by cleaning up the lodge.

It was hours later when the door swung open, sending a wave of humid air into the room. She sensed Connor before she saw him. His presence was like an airborne drug, infusing her system and heating her blood, making her entire body buzz with anticipation.

She turned, and her heart stopped when she glimpsed the look on his face.

"Xander," he said.

The other man absently looked up from the computer screen. "Hmmm?"

"Get the fuck out."

A beat of silence.

Then Xander chuckled and scraped his chair back. A few seconds later the door quietly creaked shut behind him.

Connor approached with the strides of a predator. "Did you enjoy yourself today?" he asked.

"Um. Yeah. I guess. I was messing around with the tablets and—"

"You were messing around with *me*."

Her pulse sped up at the dark gleam in his eyes.

"If you want to fuck me, come out and ask for it," he drawled. "You don't have to make excuses to come outside. You don't have to flaunt that sexy little body while I'm trying to work."

"Why would I ask for anything? You call the shots, remember?" She was surprised by how composed she sounded, when her heart was pounding hard enough to shake the walls.

"That doesn't mean you can't tell me what you want." A rakish grin stretched across his mouth. "I just decide whether or not to give it to you. But don't worry. You made your needs more than clear." He raised one eyebrow. "Take off your clothes."

Her hands automatically grasped the bottom of her shirt, then stilled as a frown touched her lips. "Why can't I say no to you?"

"Do you want to say no to me?" He was mocking her again, the way he always seemed to do. "Do you want to keep your clothes on?"

"No. I want them off. I want yours off too." Helplessness jammed in her throat. "I want to feel your skin against mine and your hands all over me."

She took a breath, struggling to make sense of her jumbled thoughts. She didn't understand the swift obedience he summoned from her. The way her brain stopped functioning the moment he voiced a rough command.

"Maybe the question I should be asking is—why am I so quick to say yes to you? I don't even stop to think about it. I just . . . do what you ask."

He stepped closer, dragging his knuckles along her jaw as his voice thickened. "The other night you asked me what your kink is. You still haven't figured it out?"

She slowly shook her head.

"You don't want to think, Hudson. You want someone to tell you what to do."

The frown returned, digging a groove into her forehead. "That's not true. I can think for myself."

"I didn't say you couldn't." His blunt fingers meandered down her neck. "I said you don't *want* to."

"That's . . . not true."

"You don't want to be in control." He touched the center of her throat, his thumb pressing into the pulse point that was throbbing erratically. "Because you're always in control—aren't you, sweetheart?"

No. Yes. She didn't even know anymore. She couldn't form coherent thoughts when he was touching her.

"That's how it is with city folk. You don't even realize you're doing it—putting up walls, guarding your thoughts, reining yourself in. You don't realize how frustrated you are. The GC gives you food and protection and so-called equality, but deep down you know something isn't right. You become hardened without even realizing it."

She was hypnotized by his eyes. His words. His callused hands sliding beneath her shirt.

"And then you come out here and your guard drops, inch by inch, until you're stripped bare." He lifted her shirt to expose her breasts, then eased it off and tossed it aside, leaving her naked from the waist up. "But even then you're still stuck in that old mind-set, so concerned about following the rules, trying to figure out what's right or wrong or sinful." His lips quirked. "Here's a little secret for you, baby—there *are* no rules out here."

He drew her zipper down, and she instinctively helped him take her pants off, lifting one leg and then the other to step out of them. He kicked the jeans away, his molten gaze resting on her skimpy panties.

"There's no reason for you to think right now. All you have to do is feel."

He cupped her pussy over her underwear, and arousal jolted through her. She was *feeling*, all right. So much sensation. Pure lust overload.

"It's exhausting, isn't it?" he murmured. "Doing what's expected of you, wanting so badly to let go but being unable to do it because you don't trust anyone but yourself." His fingers slipped inside her panties, hovering over her clit without touching it, without giving her the contact she craved. "Stop fighting it. Stop thinking. *That's* your kink—letting someone else take control, even if it's for a few hours, a few minutes."

Was he right? She was scared that he might be. But she hadn't been raised to let someone else take the lead; she'd been raised to be in control. And yet she'd been denied the outlet a person needed when all that responsibility inevitably took its toll on you.

How was that fair? Dominik and his men were allowed to do whatever the hell they pleased. They came back after their colony sweeps and were able to release their frustration and aggression and just *feel*, while she was banished to her room and ordered to bottle up her urges. Unable to feel pleasure without worrying about Dominik punishing the man who gave it to her.

Connor's finger ghosted over her clit, barely a caress, nowhere near enough, but the featherlight contact muddled her mind even more. Another thought niggled at her, trying to breach the haze of desire—who was he *really* talking about? Her? Or was it *he* who longed to let go, who suffocated under the burden of staying in control every second of every day?

She didn't have time to dwell on that, because suddenly there was pressure on her clit. His finger. Rubbing. Teasing. Sending tiny shock waves up her spine with each circular stroke. His tongue came out to moisten his bottom lip, and she watched it in fascination, the ache between her legs throbbing harder. She wanted his tongue on her, *in* her. She wanted to feel that dizzying rush of pleasure he'd made her feel last night when he'd licked her pussy with damn near desperation.

But Connor had other ideas.

"Get on the table. Lie back and spread your legs for me."

She obeyed without question. The wood table was cool beneath her back, rough against her ass. She felt so damn vulnerable as he loomed over her, his hot gaze roaming her naked body.

"Wider," he muttered.

Her legs shifted farther apart and his eyes burned into her.

She couldn't breathe. She lay there watching him, waiting. It seemed like forever before he began shedding his clothes. His jeans. His boots. His black sleeveless shirt. Each time a new patch of bronzed skin was revealed, her heart beat faster. By the time he was fully naked, all she could hear was the sound of blood rushing in her ears.

He lazily jacked his erection. One stroke, two, before he reached for his jeans and pulled a strip of foil packets from the back pocket. Condoms.

Hudson's curiosity momentarily overshadowed her lust. "Where did you get those?" She didn't imagine there were a lot of general stores in the area selling condoms or manufacturing plants to produce them, yet the outlaw population clearly had access to methods of birth control. Otherwise there'd be a lot more children in their midst.

"You can get your hands on anything if you know the right people." He gave a wry look. "The way Rylan screws his way through life, I make sure to get them in bulk."

Her answering laugh was cut short when he gripped his shaft again, the pad of his thumb absently rubbing the blunt head. Then he deftly rolled the latex on and stepped into the cradle of her thighs, but his cock stayed in his hand.

Her inner muscles clenched around painful emptiness, making her squirm in agitation. "Please."

"Please what?"

"I want you inside me. I *need* you inside me."

His other hand traveled between her legs. He slipped one finger into her pussy, not even an inch deep. A wicked tease, enough to bring a desperate plea. "More. *Please.*"

He eased in another inch.

Still not enough.

And he knew it, judging by his smug look. He was purposely toying with her.

The tip of his finger dipped into the moisture gathered at her opening before traveling up her slit. His wet fingertip rubbed little circles around her clit, scarcely enough pressure to do anything but drive her crazy with need.

"You're not in the city anymore, baby. Tell me what you want, and feel free to be filthy about it." He flashed a rare grin that robbed her of breath, one that was soft with humor instead of hard with derision. Then he pumped his cock in a quick stroke and stole the remaining oxygen from her lungs.

"Stop tormenting me and *fuck* me."

His grin widened.

"Damn it, Connor. Put your cock inside me and fuck me until I scream—"

The penetration was so deep and unexpected that the screaming part came sooner rather than later. As a wild cry left her lips, her body stretched to accommodate his size, her inner muscles tightening to keep him inside. Full. So full. Her brain turned to mush, pleasure racing through her in a dizzying rush.

"Is this what you wanted?" He chuckled, one hand splaying over her belly as he stood motionless in front of her, his cock lodged deep inside.

"Yes." Her voice cracked. "No. I want more. I want you to move."

"Like this?" He withdrew slightly, then eased back in. Slow and teasing, as if he had all the time in the world.

An anguished sound slipped out. "No. Not like that, and you know it."

"All I know is what you tell me. What you beg for."

He was lying. He knew what her *body* was telling him. He knew exactly what she needed—he just wanted to hear her say it. If she wasn't so damn needy and aroused, she might have been embarrassed by the pleas that spilled out of her mouth.

"Hard and fast," she begged. "I want you to fuck me so hard that I feel it for *days*."

Satisfaction darkened his gaze, and then his hips shot forward and he slammed deep, hard enough to shake the table. Each punishing thrust sent her mind spinning into sweet oblivion, until her entire world narrowed to the frantic slide of his cock and his hot, heavy-lidded gaze.

His pectoral muscles strained as his body bent over hers, his hands braced on either side of her head as he drove into her, fast and merciless. The new angle created friction against her clit, and her toes curled as pleasure shot through her.

Connor's mouth found hers in a blistering kiss, and then he bit her bottom lip and she suddenly tasted blood. The raw brutality of that should have scared her. Instead, it triggered a screaming orgasm that sizzled through her veins and brought stars to her eyes.

He fucked her through the powerful waves of bliss, groaning when she wrapped her arms around him and raked her nails down his back. "Fuck, yeah. Hurt me."

The raspy command made her moan. She scratched her way down to his ass and squeezed his taut buttocks, her hips rising to meet his hurried thrusts. She could feel him pulsing inside her, knew from the tight stretch of his features that he was close.

She dug her nails into his ass. "Come for me, baby." She couldn't believe the bold command had left her mouth. Neither could he, apparently, because approval glittered in his eyes and he let out a chuckle, which was cut short by a low groan that rumbled in his throat.

"Oh *hell*." He gave one last thrust and trembled on top of her, his breath hot on her neck as he climaxed.

Her body protested when he slid out. Rippled with disappointment and throbbed with rising arousal that caught her off guard. He'd just fucked her to the most powerful orgasm of her life, and she already wanted him again.

No, she was *desperate* for him again.

Shit.

If she wasn't careful, she might very well lose her head over this man.

11

It was bizarre walking into the kitchen and finding a woman there. Usually it was Xander or Kade at the stove, making soup or stew, or sometimes eggs, if Pike had paid a recent visit to the farm they traded supplies with. The men didn't make a production out of cooking—they prepared fast meals with enough substance to sustain them for another day. Nothing fancy, oftentimes not even particularly appetizing, so Connor couldn't help but gape when he saw the sheer amount of ingredients strewn on the counters. The damned woman was cooking enough food to feed an army.

And Rylan, the son of a bitch, was helping Hudson instead of performing the one task Connor had asked him to handle today.

The other man glanced up from the potatoes he was peeling and flashed a sheepish look. "Couldn't be helped, brother. She dragged me in here."

"I didn't know how to work this thing," Hudson protested, gesturing to the wood-burning stove. "We have electric ones in the city."

"I'll fix the bike tomorrow," Rylan assured him before refocusing his attention on the potatoes.

Connor swept his gaze over the counters. "Are we having company?" he said dryly.

Hudson blushed. "I wanted to cook you guys a nice dinner. It's a thank-you for letting me stay."

She stretched upward to try to reach the top cupboard, causing her ass to jut out enticingly. The tantalizing sight brought an instant dose of lust to his bloodstream. Christ, he wanted to fuck her just like that—bent over the counter as he drove into her tight pussy from behind.

"He's getting hard watching you cook," Rylan told Hudson in a cheerful voice.

She closed the cupboard and glanced over with a sigh. "I'm starting to think everything gets him hard."

She was wrong. He was usually a lot more controlled than this.

He never screwed a woman more than once. He got off, got her off, and didn't look back, didn't feel the need for a repeat performance. Not even the regulars at Lennox's could hold his attention for more than one night.

But Hudson . . . goddamn it, he wanted her again. He couldn't stop thinking about the noises she'd made yesterday. How tight she'd been. Shit, his skin still bore the gouges she'd left when she'd raked her nails down his back while he'd drilled her.

He came up behind her, his hands curling over her hips as he leaned in to kiss her neck. Her sweet, feminine fragrance surrounded him, made him dizzy. She used the same coconut-scented shampoo every cabin was stocked with, but he didn't get this worked up when he smelled the damn thing on his own head.

"Everything *you* do gets me hard." He corrected her accusation and punctuated it by sinking his teeth into her neck.

She jerked in surprise, then leaned back against his chest with a purr of pleasure.

"Tell Rylan how hard you got me yesterday," he muttered, licking a path up to her jaw. Biting that too. "Tell him what I did to you."

There was a rustle of movement, and then Rylan appeared in front of Hudson, his hands joining Connor's on her waist. "I can't wait to hear it," the man drawled.

Rylan's lips found the other side of her neck, and Connor chuckled as a full-body shiver shook Hudson's slender frame.

"*Tell* him," he commanded.

"On the table," she choked out.

Rylan chuckled too. "On the table what?"

"He—" She moaned when Connor squeezed her ass. "He . . ."

Her arousal thickened the air, her head lolling to the side as Rylan's lips devoured her neck. "Still waiting," Rylan teased between kisses. "Tell me what he did to you."

Connor ran his finger down the crease of her ass, then slid it underneath and cupped her pussy. Hard.

"He fucked me on the table, and it was—oh gosh, keep doing that." She ground wildly into his hand, abandoning all attempts to answer the question. "Please, Con, don't stop. Keep touching me—"

"Don't mind me," a sarcastic voice spoke up. "I can wait."

Hudson jumped in surprise. The spell was broken, the heat of her body gone as she hastily ducked away from him and Rylan.

Pike stood in the doorway, taking in the scene with sheer disinterest. "Didn't have to stop on my account."

Connor didn't miss the way Hudson tensed at the

sound of Pike's voice. He didn't blame her. The man was a scary motherfucker.

"I need to talk to you," Pike told him.

He followed Pike out the door, leaving Hudson and Rylan to their dinner preparations. On the front steps of the lodge, Pike lit a cigarette and blew out a thick gray cloud that matched the one darkening his eyes.

"How long is she staying, Con?"

He propped both elbows on the porch railing. "I don't know. Indefinitely, for now."

"She shouldn't be here."

His shoulders stiffened. "She's been earning her keep so far. The other guys seem to like her, and she helped us on the raid. No reason for her to go yet."

"Jesus, would you stop thinking about her pussy and start focusing on the threat?" Pike's tone was icy now. "She's got a goddamn Enforcer lieutenant on her tail."

Connor didn't need the reminder. He might be lusting over the woman, but he hadn't lost sight of the danger she could potentially bring to his door. Knox was as deadly as Dominik, maybe even more so.

"Reese will send word if Knox is heading in our direction," he replied with a shrug. "If or when that happens, we'll send Hudson on her way."

"And if we don't get word in time?" Pike countered.

"We'll figure it out, man. We always do."

Pike went silent, but Connor could feel the man's surly gaze boring into the side of his face.

"Say whatever's on your mind," he muttered. "I'm not in the mood to pry it out of you."

Pike's cheeks hollowed as he took another drag of his smoke. He exhaled abruptly and said, "Why can't you just admit what this is really about?"

Connor frowned.

"You want her here *because* Knox is after her." Pike flicked cigarette ash over the railing. "You're hoping Knox finds her, because Dominik might be with him. You *want* them to come."

It grated that Pike could see right through him. None of the other men had questioned why he was willing to protect a citizen who brought so much dangerous baggage to the table. Rylan was too enamored with Hudson's gorgeous face. Xander and Kade seemed to enjoy her no-nonsense attitude and eagerness to please. But Pike knew the deal. Pike always knew the deal.

"My plans for Dominik have never been a secret," he said coldly. "I told you exactly what I intended to do when we first met. Hell, I was on my way to find him when you and Ry showed up and decided to complicate my life."

"To stop you from your crazy suicide mission," Pike retorted, his tone equally chilly. "When we met you, you didn't give a shit whether you lived or died. You just wanted Dominik's throat."

"I still do," Connor hissed out. "You think that's changed? You think I'm going to let him get away with what he's done?"

"Boo-fucking-hoo, Con. Dominik killed your people. News flash—Dominik's killed a lot of people."

He killed my wife, you son of a bitch.

Connor slammed his lips together to stop the confession from escaping. His men knew only the details he'd been willing to give them. They knew about his need for vengeance.

They didn't know about Maggie.

Maggie was nobody's business but his. His and Dominik's. And that piece of unfinished business would only be settled once he sliced Dominik's throat from ear to ear.

"What the hell do you want me to say? Yes, I want Dominik dead. Yes, I plan on killing him the first chance I get. If you don't like that, then go. If you don't like Hudson being here, then go." He thrust an arm out beyond the porch. "Nobody's forcing you to stay here, man. There aren't any chains keeping you here, no loyalty tying you to me. To any of us. If you don't like it, then *go*."

Silence stretched between them, finally broken by Pike's tired sigh. "It might come down to that, Con." He swore under his breath. "Might fucking come down to that."

The dining room contained enough tables and chairs to seat about a hundred people.

Only six were eating tonight.

Connor could tell that little bit of math was stumping Hudson. She kept glancing at the empty chairs that were collecting dust, a slight frown marring her mouth. She didn't comment on the discrepancy, though, which was a relief because he didn't particularly feel like defending himself again about why he didn't open his doors to other outlaws.

Hell, he'd already taken in five people, and that was five too many as far as he was concerned. And the fucking irony of it was that those five people could protect themselves. They didn't *need* him. They'd just chosen to stick with him for some dumbass reason.

As for the rest of the world, well, screw it. He couldn't save everyone, and there were other communities in the free land that those seeking shelter could turn to. Lennox had told him about a bunker out east that housed more than a hundred outlaws. So there you go. All the desperate little lambs could flock there, and leave him the hell alone.

"Thank you for dinner, gorgeous. This is amazing."

Connor grinned at the reverence shining in Rylan's eyes. He had to admit he was enjoying the meal too. It definitely beat Xander's bland soups.

"You're welcome," she answered, looking pleased by the compliment.

"How'd you learn to cook?" Kade spoke up in a wary voice, which suddenly triggered Connor's suspicions, because . . . well, hell. How *did* she know how to cook? Citizens weren't in charge of their own food preparation—they ate at the city meal halls.

Hudson shifted in discomfort. "Connor told you about my father, right?"

Kade's lips curled. "He was some big-shot adviser to the council?"

She nodded. "My family got special privileges. We had our own kitchen, a cook." Hudson's voice softened. "Her name was Mary. She was sweet to me. I think it was because my mom was gone and I was the only girl in the—house."

Connor didn't miss the way she stumbled on the last word, but he wasn't sure why it raised his guard.

"I would sit in the kitchen and watch her cook." Hudson smiled. "Eventually she told me to make myself useful, and taught me everything she knew." The smile faded rapidly. "I cooked for my father and brother a few times, but my dad thought my time was better spent out of the kitchen."

An uneasy feeling tickled Connor's gut. "You never mentioned a brother."

Her expression went stricken. Pain and regret. Deep

sorrow. "I didn't mention him because he's not in my life anymore. I left him behind when I escaped." Her voice cracked. "I guess that means I have no right to miss him, huh?"

A choked sound came from Kade's direction.

"Are you okay?" Hudson asked softly.

The other man cleared his throat before nodding. "Yeah. I'm fine." He hesitated, his fingers tightening around his fork. "I left my brother behind too."

Kade didn't offer any more details, and everyone wisely kept their mouths shut.

Rylan broke the silence with an awkward cough. "Tamara's making a run into the city next week." He glanced at Connor. "She said to send a message to Lennox if there's something we want her to grab for us."

Connor shook his head. "There's nothing the city has that we can't find at the storage stations."

"That's what I told her." Rylan grinned. "She looked mighty disappointed."

Xander snorted. "Yeah, that's 'cause she wants us to owe her. The bitch loves collecting favors."

Hudson spoke up tentatively. "Tamara? I met her at the . . . at Lennox's house."

Connor hid a smile. For some reason he found it endearing that she still couldn't say the word *whorehouse*.

"She's interesting," Hudson added.

It was Kade's turn to snort. "That's a nice way of putting it."

"Seriously, don't let that beautiful face fool you," Rylan warned. "Tamara is deadly. She's probably the most powerful person in the free land, actually."

Hudson looked surprised. "How so?"

The men clammed up, and Connor stifled a sigh when everyone turned to look at him. Rylan's gaze conveyed an unspoken question, seeking permission about how much to reveal. Connor understood the reason for it. For all intents and purposes, Hudson was still a stranger to them, and a former citizen to boot. It'd been the same way with Kade when he'd first joined them. The guy had to prove himself before he was privy to their secrets.

But Connor didn't care about outing Tamara, mostly because the woman was a thorn in his side most of the time. Then again, she was also one of the few women who had no interest in sleeping with him, which he appreciated. He didn't like having to worry whether the girl in his bed might cut his balls off.

Shrugging, he turned to Hudson. "She's a smuggler."

A frown puckered her brow. "What does she smuggle?"

"Everything. She's got contacts all over the Colonies, and more than one Enforcer in her pocket."

"She bribes the Enforcers? How? With *what*?"

"Sex. Money. Who knows what else? But she's made a nice little reputation for herself. If you need something, Tamara can get it for you."

"In exchange for what?"

He repeated himself with a grin. "Sex. Money. Who knows what else?"

"Favors," Xander said glumly. "Every time I've hit her up she's asked for a favor in return. And it's always a pain in the ass. Last time, she forced me to make a three-day drive down south to pick some goddamn lavender for her."

Hudson laughed. "What did she need with lavender?"

"Apparently she knows someone who uses it to make girly body lotion and shit." Xander stabbed a roasted potato with his fork. "So yeah, I risked my neck just to pick her some flowers. Trust me, it's not worth the hassle."

Hudson still looked intrigued. "So there's a whole—I don't know—*business* side to this life? Smuggling networks, bars, places like Lennox's." She paused thoughtfully. "Are there any permanent settlements? Actual communities? Or does everyone hide underground and come out when they need something?"

"There are a few communities," Xander told her. "And yeah, they're usually in deserted bunkers, or up in the mountains, somewhere remote that the Enforcers can't easily access. Well, unless you're Reese, and then you're ballsy enough to commandeer an entire town."

"Who's Reese?" Hudson asked curiously.

Kade piped up with, "The one woman Rylan can't fuck."

Everyone laughed, including Pike, whose chuckle sounded so rusty Connor was surprised his vocal cords could support the sound.

"You mean there's actually a girl out there who can resist your charms?" Hudson teased, smiling at Rylan.

He heaved an exaggerated sigh. "It's true. Reese will get naked with everyone but li'l ol' me."

"What'd you do to her?"

Rylan gave a mock gasp of pain as he touched his heart. "Wow. It really hurts that you think I did something to deserve such appalling treatment, Blondie."

"Uh-huh. Because you're pure as the driven snow, right?"

"Damn right."

"Bullshit," Xander said. "You're a cocky bastard,

that's what you are. Serves you right that Reese is immune to you."

"She's not immune." Rylan wiggled his eyebrows. "She's just overwhelmed by my potent masculinity. A few more visits to Foxworth and I'll win her over."

Hudson turned to Connor again. "Can we go there sometime?" She immediately answered her own question. "No. That's probably not a good idea."

"No shit, little girl," Pike muttered. "You can't go gallivanting around the colony when an Enforcer lieutenant is after your ass."

A wave of tension washed over the table. Hudson bit her lip and fell silent, her gaze dropping to her plate. Pike kept eating as if he hadn't even spoken.

A sigh lodged in Connor's chest. Leave it to Pike to ruin a perfectly nice dinner.

12

Hudson had done all she could with the tablets. No matter how hard she tried, she couldn't access the program she was looking for.

She was officially admitting defeat.

"Xander?" she called from across the lodge.

"Yeah, doll?"

The nickname made her smile. All the men had taken to calling her something cute, but there was nothing sexual about it when it came from Xan or Kade. With Rylan . . . well, Rylan was Rylan. He was forever flirting with her, though she noticed he never made any advances toward her unless Connor was there. And when Pike addressed her as "little girl," it was neither cute nor sexual, because his tone rippled with disdain when he said it.

And Connor . . . every word he said was pure sex. It was impossible to even *think* his name without getting turned on, but maybe that was because the man was inside her more often than not. A week had passed since that first time in the lodge. Since then, he'd come to her cabin almost every night, rocked her world, and left her limp and sated.

It bothered her that he never spent the whole night

with her. That he kept so much of himself hidden from her. He showed her only the parts he wanted to show—lust, dominance, and the occasional flash of humor. The rest was a frustrating puzzle she couldn't solve.

"What do you need?" Xander appeared next to her chair.

"Oh." She blinked, trying to clear her head. "I needed your help with this." She booted up one of the tablets. "I'm having trouble accessing something. See this icon?"

She tapped the screen, and Xander leaned in to take a closer look. "Yeah. I've seen it before, but I think it's an old program that the city yanked from its mainframes. Never takes you further than the home page."

Hudson shook her head. "It's not an old program. They still use it now."

He eyed her skeptically. "All right. I'll bite. What's it for?"

"Communication. The Enforcers use it to send secure messages when they're out in the field, or to set up meetings, make schedule changes, that sort of thing." She hesitated, wondering how much more to reveal. "Dominik also posts the sweep schedule on there, and the weekly assignments for the men. How many in a unit, the weapons they'll need, where they're heading—"

Xander interrupted with a hiss. "How do you know all that?"

She bit the inside of her cheek. "I told you, I worked in medical, patching up Enforcers. The unit leader always had a tablet on him, and the men had smaller portable versions. They didn't hide what they were doing from me or cover their screens so I couldn't take a peek." She shrugged awkwardly. "I took a lot of peeks."

Xander studied her face before shifting to the tablet. "Tell me how it works."

"Well, when they launched the program, a box popped up asking for their log-in information. Once they entered it, they'd be redirected to other pages." She paused. "Do you think you could play around with it and see if you can get in?"

"Jesus. Of course."

She wrinkled her forehead at his very swift, very enthusiastic answer. "Oh. Okay. Thanks."

He stared at her. "Do you really not see how important this is? How valuable this information could be? We'll be able to stay one step ahead of the Enforcers. We'll know which areas they're sweeping, how many of them to expect . . . Christ, this is a potential gold mine . . ." He was still mumbling to himself as he snatched the tablet and stumbled back to his workstation.

Hudson couldn't stop the panicky sensation that churned in her stomach. Crap. Had she done the wrong thing by telling him about the program?

What if Connor and the others used the information to go after her brother?

You don't have a brother anymore.

The bleak thought was like a knife to the heart. No, she supposed she didn't. These past couple of years, Dominik had transformed right in front of her eyes. He'd become a man she no longer recognized. Cruel and barbaric. *Heartless*.

But he hadn't always been that way, damn it. Her brother had once been kind and honorable. Fiercely loyal and dedicated to keeping those around him safe.

What had happened to him?

She didn't have an answer for that, and as painful as it was, she forced herself to banish Dom from her mind. She'd known that by escaping the compound, she was permanently severing ties with her brother. She needed to put the past behind her if she wanted to have a future in this new land.

A car engine rumbled outside the lodge, bringing a rush of relief. Connor and Rylan had been out checking the motion sensors in the woods, which had malfunctioned earlier. They'd been gone long enough to worry her, but Xander had assured her they would have contacted camp on the radio if they'd run into any trouble.

Still, she wanted to see for herself that they were unharmed. "Come find me if you need me," she told Xander on her way to the door.

He didn't answer, his concentration focused solely on the tablet. She'd noticed that Kade was the only person capable of reaching Xan when he was working. If Kade interrupted him, Xander dropped whatever he was doing. No hesitation.

Hudson didn't quite understand their relationship. They weren't outwardly affectionate toward each other. It definitely didn't seem like they were sleeping together, because they didn't *act* like a couple. And yet they were clearly more than friends.

When she stepped outside, she found Rylan unloading a bag from the Jeep. Streaks of mud marred his face and clothes, and some of it was even caked in his hair.

She laughed as she approached him. "What happened to you?"

He sighed. "The rain last night turned the mountain into a mud swamp. You should've come along—we were slipping and sliding all over the place. Fun times."

"Where's Connor?"

"Went to take a shower. Which is exactly what I'm about to do." He smacked a kiss on her cheek before hurrying off.

Smiling to herself, she headed in the opposite direction, toward Connor's cabin. The door was unlocked, so she walked inside, where the sound of rushing water greeted her. Her pulse sped up as she imagined Connor's wet, naked body under the spray. Then she realized she didn't have to imagine a damn thing—she could go and see it for herself.

She eased open the door without knocking and snuck a peek at the glass shower door. No steam filled the bathroom, which told her he was conserving hot water, the way he always did.

She'd barely had a second to admire his bare ass before his head turned and those hazel eyes met hers.

"Are you just gonna stand there, or are you joining me?" The shower spray muffled his deep voice, but there was no mistaking its seductive rasp.

Hudson fumbled for her clothing so fast it was almost comical. She slid the door open and stepped into the glass enclosure, squealing when the cold water touched her skin. As shivers broke out and goose bumps appeared, she tried making an escape, but Connor stopped her by wrapping his arms around her. It didn't help, though, because his body was as cold as the water.

"Let me out of here," she begged. "I changed my mind. It's impossible to get turned on with this water temperature."

"I beg to differ." With a smirk, he glanced down at the erection jutting from his groin.

Nevertheless, he took pity on her and adjusted the faucet. Lukewarm now, but much better, and enough to thaw the ice in her bones. Then he kissed her, and water temperature was suddenly the last thing on her mind.

Hudson grabbed his wet shoulders as his tongue slipped into her mouth. Firm and insistent. Long, deep strokes that brought more goose bumps to her skin, but for an entirely different reason. She was addicted to his kisses, to the way he teased and demanded, drawing desperate moans from her throat with each stroke of his tongue.

His lips found her neck, trailing kisses along her wet skin, and she watched the water sliding down his chest, clinging to his compacted muscles, peeking through the wiry hairs on his chest. Her hands shook as she touched him, exploring the hard planes of his body and the various scars marring his flesh. Some old, some more recent. Evidence of the violence he'd known in his life, a reminder of who he was and what he fought for. Survival. Dominance.

One hand traveled over his tight abdomen, seeking out the thick erection straining between their bodies. When she started stroking it, Connor's groan bounced off the walls. "Keep touching me like that and I'll come all over your hand."

"Maybe that's want I want." She pumped him even faster, loving how his features went taut with arousal. She felt so alive when she was with him. Bold and shameless. *Free*.

She'd thought she was happy with her old life. She'd enjoyed her work at the hospital. She'd had friends among the other nurses. Sure, the compound had been a testosterone fest, but Dominik had never treated her like she was less than any of the men. Her strength had been valued, not just by Dom, but by their father, who'd made her believe she could do anything she set her mind to.

But then her dad had died, and her world had transformed. Not in one fell swoop, but in a gradual evolution, like the way the planet was slowly being destroyed. Temperatures rising one degree at a time over the course of years, decades, until one day you looked at the glaciers that had once covered the north and discovered they were gone.

Dominik had changed. The atmosphere at the compound had changed. Even the mood in the city had changed. But Hudson realized that even before that, she'd been living only half a life, because she'd never felt half the joy and pleasure that she was feeling right now.

The revelation had her capturing Connor's mouth in a greedy kiss. He stiffened for a moment, as if surprised by her passion, but then he kissed her back, his naked body crushing hers as he backed her against the cracked tiles of the shower stall. His shaft, trapped between them, slicked over her clit in a shockingly erotic grind that made her gasp.

Her response made him chuckle. With a devilish look, he did it again, and another gasp flew out.

"You're so goddamn beautiful like this."

"Like what?" It was difficult to concentrate on his words when his actions were so damn distracting. When he was fucking her clit with his cock, each wet glide sending her dangerously close to the edge.

"Wet," he muttered. "Glistening. Your skin all pink and your pussy hot against my cock."

He pushed two fingers into her core, and pleasure rocketed through her, curling her toes on the shower floor. She instinctively widened her stance, granting him better access, rocking into his touch.

"You'd let me do anything I wanted to you, wouldn't you, Hudson?"

A helpless "Yes" slipped out before she could stop it.

His eyes turned molten. "You know it'll feel good, whatever I do."

He fingered her in earnest, stroking her inner walls until she felt both full and empty, craving more, *needing* more. His cock was heavy against her hip, branding her skin like a taunt, because she knew it could fill her so much better than his fingers.

She almost begged him to screw her right there against the wall. Just drive inside her and take her to that mind-shattering place where she didn't have to think, where she could drown in the pleasure and embrace the freedom she hadn't realized had been missing from her life.

But she didn't get the chance to beg, to talk, to *blink*. Connor hauled her out of the stall, scooped her up, and kicked open the bathroom door.

"Goddamn it, I need to be *in* you." His growl sent a thrill shooting up her spine. No man had ever been this desperate for her, looked at her as if he might actually *die* if he couldn't have her.

They were dripping water all over the floor, but he didn't seem to notice. He grabbed something from the table—a condom, she realized—and her heartbeat exploded, thudding so loudly it was all she could hear. A crashing sound penetrated the frantic drumming in her ears. Connor had swept every item off the table, even the lamp, which clattered to the floor with a crash. The next thing she knew, he'd spun her around and bent her over the tabletop.

Heat sizzled in her core. He'd taunted her about this table the night they'd met, about fucking her on it. Obviously he didn't make idle threats. Or maybe it had been a promise. She didn't know or care, because his fingers were inside her again. Moving in and out in slow, shallow strokes. Her back arched and her ass thrust out, struggling to get closer.

"You're always so wet for me," he groaned. "So ready to be fucked."

She was. She was so ready that the tension was unbearable. "Give me your cock," she begged. "Please. Your fingers aren't enough. I need—"

The plea died as he plunged deep. So deep she fell forward, her elbows colliding with the table as her head nearly knocked into the wall. He filled her completely, stretching her open with each demanding thrust.

"Is this what you want?" His hoarse voice made her shiver. "You want me to fuck you like this? Hard enough to break this table? Hard enough to make you scream?"

He slammed into her again, and she actually did scream, needy and desperate. The pressure between her legs was beyond unbearable now—it was agonizing. Each time he thrust to the hilt, he hit a spot inside her that she hadn't even known existed, an ache that ran deeper than the throbbing of her clit. She squeezed her eyelids shut and rode out the intense sensations, pleasure and pain and excruciating tension that finally snapped apart like an elastic band and swept her to a whole other dimension.

Connor came while she was convulsing, his fingers digging into her hips, his breath hot against her shoulder.

She couldn't hear anything but the ringing of her ears, and her pussy was still spasming even as he pulled out and yanked her upright. His arms came around to clutch her possessively to his chest, their bodies slick from the shower, from perspiration.

"How the hell do you do this to me?" He sounded tortured as he held her even tighter.

"Do what?" she said breathlessly.

His hips flexed, and his cock ground against her ass. He was still rock-hard, still breathing erratically, as if he'd just run ten miles. "Turn me into a goddamn animal," he mumbled. "I can't think straight when I'm inside you."

She choked out a laugh. "If it helps, I can't think when you're inside me, either."

His answering laugh was strangled, laced with desperation. He twisted her body around and kissed her, moving backward as his tongue dove through her parted lips. Then he lowered himself on the bed and tugged her on top of him, his fingers sliding through her wet hair as he took long pulls on her tongue, kissing her with an urgency that floored her.

He felt it too, she realized. The overpowering need, that terrifying feeling of *not enough*. Because it was never enough, damn it. She always wanted more with him. She wanted to crawl deeper and deeper inside him, until there was nowhere left to go.

Eventually his kisses softened, becoming sweeter than she was used to. The lazy swipes of his tongue matched the strokes of his hands down her bare back.

"I like this," she whispered, breaking their mouths apart just slightly.

Something flickered in his eyes before his expression went teasing. "Making out? Or fucking each other's brains out?"

"Both. But right now I just meant the kissing part." She pressed her lips to the center of his throat before lifting her head with a laugh. "I didn't get my first kiss until I was seventeen, you know."

"That late?" He sounded intrigued. "Are you telling me all those teenage city boys didn't have the balls to lock lips with someone as gorgeous as you?"

"They were all too terrified of my brother," she admitted. "He had a strict hands-off policy when it came to me."

"Yeah? So who was brave enough to face your brother's wrath?"

"Timothy." She blushed. "He was the cutest boy I'd ever met, and I had the biggest crush on him. And trust me, he wasn't brave at all. I cornered him in the hallway after math class one day and told him that if he didn't kiss me, I'd just tell D—" She halted. Shit, she'd almost said *Dominik*. "I'd tell my brother," she quickly amended, "that Timothy had done it anyway, so since he was already going to get in trouble, he might as well get something out of it."

Connor's laughter was the sweetest sound she'd ever heard. "Jesus. Your first kiss was the result of blackmail?"

"Yep." She offered a self-deprecating smile. "But it was totally worth it. It gave me tingles and everything."

That got her another chuckle, and another happy squeeze of her heart.

"Did your brother ever find out?"

"No. I kept my mouth shut, and so did Timothy. It only happened once, though." Sadness washed over her. "All the boys were too scared to be with me. It sucked." She forced another smile. "What about you? Do you remember your first kiss?"

"Sure. It was with this girl Kara. We were both thirteen." He grinned. "Snuck away from camp one night and made out in the woods for hours."

She wanted to ask for more details—about his camp, his life, *him*—but his increasingly uneasy expression told her to tread carefully. Instead of talking, she bent down and kissed him again. Their lips met, just briefly, a soft brush of their mouths, and Hudson sensed it the moment he shut down. There was no outward change in his appearance, no stiffness in his touch, but something had shifted and suddenly he was out of reach again.

"Let me stay with you tonight," she whispered.

The change was visible now. A tic in his jaw. A flicker of unhappiness in his eyes.

"Not a good idea," he said roughly.

"Why not?"

"Because that's not what this is about."

She was so frustrated she felt like throwing something. Instead, she rolled off him and sat at the edge of the bed. "What is it about, then?"

"Fucking."

The blunt reply shouldn't have stung, but it did.

She couldn't stop the bitter note in her voice. "I'm not in love with you, if that's what you're worried about. I'm still following the rules you set, Connor. I just don't see the big deal in sharing a bed."

He sat up, and she noticed that his cock was still hard, which annoyed her. How could he be aroused right now? Didn't he care that he was being . . . what? Rude? Disrespectful? But he wasn't. He was simply being honest about what he wanted. He'd been honest from the start.

"I sleep alone," was all he said.

That stung too, especially since those three words were the equivalent of a dismissal. "Fine. I guess I sleep alone too, then."

Feeling more defeated than she ought to, she rose from the bed and ducked into the bathroom to find her clothes.

Damn it. She was getting too attached to this man. She was working too hard to "solve" him. But maybe there was nothing to solve. Maybe he really was a cold bastard who just happened to burn hot in bed.

Well, fine. She'd take it, she supposed. Stop pushing him, keep it just about sex, and take all the pleasure he was willing to give until she'd gotten him out of her system.

Anything more than that was an exercise in futility.

Connor waited until Hudson was gone before he stepped onto the porch and lit a cigarette. He didn't smoke unless he was feeling rattled. And he was feeling pretty fucking rattled right now.

His shoulders snapped straight when he heard footsteps, then relaxed as Rylan's shadowy figure ambled over from the cabin next door. The other man's face was revealed in a flash of orange light as Rylan lit a smoke of his own.

"It's okay to like her, you know."

Connor frowned. "I never said I didn't like her."

"That's not what I'm talking about and you know it. It's obvious you like her. But it's just as obvious that you don't *want* to."

His fingers tightened on his cigarette, nearly crushing it in half. "She wanted to sleep in my bed." He kept his voice low so it didn't carry in the night air.

"Lucky bastard." Rylan sighed. "It's been ages since I fell asleep tangled up with a woman."

"Next time I'll send her your way," he muttered. Except that brought an angry clench to his chest. He didn't mind sharing during sex, because it got Hudson off. It got *him* off. But he didn't like the idea of Hudson snuggling up in Rylan's bed. In Rylan's arms.

Why should it bother him, though? It wasn't like he was looking to make her his wife. He'd already had one of those, and she was buried under six feet of dirt, along with everyone else he'd ever cared about.

"Nah, you won't do that," Rylan said with a chuckle.

It pissed him off how well his friend knew him. "Yeah, well, maybe I should." He took a quick drag. "You deserve to be happy." He exhaled in a rush. "She can make you happy."

"Brother, that sounds great in theory, but we both know she's not into me like that. Yeah, she'll ride my cock until we're both limp, but she doesn't want to cuddle with me. She doesn't want to *be* with me." Rylan shrugged. "I'm cool with that, by the way. I'm not looking to settle down."

Neither was Connor. He'd tried it once, and all he'd gotten in reward was death and bloodlust.

"Don't be so quick to dismiss it," Rylan said quietly. "I think you need a woman like that in your life."

Discomfort twisted his gut. "A woman like what?"

"Who's not scared to call you on your bullshit."

An unwitting grin sprang up. "I have you for that."

"It's not the same, jackass. She challenges you." Rylan crumpled his cigarette in the ashtray on the ledge. "And she still gets your dick hard even after, what, two weeks? That's a record for you. You usually tire of them after a couple hours."

Connor didn't deny it, though it wasn't that he tired of women so much as distanced himself from them. It was too easy to get attached in this world, and getting close weakened you. It left you exposed to heartache that he wasn't willing to endure again. He didn't want anyone relying on him. He didn't want to be placed in an impossible situation again, where his choices impacted other people's lives.

"I'm turning in," he said abruptly. "Go wake up Xan if you need some more girl talk."

"You're a stubborn bastard sometimes—you know that?"

"Well aware of that. 'Night, brother."

He went inside and shut the door, putting a much-needed physical barrier between him and Rylan. Him and Hudson.

Him and the whole fucking world.

13

Cleaning out the barn was tedious work, but Hudson enjoyed having a regular task to perform. She had no idea what the men would end up using the space for, though. It would serve as a great gathering place or meeting area, but Connor remained staunchly opposed to opening the camp to outsiders.

She was dusty and grimy as she trudged back to her cabin after spending the afternoon with Kade, carrying furniture from one end of the barn to the other. Kade had agreed they probably shouldn't throw out anything they might be able to use later, so they'd dubbed one area of the barn the "storage corner" and proceeded to lug everything there.

She wanted to wash up and change before dinner, but once she got out of the shower, she decided to skip dinner altogether. It was Xander's turn to cook, and her stomach churned just thinking about the cardboard-tasting meal he'd probably serve tonight. No, thank you. She could sneak into the kitchen later and raid the pantry.

Or maybe Connor would bring her some food when he showed up at her door tonight. Last she'd checked, he was in the lodge talking to Pike about the generator, but she knew he'd track her down sooner or later. He always did.

And now that she'd decided to accept their relationship for what it was—and what it *wasn't*—she had no problem making her demands known to him. Though, really, there was only one demand: sex. Lots and lots of sweaty, dirty sex.

Luckily, he seemed more than happy to give it to her.

A knock sounded on her door, bringing a wry smile to her lips. Looked like Connor had decided to skip dinner too and go straight to dessert.

But it wasn't Connor at the door. It was Rylan, and Hudson took one look at him and ushered him inside.

"What happened?" she demanded.

He gave her a sheepish grin. He was cradling his left arm, which sported a deep gash from his biceps to his elbow. The cut wasn't gushing blood, but oozing it, and there were bits of dirt lodged in his flesh.

"I fell out of a tree." He thrust out the first aid kit that was tucked under his other arm. "Can you patch me up?"

She didn't know whether to laugh or to lecture him about his complete and total recklessness. She now understood why the men needed to stock up on bandages and antibiotics so often—Rylan really was an injury magnet.

"And don't say a word about this to Con," he added. "I already feel stupid enough without having to deal with a tongue-lashing."

Her lips twitched as she pointed to the bed. "Sit." As he settled on the edge of the mattress, she dug around in the first-aid kit. "Do I even want to ask why you were out climbing trees?"

He sighed dramatically. "No, you do not." He cursed when she pressed an antiseptic-drenched gauze to the cut. "Son of a *bitch*. I forgot about your mean bedside manner."

"Hey, there's no nice way to clean a wound. Suck it up." She dabbed at the blood before reaching for more gauze. "I changed my mind. I *do* want to know what happened."

Rylan remained silent.

She held up a bottle of rubbing alcohol. "Don't make me dump this entire thing on your arm."

He winced. "You're the devil, Blondie." His gaze found hers, sheepish again. "If you must know, I was hunting. Lost track of my prey and needed a better vantage point, so I climbed a tree. The end."

"Uh-huh." In the two weeks she'd lived at their camp, she hadn't seen Rylan go hunting even once. That was Pike's forte. "What were you hunting?"

"An animal."

"No, really? You mean you weren't tracking human prey?"

"Smart-ass."

"What was it?" she prompted. "A deer? Elk?"

"Sure, one of those."

His vague response heightened her suspicion, until a thought suddenly occurred to her, making her groan. "It was that damn wolf, wasn't it? Seriously, when are you going to give up?"

"Never," he shot back. "Not until the she-devil is good and dead. She's— Don't look at me like that. I'm not crazy, okay? If I don't kill her, she'll keep trying to ruin my life."

Hudson snorted. "Jesus Christ, Ry. That wolf doesn't have it out for you. You're imagining it."

"Jesus Christ?" he echoed, grinning at her.

She faltered as she realized what she'd said. Two weeks in the outlaw world and she was already starting to talk like one. Come to think of it, she'd shouted *Oh God* over and over again last night when Connor had been inside her.

Connor's ears must have been burning, because the door swung open and his broad frame appeared in the threshold. When he spotted Rylan, he stopped short and let out a sigh. "What the hell did you do now?"

Despite the grumbled demand, Hudson didn't miss the flash of concern that passed through his eyes. It disappeared the second their gazes locked, but not quickly enough. He could act like a heartless bastard all he wanted, but she was onto him. Just because she'd stopped pushing him to talk didn't mean she hadn't been watching him carefully the past few days. And she'd discovered that Rylan was right. Connor really was easy to figure out if you looked hard enough.

He cared deeply about his men, but he tried valiantly to hide it. He barked out orders like a military leader, but he wasn't comfortable doing it. And whatever inner battle he was fighting . . . well, it obviously took a toll on him. It made him moody at times and somber at others, but Hudson didn't walk on eggshells around him the way his friends did. Turned out she and Pike had at least one thing in common—they weren't afraid to call Connor out when he was acting like an ass.

"What makes you think it was my fault?" Rylan said with a scowl.

"Because it always is." Connor glanced at Hudson. "Is he gonna live?"

She grinned. "Unfortunately, yes."

"Shit. We were this close to being rid of him."

The lighthearted quip made her heart somersault. It happened so infrequently, seeing him let down his guard and actually laugh about things.

"Fuck you both very much," Rylan muttered.

Hudson slapped some antibiotic gel on his arm and bandaged it up. "There. All done."

She stood up, and was surprised when Connor walked up and kissed her. Which was equally infrequent—he kissed her only during sex, and if he touched her during the day, it was only to tease and taunt and drive her wild with anticipation *for* sex.

It was almost pathetic how eagerly she snatched up the affection he was dangling. She deepened the kiss before he could pull back, her tongue sneaking into his mouth and summoning a groan from him.

The naughty swirl of her tongue got her a groan from Rylan too. "Hell. You two are so hot together."

She broke the kiss at the sound of his voice, but when she turned toward him, she saw no trace of jealousy. Simply appreciation, as if he genuinely enjoyed the sight of them kissing. A glance at his crotch revealed how *much* he liked it.

Connor followed her gaze, and Hudson held her breath. She and Rylan hadn't messed around since the day in the garden. She'd wondered if maybe Connor had decided he wasn't interested in company anymore, but now his eyes gleamed thoughtfully.

"How's your dick doing?" he asked his friend. "Or did you injure that too?"

Rylan flipped up his middle finger. "My dick is just fine, asshole."

"Yeah? Then pull it out." Connor's voice went raspy. "I'm in the mood for an audience tonight."

Hudson's breath flew out. She wasn't sure she'd ever get used to the frank way these men talked about sex.

Connor raised his eyebrows at her, as if asking for permission. When her head jerked in a nod, he stepped closer and swiftly rid her of her shirt. She shivered when his rough hands cupped her aching breasts, and her nipples instantly puckered against his palms.

"What do you say, Ry? Should I make her come fast, or torment her for a bit?" Laughing softly, he drew her leggings and panties off her body.

Rylan grinned. "You already know the answer to that, brother."

Fast, she prayed. Oh God, please let him do it fast. They hadn't even gotten started yet and she was already a bundle of hot, tight nerves, so close to detonating she had to squeeze her thighs together to ease the burn.

"Torment, it is," Connor decided.

Hudson gulped as he led her to the armchair across from the bed and forced her to sit. Strong hands parted her legs as he knelt in front of her, and then his heavy-lidded gaze settled on her pussy. "Christ. You're already so wet."

She gasped when he slipped one finger inside her. Her nerve endings crackled to life, pulses of heat prickling along her skin.

Her gaze shifted to Rylan, who'd eased his pants down and was now gripping his very impressive erection. There was a rakish glimmer in his eyes as he stared at Connor's finger buried inside her.

Then that finger moved, and Hudson gasped again, because Connor had switched from a motionless tease to a furious tempo in the blink of an eye. Two fingers now, fucking her hard enough to bring a jolt of pain-laced pleasure.

Thank God. He wasn't following through on the threat to torture her. He was going to let her come. Hudson squeezed her eyes shut and gave herself over to the mounting sensations. She was close. So close. Her breath spiraled out in a rush as her pussy contracted and—

Connor's fingers abruptly disappeared.

Her eyes shot open. "You fucking *bastard*."

He clicked his tongue mockingly before looking at Rylan. "We've created a monster. She's gotten so much greedier since she sucked you off, man."

"Greedy," Rylan agreed. He gave his cock a lazy stroke as he glanced at Hudson. "Shame on you, gorgeous, calling him a bastard. You know he'll punish you for that."

He was right. The smoldering look on Connor's face confirmed it.

"Yeah, you'll have to be punished." He inched his head toward her core. "Thoroughly."

A shiver rolled through her when his lips touched her clit. His tongue flicked over her in a featherlight lick, and her hips rose on instinct, struggling to get closer. She wanted to beg for more, but she knew it wouldn't make a difference. The stubborn bastard wouldn't give her anything until he was good and ready.

The teasing began in earnest, an agonizing exploration with his mouth that turned her into a panting, whimpering mess. His tongue traced her pussy as if he were trying to memorize every inch. It skimmed her outer lips, then her inner ones, tickled her slit and traveled over her aching flesh, licking and sucking and kissing and not once making contact with the place that needed it the most. Her clit swelled, pulsed to the point of pain, but he purposely avoided it, chuckling every time she groaned in frustration.

"See? Greedy," he muttered to his friend, whose answering chuckle made her nostrils flare.

She could barely see Rylan through the mist of pleasure obscuring her vision. She heard him, though. The smug laughter, the slap of his hand on his cock, the low groan he released when Connor spread her legs wider and turned his cheek to kiss her inner thigh.

The torment started up again. Soft kisses and torturous licks. Fuck, he was going to kill her. She couldn't draw air into her lungs. She couldn't think clearly. All the blood in her body had rushed to her clit. Her entire being centered on the painful throb between her legs.

Connor licked his way up her thigh and found her folds again. She'd expected him to keep teasing, so when the tip of his tongue flicked briefly over her clit, her hips bucked so wildly that she shook the armchair.

"Oh, *yes*—"

His tongue was gone before she'd finished, and an agonized moan was ripped from her throat.

"Aw, have mercy on her, Con," Rylan spoke up. "She's squirming so hard, she's gonna break the chair."

Connor peered up at her. "You want mercy, baby?"

She was too worked up to talk, so she nodded.

"You want my mouth on that sweet little clit?"

Another nod.

He dipped his head and planted the gentlest of kisses on the tight bud. Sweet relief crashed into her when his tongue darted out for a taste. But the soft lick wasn't enough to ease the ache. Her hips lifted again, desperate for more contact.

This time he gave it to her, suckling on her clit as his thumb drifted down to tease her opening. Sensation buzzed through her, pleasure building with each brush of his thumb, each soothing stroke of his tongue.

It still wasn't enough. She shoved her fingers through his hair and tried to bring him closer, but his hair was too short to grip. Luckily, he didn't seem interested in torturing her anymore. He wrapped his lips around her clit and sucked hard, his tongue hot and insistent, coaxing her pleasure to life, sending her hurtling closer and closer to the edge.

"*Ohhh.*" She gasped for air. "I'm going to—"

No sooner had she spoken than his palm landed in a sharp smack over her clit.

The sting of pain was so unexpected that her orgasm retreated like air being sucked into a vacuum, and a wail tore out of her mouth. "I *hate* you."

His laughter heated her core. "No. You love every second of this."

She didn't.

She *did*.

She didn't even know what she felt anymore. Her body no longer belonged to her. It belonged to Connor, and it responded only to him.

"What do you think?" he asked Rylan. "Has she had enough?"

Hudson pleaded with the other man to say *yes*, to order Connor to make the unbearable ache go away, but what he did was rise from the bed and sink to his knees next to Connor.

"Nah," he drawled. "Definitely not enough."

"Agreed." Connor's evil gleam made her breath hitch. He slowly brought two fingers to her pussy and parted her folds, holding her open for Rylan.

Without missing a beat, Rylan dipped down and took over, his tongue moving seductively over her clit.

Her heartbeat accelerated as she met Connor's eyes and saw the pure male satisfaction glittering there, but her vision blurred when Rylan licked a firm circle around her clit before sucking it between his lips. Then he released it with a smacking sound and licked his way down to her entrance.

The first time he speared her with his tongue, she moaned.

The next time he did it, she came.

The orgasm caught her by complete surprise. She was wholly aware of Connor's thumb rubbing her clit, Rylan's tongue fucking her core. The thrill of knowing that two men were dedicated to her pleasure, and her pleasure alone, intensified the white-hot waves of release, and a second orgasm came without warning, different from the first but no less powerful. This time it was concentrated on her clit, a rapid, incessant throb that she felt in her fingers and toes and everywhere in between.

It was too much. Too intense. All she could do was give in to it, ride it out as her muscles strained from the force of her release and her mind fragmented into a million pieces.

Connor's heart hammered against his rib cage as he watched Hudson come apart. The complete lack of abandon, the naked ecstasy on her face . . . took his breath away.

His cock had turned into an iron spike, throbbing impatiently against his zipper. "Jesus," he hissed when she finally went still. "You're so beautiful when you come, baby."

Rylan raised his head from Hudson's pussy and released a rueful sigh. "I got ahead of myself with the tongue-fucking," he confessed. "I didn't think it'd get her off."

Connor's lips twitched. "Twice."

Hudson's gray eyes were droopy and glazed as she looked at him. "I'm sorry?"

He choked out a laugh. Damn it. He really liked this woman, probably a lot more than he ought to, but he couldn't help himself. He found her sarcasm endearing, and there was something so refreshing about her eagerness to explore her sexuality, her complete acceptance of his dominance.

Hell, he even liked the way she ordered his men around. Her bossiness made sense, considering she'd worked in a hospital and probably dealt with cranky, difficult patients on a daily basis, but he could tell it drove his friends crazy. And yet . . . they indulged her. They might grumble under their breaths as they did it, but Kade, Xan, and Rylan were quick to help Hudson with whatever new task she'd assigned herself around camp.

She wasn't like that with Connor, though. Not anymore. Not since she'd asked to spend the night with him and he'd rejected her.

During sex, she didn't hold back. She gave him every part of herself. But outside the bedroom, she kept her distance. If she had questions about the outlaw world, she went to Xan. If she wanted to talk about camp chores, she went to Kade. If she needed comfort, she went to Rylan.

It was exactly what Connor had wanted. For Hudson to be satisfied with their just-sex arrangement and stop asking for more than he was able to give her.

So why the hell was he pissed that she'd actually given him what he'd asked for?

"You're not sorry at all," Rylan was accusing her. "You wanted that orgasm."

"If it helps, you guys really did torment me before I came." She grinned, adding, "*Twice.*"

"Fuckin' brat."

Connor cut off the teasing exchange. "It's our turn to be greedy," he said roughly. "On the bed, sweetheart. I want you on all fours."

Her expression held no uncertainty or fear, just pure excitement as she did what he asked. She settled on her hands and knees, the mattress dipping slightly under her weight. Her blond hair streamed over one shoulder as she shamelessly jutted her ass in the air and twisted her head with an impish look. "Like this?"

Jesus. What a difference two weeks made. The blushing, wide-eyed innocent Connor had brought to Lennox's was gone, replaced by a confident vixen who had no qualms about thrusting her ass out at him in bold invitation.

His mouth went dry as he gazed at her pussy, slick and swollen from her orgasm. He wanted to slide inside her, screw her until she came again, but instead, he positioned himself in front of her, his knees hitting the mattress as he guided his cock to her sexy pink lips.

"Open," he murmured.

Her lips parted and he nudged the head of his cock through them. Her tongue instantly swirled around him, sending a sizzle of heat down his shaft and directly to his balls.

Rylan stood at the foot of the bed, his fist closed around his cock. He toyed with his piercing as he watched Hudson's mouth in action.

Connor's fingers slid through her hair, tightening in the silky strands when her tongue landed on the sensitive spot on the underside of his dick. "I bet your pussy feels so empty right now, doesn't it, baby?"

Her answering moan vibrated in his cock.

"Do you want Rylan to fill you up while you suck me?"

A nod now, accompanied by another deep moan that he felt in his blood.

Connor glanced at his friend and tipped his head toward the bedside table. "Condoms in the drawer."

Rylan looked puzzled for a beat, and then understanding dawned on his face as he realized what that meant. He went to the drawer without commenting. A moment later, he had a condom on and was positioning himself behind Hudson.

He ran a hand up her spine, his fingers bumping Connor's as he threaded them through her hair. His hips close enough to guide his erection between her legs even as he leaned over and covered her back with his torso. "You might have come twice, gorgeous, but now it's all about us."

Hudson's answer was an attempt to suck Connor's brain out through his cock. He lowered his focus. God, he could watch her all night, those full lips stretching around him as she worked with eager intent. Pleasure raced through him, tension rising in his balls, and his control was held on by a thread as he raised his gaze, shocked to find Rylan was still playing with Hudson.

He'd expected his friend to move like a flash, but instead Rylan waited, hips rocking as he stroked the length of his shaft against her pussy, sweeping his fingers over her back in a tender caress.

The stars in front of Conner's eyes weren't just from

the blow job anymore as a new kind of tension hit him. A hint of tightness in his chest at the building connection between them. One that didn't include him.

"Fuck her," he ordered, a harsh grate in his voice.

Rylan's head snapped up for an instant before he moved to obey, lining up and pushing in. Slow, agonizingly slow.

Hudson groaned with pleasure, and the sound reverberated against Conner's cock. Shit. If he didn't get Rylan's ass into gear, he was going to be the first to leave the party.

And still Rylan, the bastard who'd once screwed a woman so hard they'd broken through a wall at Lennox's, continued to move as if he were taking an untried virgin for the first time. Sweet and careful, his hands now stroking Hudson's hips.

Jesus Christ. Enough.

Conner tugged on the wisps of hair wrapped around his hand until his eyes met Hudson's, then pulled his cock out until the head rested on her bottom lip. "You ready for this?"

She darted her tongue over him in response, and he growled at her.

One quick nod at Rylan, and this time the man didn't ignore the order as the two of them moved in unison on her. Thrusting forward again and again, changing the rhythm so one or the other was constantly filling her, Connor sliding into her mouth, Rylan slamming into her pussy. Hudson's fingers clenched in the bedsheets, but she rocked into them in turn, as if wanting more of Rylan's cock, more of Connor's. She was always begging for *more*, and it floored him, thrilled him, because that kind of intensity was something he'd always wanted from a woman and had never been able to find.

"Fuck." Rylan's fingers dug into her waist, and he swore, holding himself deep inside her as he came.

Hudson lifted her eyes to Conner's, sucked harder on his dick, and came all over his friend's cock, rocking her hips and moaning around his engorged head, until the tension in his balls broke apart and a blinding rush of pleasure swept through his body. He spurted on her tongue and lips, and she lapped him up with tiny licks that made him shudder and gasp.

She watched him the entire time, her gaze reserved for him and him alone, and that was more thrilling than anything else they'd done tonight. Rylan was right—they *were* hot together. They burned so bright that the rest of the world faded away, and all he could see were her big gray eyes and the raw hunger that made him go up in flames every time she looked at him. That kind of fire could be dangerous. Addictive.

But right now, as he tugged her up and kissed the taste of him off her lips, he was alarmingly happy to let himself burn.

14

Hudson settled into a routine that consisted of working, eating, sleeping, and fucking.

She'd never been more content in her life.

Connor had given her the okay to start cleaning out the empty cabins, even though she knew he wasn't thrilled about it. He seemed to want to leave the cabins dusty and uninhabitable, as if doing so helped him stick to his guns about not taking other people in. But Hudson had quickly discovered a loophole to Connor's leadership—if she wanted him to say yes to something, all she had to do was voice the request during sex, and the man caved like a poorly constructed tent.

And she was shameless about taking advantage of it.

It was hard to believe that she'd been living here for only a month. She could barely remember her old life anymore, and it startled her how little she missed it.

"Do you think Pike will ever stop hating me?"

With a glum look, she followed Rylan through the woods as they searched for the motion detector that had been triggered. More often than not, the alarm that buzzed from Xander's computers was the result of an animal scurrying past the sensor or the wind knocking down a branch near it, but Connor was insistent on checking out every incident.

Rylan chuckled at her question. "He doesn't hate you."

"He's barely said more than five sentences to me—and it's been a *month*."

"He barely says five sentences to anyone, Blondie. Trust me, you're not special." He winked at her over his shoulder. "Well, you are, but in other ways."

She rolled her eyes. "Uh-huh."

"I'm serious. I've known the man for years. If he hates someone, he comes right out and tells it to their face."

"I'm curious—how did you and Pike even meet? Actually, how did all of you end up at this camp?"

"If you want the dirt on Connor, just ask for it," he teased. "You don't have to pretend you give a shit about the rest of us."

"But I do," she protested. "None of you guys ever talk about your pasts."

She couldn't deny that Connor's history intrigued her the most. She'd given up on asking him any personal questions, but that didn't mean she wasn't dying to know all about him.

"We don't talk about the past because there's not much to talk about." Rylan's tone was light, his shrug careless, but Hudson was starting to suspect that he wasn't the carefree man he pretended to be. She got the feeling that his teasing grins and easy laughter covered up a lot of pain and heartache that he didn't want anyone to see.

"Humor me," she insisted. "Where did you grow up?"

"On a farm. Much farther south than here, in what used to be Texas."

"Do you have any brothers or sisters?"

"Nope. It was just me and my folks." His voice stayed deceptively casual. "After they died I joined up with some outlaws who were still rallying for the People's Army. I was sixteen. No, seventeen, I think. That's where I met Pike, at the army training camp."

"Wow. You've known him that long?"

Rylan nodded. "Ten years." He whistled softly. "Jesus. Time passes, huh? Anyway, Pike and I moved up in the ranks and were tasked with training other outlaws who wanted to join the fight, but there was never any sort of organized effort. For all the training and boasting, everyone was too scared to make a move against the GC. Hell, they're *still* scared. Eventually we got tired of the promises and ditched the group. We were wandering around doing shit-all when we met Connor."

"Where was that?"

"Out west. The Enforcers had just wiped out his camp, and he was making his way east." Rylan grinned. "We tagged along despite his many protests. He didn't like it at first, but I finally won him over with my natural charm. It was tough—I had to work twice as hard to make up for Pike's surliness."

She laughed. "I bet."

"Though if I'm being honest, I think Con preferred Pike, at least at the beginning. You may not have noticed it, but Con's not very chatty. He and Pike got along great."

No, Connor certainly wasn't chatty. Which drove her nuts. Would it kill the man to tell her *something* about himself? At this point, she'd be overjoyed to know his favorite color.

"Anyway, the three of us came across this camp and decided it would be a good place to hole up for the winter. But we needed to gather supplies and fortify the place, which meant going on a lot of runs. We met Xander during a raid. He knew Lennox—he'd crashed at the whorehouse a few times—but Xan was a nomad, wasn't interested in staying in one place. He and I hit it off, and I convinced him to come back with us."

"And Kade came last? From the city?"

Rylan snickered. "The dumbass was being attacked by bandits when we ran into him. We saved his sorry ass and nursed him back to health. It was my idea to let him stay."

"Of course it was." Hudson had noticed that Rylan liked to surround himself with people; the only time he was ever alone at camp was when he turned in for the night. She wondered if it was easier for him to keep up his laid-back charade when he had someone to perform it for.

"And there you have it." He shrugged again. "I told you it wasn't an interesting story."

Hudson had a feeling it would have been *very* interesting—if he hadn't left out so many details. Like what it had been like growing up on a farm, what his parents were like, what dangers he'd faced as a child. But she wasn't in a position to judge him for the omissions. She hadn't been completely honest, either.

In the back of her mind she knew Dominik and Knox were still looking for her. She could *feel* it, as if their anger and frustration were being transmitted through the air like radio waves. It was an unnerving sensation that she felt often. Impending doom. Ever-present peril. Each time she found herself relaxing, that nagging feeling poked at her, reminding her that everything could go wrong at any second.

For some reason, the feeling gnawed at her now, as

Rylan took her hand to help her step over a fallen log. No sooner had the uneasiness surfaced than an inhuman shriek ripped through the forest.

"What was that?" Hudson said in alarm.

Rylan already had his rifle trained in the direction of the eerie sound. "Stay here," he ordered.

"No way." She quickly unsheathed her knife and hurried after him.

Twigs snapped beneath their boots as they moved through the brush toward the commotion. Hudson was nearly knocked off her feet when a blur of white fur flew past her. She registered four legs. A snout. Something dark and fuzzy in its mouth, but the animal disappeared into the trees before she could get a better look.

Rylan caught her arm to steady her, his rifle trained on the retreating creature. "You okay?"

"I'm fine." She took a breath. "Was that your wolf?"

He shook his head. "My wolf is black as night. Because she was created by the fucking devil."

Hudson glanced around warily. "Do you think there was some kind of animal fight?"

"Let's find out. Stay close to me, though." He smirked at her. "I don't want that pretty face of yours getting mauled. Otherwise you'll never find a husband."

She snorted, but heeded his command by sticking to his side. She hadn't come across many wild animals when she was living at the compound. The Enforcers had installed an electric fence that zapped any living creature that got too close, so the risks of getting attacked by a wolf were pretty damn low.

But there was no risk when she and Rylan finally reached the scene of the crime. No danger. No fear. Just heartache that cut her deep.

"Oh," she whispered.

"Shit," Rylan mumbled.

Hudson stared at the black wolf lying on the dirt. Blood pooled around the creature's body, not only from the throat that had been torn open, but from the mangled hind leg that jutted out at an angle.

The bloody paw prints on the ground brought a wave of infinite sadness and the sting of tears. She was suddenly reminded of the dogs that lived at the compound, German shepherds and Rottweilers that were bred to accompany the Enforcers on colony sweeps. There were no veterinarians in the city, though; animal life meant nothing to the men. If a dog got hurt, it was put out of its misery. But sometimes Dominik would secretly bring a dog to the hospital for Hudson to patch up, or at least he had before he'd turned into a callous bastard like the rest of his men.

Her heart lodged in her throat as she timidly approached the wolf, clinging to hope that maybe it was alive, that maybe there was something she could do. But it was like hoping for the sun not to rise. There was no coming back from a gashed throat.

"Goddamn it."

The chord of sorrow in Rylan's voice caught her off guard. When she turned around, she saw her own anguish reflected back at her.

"You weren't supposed to die like this, you silly bitch."

It took Hudson a second to realize he was talking to the wolf. She moved back to his side and reached for his hand, lacing their fingers together. "Is that the she-devil?"

His throat bobbed as he nodded. "I'm the one who was supposed to kill her."

Except . . . he never would have done it. His relationship with the wolf had been unconventional, to say the least, but Hudson suddenly realized how much it had meant to Rylan, how much he'd needed something to occupy his thoughts, even if that something was just a silly rivalry with a wild animal.

"No. You weren't," she said softly.

He sighed. "No. I wasn't."

They looked back at the dead wolf.

"Should we bury her?" Hudson asked.

"Nah. She's part of the food chain now."

It was a harsh way to put it, but Hudson couldn't exactly disagree. She also couldn't see how a burial was even an option, considering the dirt was packed tight and they didn't have shovels on hand.

They turned away from the wolf and headed in the direction they'd come from, but Hudson stopped in her tracks when another sound broke the silence.

She furrowed her brow. "Did you hear that?"

Rylan frowned. "Yeah. What . . . ?"

She heard it again. A half squeak, half growl.

Narrowing her eyes, she walked past the wolf's body and pinpointed the barely audible noises to an overgrown cluster of shrubs about twenty feet away. Her spine stiffened when she noticed a trail of blood leading toward the vegetation. No, leading *away* from it, as if something had been dragged out of the bushes.

"Damn it, Hudson. Let me check it out before—"

She gasped. "Oh my gosh! Ry, come here and help me."

He appeared at her side in an instant, using his rifle barrel to push aside a tangle of leaves and skinny branches until he saw the same thing she was seeing.

Wolf pups.

Hudson counted five of them, all black as night, and

her heart sank like a stone when she noticed their fur glistening in some places. Wet with blood. She bit her lip, making out another gaping throat, a throat that was so damn tiny compared to its mother's.

The tears welled up again, then spilled over and trickled down her cheeks in salty rivulets. The she-devil must have been protecting her young when the other wolf came along. And now they were all dead. She and Rylan must have imagined those growling noises.

Her vision was so blurry from the tears that when she glimpsed a flash of movement in the black mass of little bodies, she thought she'd imagined it. She blinked rapidly, trying to get her vision to focus, then dropped to her knees at the same time a small head lifted from the pile.

Fearful ice blue eyes peeked up at her. The pup had an adorable face, a tiny snout, and barely formed teeth that were bared when the animal snarled at her. Or tried to, at least. The snarl came out as another squeak, and Hudson's heart promptly cracked in two.

"Easy there, little one," she cooed. "I'm not going to hurt you."

"Hudson—" Rylan started.

Ignoring him, she leaned closer and reached for the baby wolf. It instantly made its unhappiness known by attempting to wriggle out of her grasp, but she held on tighter, even when it tried to bite her with teeth that weren't capable of breaking skin.

Once she'd secured her grip, she stood up and held her prize up for Rylan. The pup was roughly the size of its mother's head, which told Hudson that he couldn't be more than a month old.

"He's alive," she said in astonishment.

"She," Rylan corrected.

She followed his gaze and grinned at what she saw between the pup's legs. Or rather, what she didn't see.

"She," Hudson conceded, cradling the wolf pup to her chest. It was no longer wiggling in protest, but burying its face against her breasts as if it were trying to crawl into her.

"Can we keep her?" she pleaded.

He was quick to shake his head. "Bad idea, Blondie. It's a wild animal."

"No, it's a *baby*." Her grip on the wolf tightened protectively. "She'll die if we leave her out here."

Reluctance creased his forehead. "Connor will flip out if we bring a wolf back to camp. It's just another mouth to feed."

"I'll deal with Connor, and I'll feed her myself," Hudson said firmly.

She had no intention of backing down. Clearly Rylan could see that because he let out a frustrated groan. "Goddamn it. We can't—"

Loud ringing interrupted him, and they both looked around in alarm before realizing the noise was coming from the satellite phone sticking out of his back pocket. Xander was still trying to make the phones operational, and he'd ordered them to take one with them in case he worked a miracle.

Rylan looked confused as he pulled out the phone. He stared at it for a moment before pressing a button and raising it to his ear. "Yeah?"

He paused, listened, and then a huge smile filled his face.

"You brilliant son of a bitch," he crowed. "You actually did it."

Hudson was equally impressed. Wow. Xander had actually gotten the phones up and working. The man really *was* a tech genius.

Rylan went quiet for a beat, then said, "We're on our way back now." He paused again, glancing at the bundle in Hudson's arms. "Um. Yeah. You should probably go tell Connor that we're bringing home a guest."

Connor spent a very tense twenty minutes waiting for Rylan and Hudson to get back to camp. When Rylan had informed Xan that they had "guests," Connor had immediately assumed the worst—they'd come across a straggler in the woods, they'd run into a group of bandits, they'd captured an Enforcer . . .

The fluffy thing in Hudson's arms had *not* been on his worst-case-scenario list.

"What the hell is *that*?" he demanded.

"We found her in the woods." Hudson's voice held a defensive edge. "We couldn't just leave her there to die."

Connor didn't answer. He drew a long, calming breath, then turned to Rylan. "Are you out of your mind? Why would you let her bring it back here? The last thing we need is another mouth to feed."

Rylan glanced at Hudson. "Told ya that's what he'd say."

"I don't care." She stuck out her chin and leveled a determined look in Connor's direction. "I'll feed her myself. She can share my portions."

Disbelief and irritation mingled in his blood. "The damn thing can't eat *stew*, Hudson. She can't be more than a month old—she needs her mother's milk."

"Well, her mother's dead." Hudson was glaring at him now. "And she'd be dead too if we hadn't saved her."

Connor raked a hand through his hair. It was growing out and he needed to cut it, but right now he appreciated the length because he needed to grab onto something before he *throttled* the woman.

Christ, it was one distraction after the other with Hudson. Ever since she'd shown up, he'd lost sight of what mattered most to him—finding Dominik. And fine, Hudson had unwittingly brought him a step closer to that goal by telling Xander about the Enforcer comm program, but Connor knew he'd be riding Xan a lot harder about hacking it if he weren't so infatuated with her.

It was time to stop thinking with his dick, damn it. Dominik needed to be his only concern. *Vengeance* needed to be his only concern. He'd tried his damnedest to be who his wife needed him to be, and though he might have failed her in life, he sure as hell wasn't going to fail her in death.

He couldn't let Hudson keep distracting him, and he couldn't keep indulging her every whim. Allowing her to scrub and organize cabins that were better left empty. To clear out the barn so it could serve as a gathering place one day. And now she was bringing home *wolves*?

Enough was enough.

"The wolf goes," he said flatly.

Hudson's jaw tightened. "If she goes, I go."

"Fine. Then go," he shot back. "I don't have time for this bullshit. I'm not about to have a wolf running around camp and have to sleep with one eye open in case it tries to rip my throat out."

Hudson's laughter annoyed the hell out of him. She held up the tiny creature and said, "You think *she'll* rip your throat out? She still has her baby teeth! She can't even bite through the skin of a tomato!"

"She won't stay a baby forever. How do you think she'll behave when she's a full-grown wolf?"

"She'll behave perfectly, because I plan on training her." She gave him a smug look, then added, "I'm not giving her up, Con. So you can either throw us out, or suck it up."

His chest rumbled with aggravation. "For chrissake!"

A chuckle from behind him drew his attention to the porch, where Xander and Kade were watching the exchange in amusement. So was Pike, who was leaning against one of the wooden posts, his dark eyes revealing nothing, as usual.

Connor stifled another curse when Hudson dismissed him by turning to Rylan. "How do we get her some milk?"

"Um . . ." Rylan's expression conveyed visible unease, as if he knew how close Connor was to pulling out his gun and shooting his own brains out.

Jesus Christ. He couldn't believe they were even having this conversation. Wolves didn't belong at camp. End of fucking story.

Was he the only levelheaded person here?

"Don't answer that question," he snapped at Rylan. "The wolf isn't staying."

Hudson's eyes blazed. "So then you're ordering me to leave?"

He scowled at her, and it was on the tip of his tongue to follow through with the threat. To tell her to get out and take her new pet with her. But much to his annoyance, the words refused to leave his mouth, which led to a heated glare session between him and Hudson.

"I'll get the milk." The gruff announcement came from Pike.

Hudson looked over in shock. "You will?" Her tone grew suspicious. "How?"

Pike strode toward them, his heavy boots kicking up dirt with each step. "We get dairy products from a farm about sixty miles north of here. I usually pay them a visit once a month." His dark gaze flicked to Connor. "I know I'm not scheduled to go until next week, but I can take one of the bikes and leave now."

Connor was dumbfounded. "Are you insane?" He glanced at the others, none of whom had backed him up. "Have you *all* gone insane?"

Rylan shifted awkwardly.

Pike and Kade didn't answer.

It was Xander who finally spoke up. "Ah, come on, Con. Look at that little face. She's adorable."

He couldn't bring himself to look at the wolf. Couldn't look at Hudson, either. Anger burned in his blood. Anger and frustration and an odd jolt of helplessness that made him want to throw something. Jesus. He was losing control of them.

"Screw this." He clenched his teeth and took a step away. "You know what? Do whatever the hell you want. Obviously you've all lost your fucking minds."

Then he turned on his heel and stalked off.

Not even Connor's temper tantrum could dampen Hudson's spirits. After he'd stormed off, she brought the newest addition to their camp back to her cabin and proceeded to spend the next few hours petting and cooing and snuggling the baby wolf.

It was official—she was in love.

And she wasn't the only one. Xander, Kade, and Rylan had all stopped by at various points of the day to see the wolf pup, and it hadn't taken long before they were all equally enchanted.

Maybe it made her the biggest sap on the planet, but her heart squeezed whenever she looked at the wolf. The little furball had let down her guard and was clumsily exploring the cabin, poking her nose into everything and rolling around on the floor, while Hudson watched from the bed like a proud mother.

Connor might not possess an ounce of compassion, but she had too much of it, apparently.

What else was she supposed to do, though? Let the wolf die?

Still, even though she didn't regret saving the wolf, Hudson couldn't help but feel guilty that Pike was out there potentially risking his life on her behalf. He was the last person she'd expected to volunteer to help her, but as touched as she was that he had, Hudson wasn't able to relax until hours later, when Pike showed up at her door.

"You're okay," she blurted out.

He looked startled by the genuine relief in her voice. "Yeah, I'm fine," he muttered. "No trouble on the road today."

She opened the door wider, and he strode inside, a canvas bag slung over his shoulder.

"I was only able to get about two gallons, but I think you can start feeding her some mashed-up meat once her teeth come in."

"They're already starting to," Hudson told him, watching as he removed a plastic jug of milk from the bag.

The wolf pup wobbled at their feet, making a squeaky noise that caused Pike's expression to soften. Then he cleared his throat and reached into the bag again. "I got this too." He held up a small baby bottle. "Alex and Danielle's kid is two, so he's not using it anymore. Hopefully your wolf will take to it."

Her eyes widened. "Your friends at the farm have a child?"

He nodded, his expression hardening again. "Keep your mouth shut about it. You know what'll happen to them if your Enforcer buddies find out."

Hudson bristled, but decided not to touch that Enforcer comment. She was more concerned with making sure her wolf was fed. "I wasn't planning on saying anything. I was surprised to hear it, that's all." She took the bottle from his hand and unscrewed the top. "Thank you for doing this. I owe you one."

"Yeah. You do." Pike zipped up the duffel bag. "Fill the bottle and then I'll stow the milk in the cellar. It'll go bad if you leave it out in the cabin."

Nodding, she carefully filled the bottle and secured the top, then bent down to scoop up the wolf.

Pike's gaze lingered on the animal. "She'll make a good hunting partner if you train her right."

"Maybe you can help me, then," Hudson hedged.

"Maybe," he said, his tone noncommittal as he stalked toward the door. "Good night."

"Wait."

He half turned. "What?"

"Why . . . ?" She swallowed. "Why did you help me?"

"I didn't help you." He nodded at the wolf. "I helped her."

"Okay. But why?" she pressed.

Several seconds passed before he answered. "I had a dog growing up." He shrugged. "I liked him."

"Oh." She absently stroked the wolf's head as she

searched Pike's unfathomably dark eyes. "What happened to your dog?"

He made a derisive sound. "Winters were a lot colder back then. Food supplies dwindled a lot faster. So we . . ." With another shrug, he reached for the doorknob.

Her stomach churned. "You what?"

"We ate him," Pike said flatly, and then he slid out the door.

It took Hudson several hours before she worked up the courage to walk to the stables. It was past midnight by then, but she knew Pike wasn't sleeping—she felt his gaze on her the moment she entered the main room.

"Are you awake?" she asked timidly.

"What do you want?" was his brusque response.

She ventured closer, her eyes adjusting to the darkness to make out the pallet in the corner of the massive space. The wolf pup wiggled in her arms, but she didn't relax her grip. Pike made her so damn nervous, and holding on to the warm bundle was the only way to stop from fidgeting.

"I made her a little bed on the floor in my cabin," Hudson began, "but she keeps whining to come up on my bed, and . . ." She shrugged. "I'm scared I might roll over and crush her if I let her sleep with me, so, um . . . I figured you have more experience with sleeping with animals, since you had a dog, and . . ."

Pike slid up into a sitting position and waited for her to continue.

"I don't want her to whine all night, so . . . you'd be doing me a big favor if you kept her here with you."

A harsh laugh slid out. "Don't patronize me, Hudson. I'm not—" He stopped when he noticed her gaping at him. "What?" he muttered.

"You called me Hudson." She fought a triumphant smile. "You never call me by my name."

He harrumphed, which only made her lips twitch harder.

"And I didn't mean to patronize you," she added.

"Yeah? Then don't pretend you can't take care of the pup when we both know you're more than capable." He scowled. "Are you feeling sorry for me? Is that it? You think I need a furry little beast to keep my sorry ass company?"

"No. I think you *want* a furry little beast to keep your sorry ass company. I just didn't think you'd have the balls to admit it."

"Trust me, little girl, I've got the balls." To her surprise, he grudgingly held out his arms. "Bring 'er here."

Hudson's smile broke free, but she masked it quickly by pressing her lips together. She walked toward him and plopped the wolf pup in his arms, and damned if her heart didn't melt when she watched the wolf snuggle against Pike's big, muscular chest.

"Does she have a name yet?" he asked gruffly.

"Yes. But you'll probably hate it." Hudson beamed at him. "It's Hope."

Pursing his lips, he gently stroked the wolf's head. "That's a pussy-ass name for a wolf."

"I don't care," she said stubbornly. "I like it."

"Well, then," he mocked. "If you like it, then I guess it's all right."

15

Training a wolf wasn't as hard as Hudson thought it would be. She was copying the techniques she'd seen the Enforcers use with their dogs, only while Dominik's men had relied on stern words and punishment-based tactics, she used a love-and-treats reward system. The only downside was that Pike kept interfering with the process, because somehow the wolf had become "theirs," and for the past few days they'd been acting like parents bickering about their child's upbringing.

They were arguing again that morning, because Pike had decided Hope listened only when Hudson dangled treats under her nose. He was now insisting they needed to take the treats out of the equation.

"What if we're out in the woods and we need her to lie down, and she ignores us because we don't have a fucking treat to give her?" he demanded with more emotion than Hudson had ever heard him voice. Granted, the emotion was a combination of anger and annoyance, but still.

"This is the initial part of the process," she shot back. "Eventually she'll listen because she *thinks* she'll get a treat, and after that, she'll just do it on instinct."

Footsteps caught Hudson's attention, and she turned

to find Connor on the porch. His expression conveyed absolutely nothing, but she could tell he wasn't happy. He hadn't said more than a handful of words to her since she'd brought Hope back to camp. Forget sex—the man barely looked at her these days. And yeah, it bothered her, but not enough to give the wolf up, which was probably what he was hoping would happen if he continued to freeze her out.

Their gazes locked for a moment, and then he abruptly marched over, addressing Pike without even sparing a glance at the adorable wolf pup sitting at Pike's feet. "I'm driving out to Lennox's at sundown."

Pike stiffened. "What for?"

"To give him one of the sat phones. It makes more sense for us to use them to keep in touch with Lennox. We can use our radios around camp." A pained look etched into Connor's face. "I'm going to track down Tamara too, see if she can get her hands on more phones."

"I'll go with you," Pike said immediately.

Connor shook his head. "I'm going alone."

Pike shook his head right back. "You'll need backup."

"I'll be fine. I won't be staying long."

Hudson hedged in. "I can go with you, if you want. I actually wouldn't mind talking to Tamara myself. I'm hoping she can get a few things for me too."

He wrinkled his forehead. "Like what?"

Her cheeks heated. "You know, clothes, toiletries. Girly stuff."

Connor didn't ask for more details, and she was glad, because there was one item she wanted Tamara to procure that she didn't want him knowing about yet.

"All right. You can come."

His total lack of enthusiasm was more than a little

insulting. Fine, so he was pissed that she'd adopted the wolf, but couldn't he get over it already?

Maybe he has.

The uneasy thought made her body go cold. What if he *was* over it? Over *her*? What if they'd reached the point he'd mentioned in his ground rules? That if one of them wasn't interested in the sex anymore, it would end, no argument, no tears.

Her heart clenched. She didn't *want* it to end. They might be at odds right now, but she still wanted him. She was still as addicted to him as she'd been from the moment they'd met.

Oblivious to her inner turmoil, Connor turned to Pike and said, "Everyone else stays here." Sarcasm dripped from his voice. "Including your little pet."

Hudson sighed as he stalked off without another word. The man drove her crazy sometimes. It was like he was actively going out of his way to *not* create a life for himself at this camp, doing the bare minimum to survive and refusing to give everyone what they yearned for—a safe place to call home.

And yet at the same time, his presence alone made Hudson feel safer than she'd ever felt in her life. She understood why Rylan and the others had joined up with him, why they'd forced their way into his life in spite of his reluctance to accept them. Connor was compelling without even trying to be. He was a man you looked at and thought *leader*.

It marveled her to think what he could accomplish if he actually embraced the role instead of shunning it.

"Down."

Pike's irritable voice jerked her back to the present. She grinned when her gaze landed on Hope, who was sitting so sweetly at Pike's feet, peering up at him in concentration.

"Lie down," he snapped.

The wolf kept staring.

Cursing, he dropped to his knees and pounded his fist on the ground. "*Down*, Hope."

Hope blinked at him.

Pike shot to his feet, growling out another expletive. "Why does she do it when *you* ask her?"

"Two reasons—I ask her nicely and I give her treats."

Before he could break out in another lecture about spoiling the wolf, Hudson darted off with a laugh. She headed to her cabin to change into her work clothes, then hiked across camp to tackle the next cabin on her clean-the-fuck-up list.

The rest of the day flew by. After she'd scrubbed the cabin from top to bottom, she hopped in the shower and scrubbed herself from top to bottom, then donned all black and long sleeves and went to find Connor.

The sun had already set when she walked back to the lodge. Connor was waiting for her by his motorcycle, wearing jeans and a black T-shirt that stretched across his broad shoulders.

"Ready?" he said gruffly.

She nodded, too distracted by the sight of him. The stubble shadowing his jaw, the tattoos peeking out from his sleeves, the corded muscles of his arms.

Before she could stop herself, she grabbed the back of his head and yanked him down for a kiss. He stiffened but didn't pull away. He stood there, allowing her to brush her mouth over his, to lick and nip at his bottom lip until finally, *finally*, he parted his lips and his tongue met hers.

Connor groaned and deepened the kiss, taking control as his tongue teased and demanded, and although

Hudson never wanted it to end, she forced herself to wrench her mouth away.

"Stop being mad at me," she ordered. "It's hurting my feelings."

He looked unusually dazed for a second, but then his carefully composed mask snapped back into place. "Stop bringing wolves home," he grumbled.

She flashed an impish grin. "I promise not to bring another one home if you quit being such a grump about *this* one."

He rolled his eyes. "I'll think about it."

But she could tell his anger was already starting to thaw, and his touch was gentle as he helped her onto the bike.

The drive to Lennox's seemed to go a lot faster this time. As the motorcycle sped through the darkness, the wind turned Hudson's hair into a blond tornado that whipped around her head, a glaring reminder that neither one of them was wearing a helmet. Connor had explained that their helmets had been stolen a few months ago by bandits who'd ransacked their temporary camp while the men were out on a raid. He said he was on the lookout for replacements, but he hadn't found any yet. And apparently he didn't want to owe the people who *did* have helmets to spare.

That was the part Hudson still didn't fully grasp—favors. Who you did them for, who you stayed away from. It seemed unnecessarily complicated, but she was confident she'd figure it out eventually.

When they arrived at Lennox's, Connor checked the clip of his gun before tucking it in his waistband, then walked into the house like he owned the place. Hudson trailed after him, a tad apprehensive as they approached the main room.

She had no idea what carnal scene they'd be walking in on this time, but to her surprise, almost everyone was wearing clothes tonight.

There were fewer people around too, and more than half of them were women, chatting quietly on the couches. Every head turned when Hudson and Connor entered the room, but nobody seemed bothered to see them.

Connor signaled to someone behind her, then touched her cheek with unexpected tenderness. "Stick close to Jamie, sweetheart. I'm going to find Lennox."

He strode off, leaving her to greet the blonde who'd been riding Rylan to heaven the last time Hudson had seen her.

After an awkward beat, she stuck out her hand. "We weren't properly introduced before. I'm Hudson."

The woman smiled as they shook hands. "Jamie. I was rude last time you were here. I should've come over and said hello, but I was too caught up in Rylan."

Hudson had to laugh. "Yeah, I noticed that."

"He doesn't come here as often as he used to, so you've got to make every second count, you know?"

Something about Jamie's tone gave Hudson pause. And those blue eyes had softened with emotion when she'd said Rylan's name.

Shit. Did Rylan know that this girl was in love with him?

Hudson didn't think so. He would never deliberately lead someone on, and he probably wouldn't be so eager to have sex with Jamie if he knew that her feelings for him ran deep. Like Connor, Rylan went out of his way to keep emotions out of the equation.

Jamie swept her gaze over Hudson. "So. You're Con's woman, huh?"

Her discomfort promptly returned. "No, not really. It's . . . complicated."

"It always is, sweetie." Laughing, Jamie linked their arms together. "Come and meet the other girls."

For the next twenty minutes, Jamie introduced her around and talked her ear off. It turned out that Jamie and Lennox had known each other since they were kids. They'd been nomads before they stumbled across this house and decided to make it their permanent residence. Layla and Piper, who Hudson had just been introduced to, also lived there, along with someone named Nell. Everyone else just stopped by when they were in the area, and Jamie confessed that she and Lennox never turned anyone away.

Jamie's bubbly personality was contagious, and Hudson found herself relaxing as she chatted with the woman. They'd just grabbed some drinks when two men across the room signaled for Jamie to join them.

"Oh, you have to meet Beck," she gushed, tugging on Hudson's arm. "You'll love him."

"Beck" was short for Beckett. He and his friend were in their early twenties, and both had killer grins, multiple tattoos, and the kind of sexual confidence that would have made Hudson blush if she weren't used to seeing it on Connor and Rylan.

"Man, you're gorgeous," drawled Travis, Beckett's friend. "Why aren't we naked right now, honey?"

"And why the hell are you only bringing her out now?" Beckett asked Jamie with a mock glare.

"I'm new to the area," Hudson admitted.

Travis nodded. "Where you staying?"

"With friends." She kept her answer deliberately vague, and neither man pushed for details. She was discovering that most outlaws weren't as nosy as the people in the city.

Beckett eyed her curiously. "Are you sticking around or moving on?"

"Sticking around." Hopefully. The way Connor ran hot and cold on her, she really had no clue.

"Good to hear." His lips curved in a smile. "I'm looking forward to getting to know you, then."

The man was insanely appealing. He had dimples she couldn't stop staring at, and the colorful ink covering both his arms was damn near hypnotic.

Travis and Jamie drifted off and left her alone with Beckett, who, as it turned out, was the one who'd hooked Connor up with his motorcycle.

"So you're a mechanic?" she asked.

"I like to tinker around with engines, but it's more of a hobby than a job." He shrugged. "Sometimes I'll find a sweet ride and fix it up, try to trade it to someone who wants it—like Connor and his boys—but for the most part, I fix shit up for fun."

"I know nothing about cars," she confessed. "I don't even know how to drive stick."

He leaned closer, twined a strand of her hair around his finger and gave it a teasing tug. "I could teach you sometime. Trav and I live in Foxworth, which isn't too far from here."

The name rang a bell. "Foxworth . . . that's a town, right? Someone named Reese is in charge?"

"She's in charge, all right." His dimples made a reappearance. "Reese is a total ballbuster, but she's a ton of fun at the parties."

"Parties?"

"Oh yeah. We have 'em every month. It's a way to release tension, unwind, that sort of thing. Somehow they always end up turning into wall-to-wall fucking by the time the night is over." Beckett's voice lowered to a husky pitch. "You should stop by sometime. Reese doesn't mind visitors. But I'm warning you, Foxworth can be addictive. You might never want to leave—" His expression changed abruptly, playful humor dissolving into wariness.

Hudson was pretty sure what had caused it.

Connor.

She sensed him walking toward them, felt the air shift as electricity rippled up her spine. Then she turned, and there he was.

"Beckett," he said coolly.

"Con. How's the Harley working out for you?"

"Good." Connor rested a possessive hand on the back of Hudson's neck. "Nell was looking for you."

Beckett's gaze moved between the two of them before settling on Hudson. He offered a faint smile. "It was nice meeting you, beautiful. Maybe we'll run into each other again one day."

Her answering smile faded when she saw the look on Connor's face. Features hard as stone, eyes dark and turbulent.

"Go with him if you want," he said tersely, nodding at Beckett's retreating figure. "I'm sure Nell would welcome the company. She loves pussy as much as she loves cock."

Hudson swallowed the anger rising in her throat, because something about Connor's cloudy expression told her he was purposely trying to provoke her. She just wasn't sure *why*.

She studied his face, then spoke in a measured tone. "Do you *want* me to go with him?"

* * *

Connor tensed at the question. Did he want her to fuck Beckett? Jesus. Of course he didn't. He wanted to rip the guy's throat out just for *talking* to Hudson.

But he didn't want her to know how much it had bothered him to see her flirting with another man. He didn't *like* that it bothered him. Ever since she'd blatantly disobeyed him by bringing the wolf pup to camp, he'd been trying to keep his distance, but all he'd achieved in doing was punishing himself.

He was going crazy from not touching her, damn it.

"Do whatever you want, sweetheart," he said, putting on a careless tone.

She continued to scrutinize him, until every inch of his skin felt itchy and exposed. "I know I can do what I want. I'm asking you what *you* want."

His hands curled into fists.

She kept pushing. "What do you want, Connor?"

Just like that, the dam inside him splintered to pieces. "What do you *think* I want?"

He crushed their mouths together, days' worth of frustration pouring out in the form of a hard, punishing kiss. Damn this woman for sneaking past his defenses. Damn her for insinuating herself into his life, winning over his men, making it impossible to walk around camp without thinking about her.

Rather than shy away from it, Hudson welcomed the aggressive kiss. Her tongue tangled with his, sending an electric shock up his spine. Christ, he'd never met a woman who could keep up with him, whose intensity matched his own.

For all their willing enthusiasm, even the girls he'd taken right here in this house didn't hold a candle to Hudson in the passion department. Hudson dove headfirst into everything she did, whether it was kissing or fucking or training a goddamn wolf. She didn't do anything halfway. Ever.

Her body was hot and supple as she rubbed against him like a needy feline. He backed her into the wall and shoved one thigh between hers, grinding his cock against her belly. The button of her pants scraped the bulge in his, creating friction that made him groan. He was aching for her. He was *always* aching for her.

"*This* is what I want." His voice was so hoarse, it scratched his throat, and his hand trembled with need as he shoved her jeans and panties down her legs. "I want to fuck you against this wall. I want to hear you scream my name when you come."

"Then do it." She sounded far more composed than he did, but the hazy desperation swimming in her eyes belied her tone.

He moved his hand to her pussy, testing her readiness. She was already so wet, slick against his palm as he rubbed it over her. When he pushed one finger inside, she threw her head back and moaned, and Connor knew everyone in the room could hear it. But he didn't give a shit that they had an audience. He needed her too much, and he couldn't have stopped this any more than he could've stopped a tornado spiraling toward him.

He didn't take off his pants, just eased them down low enough to free his cock. Then he teased the tip over her clit and watched her eyes glaze over and her cheeks flush.

"Get inside me," she choked out.

She didn't have to ask him twice. He pushed the head of his dick past her pussy lips and plunged inside with a fast thrust that made both of them groan.

Heat.

Wetness.

Sweet Jesus. Either he'd forgotten how good it was in the three days he hadn't been with her, or—shit. No condom, he realized. Alarm bells rang in his head, ordering him to pull out, but she was so tight and so wet and it felt so good that he couldn't do anything but slide in deeper.

"Wrap your legs around me," he growled.

She did, putting herself at his mercy, handing over control. Her arms and legs wrapped around him, and now he was the only thing holding her up, the only one with the power to move. One arm kept her tight to him, while his other hand braced the wall above her head as he began to fuck her. Quick, deep thrusts that had her shoulders bumping the wall and her nails digging into his neck.

He almost blacked out when her inner muscles rippled around him. "Oh yeah, there you go. Squeeze my cock, baby."

She bore down again, and his vision wavered as pleasure shuddered through him. He quickened the pace, his body slapping hers with each deep stroke of his cock. Her breathing grew heavy, but he knew she wasn't there yet. Goddamn it, he wanted her to be. He wanted to feel her pussy milking him as she came, hear the throaty sounds she made when she let go.

"I don't come until you do," he muttered into her ear, and then he changed the angle, leaning forward so that his next thrust caused his pelvis to make contact with her clit. He rotated his hips in a hard grind, and Hudson moaned loud enough to wake the dead.

"Oh God." Her fingernails dipped beneath his collar and raked bare skin, making him grunt in pain. "Keep doing that. Please don't stop doing that."

Connor didn't stop. He went faster, slamming into

her at an angle until his cock was soaked from her excitement and all he could hear were her needy moans.

"Come for me," he rumbled.

"Make me," she gasped. "*Help* me."

"Is this what you need, baby?"

Chuckling, he reached between them and pressed his thumb to her clit, timing the contact with his next thrust, and he was rewarded by her cry of release. Her pussy clamped around him as she came, her nails digging into the back of his neck and her teeth sinking into his shoulder. He loved seeing her lose control. Loved being the one who *made* her lose control.

Her legs trembled around his hips as he fucked her through the orgasm, keeping his gaze glued to her face. So beautiful. Her eyes were unfocused, fuzzy with pleasure, and it cracked his chest wide open, the trust she so willingly handed him. She trusted him to make her feel good, trusted him not to let her fall. He'd never been with a woman who gave herself to him so completely. That trust . . . it was more powerful than any aphrodisiac. It was humbling and terrifying and so arousing that his balls tightened in warning.

His senses returned in that final moment before release hit, and he pulled out abruptly, blinding pleasure exploding inside him. As a shudder overtook him, he yanked her shirt up and spilled onto her stomach, semen coating her pale flesh, making it glisten in the candlelight.

His breathing was ragged as he met her eyes. She looked as stunned as he felt, as if she hadn't expected the fierceness of their joining, either.

"Connor." Lennox's amused voice traveled across the room.

Connor turned, stiffening when he realized that every pair of eyes in the room was fixed intently on him and Hudson. Expressions ranged from fascination to arousal, but it was Lennox's knowing smirk that grated the most. The man's silvery gaze took in Hudson's bare tits, Connor's bare ass, his come shining on her stomach. Jesus. He couldn't have marked her any more than if he'd tattooed his name on her skin.

"I need to talk to you before you go," Lennox prompted.

Furious with himself, Connor grabbed a cocktail napkin from a nearby table and pressed it into Hudson's hand. "Get cleaned up," he ordered. "I'll meet you outside."

He tucked his dick in his pants and zipped up, then stalked off, feeling Hudson's astonished gaze follow him all the way out the door.

"Well, I certainly didn't expect that."

Hudson spun around, startled to see Tamara coming up beside her. She was still breathless and tingly from that crazy, frantic sex and confused as hell about Connor's abrupt departure. The man had possessed her body like he owned it. He'd done it in a roomful of people and then walked away as if he hadn't knocked her entire world off its axis.

Avoiding Tamara's incredulous gaze, she hastily wiped her stomach and pulled down her shirt, as if what had just happened was no big deal. "You didn't expect what?"

"Honey, that man may as well have stuck a flag in your pussy and called it Connorland."

Her gaze flew up. "What?"

Tamara took a dainty sip of the drink in her hand. "Connor only fucks in the private rooms. If he did it out here where everyone could see, it was because he was sending a message. Telling everyone to keep their hands off you." The woman looked deeply impressed. "How the hell did you manage that? You must have a magic pussy, baby."

Hudson didn't answer. Her mind was too busy trying to make sense of what Tamara had said. Was that what Connor had done? Claimed her in front of everyone? Declared her as *his*? The notion was too mystifying to unpack at the moment, so she shrugged, pretending to be unaffected by it all.

Then she changed the subject.

"When did you get here?" she asked, studying the other woman.

Tamara was in leather pants and a corset again, but she'd swept her long dark hair into a knot atop her head, giving her an oddly regal vibe. "I've been here all day. I was in the back with Lennox when Con came in. The three of us had a lovely chat about satellites."

"Yeah, Connor was interested in getting his hands on more phones. Did you agree to help him?"

"Yes, and he's definitely not happy about owing me." Tamara grinned. "But Con understands that everything has a price."

"Speaking of prices . . ." Hudson smoothed a hand through her hair, which was tousled from Connor's fingers running through it. "I was hoping you'd be able to get me something too."

"I see. What do you need?"

"Birth control."

Those catlike eyes twinkled as Tamara glanced at the crumpled napkin Hudson was still clutching. "Yeah, I think you do need it. Condoms?"

Hudson shook her head. "Shots." She hesitated. "The female breeders in the city get birth control shots twice a year. Each one is good for six months."

The humor in Tamara's eyes faded, replaced with deep suspicion. "How do you know about those?"

She gulped. "Ah . . . someone told me about it. I can't remember who."

"Bullshit."

"It's true," she insisted.

That got her a husky laugh. "Again, bullshit." The woman's hard expression softened, but her next round of laughter was mocking as hell. "Give it up already, will you? I know you're from the city."

Hudson froze. "What?"

"Come on, honey. Do I look like an idiot to you? I knew it from the moment I met you. Citizens are ridiculously easy to spot." Her next pause lasted long enough to rattle Hudson even more. "Besides . . . you have his eyes."

A chill flew up her spine and turned her veins to ice. "W-whose eyes?" she stammered.

Tamara examined the room as if to make sure no one was paying attention to them, then turned back and murmured, "Dominik. You look exactly like him."

Hudson's pulse took off in a breakneck gallop.

"No," she said weakly. "You're wrong."

"Your features are softer, yes. Your hair's a shade lighter. But you two are definitely related." Tamara shrugged. "Last time you were here, I wondered why nobody else noticed the resemblance, but then I realized that not many people have ever actually seen Dominik. They know of him, and they're scared of him, but how fucking silly is that? Being scared of a person you've never even met. It's ludicrous."

Hudson could barely hear what the other woman was saying. Her head was spinning. Her muscles were paralyzed. Tamara knew who she was.

Tamara *knew*.

"You've gotta be his sister, huh?"

She started to feel light-headed. What if Tamara told Connor? What if—

"Relax, Hudson. If I were going to out you, don't you think I'd have done it by now? I know you're living with Con and the boys. I could have easily sent a message their way if I'd wanted to."

She finally found her voice, but it was unsteady, weakened by defeat. "Why haven't you?"

Tamara looked like she was fighting a smirk. "So you're not denying it, then?"

"What's the point? You've already decided you're right. But listen, whatever you think you know—"

"I don't *think* I know. I know. Period." The smirk broke free. "And your reaction confirmed it." Tamara slammed her whiskey glass into Hudson's shaky hand. "Drink. You look like you need it."

She did. She really, really did.

She practically inhaled the alcohol. It burned a path straight to her gut, but no amount of warmth could thaw the block of ice that she'd become.

"So . . . his sister?" Tamara asked cheerfully.

"Twin," she whispered.

The woman nodded.

Hudson gulped some more whiskey. "Why haven't you told anyone?"

"Because I'm a good businesswoman, and I understand that everything holds value. You want to know what holds the *most* value? Secrets."

That smug tone was irritating as hell. "What do you want from me?"

"At the moment? Nothing. That's another reason I'm so good at what I do—I look at the big picture, play the long game. Short-term gains mean nothing, not in this world."

Hudson was officially sick to her stomach, and not because she'd downed a full glass of whiskey in ten seconds flat. The thought that Tamara might hold this over her head—indefinitely—sent a wave of nausea spiraling up to her throat.

"Don't worry," Tamara assured her. "I'll give you fair notice before I come collecting. And you know what? Just because I feel terrible for upsetting you, I'll get your meds for free—how about that? No repayment necessary."

"Oh, gee," Hudson said sarcastically. "Thank you."

"Don't look at me like that. I promise you, I can be a very good ally to you if you let me." She smiled broadly. "I've got your back, Hudson."

She had her back? Yeah, right. She had a gun to Hudson's head was more like it, and she could pull the trigger whenever it suited her.

The queasiness got worse, churning and twisting her insides until Hudson was afraid she might actually throw up. She breathed deeply, trying to keep the nausea at bay and steady her frantic heartbeat. Panicking wasn't going to get her anywhere. Tamara would keep her mouth shut, at least for the time being, so there was no reason to freak out right now.

She had to relax. And breathe. And figure out how to silence her new *ally*.

For good.

16

There weren't many official marriages in the free land, not unless one or both parties happened to still believe in religion, which had been the case with Connor's wife.

Maggie's father, who'd been alive for the war and had continued his work as a minister after it, had raised his daughters to believe that a union needed to be sanctioned by God or else it wouldn't be binding. Connor had agreed to the ceremony because he wanted to make Maggie happy, but their titles of *husband* and *wife* were rare outside the city.

Most outlaws referred to their partners as "my woman" or "my man." Their commitment to each other was usually an unspoken one, unless they needed to send a message. To stake a claim in public and make it clear to everyone around them that one or both of them was untouchable.

Connor had sent a message tonight.

He hadn't done it intentionally, or even consciously, for that matter. His men messed around in the main room all the time. *He* didn't. And by doing it tonight, he'd pretty much held up a sign to everyone at Lennox's that Hudson was his. That she was important to him. He'd shown them his weakness, and although Lennox was a valuable ally, Connor knew the man wouldn't hesitate to exploit that weakness and use Hudson against him if it ever came down to it.

Hudson didn't say a word as she settled behind him for the long ride home. He appreciated her silence, because he sure as shit wasn't feeling talkative either.

With the moon shrouded by thick clouds tonight, he had no choice but to switch on the headlights, which only added to his agitation by making him feel exposed. But it was either risk an Enforcer patrol spotting the lights, or risk breaking Hudson's neck on the pitch-black road, and he wasn't about to endanger her life.

The fact that he was putting her well-being ahead of his own was a fucking mind-boggler. When had he started viewing her as part of the group? He wasn't sure how that had even happened. All he knew was that keeping her safe *mattered* to him.

They'd been driving for thirty minutes when the headlights caught a flash of movement on the side of the road.

Connor made out two shadowy figures. Had to be outlaws, because bandits traveled in larger groups and Enforcers wouldn't be walking. He slowed down instinctively, then cursed himself for it because at the sound of the engine, the dark figures halted in their tracks and began waving their arms in the air. The words *stop* and *please* and *help* carried in the night air, and Connor would've kept driving if Hudson hadn't squeezed his shoulders, her voice urging him to pull over.

Shit. He didn't need this right now.

"Stay on the bike," he ordered as he came to a stop. "We don't know what we're dealing with."

He already had his gun in hand and the safety clicked off as the stragglers stumbled toward the motorcycle. Two males. One in his forties, one in his teens. Both froze at the sight of Connor's weapon.

"Don't shoot," the younger one blurted out. "Please. We need help."

Connor swept his gaze over them, taking in their dusty clothing, disheveled hair, and the bloodstained rag tied around the teenager's upper arm.

"What happened?" Hudson asked, her gaze resting on the bloody wound Connor had been scrutinizing.

"Bandits," the older one croaked. He stepped closer, and the lights illuminated his face, revealing a swollen right eye and a split lip still caked with blood. "They jumped us about ten miles back."

Connor's shoulders instantly tensed. "How many of them?"

"At least seven."

"Nine," the kid corrected wearily. "I counted."

Hudson tried to move, but Connor reached down with his free hand and gripped her thigh, an unspoken command to stay put. "Where were you headed?" he asked the outlaws.

"South," replied the older one. "We're making our way to the coast, hoping to find a ship that'll take us to South Colony." He hesitated. "My son was stabbed during the attack. We need help . . . supplies . . . water to clean the wound . . ." He trailed off when he saw the look on Connor's face.

"There's a house about twenty miles west of here," Connor said curtly. "They'll have everything you need, give you a place to stay until you're ready to travel." He tucked his gun at the small of his back. "Tell Lennox that Connor sent you."

"But—"

"Good luck." He ignored Hudson's shocked squeak and revved the engine. The motorcycle shot forward, leaving the stragglers in its dust.

"What the *hell*!" Hudson's voice was muffled by the wind, but he could feel the anger vibrating from her body.

He kept his head low as he sped down the center line of the dark, empty road, but it wasn't the break-neck speed or the wind slapping his face that he needed to worry about. It was Hudson's fists batting at his shoulder blades as she yelled for him to pull over. His answering curse was sucked away by a gust of wind, and he slowed down only because Hudson no longer had her arms around him and he was worried she might fly off and crack her skull open on the asphalt.

"Let me off!"

Her incensed shout, accompanied by the sharp slap of her hand, triggered his own anger. "Fucking hell," he snapped as he steered onto the shoulder.

The moment the bike came to a stop, Hudson dove off it and promptly marched away in the opposite direction.

"Where the hell are you going?" he demanded.

Her boots snapped on the pavement with each furious stride, but she only made it about ten feet before she stopped abruptly, as if realizing his lightning-fast speed had managed to put at least a mile or two between them and the outlaws he'd left behind.

She whirled around, advancing on him like a ferocious animal. "What the *fuck* was that, Connor? *Good luck?*" Her gray eyes blazed, dark as thunderclouds and just as ominous. "You sent them on their way like they were garbage to you!"

His temper exploded, ripping a frustrated growl from his throat. "What did you want me to do? Pile four people onto a goddamn motorcycle? We couldn't have taken them with us even if we wanted to. The only thing to do was send them to Lennox's."

"Twenty miles!" she shouted. "Lennox is twenty miles away! It'll take them hours to walk there." Her breathing quickened. "I could have waited with the boy while you took the father to Lennox's, or you and I could have gone there ourselves and borrowed a car from someone—Beckett! Beckett has a car, and I'm sure he would have driven out here to get them. We didn't have to *abandon* them, Connor."

It took a serious amount of effort to get his temper under control. He breathed deeply, counted to five in his head, and didn't open his mouth until he was sure that something counterproductive wouldn't come out of it.

"There are bandits in the area, Hudson," he said flatly. "The kid and his pop got jumped not too far from here, which means we can't afford to be standing around arguing on the side of the road right now. You can yell at me when we get back to camp, sweetheart."

"Don't you fucking *sweetheart* me!" A helpless wobble shook her voice. "I could have at least looked at his arm! I could have checked his injuries and—"

"He was fine."

"He got jumped! You just said so yourself!" She sucked in a breath, shaking her head as she stared at him in disbelief. "What's the *matter* with you? People need your help out here. How could you not give a damn?"

His jaw tightened. "I took *you* in, didn't I?"

"Yeah, and I'm *sure* it was your idea, right? Of

course it wasn't! Kade probably convinced you to turn around. Or maybe it was Rylan. Either way, you would've been perfectly fine leaving me to fend for myself. You probably wouldn't have lost a second of sleep over it."

Impatience surged through him. "We don't have time for this right now. We have a long drive ahead of us."

She gaped at him as if she'd never seen him before. Then she went silent. So eerily silent and for so long that he was actually considering throwing her over his shoulder and tying her to the bike.

"I'm calling it," she finally said.

Connor frowned. "What?"

"You said that when one of us was done with . . . *this* . . . we should let the other one know." Her features went taut with unhappiness. "Well, I'm calling it. I'm done, Connor."

He couldn't explain the burst of pain that stabbed into him. The way his stomach twisted and his throat burned. "Why? Because I don't want to risk our necks for strangers? Lennox will take care of them, damn it." His harsh voice made her flinch, and he took a breath, softening his tone before he spoke again. "Those people have nothing to do with us. With our . . ." He faltered. "Relationship."

"You're right. They don't. But *you* do."

"What the hell is that supposed to mean?"

"It means that I'm done trying to figure out who you are."

She looked so upset he almost moved closer and pulled her into his arms, but he was afraid she'd slap him if he did.

"This isn't about sex for me anymore," she admitted. "I'm not like you, okay? I can't separate emotions from sex, at least not when it comes to you. It's different with Rylan. I know where he stands. I know who he is. I can mess around with him and not get attached, because it's just sex, just two people getting off, but . . . he doesn't make me *feel* things." Misery clung to her tone. "I feel something for you."

His breathing grew shallow.

"You're going to hurt me." Her quiet, emphatic voice sent another shooting pain to his heart. "I can see that now. I kept telling myself that you weren't a heartless bastard, that deep down you *must* care. About me, and the guys, and other people. But you don't, do you? You truly don't give a damn about anyone, do you?"

He tried speaking past the lump in his throat. "Hudson—"

"Do you even know what it's like to feel something for another person? To care about whether they live or die? To want to reach out and help someone, even if it means putting your own life at risk? Do you know what it's like to *love* someone?"

Connor's throat closed up to the point of asphyxiation. He couldn't get a single word out, and his silence only deepened the bitterness darkening Hudson's expression. Her accusations poisoned the air between them.

"Yeah, I didn't think so," she muttered.

She turned her back to him and headed toward the bike. A dismissal. A slap in the face. He stared at the high set of her shoulders, the golden hair streaming down her back, and something inside him snapped. She had no right throwing out accusations. Telling him he didn't care, he didn't *love*. She didn't know a goddamn thing about him.

"Yes," he spat out.

"Yes what?" she said without turning around.

"I know what it's like to love someone."

He saw her shoulders tense. "I don't believe you." She kept walking.

"I loved my wife."

That got her attention. No, it did more than that. She stumbled midstep, caught her balance, then spun around to face him. Her shocked expression collided with his uneasy one.

"You're *married*?"

"I was." Pain lodged in his rib cage. "She's dead now."

Son of a bitch. He wished he'd never opened his mouth. He'd wanted to knock Hudson off her high horse, teach her that she had no business making judgments about him, but now her features had softened and her eyes flickered with sympathy, and he couldn't have felt more exposed than if he'd sliced his chest open and put his insides on display.

He gritted his teeth. "Can we fucking go home now?"

"No."

Shit. He knew that look. It was the one that stubbornly said, *We're not going anywhere until I get my way*.

"What happened to your wife?"

"I just told you. She's dead."

Hudson bridged the distance between them and caught his chin in her hands, tugging it downward so he had no choice but to look at her. "How did she die?"

"How the fuck do you think she died?" He let out a ragged breath. "Dominik killed her."

Hudson's breath hitched. She looked stricken, but also confused, which puzzled him. What was there to be confused about? Enforcers killed outlaws. End of story.

"You . . . *saw* him kill her?"

Connor gave a terse shake of the head. "I didn't see him pull the trigger, but I watched him walk away from the scene." His tone held a bite of sarcasm. "I put two and two together when I found the bodies."

"You weren't there when your camp was attacked?"

The question sliced into his heart like a cold blade, because he *should* have been there. He never should've left Maggie alone.

"I was out hunting. I was the only one who knew how. The people Maggie insisted on taking in . . ." He ignored the resentment climbing up his spine. "They were . . . they were weak, okay? Women who'd always had men to take care of them, kids who'd lost their parents to disease. Maggie and her sisters were bleeding hearts, all three of them. They adopted anyone we crossed paths with." He couldn't stop an irritated curse. "There were twelve of us, and I was the only one who knew how to hunt."

Hudson hesitated for a beat, then laced her fingers through his. He let her, because he suddenly wasn't feeling too steady on his legs, like he might keel over if he didn't have something to hold on to.

"We'd heard rumors that Enforcers were sweeping the area," he admitted. "I wanted to abandon camp, but Maggie was adamant about staying. She was trying to make a home for us."

Hudson picked up on the bitter note in his voice. "There's nothing wrong with wanting a safe place to call home," she said softly.

He released a shaky breath. "No, but I shouldn't have let her convince me to stay. I knew in my gut it was the wrong move, but everyone was tired of traveling, and we had a solid camp set up. A well, an orchard, a forest in our backyard with plenty of game. That's where I was when the Enforcers came. I was tracking a deer in the forest. I'd left this kid Dan in charge—he was only seventeen, but other than me, he was the only one who was proficient with a gun." He swallowed. "I tried to teach Maggie how to shoot, but she resisted. She said that even if she knew how to, she would never be able to take a life, animal *or* human."

The memory chipped away at another piece of his heart. Maggie's compassion was one of the reasons he'd fallen in love with her. That and the eternal optimism she'd possessed. He hadn't realized until later that it wasn't optimism—it was naïveté. She'd believed that deep down everyone was good, that a gentle touch could accomplish so much more than a hard one. She'd tried to mold Connor into thinking that way too, but it had been like asking a wild animal to suppress its violent instincts. He wasn't gentle. He wasn't an optimist. He was a ruthless, cynical bastard who did whatever it took to survive.

But he'd tried, damn it. He'd tried to be what Maggie wanted, because he'd loved her and he'd wanted to make her happy. After her death, he'd finally allowed the depressing truth to sink in. Maggie had been wrong. Not just in her attempt to change him, but about the way she viewed the world.

"Her father sheltered her," he said bleakly. "Maggie and her sisters grew up on an isolated farm. They'd never encountered bandits or Enforcers, never witnessed the kind of violence that existed beyond their little slice of paradise. Their father didn't even bother teaching them self-defense, because he thought they were safe from the rest of the world, that nothing bad could ever touch them." Connor angrily shook his head. "She never stood a chance."

Hudson squeezed his hand, and he squeezed back, hard and desperate, because she was the lifeline keeping him from drowning in the memories.

Maggie's lifeless body on the dirt. The bullet hole in her forehead. Her sisters. The others.

"Dominik murdered them," Connor choked out. "I know my people, Hudson—they would have surrendered the moment he and his men showed up. None of them were trained. None of them would have fought back. Which means he opened fire on unarmed people who weren't even a threat to him."

Hudson's breathing became labored. "What happened when you returned to camp?"

"I heard the gunfire from the woods and made my way back, but it had stopped by the time I reached the outskirts of camp. There were no screams, no shots. Just silence."

It was macabre as fuck, but he'd always wondered if Maggie had screamed when the Enforcers had come. If she'd screamed when she'd watched her friends and family die. If she'd screamed before *she'd* died. Or had she still held on to hope in her final moments? Believed everything would be okay? That had been her favorite phrase. *Everything will be okay, Con. I know it.*

She hadn't known a damn thing.

"I hid in the trees," he said. "I watched the Enforcers leave the house and head for their vehicles, and I heard them talking. One of them sounded upset about what they'd done, said it wasn't right. His buddy told him that orders were orders, and that Dominik wanted them to send a message to any outlaws who tried going against the council."

"They used to give the outlaws a choice. Rejoin society, or face imprisonment." Hudson's voice shook.

"Cold-blooded murder goes against their code, or at least that's what my father told me."

"Well, there was no fucking code that day," Connor muttered. "And believe me, Dominik looked damn pleased with himself when he joined his men. He told them there was no point in disposing of the bodies. He said to let them rot." His fists clenched, and Hudson yelped, a reminder that he was still holding her hand. He quickly loosened his grip. "Sorry. . . . I didn't mean to do that."

"It's okay." She swept her fingertips over his knuckles in a soothing gesture.

"I'll never forget the look in his eyes. And that smirk, like he was proud of what he'd done. I could have opened fire on him then. On all of them. They would have fired back, and I'd be dead, but at least I could've taken a few of them down before that happened. But there was a chance some of my people were still alive, that *Maggie* was still alive, so I waited until they drove away and then I went back to camp." His heart twisted. "I should have killed Dominik when I had the chance."

"They were all dead?" Hudson whispered.

"Every single one of them."

She moved closer, leaning her head on his shoulder. "Oh, Connor. I'm sorry."

"Yeah, me too." Shame bubbled in his throat. "It was my job to protect them. To protect *her*."

"You were hunting to provide for them. You couldn't have known the Enforcers would attack."

"I told you—I *knew* they were in the area. I should have put my foot down and ordered everyone to pack up. I shouldn't have listened to Maggie."

Hudson sighed. "You did what you thought was right at the time."

"I did what was right for *her*. Not for the group, and certainly not for me, not when my gut told me it was a mistake. What the fuck kind of leader does that make me? I let my wife's big eyes and foolish pleas guilt me into making the worst possible decision for the group." He cursed loudly. "Don't you get it? I don't want to be a leader. I never wanted that responsibility."

He fumbled in his back pocket for the cigarettes he'd stashed there. His fingers shook as he lit a smoke and sucked on it so hard it gave him a head rush.

"I've been making decisions for other people my whole life. I took care of my mother after my father died. I took care of our whole group."

Resentment whipped through him, and he took another drag, then another, and another, until nothing but nicotine surged through his blood, alleviating that feeling of pure helplessness.

"I never asked to be anyone's leader. I don't want people relying on me, and I sure as hell don't want to be responsible for anyone's life but my own."

"People are responsible for their own lives," Hudson said quietly. "Nobody is expecting you to take on that burden." She hesitated. "It's your guidance they're looking for."

"Why?" he said desperately. "What the hell made my word gold?"

"I don't know. You inspire trust in people. I felt it the moment I met you." She reached up and stroked his cheek. "Out of all the people in that bar, I chose to run after *you*. To ask for *your* protection. Whether you like it or not, there's something about you that makes people feel safe."

"Well, I don't want it. I'm tired of being the one everyone looks to for answers." He dragged a hand over his scalp. "Why can't any of you see that I have no fucking clue what I'm doing?"

She let go of his hand and wrapped her arms around him, and he instinctively tensed, because comfort wasn't something he ever sought out.

"I'm sorry about your wife, Connor."

The sad whisper cracked his chest open and sent a rush of emotion to his throat. He sagged into the embrace, Hudson's body warm and solid against his, the top of her head fitting perfectly in the crook of his neck. Maggie had been slight, petite. He was always terrified he'd break her if he held her too tight, but he didn't feel like that with Hudson. He didn't think *anything* could break her.

The fact that he was drawing comparisons between the two women flooded his stomach with guilt, but he couldn't help himself. He couldn't help but recognize the strength in Hudson that Maggie had lacked.

She lifted her head, her gaze locking with his. "I'm sorry I said you don't have a heart. I know you do. I see the way you act with Rylan and the others. You *do* care about them, even if you don't like to show it."

His throat constricted, but even after he'd cleared it, his voice still sounded like it was lined with gravel. "I care about you too."

Uncertainty flitted across her face. "You do?"

"I know it might not seem like it, but I really do care. You . . ." He pressed his lips together, then forced himself to continue. "You make me happy."

Surprise widened her eyes. Surprise, and something akin to guilt, which made no sense at all, because she had no reason to feel guilty.

"Connor." She visibly swallowed. "I need to tell you—"

God. No. He couldn't hear another parting speech, not after he'd laid himself bare to her. He coughed, flicking his cigarette on the pavement. "It's fine, sweetheart. I understand why you want to end this, and I respect your decision, okay? I promise it won't be uncomfortable at camp. I'll—"

She cut him off with a kiss. "Shut up," she mumbled against his lips.

Connor would've thought laughter was impossible after everything they'd discussed, but somehow a chuckle popped out of his mouth.

Hudson swallowed the husky sound with another kiss. Warm and firm and confident. Then she drew back, her mouth millimeters from his as she whispered, "Nothing is ending, Con." Her palms stroked his cheeks as she brushed her lips over his again. "It's just beginning."

17

Air. No air.

Connor's hands were a tight vise around her throat, his eyes more red than hazel as they gleamed with pure, naked hatred. He was going to kill her. He was going to squeeze the life from her body until she was dead. Dead like his wife. Dead like Dominik. He'd killed her brother and now he was about to kill—

Hudson woke up, gasping for air.

Her hands shot up to her throat, then faltered, as if they were surprised to find it intact. The dream—no, the *nightmare*—had been so real, she could still feel Connor's strong grip crushing her windpipe, and her lungs burned as she sucked in fast, gulping breaths that made her weak and dizzy.

The scariest part of all was that the dream—the *nightmare*—wasn't a figment of her vivid imagination. If Connor came face-to-face with her brother, he *would* kill him. And if he was feeling bloodthirsty enough, he could very well decide to kill *her* for being the twin sister of his enemy. For lying to him.

She still couldn't wrap her head around everything he'd told her tonight.

Her brother had killed Connor's wife.

Connor had been *married*.

Taking another breath, Hudson climbed out of bed and stripped out of her sweat-soaked clothes. The cabin suddenly felt too hot and suffocating, so she stepped outside, unconcerned by her nudity. It was too late for anyone else to be up, and although it was still humid out, the air was cooler on the porch than it was inside.

She stared up at the black sky, her heartbeat slowly regulating as she drew more oxygen into her lungs, and she found herself thinking about her brother. He was a night owl too, and she wondered if Dom was standing outside right now, staring at the same moonless sky.

Or maybe he was out slaughtering people.

Bile burned her throat as Connor's story buzzed in her mind. It didn't make sense, damn it. Dominik didn't kill outlaws in cold blood, not unless he was defending himself. He always gave them a chance to reintegrate first.

Not always, a cynical voice reminded her.

Her stomach twisted. No, these days Dom didn't give the outlaws a choice. He'd stopped following the code, the one her father had put in place when he'd created the Enforcer unit all those years ago.

But Connor had said his wife had been killed two years ago. Dom had still been . . . *normal* back then, hadn't he?

She bit the inside of her cheek, trying to pinpoint exactly when it was that Dom had started exhibiting the violent, aggressive behavior that had eventually led to her escape. He'd begun to unravel after their father's death, so . . . a little over two years ago, she realized with dismay.

It was definitely possible that he had murdered Connor's group.

But . . . did he deserve to die for it?

Yes.

The voice in her head was swift and unforgiving, but her heart squeezed so painfully at the thought of seeing her brother dead that her ribs actually hurt. Whether he deserved it or not, he was still her twin brother. He'd been her best friend and her confidant. Her protector. Could she really stand by and let Connor exact his vengeance on Dominik?

"What are you doing out here, sweetheart?"

She jumped at the sound of Connor's voice. "Oh," she squeaked. "I . . . ah . . . had a bad dream."

He approached from the neighboring cabin, and her cheeks heated when she realized she was buck-naked. Connor's gaze lingered on her bare breasts before rising to her eyes. "You okay?" he said gruffly.

She nodded. Then she shook her head, misery sticking to her throat. "Do you . . . ?" She swallowed. "Do you think people can turn evil? Or are they born evil?"

Surprise flickered in his gaze. "Uh. Well, I don't know. That's kind of a deep question for this time of night."

A weak smile lifted her lips. "Yeah. I guess it is."

He came up beside her, hesitated, then wrapped one arm around her and pulled her close. Hudson rested her head against his shoulder, breathing in his familiar scent, woodsy and masculine, strong and reassuring.

"I think they're born evil," he finally said.

Her chest started hurting again. "Yeah?"

"I think good people can do bad things, but that doesn't make them evil. But evil people . . . they're born with poison in their hearts. They might try to hide it, or go years fooling people and pretending to be good, but the darkness is always there, waiting to come out."

Hudson thought about Dominik when he had been a little boy. His kind eyes and angelic smile. The way he'd adored their mother and idolized their father. He'd been such a sweet kid. He'd been a sweet man too, before he'd changed.

Changed . . . or simply unleashed the evil that had always lurked in his heart?

No. She didn't believe that. He wouldn't have been able to fool her. She *knew* him, inside and out, and she refused to believe that her own twin had been a monster all along and that somehow she hadn't picked up on it.

"It's in their eyes," Connor mumbled. "You can see the darkness when you look into their eyes."

She hesitated. "Did you see the darkness when you looked at Dominik?"

He gave a curt nod. "Yeah. I saw it. I *felt* it." His hand tightened on her shoulder, trembled with barely restrained violence. "He walked up to that Jeep after killing a dozen people, and he looked so damn smug. No, he looked *happy*. His eyes were shining. Those dark eyes, black as night, shining brighter than the fucking sun, as if wiping out a camp of innocent people was the greatest gift he'd ever received."

Something about the embittered speech troubled her, but Connor didn't give her time to think about it. His grip loosened, his lips tender as he brushed a fleeting kiss on her temple. "It's late. You should go back to bed."

She managed a nod, still trying to figure out what

had bugged her, but she pushed her thoughts aside and headed for her door. "I'm sorry if I woke you."

"It's okay." He watched as she turned the doorknob, then cleared his throat. "Can I come in?"

Her forehead wrinkled. "I don't . . . um . . . I'm too exhausted to have sex, Con."

He shifted, looking peculiarly nervous. "Not for sex. I, ah, thought we could . . . sleep together."

It was impossible to control the shock that slammed into her. "But you sleep alone," she reminded him.

Connor's gaze was so intense it sent a shiver through her. "Maybe I don't want to do that anymore."

"Oh." Her pulse sped up as joy and hope erupted in her chest, but she was too afraid to ask what his change of heart signified. "Come in, then."

They entered her dark cabin, Connor shutting the door behind him as Hudson slid between the sheets. He stripped, his clothes rustling as they fell to the floor, and a moment later he crawled in next to her, his warm, naked body pressed up against her. A contented sigh slipped out as she snuggled closer, her back settling against his chest as he draped a possessive arm over her.

"Good night," he said gruffly.

"Good night," she murmured.

She sighed softly, cocooned by Connor's warmth and the bliss of having him there with her. And maybe she would've even fallen asleep, maybe she would've slept peacefully in his arms all night long, if something hadn't dawned on her.

Those dark eyes, black as night . . .

Connor's angry words clicked a switch in her brain, solving the uneasy puzzle that their conversation had left her with.

Dominik didn't have dark eyes. He had light gray ones. So light they resembled the transparent icicles that formed on the roof of the compound every winter.

The man Connor had witnessed leaving the bloody scene of the crime . . . the man who'd slaughtered Connor's wife and the rest of his people . . .

It couldn't have been her brother.

18

Hudson woke up to the feel of Connor nuzzling her breasts and the erotic scrape of his stubble against her naked flesh. He did this often now, waking her up in the middle of the night with his mouth or his hands. Coaxing her body to life while her mind remained blissfully drowsy, consciousness slowly floating back to her with each stroke of his fingers and brush of his tongue.

He'd spent every night in her bed for the past two weeks, but she knew she was living on borrowed time. Tamara knew who she was. All it would take was one visit from the woman and Connor would know the truth too.

Hudson had to tell him herself. She'd already decided to, the night he'd told her about his wife's death, but every time she thought she'd worked up the courage, the words refused to leave her mouth and—

Oh *fuck*, that felt good. His mouth was on her nipple. Hot suction and the slightest scrape of teeth, rough enough to bring a sting of pain, but he soothed it rapidly with his tongue, a long lick that distracted her from her thoughts and summoned a happy little sigh.

His chuckle warmed her nipple. "Was wondering when you'd wake up."

The cabin was bathed in darkness, so all she could see was his head between her breasts. "How long have you been at it?" she teased.

"Playing with your tits? A couple minutes."

"Pervert."

It was too dark to see his face, but she felt him smiling, the curve of his mouth tickling her breast. "You love it."

She certainly did.

She loved it even more when his hand traveled toward her stomach, circling her belly button before stroking a path down to her pussy. Rough fingertips grazed her clit in a sweet caress that made her suck in a breath.

"My favorite sound in the world," he told her.

"What is?"

"That breathy little noise you make when I do this." He rubbed her clit with the pad of his thumb, and sure enough, a breathy whimper was his reward.

Connor's lips traveled to her neck, planting slow, torturous kisses in time to the slow torturous strokes of his thumb on her clit. His erection was heavy against her hip, and he moved in a slow grind, branding her skin with the hot evidence of his arousal.

She never knew what to expect from him. Whether it would be hard and fast. Filthy and demanding. Languid and teasing. But one factor remained unchanged—the hunger. He was always as hungry for her as she was for him. It didn't matter if Rylan was there. It didn't matter if they were alone, or being watched by every person in Lennox's playroom. Connor could fuck her in front of five hundred people and he'd still be the only one she'd see. Just him, with his rough voice and his wicked touch, and the way he looked at her like she was the most beautiful woman he'd ever met.

She grasped his chin as his lips teased her jaw, tugging his head up and molding their lips together, and the only thought in her mind was *perfection*. Their mouths, their bodies, *everything*. They fit so perfectly that emotion clogged her chest and her hands became frantic, reaching for his cock to guide him between her legs.

"Hold on, baby. We need—" He let out a husky groan as she stroked his erection. "Condom," he choked out.

He leaned over her and fumbled for the night table, and then he was back where she wanted him, the blunt head of his cock nudging her opening.

She was so wet and ready for him that his entire length slid inside her with ease. Filling her, stretching her, and the sense of completion that washed over her extended far past the delicious way his body completed hers. *He* completed her. He was intense and fierce and beautiful, and there was no one else she wanted to be in this bed with. No, in this *world* with.

"Don't hold back," she murmured when he tried to go slow. "I need . . . all of you. I need to feel every inch of you."

Her hips moved in a frantic upward thrust, and he hissed in surprise before quickening the pace.

"Harder," she begged.

"Jesus." His features went taut. "No, I'm going to hurt you."

The same words she'd thrown at him on the side of the road. *You're going to hurt me*. But he wouldn't, not anymore, not now that she knew what he'd gone through, what had shaped him into the man he was. He wasn't heartless. He was just a little bit damaged. But he was *hers*, damn it.

"More, Connor. I *need* you."

Groaning, he rose to his knees as he set a hard, relentless rhythm that had his cock slamming into her without mercy. She felt each deep stroke between her legs, in her fingers and toes and the tips of her breasts. When she came, it was in an explosion of white-hot pleasure that blinded her, seared her from head to toe. Her entire world was reduced to Connor, and the heat in his eyes, and the way he groaned her name as he sagged on top of her and shuddered in climax.

"*Christ*." He was breathing as hard as she was, his sweat-slickened chest plastered to hers as they both recovered.

Watching him dispose of the condom stole the lingering pleasure from her body and replaced it with prickly unease, because it reminded her of the birth control she'd requested before Tamara had stolen the one piece of insurance Hudson had counted on for her survival—that nobody but her knew who she really was.

Not many people have ever actually seen Dominik . . .

Tamara's words suddenly came to mind, solidifying the idea Hudson had been toying with for days now. What if the man Connor had seen leaving his camp hadn't been Dominik? That would mean Dominik hadn't been responsible for his wife's death. It would mean that she could tell Connor who she was, and he might not hate her.

But she wasn't ready to tell him yet. She wasn't ready to lose *this*—his heavy body against hers, his lips trailing kisses on her neck as he came back to bed and settled beside her.

She rested her head on his chest, the even beating of his heart tickling her ear. "Was it like this with your wife?"

The question popped out before she could stop it, and Connor instantly tensed, his pectoral muscles tightening beneath her cheek. His chest rose on an inhale, then fell as the air seeped out of his lungs. "What do you mean?"

"The way it is with us." She paused, struggling to put it into words. "Intense. Frantic. It's like . . . I can never get enough of you."

Connor was silent for a moment. "No," he admitted. "It wasn't like this."

"What was it like, then?"

"Different."

She couldn't help but laugh. "That's very diplomatic of you. You can say *better*, if that's what it was." But the notion stabbed her heart.

"That's what it was, though—different." There was another beat, long and strained. "She didn't like this side of me."

Hudson frowned and rose onto her elbow. She could barely see his face in the darkness and it bothered her, so she hastily reached for the lighter on the bed table and lit the candle beside it. The yellow glow that filled the room emphasized Connor's pained expression.

"What side?"

"When I was rough in bed." He rested an arm over his forehead, not quite shielding his face from view, but casting a shadow over it, making it hard to read his expression. "Or when I was too intense. It scared her, I think."

Hudson's frown deepened. "But that's who you are. You're intense."

His answering chuckle sounded sad. "I guess she didn't like who I was, then."

"I don't think that's true. I think she loved you."

He nodded. "Yeah. She loved me." His arm dropped to the mattress, long fingers tightening in the sheets. "But she didn't know me, not completely, anyway. I learned pretty fast to hide certain parts of myself from her. I wanted her to be happy, and . . . well, that part of me didn't make her happy."

The admission drove slivers of displeasure into Hudson's skin. Connor's dominance, his intensity, his roughness . . . they were an important part of who he was. It was the reason he'd survived this long in such a primitive, unforgiving land. How could his own wife not understand that?

"You must have really loved her, if you were willing to change who you are," Hudson whispered.

His voice shook slightly. "Maggie was . . . she was like a beacon of light in the midst of so much darkness. I've never met anyone who *smiled* so much. I didn't understand it, but I knew I wanted it. I wanted to feel that light touch in my life and find out how she did it—how she lived without fear." Connor's tone sharpened at the edges. "But that's not possible, not in this world. It took me a year with Maggie before I realized what was really going on. It wasn't that she'd found a way to bring light to the darkness—she genuinely didn't recognize that the darkness was there. She was living in a fantasy."

The notion made Hudson sad. "So are most of the people in the city."

"Yeah, but at least they're *safe* in the city, as long as they follow the GC's rules. Out here you can't afford to be that naive."

"How long were you married?"

"Three years." He tugged on her arm. "C'mere. I don't like how far away you are."

They were only a foot apart, but she humored him by nestling close to his side again. His fingers immediately slid through her hair, stroking it gently, and she couldn't deny she liked this sweet, relaxed part of their relationship as much as she liked the raw passion of it.

Something had shifted between them since the night they'd driven back from Lennox's. Connor was still as gruff and controlled as he'd always been, but he was also more tender. He *laughed* more. And he'd even warmed up to Hudson's wolf. He no longer frowned when Hope scurried at his feet, and he never complained when the wolf pup slept at the foot of the bed on the nights that Hudson stole her away from Pike.

"Why didn't you guys stay on the farm?"

"Hmmm?" he said absently, toying with her hair.

"You said that Maggie's father raised her and her sisters on a farm, right?"

"Yeah. I came across it after my mother died. I split from my other group, handed leadership over to one of the other men, and hit the open road. That's where I met Maggie."

"So why didn't you stay there?"

He sighed. "Because it burned down."

"Oh shit. How?"

"Maggie's father had a heart attack. We were asleep upstairs and didn't hear him get up, but I guess he woke up in pain and went downstairs. He lit a candle, and then he must have dropped it when he passed out. The fire spread to the drapes and it all went to shit from there. The smoke woke me up, and I got Maggie and her sisters out of there. Found Darren downstairs and hauled him out too, but he died on the front lawn while we watched the house burn."

As an ache shuddered through her heart, Hudson reached for Connor's hand. "I'm sorry."

"I think that's why Maggie was so insistent on staying in that last camp. The house reminded her of the one she'd grown up in. It reminded her of home." His chest rose sharply again. "And, well, you know the rest. I made the wrong call, and my people paid the price for it."

Trepidation scurried up her spine, but she forced herself to continue on the course she hadn't even realized she'd set. "Connor . . . I have to ask you something."

He gave her hair a gentle tug, tilting her head so he could see her eyes. "What is it?"

"The day that Maggie died . . . You said you saw Dominik leaving your camp and talking to his men."

"Yeah . . ." Wariness creased his forehead.

She took a breath. "What did he look like?"

"Why are you asking me this?"

"Please. Just humor me and tell me what he looked like. Hair color, eye color, all the details you can remember."

Connor sat up and rubbed his jaw, looking unsettled by the request. "Dark hair," he muttered. "In a buzz cut. Dark eyes, more black than brown."

Her heart sped up. "Any facial hair?"

"Goatee, but it was more scruffy than groomed. Why?"

A sick feeling crawled up to her throat. "What else? Was he tall? Short?"

"Average height, I guess. Definitely shorter than me, but taller than you. Stocky build, barrel chest . . ." Looking suspicious, he repeated himself. "*Why?*"

"Because . . ." She exhaled slowly. "I don't think the man you saw was Dominik."

"Bullshit. It was him."

She shook her head. "Dominik has blond hair and light eyes. And he's tall, even taller than you. Six foot five."

Connor was stricken for a moment before responding with the firm shake of his head. "It was him, Hudson."

"Did his men call him Dominik?"

"Well . . . no," he admitted with a frown. "They called him 'boss.' And 'sir.'"

"But nobody ever called him by his name?"

"Where are you going with this?"

"The man you described . . ." She choked down her nausea. "That's Knox."

Connor's alarmed gaze flew to hers.

"You described *Knox*, Con. The hair, the eyes, the goatee. And he's Dominik's second-in-command—the men always address him as 'sir' in the field." Hudson's heart continued to race. She wasn't sure if it was because of the relief in confirming that her brother hadn't killed Connor's wife, or the rage of knowing that Knox had.

"No," Connor said stiffly. "You're wrong."

"I've seen Dominik. I know what he looks like, and that's *not* it. I've also seen Knox, and trust me, that *is* it." She met his mistrustful gaze. "This means . . . you've been after the wrong man."

The accusation turned his features to stone. "No. It just means I need to add another man's name to that list. Because even if Knox is the one who pulled the trigger, who the fuck do you think gave the orders, Hudson?"

Panic shot through her. "Knox could have acted on his own."

"Jesus. When did *you* become naive? Knox acts under Dominik's orders. Dominik *sent* him out into the colony to hunt outlaws." Connor jumped off the bed and strode naked to the chair where he'd left his pants. He dug in the pockets until he found what he was looking for—a pack of cigarettes, which he almost crushed in his hand as he stalked to the door. "I need a smoke."

Hudson bit her lip. "Do you want me to come out with you?"

"No," he muttered. "I need to be alone for a minute."

The door shut behind him, not quite a slam, but loud enough to make her jump, to bring a rush of helplessness to her chest and a chill to her bones.

She'd hoped that learning Knox was to blame for Maggie's death might lessen some of Connor's hatred for Dominik. That it might make it easier for her to tell him the truth.

But apparently that was hoping for too much.

By the time morning came, Connor was feeling centered again. The bomb Hudson had dropped on him had messed with his head and kept him up most of the night, analyzing and second-guessing every move he'd made these past two years. Raiding as many storage stations as he could in the hopes that Dominik might be there. Hitting up anyone he crossed paths with for information. He'd even swallowed his pride and asked Tamara for the location of the Enforcer compound—only to discover it was the one thing on the planet the bitch *didn't* know.

All that time wasted, hunting Dominik, searching for a man who hadn't even pulled that trigger. It was a disheartening notion . . . until he reminded himself that it didn't matter who'd pulled the trigger. Dominik was still every much to blame for Maggie's death as his lieutenant was. The council issued orders, and Dominik enforced them. He'd known damn well what he was asking of Knox.

Still, it was with a new sense of purpose that Connor walked to the lodge that morning. He wanted to check if Xan had made any progress with the communication program, but just as he reached the door, Xander burst out of it.

The other man halted. "Shit. I was coming to find you."

Connor instantly went on the alert. "What's wrong?"

"Lennox called on the sat phone. He was paying a visit to Foxworth and came across an Enforcer on his way back. A deserter." Xander shrugged. "I guess Hudson was right—there really are deserters in the Enforcer camp."

"Please tell me Lennox captured the bastard."

Xander's lips twitched. "Damn right he did."

Connor didn't believe in a higher power, but . . . fuck. He'd just renewed his mission to find the men who'd murdered his wife, and suddenly an Enforcer deserter was handed to him on a silver platter? If that wasn't a sign from God, he didn't know what was.

"Lennox took the deserter to the abandoned mill near the river," Xander told him. "He called to see if you wanted to interrogate the kid."

If Lennox had been standing in front of him right now, Connor would have kissed him square on the mouth. "Call him back and tell him I'm on my way."

Xan nodded. "You want me to go with you?"

Hudson's voice joined the conversation. "Go where?"

Connor turned to find her approaching, and he was momentarily distracted by the thin white tank top that outlined the hard buds of her nipples even through her bra. Her hair was braided down her back, but a few strands framed her face, catching in the sunlight as she walked toward them. Christ. She was so beautiful that sometimes it hurt to look at her. And it was getting a lot harder to keep his emotions under control now that she slept in his arms every night.

"Lennox captured an Enforcer," Xander told her.

Hudson's eyes widened. "Really?"

"He's got him stashed at a warehouse about an hour from here," Connor said briskly. "I'm heading there now to have a chat with him."

Her surprise dissolved into wariness. "To question him about Dominik? And Knox?"

Connor nodded.

She let out a breath, then nodded back. "I'm coming with you."

He could've said no, but he knew she'd only argue with him. Besides, he didn't *want* to say no. He never would've dreamed of placing Maggie in a potentially dangerous situation, but it was different with Hudson. He'd seen her handle a knife, and when he'd teased her about how she had all those guns stashed in her bag but probably didn't know how to use them, she'd proved him wrong with an impressive shooting display that even Pike had broken out in applause for.

"You can ride with me," he said. "But go find Rylan, will you? I want him to come too."

She looked oddly shaken up as she hurried off, but Xander spoke before Connor could ask him if he'd thought Hudson looked a bit pale. "Do you want me to radio Pike?"

"Where's he at?"

"He took Hope to the woods. I think they're doing some more training."

Connor shook his head in amazement. Pike was still the same surly bastard he'd always been, but when it came to that wolf . . . Christ, he was a different person. An endless well of patience, and more affectionate than Connor had ever seen him.

"Yeah, radio him," he answered. "But not to come along. I want him to stick close to camp while we're gone. Kade too."

As Xander disappeared into the lodge, Connor headed to the garage to fill up the gas tanks for the trip, hoping to hell that it wouldn't be a waste of fuel. All the Enforcers he'd questioned at storage facilities had refused to reveal the location of their compound before he'd killed them. But depending on what had made him flee, this deserter might be the exception to that rule.

Twenty minutes later, they drove away from camp, Connor and Hudson on the Harley while Rylan rode the beat-up Ducati he'd finally gotten around to fixing. Their tires ate up the long stretch of road, following the river toward the industrial area that had lain abandoned for decades. Textiles warehouses and run-down mills came into view, the chain-link fences that had once served as security now sagging in some places and fully collapsed in others.

Connor slowed down when they reached the old lumber mill, where rusted machinery and rotting logs were scattered around, forgotten in the chaos that had destroyed the world. Colorado was one of the few states that had been almost untouched by the war, which was why so many outlaws had ended up there. Too many for Connor's liking, because the growing outlaw population in the area was like a magnet for the Enforcers.

He and Hudson slid off the bike. Rylan came up beside them, drawing his gun from his waistband and checking the clip. There was another motorcycle parked on the dirt—Lennox's ride, and the shiny black paint job was clearly the work of Beckett, who practically lived in the mechanic shop in Foxworth.

Lennox strode out of the building, a rifle propped on his shoulder. "You got here fast," he remarked.

"Had nothing else to do," Connor drawled.

Lennox saw through the relaxed front. "I'm sure." He raked a hand through his messy hair, the tattoos on his forearms flexing with the movement. "Dude's not saying a word, by the way. I didn't rough him up for answers, because, well, honestly, I don't give a fuck. It makes no difference to me where their headquarters are."

Connor headed for the door. "Yeah, well, it makes a difference to me."

He felt Rylan on his tail, but Hudson had stayed put, and he glanced over his shoulder with a frown. "You coming?"

"I think I'll stay out here."

Connor suddenly understood why her face looked ashen. She'd escaped the city because of men like the one beyond that door. Of course she wouldn't want to be around any Enforcers, not when one of the most dangerous Enforcers was determined to make her his bride.

The thought made Connor's blood boil. No fucking way was he letting Knox get his hands on Hudson.

"Don't worry. I'll keep your girl company," Lennox said, mistaking Connor's anger for concern.

Then Lennox suggestively wiggled his eyebrows at Hudson, and Connor promptly leveled a glare in his direction. Also known as *touch her and say good-bye to your balls*.

"Message received," Lennox said with a grin.

The smell of sawdust and wood rot hit Connor's nostrils the second he entered the building. Exposed beams and piping made up the main room, and for all his bullshitting about how he didn't care, Lennox had taken the time to tie his hostage to one of the wooden beams.

Brown eyes widened in fear when the young man spotted the newcomers. His features strained as he fought the knots binding his hands to the beam behind his back.

"Relax, kid. We're not going to hurt you," Connor said. "We're just here to talk."

He stuck his gun in his waistband and stepped closer. The deserter still wore part of his Enforcer uniform—black tactical pants with red stripes down the sides and a lightweight zip-up jacket. But he'd stripped the Enforcer logo off his breast pocket, leaving a gaping hole in its place. As if any outlaw would be stupid enough to see him and *not* immediately know him for what he was, with or without the logo.

"Then you're wasting your time." The deserter spoke with a surprising amount of bravado for someone in his position. He also couldn't have been older than nineteen, which only made his arrogant tone seem even more out of place. "I already told your friend I'm not saying a word."

With a faint smile, Rylan cocked his weapon. "You sure about that?"

"Yes. Whatever you do to me is nothing compared to what they'll do if I talk." Then he pressed his lips together and tipped his head as if to say *do your worst*. Only the trembling of his body revealed how terrified he actually was.

Connor stifled a sigh. Shit. He wasn't in the mood to torture anyone, especially a kid who probably hadn't even screwed his first woman yet.

But damn it, he *needed* that location.

And he was willing to go to any lengths to get it.

Hudson's stomach was in knots as she waited outside the mill. She'd been pacing for the past fifteen minutes, straining to hear what was going on inside, but if the men were talking, their voices were too soft to make out. She didn't dare get too close to the door, which was gaping open. She couldn't risk the Enforcer recognizing her.

Lennox had given up on making conversation with her. He was now lying on the dirt with his head propped in his hands and tilted up at the clear blue sky, his eyes closed as he basked in its rays.

She grew more and more nauseous with each passing minute. Worst-case scenarios flashed in her mind, and she could practically see the deserter regaling Connor and Rylan with the story of how Dominik's twin sister had escaped the compound, how everyone was looking for her. Connor would casually ask, "What's her name?" and the kid would say, "Hudson."

And then the only person staring down the barrel of Connor's gun, begging him not to pull the trigger, would be *her*.

When she heard the men's footsteps, her heart lurched and her breathing quickened, but there was no gun in Connor's hand when he walked out the door. It was poking out of his waistband instead. And rather than the fury and betrayal she'd expected to find in his eyes, all she saw was sheer disgust.

"He's not talking," he announced.

Lennox's eyes snapped open. "Told ya. He's a stubborn little bastard, huh?" He hopped to his feet and approached the group. "I didn't hear any screams."

"Didn't have the heart to wail on him," Connor admitted. "He's just a kid."

"How old is he? If he's that young, he might be a trainee." Hudson was surprised by how calm her voice sounded when her windpipe was clogged with terror.

Rylan shrugged. "I'd put him at eighteen or nineteen."

"Can I go in to see him? He might talk to me." Her stomach churned. "Actually, there's a chance I might even know him. I didn't have much contact with the recruits, but I did meet a few of them when I was working at the hospital."

Lennox sucked in a sharp breath. "You're from the city?" His head swiveled to Connor. "Why the hell didn't you tell me that?"

"Because it's not important." Connor shrugged. "She's one of us now."

Her heart soared when he said that, but it didn't stay airborne for long. It plummeted even faster than it had flown, twisting in the pit of her stomach. She had to tell Connor the truth. She *had* to. But not here, and especially not in front of Rylan and Lennox.

It would have to wait until they got back to camp, but no longer than that, because he considered her one of *them,* damn it. If she didn't come clean soon, the guilt was liable to eat her alive.

"I guess it wouldn't hurt to give it a shot," Connor said in reply to her offer. "C'mon."

He took a step to the door, but she stopped him by touching his arm. "Let me talk to him alone," she said quietly.

"What for?"

"He obviously doesn't trust you guys," she pointed out. "If you come in with me, he'll probably clam up again, but if I go in there alone . . ." It was her turn to shrug. "He might respond better to a woman. See me as less of a threat."

Connor thought it over. "Yeah, you could be right about that." He quickly affected a stern tone. "Don't get too close to him, and keep your gun on him at all times. He's tied up, but those fuckers are well trained. You never know what they'll do."

Nodding, she withdrew the pistol she'd tucked into her boot, then released the safety and headed for the building. She felt Connor's eyes boring into her back with every step she took. Not suspiciously, but *protectively*, as if he was worried that the deserter might find a way to hurt her. She was worried too. Who knew what the kid would do if he recognized her? He might shout out her name loud enough for everyone in a five-mile radius to—

She didn't know him.

Relief flooded her body as she encountered a total stranger. Light brown hair, wiry body, and completely unfamiliar features.

But the relief drained away when the kid's eyes widened at the sight of *her*.

Shit. They might not have met before, but like Tamara, he'd clearly picked up on her resemblance to Dominik.

"Holy shit," he blurted out.

Hudson instantly raised her finger to her lips. "Keep your voice down."

He looked alarmed, gazing past her toward the open door, then shaking his head as if he couldn't fathom what was happening. "You're . . ."

"Shut. Up," she hissed.

"But . . ."

Hudson moved closer, but heeded Connor's order to keep her distance. Leaving three feet of space between them, she squatted on the dusty ground and rested her pistol on her thigh. "They'll kill us both if they hear us."

"Why . . . ? How are you here?" His voice lowered to a whisper. "You're Dominik's sister, aren't you? You look just like him." Panic flickered in his eyes. "They're all looking for you!"

The nausea returned in full-force. She should've known better than to hope her escape was no longer a priority for Dom. "They're still sending out search parties?"

The kid nodded fervently. "One a day. Knox—" His mouth slammed shut.

"Knox what?" she demanded.

"He's on the warpath. He demanded round-the-clock searches, but Dominik turned down the request, and the two of them had it out in the courtyard a couple weeks ago."

Her mouth puckered in a frown. She wasn't surprised to hear that Dom and Knox had argued—the two of them had been at odds for as long as she could remember. That's why she'd been so shocked when Dominik had informed her she had to marry Knox.

What surprised her now was hearing that Dominik

was limiting the search for her. She had assumed he'd be desperate to find her and bring her home.

"It was bad," the kid admitted, still talking about the fight. "Really bad. Knox got Dominik on the ground and snapped his wrist, but Dom somehow fought through it and broke Knox's nose. They would have killed each other if Cruz and Dalton hadn't stepped in to break up the fight."

Shit. An argument was one thing, but a full-on fistfight? With broken bones? It was rare for Dominik to get violent with his own men, even ones he didn't like.

"I don't know . . . Maybe it's the drugs, or maybe they're all fucking crazy. Either way, I had to get out. I—"

"Wait. Back up," she ordered. "What drugs? What are you talking about?"

"You know, the pills." He shrugged. "Well, now it's injections. The commander says they get results faster."

Hudson had no clue what he was talking about. The only pills she'd ever seen her brother take were the vitamin boosters that every man in the compound swallowed on a daily basis.

Her throat grew impossibly dry. "What do the pills do?"

"I'm not really sure. The commander says they keep you alert, you know, help you focus, and something about blood clots and healing faster . . . I honestly don't know half the stuff he was saying. But it's all bullshit. The only thing the drugs did was give me headaches. And the other guys in my training class . . . they . . ." His hard expression collapsed. "The pills messed them up too, made them violent and angry and turned them into strangers."

She felt sick. What the hell were the Enforcers taking? Some kind of aggression drugs? Steroids, maybe?

Hudson's mind raced as she tracked Dominik's behavior as far back as she could. He'd been taking the boosters since his Enforcer training, so . . . since he was seventeen. Hudson's father had worked closely with a chemist at the city lab and a nutritionist to create the cocktail, and Dom had still been normal at that age, so the drugs couldn't have had a negative effect on him, not back then. She knew Dom was still taking the cocktail, though. And their father had died two years ago, which was when her brother had started to change.

"Did Dominik ever say anything to you about the drugs?" she asked.

The kid shook his head. "I barely spoke to the guy. Cruz was my training instructor, so he was the only authority figure I ever had contact with."

Her mind spun faster as she tried to put the pieces together. Dom's behavior had changed once Commander Ferris had taken over for their father. Hudson had always hated Ferris. The man was a cold bastard. Rude, short-tempered, and self-entitled, and he lacked the diplomacy that Hudson's father had possessed, that enigmatic combination of ruthlessness and compassion that had made Arthur Lane such a strong leader.

She wouldn't put it past Ferris to give his men drugs. But she knew her brother. He would never willingly take anything that screwed with his head.

Had Ferris altered the vitamins without Dom's knowledge?

Her pulse sped up at the thought. God, if that was true, then . . .

Dominik was as much of a victim of the GC as the outlaws he'd been hunting.

"Cruz is fucked in the head too. They're all fucked in the head. They're killing them! They *make* you kill them."

She tensed. "Kill who?"

"Outlaw prisoners," he mumbled. "It's the final test you need to pass if you're accepted into the program. They bring out an outlaw and make you kill them. Cruz says it's supposed to prepare us for taking a life in the field, but it's sick! It's fucking sick, and I had to get out—don't you get it?"

Hudson inhaled slowly. "What's your name?"

He faltered. "Max."

"Okay. I want you to listen carefully to me, Max." She let out the breath. "I'm going to tell my friends to let you go."

Gratitude flooded his eyes. "Thank—"

"On two conditions," she cut in.

His mouth snapped shut.

"One, you get as far away from here as possible. Go to the coast, find a way to another colony, just get the hell out. We both know what Dominik does to deserters." Did she, though? The punishment for desertion used to be imprisonment. For all she knew, it could be execution now. "And two, you can't tell anyone you saw me."

"Deal," he said without delay.

"I want your word." But even as she voiced the request, she had to wonder what the point of it was. Dominik had given her his word too when he'd promised to protect her, and look where that had gotten her. Swallowing, Hudson softened her tone. "Please. Prove to me that someone's word still means something."

Max's expression went somber. "I promise to run like the wind, and I promise I won't tell anyone I saw you."

"And that includes my friends out there. Don't say a word to them about who I am."

"I won't."

"Good." She rose to her feet, brushing dust off her jeans. "I'll be right back."

When she stepped outside, all the men snapped to attention. Whatever conversation they'd been having was abandoned as Connor marched up to her.

"Did you get anything?"

Hudson nodded.

"Son of a bitch." He looked impressed. "He told you where the compound is?"

She nodded again. "I promised him we'd let him go in exchange for the information." When Connor stiffened, she hurried on. "There's no reason to hold him prisoner, Con. You said so yourself—he's a kid."

Rylan spoke up grimly. "He's still an Enforcer."

"Not anymore," she corrected. "If we let him go, he won't stick around in the area and cause trouble, not with the Enforcers hunting him. The kid wants to live. He's planning on leaving the colony."

Lennox piped up. "Well, *I* don't want him. So as far as I'm concerned, he's free to go."

Connor still looked unsure. "What did he tell you? What if his intel is bullshit?"

"It's not. The Enforcer compound is about fifteen miles north of the city. I can even draw you a map—he was very detailed about the location."

He hissed in a breath. "What's the security protocol?"

"Impossible to breach," she admitted.

His eyes gleamed. "Nothing's impossible."

"Fine, not impossible. Just suicidal. There are two hundred men living on the compound. The barracks are located in the west building, training areas and offices are in the main one, and the senior Enforcers have their own quarters in the east building."

She recited the details from memory, because she was describing her home, the place her father had moved them to after her mother died when Hudson was eight. There'd been no reason to stay in the city after that. Her father had thrown himself into his work, deciding he'd rather raise his children in a testosterone-fueled military facility than in the cozy house they'd had in the city.

"A twelve-foot electric fence surrounds the compound," she said flatly. "Trip wires and land mines on the perimeter and security cameras and motion sensors situated about five feet apart. There are guard towers on all four corners of the property, with four armed guards posted on each tower."

Lennox whistled. "Je-sus. The kid really *was* detailed."

Connor looked unhappy with the report. "Could he be exaggerating?"

"I don't think he is. My father told me their security was intense. If anything, there's probably a lot the kid left out." She implored Connor with her eyes. "You can't ambush the compound. It's not like the storage stations, not by a long shot. If you want to get to Dominik"—her heart ached at the thought—"you'll need to do it outside the gates, because they'll shoot you down like a dog if you get within a hundred feet of the fence. Oh, and speaking of dogs—I forgot about that. There are guard dogs patrolling the inside of the fence."

He rubbed his jaw, and she could see his brain working over the implications. Then he gave a brisk nod. "I'll think on it. But you're drawing me that map when we get back to camp."

"And the kid?" she pressed. "Can we let him go?"

He glanced at Lennox. "You tied him up. You can cut him loose."

"Yes, sir." Rolling his eyes, Lennox strolled toward the building. "Thanks for the lovely visit," he drawled over his shoulder.

Rylan drifted over to the motorcycles, but Connor didn't follow suit. Instead, he surprised Hudson by taking a step closer and cupping her cheeks with his hands. He kissed her, sweet and gentle, the warmth of his lips doing nothing to ease the chill that had plagued her body since she'd decided it was time to tell him the truth.

When he pulled back, unmistakable gratitude shone in his eyes, and then he uttered two words that made her want to cry.

"Thank you."

19

Connor got the feeling Hudson was avoiding him. Granted, they'd both been busy since they'd returned to camp. Hudson had been cleaning out another cabin while Connor was with Xander in the lodge, but now that night had fallen, she continued to stay away. And Connor didn't like it.

He knew she was worried about him, but he wished she'd quit stressing. He wasn't about to storm the Enforcer compound like a paratrooper from the old wars—he was smarter than that. Now that he had the location of Dominik's base, it was time to start making plans, and not the half-cocked kind. Carefully strategized plans.

It was why he'd spent the day riding Xander's ass about the communication program. If the Enforcers used it to send messages, then Connor could use it to his advantage and find a way to get to Dominik through the program. But Xan wasn't making any headway, no matter how many times Connor ordered him to work harder.

A knock on the door interrupted his thoughts. The sound was soft and feminine, which told him Hudson had finally decided to stop hiding from him. About time. It was nearly midnight, and he was surprised he'd allowed her to keep her distance for this long.

He let her in with a gruff hello, and she looked exasperated as she walked into the cabin. "Xander said you were driving him crazy today."

"I'm surprised he phrased it that nicely," Connor said dryly.

"He didn't." She grinned. "I was trying not to hurt your feelings."

Yeah, he could only imagine the kind of expletives that had left Xan's mouth.

"I may have been a *little* overbearing today," he admitted, albeit grudgingly.

"A little? He said you threatened to chop off his fingers and feed them to the wolf if he didn't type faster."

Connor snickered.

"You can't bully him into making the program work. Technology can be a bitch sometimes."

"I wouldn't have to bully him if he spent more than ten minutes a day on the damn thing," Connor protested. "Honestly? I think he's stalling."

She frowned. "Why would he do that?"

"Fuck if I know. But I want that program up and running."

"And you always get what you want, huh?"

Her tone was half teasing, half resigned, and it brought a devilish smile to his lips. "Yeah, I do." He arched one eyebrow. "You wanna know what I want right now? You. Naked. On my bed."

"Oh really?"

He eased closer, teasing his thumb over her cheek. "Yes. That's exactly what I want." He pinched her bottom lip between his fingers. "Are you going to give it to me?"

Her gaze locked with his, and her expression became impossible to decipher. "No."

He blinked. "No?"

"No," she repeated. Her voice went husky, thoughtful. "You won't get what you want, Con. But . . ." Those gray eyes softened with an emotion he once again couldn't puzzle out. "I think I'm going to give you what you need."

Before he could respond, she planted her hands on his chest and gave him a little shove. "Get on the bed."

Her fortitude unnerved him, but he was too turned on to argue. It was impossible for this woman to say the word *bed* without his dick getting hard, and he was sporting a noticeable erection as he stretched out on his back, waiting to see what she did next.

She began to undress, and he couldn't take his eyes off her. Sweet curves and sun-kissed skin were revealed with each discarded item of clothing, stealing the breath from his lungs. She unclasped her bra and let it drop to the floor, then undid her braid and smoothed her fingers through her hair. The golden strands covered her breasts, but her pink nipples peeked through, making Connor's mouth tingle with the need to taste them.

When he tried to sit up, she pointed to the mattress. "Lie back."

He reluctantly lowered himself back down, his heart thumping as Hudson climbed on the bed and straddled his thighs. Warm hands slid beneath his shirt, delicate fingers stroking his pecs before finding his nipples, rubbing the hard, flat disks until he groaned in abandon and reached for her again.

"Bring your tits to my face, damn it."

"No." She intercepted his hands and forcibly moved them behind his head. "You don't get to bark out orders. Not tonight."

He frowned.

"You're always giving everyone else what they need." Her voice cracked slightly. "Me, Rylan, the others. Just this once, let me give you what *you* need."

She tugged his shirt up, nudged his arms so he could help slip the fabric over his head, then gripped his wrists and moved them back to his nape. "Leave your hands there. Let me take care of you."

Uneasiness washed over him. "Hudson . . ."

A faint smile lifted the corner of her mouth. "God, look at that frown. This freaks you out, doesn't it?" Her breasts swayed seductively as she leaned forward, using her thumb to smooth the deep crease in his forehead. "I knew it would." She paused. "I figured it out."

"Figured what out?"

"You," she said simply. "You're always in control, Con. You can't give it up. Ever. Hell, you know shit-all about technology, and yet you sat on Xander's ass all day, ordering him around, because you can't *not* be in control."

The frown returned, but she caressed it away again, while her other hand rubbed soothing circles on the center of his bare chest.

"I thought that maybe you were on some kind of power trip, but now I know that's not true." Her fingertips touched the patch of skin above his heart, and he knew she could feel it hammering against her palm. "You're scared that if you don't stay in control, someone will get hurt."

A powerless sensation eddied in his gut. "Hudson—"

"But it's okay to let go, remember? That's what you

told me when I first got here, that sometimes a person needs to hand over control and just let themselves *feel*." She planted a gentle kiss on his collarbone. "I want you to let go tonight." Her lips traveled up his throat, leaving goose bumps in their wake before hovering over his mouth. "You don't have to do everything alone, Con. You don't have to be strong for everyone else." She kissed him, firm and reassuring. "We all trust you, but you need to trust *us*."

Something akin to panic fluttered up his spine. He was in no way immobilized. He could move his arms. He could push her off him.

But he was trapped.

It was the same way he'd felt after his father died and he'd had no choice but to step up and take care of the group. The way he'd felt whenever Maggie had pleaded with him to give her the home she so desperately yearned for. When she'd convinced him to go against his better judgment and play along with her fantasy of what the world was.

"Trust me," Hudson whispered. "Tonight you don't have to think, or issue orders, or take care of anyone. Trust someone else to take care of *you*."

"I . . . don't know if I can," he whispered back.

"You can." She kissed him again, but his lips remained paralyzed. "You're going to lie there and shut that sexy mouth of yours, baby."

A grin tickled his lips.

"I mean it. Keep your hands to yourself, and no filthy commands." She pulled his belt free of the buckle and dragged his zipper down. "You don't need to tell me what'll make you feel good." When his cock sprang up, hard and eager, she gripped the base tight enough to make him grunt. "I already know."

Jesus, she did. She knew so fucking well, and the rough stroke she gave him brought black dots to his eyes.

This time when she kissed him, he responded. Lips parting just enough for his tongue to sneak past them and into Hudson's mouth. She quickly chased his tongue into his mouth, kissing him so deeply they were both gasping for air by the time they broke apart.

The silence was eerie. He was used to hearing himself tell her what to do: *Suck harder, spread wider, come for me*. Tonight she needed no instruction. His body belonged to her, and she knew it. She *took* it, warm lips and clever hands traveling over every inch of his flesh until there wasn't a part of him she hadn't branded with her touch.

When her mouth closed around his cock, a command almost slipped out. "Suc—"

He stopped abruptly, and she peered up with a chuckle. "Aw, look at that. You're learning." Her breath tickled his shaft, tongue darting out to taste the pearly drop at his tip. "You're going to be good, aren't you, baby? Sweet and submissive and silent while I have my way with you." She licked his crown in a slow, wet circle. "You're going to let me suck your cock until you can't remember a time when my mouth wasn't bringing you pleasure."

Jesus.

She didn't let up, whispering sinful words and filthy promises against his skin as she used her tongue to test his control. Each hard suck was followed by a taunt. Each sharp pump trailed by a satisfied laugh, as if she knew she was stealing his sanity, turning his brain to mush. The role reversal should have terrified him, but it only turned him on, so much that when he suddenly climaxed, it caught him by complete surprise.

A shock of pleasure rocketed through him as he came in her mouth, but his hips stayed motionless, as if his body knew that Hudson would give it what it needed. And she did, her fist pumping him through the release as her mouth stayed glued to the head of his cock, swallowing every drop of pleasure she summoned from his body.

It was a heady feeling. Letting go. Letting her take charge.

Connor stopped thinking. Stopped wondering what she was going to do next. He closed his eyes and let himself feel, and when the mattress dipped and her pussy bumped his lips, his tongue came out on instinct, licking and probing until Hudson was groaning as wildly as he was. He wanted to feel her coming on his face, feel her clit pulsing on his tongue, but she denied him, rocking into him until she was wet and swollen, and then she was gone.

His eyes stayed closed. He waited. Trusted that the course she'd set would take them both where they needed to go. His cock was already hard again, a painful weight against his stomach, aching for relief.

He shivered when she ran a hand down the center of his chest. A teasing stroke. Gentle fingers gripped his shaft as she stretched a condom over it.

"This isn't so bad, is it? Trusting someone else to take care of you?"

No, it wasn't bad at all. It was good. So fucking good, and he was never going to forget—

She impaled herself on his cock, and his brain imploded. Shut down completely. It was sensation overload. The tight clasp of her pussy. The pressure in his balls. She rode him hard, her nails digging into his pecs as her hips moved and her inner muscles bore down on him.

"Touch my clit, Connor. Rub it. Make me come."

His hand shook as he brought it to the place where they were joined. He pressed his thumb to that tight bud, flicking and stroking in time to the wild grinding of her hips. When she cried out in orgasm, he felt it in his cock, in his blood. It was almost enough to send him flying over the edge again, but not quite, and Hudson was so attuned to his body's responses that she leaned forward and kissed him, whispering another order even as she trembled in release.

"Fuck me hard. Now."

The control he'd barely had to begin with snapped like a frayed piece of rope. His hips rose in an upward thrust, hard and deep, over and over again, filling her to the hilt as he wrapped his arms around her and held her tight to his chest.

Ecstasy. He'd thought he'd known what that was, but everything he'd felt in the past, all the sex and blow jobs and orgasms . . . a blurry photograph compared to the vivid canvas flashing in front of him. Release came in a warm, soothing wave that washed over him, loosening muscles that were always coiled tight, breaking apart the armor that surrounded his heart.

"I . . ." His voice was gravel. He took a breath, stroking the small of her back. "Jesus Christ, baby." Another breath. "I . . ."

She slid off him before he could finish, and his body couldn't comprehend it. The loss of her warmth, the sudden emptiness.

"Hudson?" he said warily, because her stricken face was even more mystifying.

She opened her mouth. Closed it. Opened it again.

"What's wrong?"

Guilt passed across her features, just another bewildering puzzle piece that made no sense to him.

"I . . ." Her shoulders sagged, her breath coming out in a wobbly rush. "I'm Dominik's sister."

It wasn't the right moment to tell him. Not with Connor's sated eyes peering up at her and his naked body sprawled on the bed, free of the tension that always seemed to plague it.

Hudson wished she could take back the words, at least for tonight. She wanted to take them back and save them until morning, so the sunshine could temper the hard edges of the truth and this beautiful moment could be preserved in her memory without her confession having tainted it.

But she'd just spoken to him about trust, damn it. She'd made love to him with every breath she had, and Connor had finally—*finally*—lowered his guard and given her that part of himself he'd been holding back. And now with three measly words, she was about to lose him again. She knew that, and it broke her heart, but the truth had flown out of her mouth before she could stop it. Because in that pure, shining moment of open trust, she hadn't been able to lie to him anymore.

Because she loved him.

His stunned gaze focused on her face. "You're . . . what?"

"I'm Dominik's sister." Her hands began to shake, so she pressed them to her bare thighs. "His twin, actually."

Connor blinked. Just one blink, while a multitude of emotions streaked across his face. Confusion sharpened into suspicion. Suspicion darkened to anger. Anger became . . . horror. Horror and betrayal and a glitter of menace that made Hudson wince.

When it finally dawned on him that she was telling the truth, Connor shot to his feet. Every muscle in his body coiled tight, from the tendons of his neck to the arches of his feet, and the dark cloud on his face gathered in strength until his eyes were more black than hazel.

"You . . ." He hissed out a breath. "Are you goddamn serious?"

She nodded weakly. "I should have told you the night we met, but I was afraid if you knew who I was, you wouldn't help me. I was afraid you'd kill me."

"You're damn right I wouldn't have helped you!" The venomous response matched the poison in his expression.

"Everything else I told you was the truth," she said desperately. "I ran because I was supposed to marry Knox. I didn't know that my father—" She stopped, realizing in dismay that everything she'd told him *wasn't* the truth. "My father wasn't an adviser to the council," she admitted. "He was a councilman. One of the founding members of the GC."

A muscle twitched in Connor's jaw.

"But his main job was commander in chief of the Enforcers. Dominik is in line for the position once he can't work in the field anymore." She swallowed, remembering the final truth she'd kept hidden. "I'm an Enforcer too, at least unofficially."

Those cold eyes landed on her wrists. "You're not marked."

"Yes, I am."

Her heart pounded as she swept her hair back. Avoiding Connor's gaze, she wet the pad of her thumb with her tongue, then rubbed it vigorously over her nape to wipe away the makeup. Her thumb came back stained with flesh-colored powder, and then she angled her head so Connor could see the compass rose on her neck.

He released a vicious expletive.

"It's just a title," Hudson said miserably. "I was never officially trained or sent into the field. I think my father only marked me because he didn't want me to feel like Dom was better than me." Desperation rose again. "I worked in the hospital, just like I told you, and I escaped because of Knox, just like I told you. The only part I left out was my father's real position and that Dom is my brother."

Connor stared at her for one long, terrifying moment.

Then he exploded.

"Your brother killed my wife!"

She swallowed. "No. Knox did."

"Same fucking thing!" He yanked his pants on and zipped them up, and when he noticed she was still naked, it only seemed to make him angrier. "Put your goddamn clothes on, Hudson."

She got dressed in a frantic rush, her body shaking so wildly she was surprised she was able to stay on her feet. She'd expected Connor's fury. She hadn't expected the hatred.

"Please don't look at me like that." Her voice cracked at the same time her heart did. "I'm still the same person I've always been. And I know my brother has done awful things, but . . ." A lump filled her throat. "But I think the new commander might be drugging him. Max told me—"

"Who the fuck is Max?"

"The trainee. When I talked to him this morning, he said the commander is injecting the Enforcers with aggression drugs. It's screwing with their minds." Tears welled up, making her voice wobble harder. "Dominik didn't used to be a killer. He used to be fair to the outlaws—"

"Fair?" Connor roared.

She flinched as if he'd struck her. "No, not fair, but he never murdered them without provocation before. He's . . ." A few tears trickled free. "I don't think he knows what he's doing."

"Jesus Christ. Do you expect me to feel sorry for that bastard?" His razor-sharp tone cut her straight to the bone. "Have you seen how people live out here, Hudson? Hiding and running and struggling to survive. The Enforcers either drag our asses to that prison they call a city, or they kill us if we choose not to go. Because of your *father* and the 'system' he implemented. Because of your *brother*, who fucking enforces it."

"My father and my brother," she echoed. "Not *me*. You said so yourself—I'm an outlaw now. I'm one of you."

He stared at her.

"I'm not like them." She tasted salt in her mouth as the tears fell harder, coursing down her cheeks and catching on her lips. "I help people. I care about people. I care about *you*." She wiped her cheeks with both hands. "No. I *love* you."

Stony silence was the only response she got.

"I love you, Connor," she said fiercely. "And I'm not like Dominik. You *know* that."

"I don't know a goddamn thing apparently."

"You know me," she insisted. "I never lied about how I felt for you, and I know you feel it too. This thing between us is real. I promise you it's real."

"Yeah? This is real?" Acrid bitterness oozed from his every word, his every pore. "Then prove it."

"What?"

"You want to convince me that what we have is real? That you actually give a damn about me despite the fact that you lied about who you are?" His lips tightened. "Then fucking prove it."

"H-how?"

"Take me to Dominik."

Her heart dropped to the pit of her stomach. "What?"

"Take me to him, Hudson. Knox too. Stand by my side while I wipe their sorry asses off this sorry excuse for a planet."

It was hard to breathe. The forbidding gleam in Connor's eyes was so hot and visceral it singed her skin and closed up her lungs. She bit the inside of her cheek hard enough to draw blood, and the coppery flavor coated her tongue and throat, threatening to choke her.

"No," she said. "I'll find a way to get you to Knox. But not Dom. Please." Her face collapsed from the force of Connor's murderous glare. "He's my brother."

"He's a killer."

"He didn't kill Maggie." A strangled sob flew out. "I understand why you want vengeance, but Dom didn't kill her. And even if he had, I still wouldn't be able to stand there and watch while you killed my brother."

"The same brother who was willing to marry you off to a man you despise?" Connor spat out.

"Whatever he does, good or bad, he's still my brother.

He can go to prison for the rest of his life to pay for his crimes. He doesn't have to die for them."

Another silence stretched between them, a deep, gaping chasm that Hudson knew she'd never be able to cross. Connor was slipping away from her by the second, his empty eyes and hard jaw telling her everything that his silence couldn't.

When he spoke, she didn't expect the hoarse unsteadiness of his voice.

"I'm only going to say this once." His breathing grew ragged. "Take me to Knox and your brother, and you and I can wipe the slate clean. I'll forget that you lied. Maybe I'll even trust you again one day. It might take some time, but you know me, Hudson—I don't make false promises. I'll try to forgive you."

The sheer arrogance of that statement sparked a burst of indignation. "And if I refuse?"

"Then you leave this camp and never come back."

All the oxygen left her body in one shocked rush. "Are you serious?" she snapped, trying to keep her rising anger in control. "If I don't take you to my brother so you can kill him, you're going to *exile* me?"

His curt nod made her want to slap him. He'd told her he was a ruthless bastard and that he wouldn't hesitate to slit her throat if she betrayed him, but this . . . *this*?

They stared at each other for what felt like an eternity. She waited for him to back down, but he didn't. He waited for her to give in, but she didn't.

She refused to sacrifice her brother's life, especially when she wasn't certain that Dominik was even in *control* of his life. If Ferris had turned him into his pet monster without Dom's knowledge or consent, then he wasn't at fault for his actions.

"I won't do it," she said quietly.

Connor's gaze flickered with disappointment. Maybe even regret. But then his lips curled and his head tipped toward the door.

"Then save your declarations of love for some other fool and get the fuck out of my camp."

20

He'd banished her.

He'd actually banished her.

Her duffel bag, one of the Ducatis, and her life—that's what Connor had sent her away with, and even hours later, Hudson was reeling from the shock of what he'd done. He hadn't allowed her to say good-bye to Rylan and the others. He hadn't let her say good-bye to Hope. He'd simply cast her out in the middle of the night as if she were a piece of trash, while the people she'd come to care about slept in their cabins, oblivious.

Would Rylan have tried to stop her from going? Would Xander? Kade? Pike?

She would never know the answer to that question now.

Her eyes were dry—finally, *blessedly*—as she killed the engine in front of Lennox's dark house. She'd cried herself stupid on the long drive, but she was all cried out now. The wind battering her face hadn't helped, and as she dropped the kickstand and headed for the door, she knew her red, swollen eyes were broadcasting the devastation she'd endured tonight.

It was late. So late that Lennox and the girls were no

doubt asleep and would probably mistake her for an intruder and shoot her on sight. She almost hoped they did. She couldn't imagine a bullet hurting any worse than the agony she was already feeling. If anything, it would put her out of her misery.

So fucking ironic. She'd chosen her brother over Connor, and yet chances were she'd never even see Dom again. As much as she wanted to warn him about the drugs he might be taking, she wasn't going back to the compound, not when Knox was still there. She wasn't going anywhere near that sadistic bastard.

Irony, all right. She was alone. No Connor. No Dom. Nothing but an empty hole in her chest where her heart used to be.

As she knocked on the door, she found herself praying that Tamara was there. At this point, the woman might be Hudson's only hope of landing somewhere safe. Maybe she'd even join up with the bitch, she thought bitterly. They could be partners in crime, smuggling goods through the colony together, two cold-hearted women who were feared and unloved.

Hudson jerked when the door swung open and the barrel of a shotgun appeared in her face.

Lennox lowered the gun the second he recognized her, his brows drawing together. "Hudson?"

She opened her mouth, but all that emerged was a shaky sob.

"What's going on, love?" Then he stiffened. "Connor—?"

"He's fine," she said quickly. "They're all fine. I . . . I didn't have anywhere else to go."

"Len?" a female voice said urgently. Jamie materialized beside Lennox, wearing a short white negligee and holding an assault rifle. The intimidation in her eyes dissolved into deep concern when she spotted Hudson. "What happened?"

"We hadn't gotten to that part yet." Sighing, Lennox held out his hand. "Come in, love. I think you need a drink."

Hudson's shoulders sagged in defeat. She took his hand and followed him inside.

"What do you mean, she's *gone*?" The incensed demand came from Xander, who was staring at Connor as if he'd donned an Enforcer uniform and opened fire on their camp.

They were all looking at him like that, their expressions ranging from outrage to disbelief, and damned if their judgment didn't evoke both those responses in *him*.

They would have done the same thing, each and every one of them. That's how it was in this land. You didn't live with your enemies. Hudson was lucky he hadn't *killed* her, for chrissake. Banishment was a goddamn vacation compared to what he could've done to her.

"She's Dominik's twin sister," he snapped.

He was greeted by four shocked faces, but the understanding he'd expected to find, the *support*, was glaringly missing. Not a single one of them looked as if they believed that Hudson's connection to Dominik justified what Connor had done. Not even Rylan, who always unfailingly had his back.

"She lied to us," Connor muttered.

Contempt laced Xander's tone. "We already knew she was from the city. Who the fuck cares who she's related to?"

Fury scorched up his spine. "She's related to the man who killed my wife, you bastard."

The men looked shocked again, but Kade was the

only one brave enough to speak up, though his voice was lined with apprehension. "You were married?"

"Yes, I was fucking married. And I slept with the sister of the man who *killed my wife*." Revulsion tore a path down his throat and twisted his insides, making him feel like he'd swallowed a handful of razor blades. "You honestly think I could let her stay here after learning that? What the hell is the matter with you guys?"

A whining noise had him whirling his head at the furry creature in Pike's arms. For fuck's sake, even the wolf was looking at him with baleful eyes, as if he'd betrayed her. As if he'd betrayed all of them.

Pike stroked the wolf's head to calm her before flicking his expressionless gaze in Connor's direction. "Where did she go?"

"How the hell am I supposed to know?" The defensive note that crept into his voice pissed him off. "I gave her one of the bikes, okay? She has her gear, weapons, enough food to last a few days. I didn't send her away with nothing, all right? But she couldn't stay here."

"Lennox's," Xander said decisively. "That's the only other place she knows."

Kade nodded. "Yeah, she would've gone there."

The men conversed as if Connor hadn't spoken, as if he weren't even *there*, and he listened to them in disbelief, unable to fathom what was happening right now. Even Rylan was avoiding his gaze. His own best friend couldn't stomach the sight of him.

"This is unbelievable," Connor growled. "You bastards took it upon yourselves to call me your leader. I didn't want the damn job, but you gave it to me, and I've done everything in my power to make decisions that I feel are best for this camp. And now I make a call you disagree with, and that's it? You've written me off?"

Rylan finally spoke up, cold and measured and gratingly self-righteous. "You didn't kick her out because it was the best decision for camp. You did it because it was the best decision for *you*. Because she hurt you and you lashed out like a goddamn lion with a thorn stuck in its paw."

Connor ground his teeth together, trying hard to control his temper. "You're saying you would have continued to trust her? Knowing who her brother is and what he's done?"

"What *he's* done. Not her." Rylan's blue eyes flared with annoyance. "Hudson isn't responsible for her brother's choices, or his actions."

"She lied to us, Ry."

"Because she knew exactly what would happen if she told the truth. She knew you'd react like this." Rylan dismissed him just as the others had, turning to Xander to issue a sharp command. "Reach out to Lennox on the sat phone and find out if she's there."

Xan took off without a word, Kade hot on his heels.

"Gas up the bikes," Rylan told Pike. "The Jeep too."

Pike left with a nod, still cradling that damn wolf as if she were his own young.

Alone with Rylan, Connor drew a ragged breath and met the eyes of the only real friend he'd ever had in this sorry world. "What the hell are you doing, man?"

"Getting her back," Rylan said evenly.

His gut clenched. "I won't live here with her."

Rylan hurled Connor's own words back at him. "Then go. There are no chains keeping you here, remember? You don't want to be our leader? Well, fine, brother. Maybe I don't want to follow someone who makes impetuous decisions without consulting the rest of the group. Someone who throws an innocent woman to the mercy of this goddamn wasteland just because she was scared to tell you about her past. I wanted you to lead, not terrorize, and if you took even a second to think about it, you'd understand why she hid the truth from you."

Connor had never heard his friend sound so impassioned. Or so disgusted. "I gave her a choice," he mumbled.

Rylan looked startled. "What?"

"I told her she could stay if she led me to Dominik. She refused."

There was a beat.

Then an incredulous hiss.

"Jesus Christ, Con! What kind of coldhearted move was that? Did you think she'd happily lead you to her brother so you could *kill* him?" Rylan threw his hands up before Connor could answer. "You know what? I can't even look at you right now. You'd better get your head on straight, Connor, because we're going to bring that woman back whether you like it or not. Because she's one of *us*. So you can either be here when we get back, or you can be gone." Rylan squared his shoulders. "I don't give a shit either way."

"Are you sure Tamara is in Foxworth?" Hudson asked as she accepted the coffee mug Jamie held out to her.

They were sitting at the counter in Lennox's kitchen, going over Hudson's plans as waves of humidity rolled in through the open windows. The sky was overcast, hinting at a downpour, but as much as Hudson welcomed some rain to temper the heat they'd been dogged by, the dark clouds were simply a reminder that summer wouldn't last forever. It was already August, and she wanted to have a solid plan and a place to live before autumn came and temperatures dropped.

"That's where she said she was headed." Lennox took a quick sip of coffee, then raked a hand through his messy hair. "But if you want to catch up with her, you'll have to leave soon. Tam wasn't planning on staying long. She mentioned something about a trip to East Colony."

A burst of excitement went off inside her. East Colony. If Hudson hurried, she could track Tamara down and convince the woman to take her with her. A whole new colony. An entire ocean separating her from Knox.

And Connor.

Pain shot straight to her heart at the thought of never seeing him again. When she'd left the Enforcer compound, she hadn't imagined she would fall in love with someone, and yet she'd fallen so hard and fast for Connor that she couldn't remember a time when she *hadn't* loved him.

She loved the bastard even now. Even after what he'd done, even though he'd proved to be as ruthless as she'd suspected him to be from the moment they'd met. She loved his strength and arrogance, his gruff voice and rough caresses. She cherished those rare moments of ease and laughter, when he dropped his guard and made himself vulnerable to her. She loved every fucking thing about him, the good and the bad *and* the ruthless.

But she'd made her choice, and she couldn't go back on it now, because no matter what her brother had done, she refused to have his death on her conscience. She and Dominik had shared a womb. They'd spent every waking hour of their childhood together. She would never be able to live with herself if she led Connor and his loaded rifle to her brother's doorstep.

"I still think you should stay here," Jamie insisted, as she'd been insisting all morning.

And risk running into Connor? No way. Hudson knew the men would wind up here sooner or later, and her stomach roiled at the thought of facing Connor after she'd offered him her love—her *heart*—and he'd crushed it into dust between his fingers.

"I can't," she said, wincing at the audible crack in her voice.

Lennox cursed softly. "What the hell did that bastard do to you, love?"

"Nothing." Sorrow curled around her throat. "It was my fault. I lied to him, and he reacted the way anyone would have reacted."

But had he? Would Rylan have thrown her out? Would Lennox? She wasn't sure, but she also wasn't about to share the sordid details with Lennox and find out. Her only course of action was the initial one she'd set months ago—to get as far from West Colony as possible. She simply had to treat everything that had happened in between like a tiny hiccup.

Meeting Connor . . . loving Connor . . . it was all just a fucking hiccup.

"I don't like the idea of you going to Foxworth alone," Lennox admitted. "You've never met Reese before. She's suspicious of strangers."

"Beck and Travis have both met Hudson," Jamie pointed out. "They'll vouch for her."

"If they're there," Lennox said somberly. "Those

two spend half their time combing the colony for cars to fix up." He sighed. "I'd come with you, but I don't like leaving Jamie here alone."

The blonde rolled her eyes. "I can take care of myself, asshole."

"Of course you can, love. I just don't like leaving you."

Hudson didn't miss the way he looked at Jamie when he said that. Tenderly. The cocky rogue had vanished, replaced by a man who . . . Oh hell. He was in love with Jamie.

And Jamie was in love with Rylan. Not only that, but she didn't seem at all affected by Lennox's rakish good looks and magnetic charm. It was obvious from the way she treated him that she viewed him as nothing more than the best friend she'd had since childhood.

Thinking about the love triangle that neither Rylan nor Lennox probably even knew they were part of made Hudson's head spin, so she pushed the thought aside and focused on more pressing matters.

"I'll be fine on my own," she assured Lennox. "I don't want to put your life at risk."

"No, it's not safe to travel alone." He glanced at Jamie. "Are you sure you're okay with manning the fort while I'm gone?"

"Seriously, Len. Insult me one more time and I'll carve your balls off with this spoon." With a sweet smile, Jamie waved the spoon in question before using it to stir her coffee.

"Jesus, woman. Leave my balls out of this." His trademark grin returned as he glanced over at Hudson. "We'll head out in thirty. Why don't you grab something to eat while I gather some gear and gas up the—"

He didn't get a chance to finish his sentence.

The gunshots that exploded in the air shook the walls, causing Jamie's mug to slip out of her hand. It hit the floor and smashed to pieces at the same time heavy footsteps pounded on the hardwood floor as multiple intruders entered the house. Another gunshot rang out, followed by a loud crack and a deafening crash, as if pieces of the ceiling had snapped off and fallen to the ground.

Hudson's pulse raced in panic.

They were under attack.

Eight hours. Rylan and the others had been gone for eight hours, and Connor couldn't fight the gnawing worry that something was wrong. Lennox had confirmed over the sat phone that Hudson was with him, but it took only three hours to reach his place. Three hours there, three hours back. Connor tacked on an extra hour for Rylan to sweet-talk Hudson into agreeing to come back, and that totaled up to seven.

They should have been back by now, damn it.

Unless they'd stayed for a drink, or to shoot the shit, or . . . Hell, maybe they weren't *coming* back. Maybe they'd decided his shitty leadership wasn't worth coming back to.

But no, they'd be back. Or at least Pike would, because no way would the man leave the wolf behind. Hope had planted herself in Connor's cabin the moment the others had left, and she'd been staring accusingly at him ever since. She didn't seem to like the rain, though. Each time a boom of thunder rumbled in the sky, she whimpered and burrowed her head into the mattress. Whenever Connor tried to reach for her, she snarled at him.

Jesus. He really had no allies left.

"Relax, beast. I'm going to make it right." His voice came out in a hoarse rasp. He'd smoked so many cigarettes today, he was surprised smoke wasn't blowing out of his pores. He hadn't given in to the temptation to drink himself stupid, though. He couldn't be piss-ass drunk when the others returned. When *Hudson* returned.

He needed to be sober when he told her he loved her and threw himself at her feet to beg her forgiveness.

You didn't kick her out because it was the best decision for camp. You did it because it was the best decision for you. *Because she hurt you and you lashed out like a goddamn lion with a thorn stuck in its paw.*

Rylan's accusations had been running on a loop in his head for eight hours straight, and not even the rain pounding relentlessly against the roof could drown them out.

It had taken only about twenty minutes for the words to sink in, and by then his men had already been gone. So had any vehicle he could've used to hightail it over to Lennox's, which left Connor with no choice but to stay behind and think about what an asshole he was.

"I screwed up, okay?"

Hope cranked open one eye before lowering her head again. Unimpressed.

He didn't know what possessed him to defend himself to a *wolf*, but he couldn't stop the desperate words that poured out of his mouth. "I let my pride and temper get to me. I fucking know it, so quit looking at me like that."

The wolf didn't even blink. Her eyes were no longer ice blue, but contained a yellowish tinge now. Eventually they would change color completely. Yellow-gold most likely, the same shade as the she-devil that birthed her.

"I love her." Three tiny words, yet they sounded rusty leaving his mouth. Foreign. He cleared his throat, testing them out again. "I love her."

Goddamn it, he did. So much that it hurt to think it, *feel* it. He hadn't thought he'd ever love another woman after Maggie. He hadn't wanted to. But Hudson had snuck past his defenses with her stubborn gray eyes, her eager sensuality, and that remarkable combination of strength and compassion that never failed to amaze him. The things he loved about her were different from what he'd loved about his wife. He'd been drawn to Maggie's sweet innocence and sunny smiles, and her softness had soothed him, at least at the beginning. But Hudson . . .

"She stands up to me," he told the silent creature at his side. "Which you should be fucking grateful for, beast. Otherwise you wouldn't even be here." A chuckle slid out, as hoarse as his voice. Shit, he really needed to stop using smoking as a stress reliever. Damn habit was going to kill him.

Yeah, he really did like her bossiness, though. The way she ordered him and his men around as if she'd known them for years. And he fucking loved how protective she was. Of Pike, when she came to his defense each time the men mocked him about being a grumpy bastard. Of Kade, whom she never once pushed to talk about his life in the city. Xander and his tech gadgets. Rylan, every time he pulled a stupid stunt and got hurt. And . . . hell, she was even protective of her brother, monster that he was.

She'd lied about being Dominik's sister, but Rylan

had been right—Connor needed only to stop and think about it, and he got it. He would've done the same thing if it meant ensuring his survival.

Christ, he was such a bastard. He'd *exiled* the woman he loved. If he was lucky enough to earn her forgiveness, he knew he was going to spend the rest of his life making it up to her.

Hope whimpered suddenly, and Connor ran an awkward hand through her fur. Surprisingly, she let him. "It's just thunder," he assured the pup.

But clearly her hearing was more fine-tuned than his, because she shot up to all fours and darted toward the end of the mattress, gazing intently at the door. Since she'd yet to master the act of jumping on and off the bed, Connor scooped her into his arms and marched to the door, throwing it open just as headlights appeared in the driveway.

His heart soared with joy and sank with dread simultaneously. Unconcerned about the rain pouring down on him, he ran toward the approaching vehicles.

Too many of them.

Connor shifted the wolf to one arm and withdrew his nine mil, relaxing only when he recognized the pickup truck that pulled in behind the Jeep. Lennox's. And the black SUV that tailed it was the one Beckett had procured for Jamie.

His body hummed with unease. Shit. Something had happened. Something really fucking bad, because there was no other reason why Lennox and Jamie would be here—and Layla and Piper, he realized, as the two women climbed out of the SUV. It wasn't until everyone had gathered on the driveway that he understood how bad the situation was.

Because Hudson wasn't with them.

"Where is she?" he blurted out, his gaze traveling from one solemn face to the next.

The silence was worse than anything they could have said. It flooded his brain with grisly images that quickened his pulse and brought bile to his throat, and he stood there frozen in place as the rain fell over him.

Pike was the first one to speak. "She's gone."

"What do you mean, she's gone?" The outraged demand sounded familiar. He realized it was the same one Xander had shouted at him this morning after he'd confessed to sending Hudson away.

Rylan spoke up next, his grim voice muffled by the relentless downpour.

"Knox took her."

21

The rest of the story came out faster than Connor's panic-ridden brain could keep up with. Jamie's sobs mingled with the slaps of the rain hitting the dirt as Lennox described the attack on their house. The gunshots. The shouts. The bullet that had ripped into Nell's abdomen when she'd stumbled out of her room to find Enforcers swarming the corridor.

"Nell?" Connor's head snapped up, and he gazed past Lennox's shoulders at the SUV behind him. "Is she . . . ?"

"She's dead." Grief swam in Lennox's eyes. "The rest of us would be dead too if it weren't for Hudson. The Enforcers stopped firing when they realized she was in the house. The lieutenant . . ." Lennox hesitated. "He called her his wife."

Acid rose in Connor's throat. Swallowing it down only succeeded in ripping his stomach to pieces.

"They were in the area looking for her, Con. And she . . ." Lennox trailed off.

"She made a deal with him," Jamie filled in with a sniffle. "She said she'd go with him if he promised not to hurt the rest of us."

His stomach clenched. Of course she had. Hudson

would never let people she cared about get hurt, even if it meant sacrificing herself.

"And then they left." Jamie shook her head, visibly confused. Amazed. "I thought for sure they'd kill us. But they just left."

"We didn't stick around after that," Lennox said grimly. "I don't care what that bastard lieutenant promised. He has our location now, and I'm not dumb enough to believe he won't send a cleanup crew to take us out. So we packed our shit and took off. We were headed for Foxworth when we ran into your boys on the road."

Connor took a deep breath that burned his lungs to ashes. "Knox probably took her back to the compound." He gnawed on the inside of his cheek. "We have to get her back."

"The city is nine hundred miles from here," Xander reminded him. "We're looking at a fifteen-hour drive, and that's not accounting for roadblocks or fuel stops."

"You don't happen to have a chopper lying around here, do you?" Lennox said dryly.

"No." Connor cursed. "But we both know someone who does."

"Reese." Rylan's expression lit up. "Wait—you're saying we get Hudson back *and* I get to pay a visit to Foxworth? Fuck yeah."

Fuck no, more like it. The reigning queen of Foxworth did indeed have a helicopter. It was a military chopper abandoned after the war, designed for speed. It'd get them to West City in five hours or so, cutting their travel time in more than half.

Unfortunately, Reese wasn't one to hand out favors at the drop of a hat. "She won't let us use it," Connor muttered. "It'll cost her too much fuel."

"You'll owe her big," Lennox agreed.

Yes, he would. But he was willing to pay the price. He'd give Reese whatever the hell she wanted as long as it meant having Hudson safe in his arms again.

Speaking of his arms, Hope was struggling to get out of them, straining her head in Pike's direction. Connor thrust the wet ball of fur into Pike's arms, then swept his unfocused eyes over the group. They were all staring at him, waiting, as if they expected him to make a decision, issue an order.

Jesus, he wasn't even capable of reciting the alphabet right now, but somehow he got his brain into gear and found his voice. "Kade, take Lennox and the girls to the cabins Hudson cleaned out. Ry, you need to get to Foxworth." They'd have to pass through Foxworth on their way to the city, but he might as well send Rylan there ahead of them to butter Reese up. Maybe this time she'd actually fall for his charm.

"Pike, you're on first watch. We need to guard the camp in case there are still Enforcers in the area." His tone went deadly calm. "Xan?"

"Yeah?"

"You're going inside and getting that comm system working, or God help me, I'll—"

"Already done."

Connor blinked. "What?"

Xan shrugged sheepishly. "I got the program running three days after Hudson told me about it."

His mouth fell open. "You did?"

Xander nodded.

"You . . ." Connor blustered, shock and anger warring for his attention. "Why the *fuck* didn't you tell me? And what the hell were you doing yesterday when I sat beside you for hours?"

"Well, ah . . . I wasn't doing anything. Just messing

around with an old program I'm recoding." The other man shrugged. "And I didn't tell you because I was trying to stop you from making the biggest mistake of your life."

The anger won out.

Combined with the overwhelming worry for Hudson and the bone-deep shame over what he'd done to her, his blood coursed with a lethal cocktail that had him grabbing Xander by the collar. "A mistake? Because I'm trying to find the man who killed everyone I ever cared about?"

Xander was unfazed by the death grip on his shirt. "You'll be shot down if you get within five feet of him, Con. Do you really think your wife would have wanted you to die avenging her?"

He released Xan, stumbling backward with a grumble. "You still had no right keeping that from me."

"I made a decision I felt was best for the group."

Xander was mocking him now, and Connor would've slugged him in the jaw if they didn't have more important issues to deal with. He jabbed a finger in the air, inches from Xander's nose. "I'm kicking your ass for this later, Xan. I mean it."

The man's lips twitched.

"But it'll keep." He broke out in an urgent stride toward the lodge. "Right now I want you to load up that comm program so we can figure out a way to get my woman back."

Her quarters were untouched. Unchanged. Hudson looked around the spacious room, with its huge bed and cozy sitting area, and it felt like she'd never left.

"Look at me, you little *bitch*!"

A strong hand forcibly yanked on her hair, reminding Hudson of *why* she'd left.

Knox's dark eyes blazed as he sneered at her. He hadn't stopped sneering since he'd dragged her out of Lennox's house and thrown her in the back of the Enforcer truck. He'd ridden up front with his driver, and during the chopper ride to the compound he'd sat next to the pilot, as if Hudson's presence were inconsequential to him. As if she were a piece of furniture that didn't bear acknowledgment.

Now, in the privacy of her old room, he'd dropped the mask of indifference. Fury and disgust had his whole body trembling as he shook her so hard her teeth rattled.

"You have no idea how much shit you're in," Knox spat out. "That stunt you pulled? Running away? I'm going to make you pay for it, Hudson."

She didn't answer. A long, vacant stare was all she gave him, because experience had taught her that talking back to Knox only intensified his rage.

She'd known him since they were children, and she'd loathed him even back then. He'd been a smug, spoiled child who'd grown up to be an arrogant, violent psychopath. His sadistic tendencies and brutal efficiency made him a good Enforcer, and that was the only reason Hudson could think of that would make her father consider Knox for her husband. Her father's compassion had been trumped only by his obsessive devotion to the Colonies, and on paper Knox had probably looked like the perfect candidate to head up the new Coast Colony.

But Hudson knew better. Knox would run the place to the ground with his blind rage and complete lack of empathy.

"*Say* something, bitch."

She laughed without an ounce of humor. "Bitch, huh? Is that going to be your pet name for me when we're married?"

The sharp backhand nearly knocked her off her feet. Her cheek stung from the force of the blow, and she pressed her palm to her face in shock as Knox smirked at her.

"I'm going to call you whatever I want when we're married. And I'm going to do whatever the fuck I want to do to you."

She yelped when his hand closed over her left breast. He squeezed it hard enough to make her eyes water, and her knee came up instinctively, slamming into his groin.

Knox staggered back in pain, glowering at her. "You're going to wish you hadn't done that." He advanced on her again, but wisely kept a foot of distance between them this time. "I'm not weak like your brother, and I'm not going to stand for this bullshit when we move to the coast."

She shook her head incredulously. Did he honestly believe she would willingly follow him to a whole new colony and be his wife? She'd rather die first.

Before she could stop it, the last devastating image she'd seen at Lennox's house flashed in her mind. That redhead's body—Nell—on the hallway floor. Blood pouring from the wound in her abdomen as Layla hovered over her and screamed for the Enforcers to leave them alone.

Hudson hadn't known Nell at all, but her heart still ached for the loss. For Lennox and Jamie's loss. Knox would have murdered everyone in that house if she hadn't agreed to come home with him, but just because she was here now didn't mean she'd forgotten what he'd done or what he was capable of.

"I want you to listen to me, and listen good," she hissed out. "I am not your wife. I will never be your wife. I will slit my own throat before I let that happen, *bitch*."

His face turned red, the deep color emphasizing the bruising around his nose, which was more crooked than it had been the last time she'd seen it. Dominik had broken it, she remembered. And maybe it made her as bloodthirsty as everyone else in this ruthless world, but she wished her brother had smashed Knox's goddamn face in and turned it to a bloody pulp.

The door swung open before Knox could respond, and relief flooded her belly when her brother walked in.

There was a split second of silence. A multitude of emotions traveled from his eyes to hers.

Dominik opened his arms.

Hudson hesitated. She hadn't forgotten what he'd done to her, either. What he'd done—and was still doing—to the outlaws outside the city walls. But when she saw his anguished face, some of the anger chipped away, leaving her with a deep ache of sorrow. This was her brother, damn it.

Good or bad, he was still her brother.

She dove into his open arms, tears stinging her eyelids as she returned the tight hug he gave her.

"Hey, sis," he said hoarsely, and then his voice sharpened as he snapped at Knox over Hudson's head. "Leave. *Now*."

"I'm not going anywhere," the other man snapped back. "She's my wife."

"No. She's a name on a marriage contract," Dominik

said coldly. "Which, in case you've forgotten, I haven't even signed."

Hudson looked at her brother in surprise. He *hadn't*? She thought back to the contract he'd handed her before she'd escaped, but she hadn't paid attention to the signature lines, because the bride and groom didn't get to sign a damn thing. Only three signatures were needed to approve a marriage—those of a West Colony councilman and two approved individuals who endorsed the marriage, usually family members or employers. All three had to be alive and kicking at the time the contract was signed, so with her father gone, it had been Dominik's job to endorse.

"I suggest you get the hell out of here before I have you thrown out," Dominik finished. "I haven't seen my sister in two months. We'd like some privacy, please."

Please. So polite. Hudson might have even believed he was being genuinely cordial if it hadn't been for the purple vein throbbing in his forehead.

The two men stared each other down, but Knox was the first to look away. With a muttered expletive, he stalked out of the room and slammed the door—but not before Hudson caught a glimpse of the armed Enforcer posted outside of it.

"Am I prisoner here?" she demanded.

Dominik's gray eyes, so much like her own, flickered with regret. "Yes. Commander Ferris ordered twenty-four-hour surveillance on you when he heard you'd been located." His features strained. "He plans on interrogating you tomorrow morning. He's going to demand all the intel you gathered when you were in outlaw territory."

Her lips tightened. "I'm not telling him a damn thing."

Dom sighed. "Yeah, that's what I figured you'd say."

She searched her brother's face, desperately trying to find a trace of that darkness she and Connor had talked about. The evil he might be harboring. But all she saw was sorrow. Deep, soul-sucking sorrow.

"Why didn't you sign the marriage contract?" she whispered.

He surprised her by chuckling. "Oh, come on, H. We both know I was never going to let you marry that bastard."

Her eyes widened. "What? But you said . . ."

"I said a lot of things. It's what I *did* that you need to be focusing on."

Her blank look summoned another heavy sigh from him.

"Shit, Hudson, why do you think I sent you out in the field the day after I showed you that contract?"

Her breath caught in her throat.

"Because I knew you'd run." His smile was gentle. "I know you better than I know myself, H."

Her mind reeled as she absorbed the new information. He'd been *protecting* her?

She hadn't even questioned his orders that day. An Enforcer had been injured—of course Dom had dispatched her to help. Except . . . he could have sent any of the other nurses. But he'd chosen *her*.

To give her an opportunity to escape.

"What's happening here, Dom? It must be something pretty awful if you were willing to let me go."

"I don't know," he said miserably. "Ferris has been riding my ass since Dad died. He's put all these new protocols in place, and he killed the outlaw surrender program because he doesn't want them living in the city. He thinks they don't deserve it, that there's no hope for their rehabilitation. He'd rather just see them all dead."

Dominik raked his hand through his blond hair. It was messy, growing out, as if he didn't care about keeping up appearances anymore. "I'm . . ." He puffed out a breath. "I'm so angry, Hudson. All the time. I get these urges to . . . to rip people *apart*. And I wake up sometimes and don't know how I even got back to my room. I don't know what's happening to me."

Fear skittered through her. "I think I do."

"What? How?" he said in surprise.

"I met one of your trainees on the road. Max?"

Dominik sucked in a breath. "Max is alive? He dropped out of the program and killed two guards on his way out of the city, but the kid's soft. I didn't think he'd last a day out there."

"He made it far enough to run into me and my group. And he told me that Ferris is giving the trainees injections."

Dominik nodded. "Vitamins."

"No, I don't think so. Max noticed serious personality changes in the other recruits, guys he's known his whole life. I think Ferris is giving you guys some kind of aggression drugs." She bit her lip. "I think he switched your pills out after Dad died."

Dominik paled. He rubbed his bloodshot eyes, looking more tired than Hudson had ever seen him. "Fuck. That . . . would make sense." He pinched the bridge of his nose like he was warding off a migraine.

She let out a breath. "Did you know about Dad's plan for me to marry Knox?"

"No," he said immediately, his tone vehement. "I didn't. I promise, Hudson. You *know* how hard I fought him when he decided that Knox would be the perfect lieutenant for me. But there was no arguing with the old man, so I sucked it up. I tolerated Knox because he's a good soldier, but I never would have agreed to let him marry you."

She believed him. She knew when her twin was lying. Although his eyes looked desperate and angry and confused, there was no dishonesty there.

"What's going to happen to me now?" she asked as a wave of exhaustion washed over her. "Will I have to marry him?"

Dominik was quick to reject that. "No way. That's never going to happen."

"He thinks it will."

"He can think whatever the hell he wants. I won't let him touch you." Determination hardened his jaw. "I found a way to get you out once. I'll do it again."

Their hushed conversation halted when a knock sounded on the door. Dalton, one of Dominik's higher-level Enforcers, appeared in the doorway with a sleek silver tablet in his hand.

"I'm sorry to interrupt, sir, but . . . well, uh, the men are a bit confused."

Dominik's brow puckered. "About what?"

Dalton held up the tablet. "The order you posted. Nobody is sure what it means."

"Be more specific," Dom snapped. "I post a lot of orders."

"The meeting tonight." Dalton fidgeted in discomfort. "Was this supposed to go out to the general boards? Should I gather the men?"

"For *fuck's* sake, I have no idea what you're babbling about." Dominik stuck out his hand, gesturing to the tablet. "Give it here."

Hudson watched as her brother scanned the contents on the screen, his frown deepening.

"This is obviously some kind of tech error," he muttered. "I didn't schedule a meeting for tonight, and I'd certainly never arrange for it to happen outside the gates."

Hudson's heart flipped as a thought occurred to her.

Her gaze snapped up at Dom, and he tensed slightly, as if sensing she had an answer to the mystery. They'd always been able to read each other with nothing more than a look, and so she wasn't surprised when he turned to Dalton and barked, "Give us a moment. I'll be right out and we'll go clear this up."

But he didn't hand over the tablet, just tucked it under his arm nonchalantly, as if he'd forgotten it wasn't his own.

The moment the door closed behind Dalton, Hudson snatched the device from Dom's hand and eagerly read the message. It was brief and to the point. *Meeting. Four a.m. Two clicks west of the rear gate.*

A smile sprang to her lips. "Oh Christ. He actually did it."

"Who?" Dominik said uneasily.

"My friend . . . one of the people who took me in . . . he's a hacker." She swallowed. "We found some tablets when we were out gathering supplies and I told him about the program. He must have found a way to get it to work."

"These are your friends?" Dominik tapped the screen as he skimmed the message again. "Why would they send this? They came to rescue you?"

"Ye—" She halted when she realized that might not actually be true.

Yes, they could have come here to rescue her.

Or they'd come to kill Dominik.

"I don't know," she said quietly. "When I was with them, I found out . . ." She took a breath. "You ordered

Knox to sweep an outlaw camp in the west about two years ago. He didn't give them a chance to surrender. He killed them all, and one of them was my . . . my friend's wife." She stumbled on the word *friend* because Connor was so much more than that.

Connor was *everything* to her.

"He blames you for her death," she admitted. "There's a chance he'll kill you if you show your face."

"Then he'll kill me," Dominik said simply.

She gasped. "Dom—"

"This could be our only chance to get you out of here again," he cut in. "If I have to give up my life so you can rejoin your people, then so be it."

Her people. It was surreal, difficult to absorb, but so damn true it made her throat hurt. She didn't belong in this compound anymore, and she didn't belong in the city.

She belonged in the free land. With or without Connor.

Dominik lifted his chin in that stubborn pose she'd seen her entire life. The same one she donned when she was about to dig her heels in. "I'll tell the men that the message was a communication error and make sure they know there's no meeting on the schedule." He paused in thought. "We've got four hours. Plenty of time for me to figure out how to get you out of the compound."

She attempted another protest. "Dom—"

"Don't you *fucking* argue with me!"

She recoiled.

And when he took a menacing step toward her, she was genuinely afraid.

"Oh fuck." He staggered to a stop and sucked in a breath, his fists slowly loosening. "*Fuck*." A stricken look seized his features. "I'm sorry. I didn't mean to snap. I wasn't going to . . . hurt you . . . I promise . . ."

He transformed in front of her eyes, reverting back to the little boy she'd grown up with. He looked so confused and upset that her fear faded and her heart throbbed, spurring her to throw her arms around him again.

"It's okay. I know you'd never hurt me." When she felt him shaking against her, she hugged him tighter. "I love you, Dom."

"I love you too."

They stayed like that for a few minutes, until Dom finally dropped a kiss on her cheek and stepped out of the embrace. Clearly shaken up. "I need to make arrangements." His stride was weary as he headed for the door. "I'll be back as soon as I can."

22

"How did you get rid of the guard?" Hudson whispered a little more than three hours later. She gazed at the empty corridor outside the door of her quarters, then at Dom's tired face. "Won't Ferris be suspicious?"

"Trust me, he's not happy about it," Dom whispered back. "I was on the phone with the bastard for more than twenty minutes, listening to him fume about it. But I told him that no matter what you've done, you're still the daughter of the man who founded the Global Council and therefore you deserve to be treated with respect." He smiled faintly. "I also reminded him you were in the same training class I was and that if you wanted to escape, one guard at your door wasn't going to stop you."

She grinned back. "Damn right it wouldn't."

They fell silent as they crept down the fluorescent-lit hallway. The building primarily housed offices and living quarters, so they moved cautiously and soundlessly to avoid the risk of waking anyone. Hudson's legs trembled with each step she took. She wasn't sure what Dom's plan was, how they were going to walk out of the gate unseen, but she hoped that whatever he'd come up with, it wouldn't result in the two of them dying in a hail of bullets.

It was eerily quiet outside when they emerged from the building's rear exit. They stuck close to the brick wall, which was bathed in shadows. Hudson glanced up at the roof in surprise. Normally there was a floodlight shining down on the back door.

Dominik raised a brow. "Bulb must be busted," he murmured. "I should really get maintenance to look into that."

She choked down a laugh, but all traces of humor died when she gazed at the lit-up area beyond their shadowy nook. The pavement gleamed under the bright lights, the silver links of the massive chain fence winking as if to taunt at her. Hudson peered up at the guard tower a hundred yards away, then studied the security cameras mounted on every fence post. Her uneasiness steadily rose.

How on earth did Dom think they'd make it all the way to the gate without being spotted?

To her shock, he raised his assault rifle and strode forward.

"What are you doing?" she hissed out.

He gestured for her to follow him. "It's all right. The cameras along this side of the fence have been disabled." Another grin flashed her way. "Regularly scheduled maintenance, which requires a total reboot, of course. But we've only got nine minutes before they're back online. Stay tight to the wall so the tower guards don't see us. It'll be okay."

She hesitated for only a second before deciding to trust him. This was her twin brother. She had to believe that he wouldn't betray her. That he wasn't leading her into a trap.

And if he was . . . well, then she'd take the *screw you* that the universe had handed her and accept her fate.

Because maybe she was simply destined to be betrayed by everyone she cared about. Her father had arranged for her to marry a monster without telling her. Connor had cast her out without batting an eye. At this point, a betrayal from Dom wouldn't be any worse than what she'd already had to deal with.

Her brother led her to the edge of the compound, halting when they were twenty feet from the gate—and the guard tower.

"Use this to open the gate."

Horror swamped her stomach when he tucked a key card into her hand. "No. If I use your card they'll know you helped me."

"It's not my card." His eyes twinkled. "You left it behind the day you escaped, remember?" His tone went serious. "It's still active—I checked. The system will log that you used it, but I'll just claim you had it stashed in your room and nobody thought to search for it."

"Or . . ." She dug her teeth into her lower lip. "You can come with me."

He was quick to shake his head. "I can't."

"You can. You don't have to stay here, Dom. You can start a new life in the free land, a real *life*, without drugs and rules and all the bullshit the GC feeds us."

His jaw set in a tight line. "I have unfinished business here."

Alarm rippled through her. "What are you planning to do?"

"I'm not sure yet, but I'm damn well going to do *something*. Not everyone on this compound is evil. There are good men here, and Ferris is drugging us and messing with our heads so we can go out into the colony and murder innocent people. I can't let it go on."

"Then I'll stay and help you," she said firmly.

He was just as firm. "You're not safe here. Things are changing, and not for the better. All these new rules being put into place . . ." He shook his head again. "You're safer in outlaw territory, H. I don't know if I'll be able to protect you if you stay here."

He reached into his inner pocket, pulled out a small device and pressed it into her palm. It was a phone, she realized. Sleek and lightweight, with fewer buttons than the cell phones she was used to seeing.

"I won't be able to use this outside the city," she reminded him.

"It's not a cell. It's a satellite phone. You can use it to send text messages too. When you get settled, send me the coordinates of your location. I'll do whatever I can to keep the colony sweeps away from that general area, but . . . I don't know how much longer I'll be in charge."

"Promise me you'll leave if things get worse. Promise you'll call me, and I promise you'll be welcome wherever I wind up."

He visibly swallowed. "I promise."

Hudson nodded in relief. "So now what?"

Dom tipped his head toward the tower. "When I give the word, I want you to go to the gate. I'll deal with the guards." He unclipped the radio from his belt. "The second that gate opens, I want you to run, H. Run as fast as you can. You should be able to make it to the woods before they spot you, but if they do . . ." He lifted his rifle. "I'll cover you."

Her throat clamped shut. "They'll kill you."

He seemed unfazed by that outcome. "Run and don't look back, okay? You know where all the trip wires are, and the motion sensors on the north perimeter were disabled in the reboot. Get at least ten yards past the perimeter line, and you won't have to worry about triggering any alarms." Frowning, he glanced at his watch. "Four minutes until everything's back online. Time to go, sis."

Her heart clenched. "I don't want to say good-bye to you again."

"Hey, at least this time there *is* a good-bye." He ruffled her hair good-naturedly. "You skipped out without a word during your last jailbreak."

She had to smile. "Yeah. Shitty move, huh?"

"Yup. Now give me a hug and get out of here already."

Hudson wrapped her arms around him, forcing herself to remember this moment: her brother's solid chest against her cheek, the warmth of his embrace, the pride in his eyes. Then she released him and whispered, "I'll see you soon," and hoped like hell that those words would come true one day.

The next few minutes were a blur. She wasn't sure how she managed to make it to the gate without stumbling over in terror, or how she swiped the key card without dropping it five times beforehand. She wasn't sure what Dominik did to lure the guards' sharp gazes away from the clearing, or if he even had. All she was aware of was the asphalt beneath her boots as she ran as if her life depended on it.

Her lungs burned, the late-night wind slapping her face as she raced toward the tree line. She didn't dare look over her shoulder to check if the tower guards had spotted her. She just ran. She ran fast and hard, praying that nobody fired at her, that she'd reach the trees before the guards noticed that she—

She'd made it.

Hudson couldn't contain her astonishment as she

sprinted into the brush and out of sight of the tower. No shots. No yells. Nothing but the sounds of twigs snapping beneath her feet as she flew past the motion sensors toward freedom.

Holy shit, she'd done it. She'd escaped—again. She'd fucking done it, but still she kept running, fueled by a sense of triumph that surged with her movements as she put as much distance as she could between her and the compound.

The forest was pitch-black, but she knew every inch of it. She and Dominik had played out here when they were kids. They'd hunted with their father and combed the woods, building forts on the days Dominik got to choose the activity and picking flowers when it was her turn to choose.

Two clicks west. That's what Xander's message had said. Hudson had no idea if she'd even traveled a mile yet, but she didn't see any faces or hear any voices as she hurried through the forest.

She hoped Connor and the others were out there somewhere waiting for her. If they weren't, it would make her journey a hell of a lot tougher, but she'd done it once, and she could do it again. She had her knives and the two pistols Dom had given her. She had her brains and her courage and a deep-seated will to survive, and any one of those things could get her as far as she needed to go.

She quickened her pace, cheeks flushed from exertion, lungs aching. She had to be getting close to the rendezvous point. A glance at the tactical watch Dom had strapped to her wrist revealed that it was ten minutes to four a.m. And she'd already vowed to wait no more than ten minutes past that.

If Connor and the men didn't show by then, she

would keep running. Make her way to Foxworth to find Tamara, or try to track down Lennox and—

"Going somewhere?"

The deceptively pleasant voice had her staggering to a stop. Hudson whirled around in time to see Knox step out of the darkness, the red stripes on his Enforcer uniform glinting beneath the shards of moonlight slicing through a gap in the trees.

She drew her weapon, but not fast enough.

Knox charged forward and knocked the gun out of her hands, and in the blink of an eye, she was flat on her back and he was on top of her.

His hands wrapped tightly around her throat.

I'll be there.

That three-word reply was the only response to Xander's message, and Connor couldn't even be sure it had come from Hudson. Still, that hadn't stopped him from boarding the chopper, from flying straight into city airspace and risking getting shot down by an air patrol.

But the risks didn't matter. Nothing mattered if Hudson wasn't with him.

The scream that suddenly pierced the air was not shrill. It wasn't even loud. But Connor felt the muffled, shock-laced sound right down to his bones.

"It's her," he murmured to Rylan, whose shoulders had stiffened at the sound. The men had stayed hidden for the past twenty minutes, after spending an hour scouting out the area to ensure they weren't walking into an ambush.

"Could be a trap," his friend murmured back.

He didn't give a shit if it was. He'd recognize Hudson's voice anywhere. She was here. Somewhere in the woods.

Under attack.

Pike spoke up from Connor's other side. "Gotta check it out either way."

It was only the three of them, because Reese was an obstinate bitch and she'd refused to let anyone else accompany Connor on his mission, claiming that the added weight on the chopper used up fuel she couldn't afford to spare. She'd allowed Pike to go because he was the only one of the men who knew how to pilot the damn thing, and Rylan, well, Connor suspected she just wanted him out of her hair. But he wished to hell the woman had consented to letting him bring a bigger crew.

"I'm going out there." Connor raised his rifle and stepped out of the thick cluster of vegetation, Pike and Rylan quickly following suit.

They moved in unison through the brush, their years of hunting and survival skills making it easy to walk without making a sound, without disturbing the forest or alerting anyone to their presence. The farther they went, the closer the voices got. Muffled, hissed. Stilted words Connor couldn't make out but that sent a chill up his spine regardless.

"Promised . . . coast . . . damn well gonna get both . . ."

Connor's muscles tensed. A male voice, harsh and furious.

"*Make* you obey . . . understand?"

He slid behind a thick tree trunk and signaled to the men. They froze, taking cover nearby. Connor held up his hand to order them to stay put, because there was no point in all of them getting their heads blown off tonight.

If this was a trap, then he'd be the only one walking into it.

Rylan looked unhappy with the call, but a firm shake of Connor's head had the man maintaining his position.

Adjusting the grip on his rifle, Connor continued forward alone. The voices got louder, a vicious stream of words that became more and more audible.

". . . don't care if I have to beat you senseless every morning—you're going to do what I say. You hear me?"

There was a moment of silence. Connor eased behind another tree. Waiting. Listening.

"I'll keep you on a fucking leash if that's what it takes. Your father and I had a deal! A new colony—for *us*, damn it. For you and me to mold and enforce and rule over."

"You're a delusional bastard."

Connor nearly dropped his weapon. *Hudson*. Jesus, he'd been right. It was her. Which meant that the man spitting out venom at her had to be Knox.

"You want to put me on a leash? Go ahead. I'll still find a way to beat you." Hudson let out a wild laugh. "I said I'd kill myself before I married you, but you know what? Forget that. I'd much rather kill *you*."

A roar of pain sliced the air. It was followed by a grunt, then a fleshy thwack and a loud thud, as if something—or some*one*—had fallen to the ground.

Connor charged forward without a single thought to his own safety. He burst through the trees in time to see a dark figure launch itself at Hudson's prone frame. Relief exploded inside him when he realized she was still alive, but the sight of Knox looming over her ignited a different kind of explosion.

Pure rage.

He flew at the other man, smashing the butt of his

rifle into the back of Knox's head as he heaved him off Hudson's body. But the bastard's skull was thicker than he'd expected, and the blow didn't knock him unconscious. Knox fell on the dirt, then bounced to his feet with military speed that caught Connor by surprise.

"Don't fucking move," Connor growled as he trained his rifle on Knox's chest.

The man froze, wild eyes snapping up to meet Connor's.

Those *eyes*.

All the breath left his body as he stared at the man who'd murdered his wife. In a heartbeat, he was transported back to that day. Watching from the woods as this man—this *killer*—had sauntered up to his fellow Enforcers as if he were king of the world. Smirking, *bragging* about what he'd done.

"Who the hell are you?" Knox spat out.

Irony. There it was again. The man who'd haunted his nightmares for two years didn't even know who he was. Didn't even realize that he'd destroyed Connor's life by the simple act of pulling a trigger.

"I'm the man who's going to kill you," Connor said softly.

And, yes, it *was* simple. Squeezing that trigger was the most natural motion his hand had ever made. He just . . . squeezed. Once. Twice. Three times, and then Knox's body tumbled to the ground, and the evil eyes that had haunted Connor for so long lit up with panic before going glassy, unfocused, and finally . . . lifeless.

His breathing grew shallow as he lowered his weapon. He slowly turned to Hudson, who was still lying on the dirt, who hadn't even made a sound when he'd put three bullets into another man's chest right in front of her.

But her expression conveyed no fear. No recrimination. Her gaze never wavered as she locked it solidly on his, and when he leaned forward and held out his hand, she took it without hesitation.

"You're here," she whispered as he helped her to her feet.

"I'm here," he said gruffly.

She glanced at the motionless body sprawled two meters away, and a flicker of emotion crossed her eyes. Triumph. Or maybe satisfaction. Either way, she didn't seem devastated by the loss. She simply stared at the pool of blood forming around Knox's chest as if mesmerized by the crimson puddle.

When she turned back to him, she looked calm and alert. "Why?"

He swallowed. "Why what?"

"Why are you here?"

His pulse quickened. He knew what she was really asking him, and his palms went damp as he struggled to find the right words. But he wasn't good with words, damn it. He didn't have Rylan's easy charm or Kade's city vocabulary, or the dry quips Xander always seemed to have handy.

All he had was . . . the truth.

"Because I—"

"Hudson!" a male voice interrupted. "Where the hell are you?"

Connor's rifle shot back into position, taking aim on the trees behind Hudson's head just as a frantic figure came into sight.

"Dom?" she blurted out, whirling around.

"Holy fuck, you're okay!" The man's voice was weak with relief. "Knox left the compound before us. I only found out when I got back and saw that he'd signed out, claiming he was going out on a patrol and—" He stopped when he noticed the dead body, a harsh curse sliding out. "Shit." Then he went frozen in place as he noticed something else.

Hudson realized it at the same time, her shocked gaze flying to Connor.

"Don't," she begged.

It took him a second to understand what they were both seeing. He still had his weapon trained on the newcomer, aimed right between the man's eyes. Gray eyes. The exact shade as Hudson's.

Connor blinked, startled by the resemblance. Dominik's features were chiseled and masculine compared to Hudson's soft, feminine beauty, but anyone could see that they were related.

This was Hudson's brother. The head Enforcer of West Colony. The man who was responsible for the colony sweeps.

"Please, Connor. Don't."

Hudson's voice penetrated the angry mist. Connor turned his head and bit his lip when he saw the anguish etched into her face.

"He's going to make it right. He's made mistakes, but we've *all* made mistakes. We've lied and we've stolen and we've killed, but it doesn't have to be like that anymore." She looked pleadingly at her brother. "You're going to make it right—aren't you, Dom?"

"Yes. I am." Dominik's gaze stayed on Connor's, and though his voice had softened when he'd answered his sister, it rang with resignation as he addressed Connor. "Do what you have to do, man. My head's fucked up enough as it is. A bullet might make everything better."

Hudson gasped. *"Dom."*

"It's true, H. I don't know what they're giving me.

Who knows? Maybe the drugs will bring about a slow, painful death." Dominik nodded at Connor. "I'm sure that would make your friend pretty happy."

"She's not my friend," Connor said roughly. "She's my woman."

Dominik's eyebrows shot up, and then his lips twitched with amusement. "Keeping secrets from your twin, huh, sis?"

Her cheeks reddened. "I didn't say anything because I had no idea what was going on between us and— Jesus, why am I explaining myself?" Her voice became colder than ice as she turned to Connor and said, "If you pull the trigger, you will never see me again, Con. I will never forgive you, and you will *never* see me again."

She meant it. He could see the promise of it in her eyes, and the thought of letting her walk away from him again was . . . unacceptable.

Letting out a breath, he bent down and laid his rifle on the ground. Then he straightened up and met Dominik's startled gaze. "I surrender."

Hudson's brother blinked. Then he laughed. "Um, nobody asked you to do that, buddy. Pick up that weapon and get my sister the hell out of here."

It was Connor's turn to blink. "You fucking serious?"

Hudson snickered.

"Of course. I don't understand why we're still standing around talking," Dominik said in exasperation. "If you're not going to shoot me, then get lost already. Hudson says you're good people, so *prove* it. Keep my sister safe."

Either he'd gone crazy, or that was actually grudging respect flowing through him. It both enraged and mystified him, but Connor didn't waste time analyzing either response.

He nodded at Dominik, then met Hudson's beautiful gray eyes. "Come on, sweetheart. It's time to go."

The drive to the landing strip was a festive one. Rylan had hugged the living daylights out of her when she and Connor had rejoined the men, and even Pike had looked happy to see her. But Connor . . . he'd clammed up on her. He'd referred to her as his woman in front of Dominik and then acted as if it had never happened, sitting silently behind the wheel as they sped away to safety.

Hudson hadn't asked where they'd gotten the car. She hadn't asked how they'd managed to find a working helicopter. She'd simply basked in the joy of escaping the compound with her skin intact and allowed that feeling of liberation to fuel her patience.

Now that patience was wearing thin, and Connor's silence was grating on her nerves, so the first thing she did when they got out of the car was address Rylan and Pike with a stern look. "I need to talk to Connor. Alone."

Both men seemed to be fighting grins.

"Yes, ma'am," Rylan drawled. He smacked Pike on the arm. "Come on, pilot. Let's get the lady's ride ready to fly."

The moment they were out of earshot, she advanced on Connor with single-minded purpose, enjoying the way he gulped.

"You didn't answer my question," she said accusingly.

"Ah . . . which question was that again?"

"Playing dumb, are we? Fine, let me be more clear."

She met his adorably awkward gaze. "Why did you come back for me?"

She half expected another stalling tactic, but she should've known better than to think that Connor would beat around the bush.

"Because I love you."

Her mouth fell open. "Oh."

"Oh?" His lips quirked. "That's really all you have to say?"

"No, I have a lot to say, actually. But it can wait, because right now I just want to do *this*."

She raised her hand and slapped him right across the face.

A loud snort sounded from the vicinity of the chopper, but Hudson was too furious to check which one of the men was taking so much amusement from her very genuine indignation.

"You *exiled* me! What the *fuck* is the matter with you, Con?"

He rubbed his cheek, but the smile didn't leave his lips. "You can hit me again if you want. God knows I deserve it."

Hudson glared at him. "You *do* deserve it. And trust me, that won't be the last slap you'll be getting from me. You might have let my brother go—and I'll never forget that or stop being grateful for it—but that doesn't mean I'm going to forget what you did back at camp. I'm going to bring it up every time we get in a fight, and every time you piss me off or annoy me or tell me I can't do something. Every damn time, Connor! You've officially made it possible for me to lord this over your head for the rest of our lives."

"The rest of our lives, huh?" His voice thickened. "Does that mean you still love me?"

Her annoyance slowly seeped away. She shot him a thoughtful look and said, "Do I still love you? I don't know—what do *you* think?"

"I think I screwed up. I think I acted irrationally and made the biggest mistake of my life when I forced you to leave. I think I let my need for revenge blind me from what really matters to me." Vulnerability creased his rugged features. "I think you might be the best thing that's ever happened to me." His voice shook. "And I'm afraid I've lost you."

The earnest words cracked her heart wide open. Without a word, she moved closer and cupped his face with her hands. "You haven't lost me. I'm right here." She gently stroked the red mark her palm had left on his cheek. "And I never stopped loving you, you ruthless bastard."

The corner of his mouth lifted. "Do you forgive me for exiling you?"

"Do you forgive me for lying to you?"

"Yes." No hesitation. Just steadfast sincerity.

"Good. Because I forgive you too." She leaned up on her tiptoes and brushed a kiss over his lips. "I promise I'll never keep anything from you again, Con. But you have to promise not to shut me out. This is only going to work if we're completely honest with each other. If we *trust* each other."

"I know." His rough fingers stroked her cheek. "I trust you, baby."

Her heart soared when their lips met again, and this time the kiss was not fleeting, but endless. It warmed her belly and curled her toes, wrapping around her until her surroundings faded and the only thing she was conscious of was Connor's hot, eager mouth. His wicked tongue. His big hands sliding to her waist, then lower, caressing her bottom and—

"Hey, assholes, can we speed this up?" Pike called.

"Seriously," Rylan agreed. "Either get to the sex, or stop, because watching you suck each other's faces is kinda nauseating."

Hudson's laughter was muffled against Connor's lips. "Should we get to the sex, or stop?"

"Let's save the sex for later. I'm gonna want to take my time with you once I get you naked." Chuckling, he reached for her hand. "Are you ready to go home?"

Hudson planted one last kiss on his lips. "Never been more ready in my life."

Epilogue

Connor stood on the lodge porch, stifling a sigh as he watched Rylan and Lennox unload an ornate vanity table from the back of Lennox's pickup truck. Jamie was monitoring their every move as well, hands on her hips as she ordered Lennox to be careful with her prized possession. Which brought a wry smile to Connor's lips, because it seemed like everything she'd asked Lennox to bring over from their former residence was her "prized possession"—Connor had never met a woman who owned so much *stuff*.

A soft laugh came from behind him as Hudson stepped out of the lodge and joined him at the railing. "They're really making themselves at home, huh?" she remarked.

Connor slung an arm over her shoulder and pressed a kiss to the top of her head, breathing in the coconut scent of her shampoo. "Ha. Like this isn't exactly what you wanted, to turn this camp into one big happy community."

She grinned at him. "I won't lie—it's nice having other women around. You know, some estrogen to temper that testosterone fest you guys had going on."

He chuckled.

She rested her head on his shoulder, her tone becoming serious. "So what are you going to do about Reese's summons?"

His good humor faded at the reminder. When they'd gone to Foxworth to ask to borrow Reese's chopper, they'd given the woman one of the sat phones, since Lennox didn't need it anymore now that he was living at camp. Connor had told Reese to contact him when she decided what she wanted in exchange for the use of her helicopter, but she'd remained radio silent for the past couple weeks. He'd hoped that meant she'd forgotten about the favor.

But that was hoping for too much.

"What else is there to do?" He let out a breath. "I'll head out there next week like she asked and find out what she wants."

Hudson bit her lip. "What if it's something dangerous? Or insane?"

"We'll cross that bridge when we get there." When her worried expression didn't ease, he pointed out the silver lining. "Hey, at least the roads will be safe. Your brother is making sure to keep the sweeps away from us, remember?"

His words had the opposite effect—she looked even *more* worried now. Shit. Maybe reminding her of Dominik hadn't been the best move. Hudson's brother had contacted them the day after they'd returned to camp, sending a message to the phone he'd given her to tell them that he was all right, still in charge, and doing everything in his power to keep their area Enforcer-free. Connor wasn't sure how long that would last, but for the moment he was grateful for Dom's efforts.

Christ. Never in a million years had he thought he'd ever be *grateful* to Dominik.

"I wish he'd just leave the compound," Hudson said softly.

"He'll be okay, sweetheart." But Connor was in no way confident of that.

"Hudson!" Jamie's excited voice interrupted them. The woman hurried over when she spotted Hudson on the porch. "Do you want to help me and Layla decorate our cabins?"

For once, Connor was grateful for Jamie's obsession with making herself at home, because her question succeeded in relaxing Hudson's tense shoulders.

"Sure," Hudson replied, and then she linked her arm through Jamie's.

Footsteps sounded from the door again, and this time it was Xander who sidled up to him, his dark eyes focused on the commotion in the courtyard: Rylan and Lennox lugging the table. Hudson and Jamie walking down the path. Pike appearing in the clearing with the wolf in his arms.

Xander sighed, but when he spoke, he sounded more amused than annoyed. "It's the dawn of a new era, huh?"

Connor's gaze rested on Hudson's sexy backside, her long blond hair cascading down her back, the ease and confidence of her gait. She stopped suddenly, turning to toss a smile at him over her shoulder, and his heart overflowed with emotion.

"Yes," he murmured. "It is."